William P Mallory

They Don't Let You Scream Here

They Don't Let You Scream Here
by William P Mallory

The Man in the Window
Pilate's Dilemma With a Witch
Catcherman and the Great Madness
The Vanishing Tree

A special thanks to Susan Latta and Ed Lambro

For my Parents and my Brothers

For Bill

They Don't Let You Scream Here

The Man in the Window

An ominous dark cloud loomed over the simple town; no one expecting such a foreboding sign, not even Oliver. More sinister things have happened to men. Women have always been protected from certain things supernatural. The wind parts for only a few. In microcosm universes maybe some things are more equal, more apt to the laws of nature, rather than the laws of man. Dr. Oliver put his glasses back down on his desk, and leaned back in his chair, creaks echoed across the hard wood floor. His window was just above him, it over looked the beautiful commons and Herth Avenue. It was pleasant and easy on the eyes, a heartfelt home outside of his own; be his imagination unto what is given to him. The sun was cusping the trees in its hypnotic tug. The color of the leaves orange, yellow and red pasted the street-way, a fairy's delight for onlookers and adventurers of any age. Very little green remained but on the lawn of the commons, down the street at the intersection. Class had just ended. The semester was half the way through. It was difficult. The students were all full of new fears, new anxieties, and new domestic problems he never dreamt of hearing until teaching here, at Pristol University. The bell had rung, and the students have left the building.

Dr Oliver leaned back forward in his chair, took a good breath and stood himself up, walking beside his desk to get a good look below. A thought of 'day one' passed him by, eager students waiting to meet their new teacher, another block in the brick wall. Another reason to be forgotten two years down the line. Maybe you won't, but most subconscious people will rarely bring up Critical Thinking 2, only to remember what, exactly?

Dr. Oliver walked out into the hall. The University was tied to a set of brick buildings, it wasn't much on the annex side of life, but it was still school. And no good fool there was to tune in, turn on, and drop out. No good fool tis done such a thing any less wiser.

Oliver picked up his case and looked around the room, seeing if he had forgotten anything. He was off to a twister of a weekend, and he knew it. The storm coming in wasn't going to help. But that's mother nature, and somewhere down deep we learned way early on in life that mother nature makes the calls, and we as humans bend around her. Most days are normal, most days are easy to deal with. Wake up, go to bed, wake up go to bed. Sunshine blaring its ways between intervals. Then a storm comes, and that doesn't usually turn the ears upward, it puts the ears on high alert. Pristol University was on the river, across from the old broken down King's Brewery that put most people to work in the 1940's and 50's. Now its a hangout for college kids and weekend puff parties. Oliver looked again, because it was natural as well for him to behave more like an OCD leprechaun and less like a college professor, teaching English, and two classes on the Paranormal in Literature. Where he was going this weekend had more to do with the latter; but then again, most literature is based in the echoes of voices passed. Ghosts.

He got into his car, looking up at the window that housed his small introverted office. It wasn't a far walk at all to his space. It was a perk on campus to drive right up and out, walk across the street and into the David Born Building, or just the Born Building as most students know it by. He turned down the window, put the key in and turned the ignition. WPSC was fine tuned in, lunch with Barry and the Screamers. Playing odd ball recordings from the 70's on up. Some jazz funk opera was tearing through the speakers like the band was on the hood of the car. The day looked bright on the inside, but the outside looked like rain. And lots of it. Oliver put the car in reverse and backed out of his spot, put it in drive and kissed the sweet ass week behind, driving around the circle and down the main driveway. University Road. Who could be more original, who could be more direct naming streets 150 years ago, knowing full well they'd only sound more redundant with age.

Oliver's chainsaw massacre of a car didn't mind the fall, but when winter came it was another story. His 1978 Charger started up and was halfway down the road when he stopped, thought of something, couldn't quite put a finger on it. It was the grass, the lawn on his left. The Great Lawn. It was fluttered with orange and yellow, red leaves, students were running along by the path, that led to the river. But there was something else. A deja vu. Something he saw in a dream, a fragment, a moment caught on the celluloid in his brain. He sat there behind the wheel, spaced out into the never ending abyss that University Road alluded to, a place with no end. Oliver looked again, to his left, at the field. Again the same reaction, he turned his eyes ahead again, a road, the road ahead. The road less traveled, how ever it went. Why Robert Frost took over his mind, misguided his process onto what just happened; none the less, Oliver took his foot off the break, and put it back on the gas. A minute later he was making a left onto yet another big idea of a street name at the town hall a century or so ago. Main Street. Main Street, Pristol.

The street was narrow, Main Street, main line, a fine vein to siphon from. Parallel Books, The Orange Cafe, Vintage Highlights, The Pristol Library at the end, two old gothic churches, St. Elizabeths, and House of the Savior. House of the Savior was more of a cult takeover. It used to be Johns Baptist and was sold on high taxes in the area. Rich hipsters took over and that was the beginning of the end. Walton's Homeless Reach-out was across the street, and an old style A&W Rootbeer sat parallel to Anderson Park. Across the street from the Library. One block down and it's bar avenue. The Crow, The Stupid Animal, Wishes and Wine, Hollow 8. Hinnigans, and The Tapestry. And a few others that tap themselves off of the off streets. Main Street carried its way downward, slipping its way into where alcohol takes you, into the cheaper rents, and less cared for homes, less tidy sidewalks and stores becoming hide outs for small drug deals on small corners. On the weekends during Rush Week, they shut the streets down and the students go ape for ten hours. Halloween comes after, and that's a whole other hoodlums' holiday. Jack O Lanterns on every doorstep, creeps come on and claim their turf, a night back to get their lost dignity.

Oliver came to the light, the first of four that put a hick-up in the flow. He stopped to a slow halt, nothing was bothering him much. The house, maybe a little. The odds and ends he wasn't told, the gaps, the holes. It was a simple job. He got to thinking. The light before him was red. Just a second or two more. He turned his head left, and looked at the Shady Eye, a gaping hole for a bar, left for the few die hards in the Generation X era. A woman was standing in front of it. She was wearing a yellow over coat and smoking a cigarette, tapping it in front of her. Then it happened again, at that moment he came to a strange recollection of seeing her somewhere else, but not in this world maybe. But it was a feeling of being somewhere else, a different time. Not of the one he's known. Maybe one in a dream. He couldn't quite grasp where or when, but he knew he'd seen her, the sign above, having its cryptic overtone in its own dark shadow; it was all too familiar. Yes, he knew he's been here before, at this light, looking left, being there. Two harrowing deja vu's in one day. The light turned green and he put the gas back on, driving through, looking left when he could, then through his drive side mirror. The girl, still puffing away, standing in the lighted darkness, in her own, where she was. Oliver made a point to himself; he was not her and she was not him. Five seconds later the rain started to fall. Oliver turned the wipers on and drove through the next green light.

One half mile further down the road, on the right sat the infamous and rather ominous historical building. It was property of the town, and the town board ran the meetings on the future of the building itself. It was an interesting building. Brick, all of it, eight windows on the outside, two for every room showing. There were four bedrooms in the house, now turned into offices, and below the main entrance and foyer, the living room and kitchen quarters. Some of the rooms are still for show, like the attic hosting a secret bible. Some rooms are for use to keep the historical buildings in town standing. It was an effort. Edgar Topstow was the keeper of the quarters. On Saturday, Kate came in to curate the tourists, as well as the tours.

It was Friday afternoon, and Oliver was to meet Edgar roughly around 4:00. As Oliver pulled into the house, which was adjacent to about three acres of land on each side, surrounding the house with flush meadows and tall oak trees. It was a beautiful lawn to admire come autumn; and for a glimpse, Oliver saw how awe inspiring it all was. It was a thrill for a second, an uplifting of his spirit, and he felt it. He pulled his Charger up, parked it in the space provided. There was only one other spot taken, the rest were for the ghosts, Oliver laughed to himself. He shut the engine off. Looking out of his window he

8

gazed on the house. The parking lot spoke to the east side of the building, not the front. The front of the house faced Main Street, a good two acres from the road. Oliver thought of its history, the job. He looked up at the windows, as if he was actually going to get a glimpse of the figure, the one that is rumored, tallied up in all local folklore, people have seen him. That was all he knew, well; he knew a little more. He knew about the house, and that was the main reason he was there. To photograph the house. To record the house. Catch a ghost, something like that. Or so he thought.

He walked across the broken navel of an entrance, cobble stones and romantic mid-afternoon skies. Dire and dark as the the forbearer's name, Edgar. Oliver liked the sound of it. The walkway up to the door, sheets of black broken slate, each side small baskets of yellow and orange carnations sat un-wilted and cared for. The knob on the door was anything but ordinary. It was a lion of cast iron with the knocker coming out of his mouth. It wasn't very original as it was unique. Oliver knocked on the door. Immediately he could hear someone's footsteps coming to the door. A second or so later they answered, and the door was swung open from the inside.

"Well, hello. You must be Dr. Oliver Whisk."

There standing before Oliver was a charming looking young woman, intelligent looking, bright and cheerful. She stood there as if she was looking forward to the weekend as much as he was. "Yes, I am, Oliver Whisk."

"Oliver Twist?" She laughs.

"My parents had a sense of humor, or just literary junkies."

"Well, do please come in. I'm Kate Warren."

Oliver walked inside. Kate felt at ease, she looked outside, at the day, at the clouds above, coming in fast. "You beat the storm. And a night for it."

"You are Edgar's assistant? I presume?" Oliver made it polite.

"Yes, I am. I just got here this past Spring. I've been keeping with the place, and so much. The tours are quite fun. They come on the weekends. But since tomorrow we'll be closed so that you can have your full attention on your work here. I'm not sure if Edgar told you that he put me on the job as well, as your assistant."

"Yes, I mean he has told me, mentioned it. And yes, that sounds great. Where is Edgar. He is presumably punctual, no?"

"You're funny. Of course. He's upstairs, he knows you're here. He wanted to grab something. Quick, come with me." Kate led the way as Oliver walked right behind her, eventually catching up as they entered the main room.

"This is the living room quarters." Kate looked around as if the house was hers, with a sense of childhood pride. "Upstairs are the bedrooms and the study, as well as a small bathroom. The kitchen is through that door." She pointed through the hallway and the door adjacent. But something grabbed her shy of a centimeter, her body turned left a hair too far, her head back an inch too fearsome to recognize, as if she knew something no one did, maybe she could hide it, maybe she'd save it. But before the feeling went, Oliver caught her face, there in the limbo of the moment. The picture frame stood still in his mind, her chin, her nose, her eyes, her hair; but most importantly, her. That feeling came back, like back at the bar with the girl and her cigarette, exactly that feeling. He looked at her, she was coming back around.

"There, through there. And upstairs. Yes upstairs." She gathered herself, as if she felt it too. An odd look on her face slowed herself down even further than she was. The clocks on the walls melted in her ear, the second hand on the wall ticking, slower and slower.

He looked back, the knowing that comes with epiphany, with second sight. The room opened up, an imaginary library sprouted before his eyes, the history of the place, it all came fluttering before him, names, dates, celebrations, horrifying deaths, wars of meaningless gripes. As if he could see it, for a second or so, as if he were there.

She looked at his face. "Strange I must say. You look like you've seen a ghost my friend."

"It is strange, it's the third time today, a deja vu, out of nowhere. It was like I knew you from somewhere else. This place. This place had something to do with it. That's what it was saying." Oliver looked around the room. Mystified, glued to the brief flash of novelty, like seeing stars in your head, slowly watching them before your eyes disappear.

"That is strange. I felt something too, but not a deja vu. Something else. I'm not sure what to say it felt like. It felt kind of sad in a way. Strange." Kate walked towards the staircase. Just as she did, the sound of footsteps on wood came clear to the smaller sized giant coming down them.

"Well, hello hello. If it isn't the good Doctor himself." A man appeared from the gallows it presumed.

"Edgar, it is good to see you." Oliver's smile engrossed the moment. He hugged Edgar.

"I see you've met my charming magician of an assistant. She carries the place for us. People might think, well, it's just an old house. But they don't understand we're washing bricks, keeping the lawn, the dirt that comes in here every Saturday.

"Yes, I'm the one who cleans that up." Katie freezes the moment.

"Yes she does. Thank you, I would have kindly given you the merit well deserved my good friend, if you'd of waited a second longer."

"I know, I'm just messing around boss. Of course I know that."

"I know, let me talk to Oliver. Check upstairs and make sure its in order for my man and we'll get things going on the right path for the weekend."

The moment grew cheerful, despite the darkness in the room. There was very little light; and with the clouds as dark as they were, it wasn't making it easier. A silence took over. Oliver looked at Kate and thought of a few seconds before, before Edgar walked down.

"Great, I will do just that." Kate walked up the stairs and into the upper deck of the house. Her foot steps were more than audible, as if the wood in the house creaked with some old bones of herself.

"Come in here my friend," Edgar took Oliver's arm, pulled him down the hall and into the kitchen. "In here. This is the room I'm not too fond of lately. The angles, the wood, something about it. I've come in four or five times where things moved across the room where I'd lay them down ten minutes prior in another place. The same thing happens upstairs in the bedroom. The one on show. Well, the doll, Betsy, she moves herself into the pantry closet. I've found her there a few times. The clock stops at 1:10 am sometimes, you kind of have to jiggle the second hand and it starts up again. I'm not sure if that has anything to do with anything." Edgar pulls out a cigarette, tugged his brown corduroy jacket. "I'll tell you, I'm really trying to quit these things."

"You should. I quit four years ago. What else. What's with the rumors of the man in the window."

"Ah yes, the man, or the older boy some say. The boy drowned in the river you hear, the boy fell off the roof, the boy was killed by his brother, oh and this one, the boy got hit in the head by a horse." He looks, up out the window in the kitchen. "The man, yes. He committed suicide. Or you hear sometimes his wife left him and he bricked himself up in the wall." I hear that one, but over active minds of Poe fans will believe that one most of all. Well, none of 'em are true, at least what I've gathered. What is true, yes there is a man. I've seen him. I've seen him three times. Once walking across the hall into the kitchen here. Once coming down the steps after midnight. And I saw him once from the lawn, at a picnic. I saw him in the window, and he seemed to be looking at me. It wasn't far from my sight. And then he walked away from the window. I had to catch a second glance but I saw him clear as day as the day it was."

"What else. You didn't drag me here for a few moving dolls and a man in a window. What else?"

"I'm getting packages. Usually I wouldn't think anything of them. And most of the time I'm good with ghosts, but I think they're related." Edgar dragged him into the hall and back into the living room. There was a couch and a chair, an old desk and an old bell on the wooden floor. Edgar walked over to the desk and handed Oliver a package. "Here look at this."

Oliver took the package from Edgar's hand. It was small the size of a paperback. "You didn't open it."

"I didn't have to." Edgar looks wide eyed and excited.

"What do you mean? You know what's inside?"

"Look at the return address."

"Topstow 477 Oxford Street, Pristol MA 32867" Oliver spoke out the address, to confirm what he was reading, curious.

"What do you see?"

"Oh wow," Oliver looked perplexed, a sense of confusion was leaving. "It's your last name."

"It's also my address." Edgar took the package back. "I know what's inside this package because I was the one who mailed it."

"Look at the stamp."

"Oct 11 2006."

"Exactly."

"You mailed this 12 years ago?"

"I did."

"Why would you mail this 12 years ago?"

"Because it was really last week. I was walking in the hall, and into this kitchen when I came out through that back door, things were different. I noticed right away. All the cars looked older. Oliver, what I'm saying is that I went back in time. And it happened at 1:10 am. I was up and finishing up and walked into the kitchen. I was in 2006. I walked around, tried to believe what happened, it was late so I went back to the lot and my car wasn't there. There weren't any cars in the lot, so I walked and wound up in a bar and everyone's clothes were a decade out of whack, it wasn't that obvious, things don't change that much. I was trying to hold my own at that point. Then it occurred to me that no one was holding cell phones, or their cell phone wasn't in their hands, so it got me guessing. So the next day I bought a book, and mailed it here. Just to see if I could prove anything. I bought Catcher in the Rye, and I asked someone to sign it and date it inside. In the pub, he did it. There was a picture booth in the bar, so I said I'll pay if you to pose with me, you and your girlfriend. Just a photo of them smiling in the machine. They did it. And I slipped that in there too."

"That's what's in the package?" Oliver looked at his friend, wondering if Edgar had gone off the deep end. Wondering if there was a portal in his compound kitchen. He looked at the package in his hand, then without delay he asked. "May I?"

"Be my guest." Edgar still wide eyed and enthusiastic.

Oliver ripped open the edge on the top of the envelope, peeling it down. He looked inside the open flap, a book and a photo. He pulled out the book. Catcher in the Rye, inside was a photo. It was Edgar, same age as he looked now, nothing changed. But he was in a different world no doubt. The man next to him had hair that stuck strait up from overused gel, the girl had her hair as well, very curly it looked. Her bright pink tank top, her stone washed jacket she was wearing. And then there was the note inscribed.

Hey thanks for the beer. I hope you get back to your friends. Oh and the date is October 11th 2006.

Oliver looked at Edgar. "You're putting me on. This is nothing. I mean, it's something. What the hell. Where did you get this taken?"

"In the bar, no I'm not putting you on. I met them. And that's not it, look over there." Edgar points towards the desk, on top are ten or so packages. "I opened some of them. Well, because I only sent one package. But shortly afterwards these came. From strangers, books, people writing letters looking for help. I think I may have opened up something by sending myself this book and picture."

Oliver looked spooked, a little. Nothing he couldn't handle. He's seen it all. Kate was coming back down the stairs.

"Well Sir Edgar Allen, it looks good." Kate turns to Oliver. Again a sense of knowing, a small fairy dust worth of deja vu, but not like before. "I see he's told you about the packages." She looks in Oliver's hand, him holding Catcher in the Rye.

"Yes, he has. Very strange. What does this do with the man, the man in the window."

"I think he's from there. I think he's hanging around here, maybe got hit off or died back there only to say something." Kate looked at Edgar, as if he's heard this particular theory before, and she knows he has.

"Sounds reasonable. But this house has been here some time. I mean it's a tourist attraction now. Of course there are going to be a ghost or two hanging around." Oliver laughs it off. They all chuckle.

"Yes, but that's not it. Not so much the ghosts as the feelings, and the things moving. Down here too. Right there. That bell, weighs about a hundred fifty pounds of solid iron. Well it's been there all week, just sitting there. Tuesday morning I came in and Kate comes up to me and tells me the bell was on the other side of the room. Next to the piano."

"It's true. And there were also eight glasses lined up on the kitchen counter that were in the cabinet. They were just lined up in a row. And the spooky thing was that there was a feather on the last one, on the top of the glass, just laid out. That got me." Kate shivered, she felt the feeling again.

"A feather?" Oliver exemplified.

"Yes a feather," Kate confirmed in a dazed almost stupefied reply.

"That's weird." Oliver exclaimed.

"It is weird." Kate looked at the clock. "And that clock is weird. It stops."

"I know, that's what Edgar was saying. Every night at 1:10."

"Is there something about that time other than that's when the portal door opened up?"

"Yeah, that's when the man comes. I've seen him in front of the attic door one night I was up there." Kate started to feel creeped out a bit. She backed up, took up composure and relaxed herself. "I don't know. This place, if you go there, can open up portals in your mind. It's shaped like a box, like a cigar box; but it's got powers. I feel it."

"She's right Oli, it does. It's why I called you in. And why I'm counting on some concrete proof come this Monday. There's a letter and some directions of safety on the kitchen counter. Here are the keys. Good luck Oli."

Edgar walked over to the door, picked up his umbrella, then his coat. "I'm sorry I have to go so soon. You're equipment is in the car?"

"Yes I will get it. Thanks."

"Well, Kate will fill you in more. I really do have to go. I just wanted to pass the torch."

"I understand." Oliver looked confused a bit, not much, but didn't quite get the hurry on Edgar's departure. Maybe slightly. "I have

Kate. Thank you for leaving me in good hands. I appreciate that. You have a good trip."

"Thanks," Edgar said. Put on his coat and opened the door. The blackness outside came in like a cold front. Large dark clouds moved in like painted globs of oil ivory. It looked like rain, and Edgar was correct assuming the worst. "Bucker down here. Kind of funny how much the weather is playing her part on your expedition."

"True, my friend. Very true. Cheers. We'll talk Monday."

"That we'll do. Have a successful weekend and we'll talk Monday on the morning. Good luck." And with that, Edgar walked through the front door, down the stoop, and cobble walkway, turning his head left and right, at the point of barely being rescued by a bell. A bell that moves.

Oliver and Kate watched Edgar walk across the pavement and into his car. He looked back with a slight wave, almost apologetic. He got into his Saab and drove off. A dark plethora of moving clouds rattled the sky softly, rumbling; for they too had an ominous foreboding. A pair of lightning bolts split the sky, crashing down soundless from the black sky. Moments later, as thunder usually does, the sound of an angry god came echoing not far behind. Not far behind at all.

"He's a funny one," Kate saying a little soft, harmonious with the wind, as if speaking for it.

"He is. I give you that." Oliver laughs, inquisitively.

"This storm too. I like storms. I do. This one looks a little creepy. I have to say."

"Oh all part of the charm. Don't you think?" Oliver laughs. Kate laughs right behind, though a little hesitation, for a little fear to come in. "Really, I wouldn't be afraid of this. I mean we have candles, a radio, a fireplace."

"The fire place doesn't work. It's been sealed up on top." Kate's feeling of comfort turns slightly, though she does believe her new friend, thinking everything was going to be alright. She wanted to fight her gut, she really did.

"That's alright. Really. We have the lamps. 200 years old and I'm sure they still work. Well, come on, let's get the stuff. You want to give me a hand. I'm sure he's around the bend by now." They both laugh.

"Sure, I'll be glad to help. Lead the way Captain."

"I'm good at that. Sure thing."

They both head down the front stoop. The black sky was spellbinding and hypnotic. The car was parked in the lot, and there weren't any other cars left.

"This is a nice car Oliver."

"Oh this piece of shit. Thanks. It gets me there." Oliver opens the hatch, reaches behind the seat and pulls out some camera tripods, then a bag with three video cameras, a manual 35mm, a lap top, some EVP mics and some other minor ghost hunting gear. "Not sure what we're going to catch. But if there's something, maybe we got a chance to catch it. I think energy has a lot to do with catching a ghost on film." Oliver ducks his head back out from the car.

Kate is standing next to him, like a friend in the mist. "I think you're right. Maybe we will. They say the ghosts come out in a storm. Maybe that's true too."

"That man too. I don't know. Maybe put a video camera on the window from a pod outside." Oliver looks at the sky. "Here, grab these." He hands Kate a bag of equipment and a flight case of video gear. "I'll take the rest." He looks up at the looming sky, and quickly brought his eyes back downward. "Yes, come on. Let's head in."

Kate took the remaining bags and put them in her hands, a little heavier than she had anticipated. Carried on like a soldier. Right by his side. Light rolling thunder shook the ground, ever so lightly.

They walked back over the small street that separated the parking lot from the house. The lot has been there since the doors opened, and the first man Larold Harney built it back over 200 years ago, in 1762. The house had housed George Washington, John Adams, Thomas Jefferson, and some laymen, congressmen, and famous guests from time to time. It finally shut its doors as a family owned estate and opened as a museum in 1976, as a celebration to the Bicentennial.

Oliver swung the door open, stepping back into the living room. He put the bags down. Thought, looked around. Kate was right behind him. The thunder silenced in half as soon as Kate had shut the door behind her. There was a sense that the two of them were alone, on a journey of sorts, unplanned.

"I thought it was black out there, it's only getting darker. It's October, but its dark for 4:30."

"It is. It looks eerily spooky out there. I don't think I've seen clouds like that." Kate put the bags down. "Here you want them?"

"Yes, that will do. I'll plug in the lap top, it will give me an overview of the map out. It's not a very big place, but still there is a lot to cover. I've covered bigger places in the past, working for the Paranormal Mist."

"That name rings a bell." Kate says.

"It's a small paranormal magazine, runs itself out of Jersey. They're done now. That was some 10 or so years ago. I was in college out there so I wrote a few articles with them, took a few shots, stayed in a few places. Cool stuff." Oliver looked at Kate. "Hand me that bag, the one there." He points to the leather bag holding the video cameras.

"Yeah, here." She reaches down and picks up the bag next to the piano. "Sounds cool. Well this is my first paranormal experience. I'm an intern at Harvard and doing paranormal studies and history of haunted houses." She looks for a seal of approval, finds some.

"Sweet, wish we had that course in our school."

"It's an elective." She laughs.

"Still, none the less. It's a class. Well, I'll try and give you your money's worth."

"I'm excited about it. When Edgar told me of the weekend, I was thrilled. I heard of your recent work and studies around the town. Well, I've heard of you anyway. So I was looking forward."

"Thank you. Now that bag, over there. The red one. Take out the tripods and set them up. We'll put them here, one in the hall way. I have a set camera for the kitchen. The room upstairs will need a tripod. The one with the window."

"This is so cool!" Kate explodes in mild excitement.

"It is. Isn't it?" Oliver agrees. They nod, and laugh.

Oliver digs into a few of his bags, takes out cables, then walks a few steps and grabbed his carry on that was sitting on the piano bench.

He took a laptop out of it and placed it on the piano frame. "Do me a favor, find me an extension chord, and plug this into the outlet over there." Oliver points to the socket.

"Sure thing Captain." Kate grabs a big orange chord from one of the bags and walks over to the wall and plugs it in. Above her sat the living room window. There were three in the room, two on one side, and one behind the piano. Kate stood up and looked outside. The clouds were like a thick vapor of gigantic black osmosis. Little drops began tapping on the window. Kate looked at them like invaders from another world, lonely little beings falling from the heavens. "It's beginning to rain."

"Is it now? Well, that was expected; as I believe by the looks of those clouds, we're in for a night here." Oliver takes the chord end from Kate and plugs the computer chord into the orange monstrosity. He then immediately turns on the power button, and alas. "We have touched down, Houston. We now have power. Awesome!" Oliver smiles a big grin, his delight in the passion for the paranormal comes alive. Kate can see it on his face as she too agrees with a look of excitement. There was a moment there. The smile, then a stroke of lightening, then another deja vu. And Oliver stood in his tracks. This time thinking he may have gotten a little too much information, as if a little too much was being told to him in the millisecond of time that came and vanished like wind through an ally. "I've been here." Oliver stares into the window, looking strangely and fantastically mesmerized. "I've been here before."

"What is it?" Kate puts a freeze on her focus, her job. "Here? Are you having a deja vu?"

"Yes, I just had one. I was in this house before. A long time ago. I was somebody, someone special I think, but it wasn't my house. This wasn't my home. I was visiting."

"That's strange indeed." Kate lets loose of the chord a little. "Anything else? Did you catch a time period?"

"I don't know, it wasn't that long ago, that's what seems odd. It was as if it were just yesterday, or maybe a decade ago, or two maybe. But it was in this lifetime. That's what's odd. I was never here before. Though I knew every corner, as if I've been here a few times, or spent some time here. That's all I know." Oliver looks at his computer. The program is on and full frontal, ready to go. "Here, let's get back to it. I need you to go back outside while we have a little light, and harness this video camera to the tree with the best view of the window."

"Sounds good." Kate takes a tripod from the red bag and heads outside. She walks towards the front door, and reaches for the handle. She opens the door, and again stops in her tracks. The same feeling, as if she'd been here before. As if she had found herself in the same position. But this far from the living room, and her mission on her mind, she decided to let the feeling pass, and walk out in the dark outside, with the dark clouds. Into the unforeseen. Closing the door behind her, thoughts of the house came up upon her, like a heavy winter coat. A sense of need, a fear of abandonment almost gave her a slight panic sensation, but it quickly left as soon as it came.

Kate Warren walked over the sidewalk and towards the big oak on the front lawn. The monstrous tree ached in years, hanging its branches like wooden sad poetry, leaves that were left, dangled in surrender. The wind was picking up. Kate looked back at the house, a lonely building with nothing but stories, she thought. The rain began to come down in bigger drops. She thought of a comedy with Steve Martin and Eddie Murphy, Chubby Rain. When she came to the tree, it was as if taller, as if more sad, and so much left unsaid. She felt a need to know the tree's thoughts, its secrets, and forgotten memories. She wanted to know more than the time allowed, as if the tree told her there wasn't enough time, and that it's all not worth the effort. The party was over, the Great Gatsby is long gone, and the woman driving up to the house at the end of the novel probably never saw it more clearly. The party was over. Kate looked up at the window, from under the tree, there in the middle of the front lawn. It's a good spot, she thought to herself. Perfect. She harnessed the tripod against the tree, and wrapped a good two feet of rope around it's frame. She took the video camera from her bag and placed it in the holder. Perfect again, she thought. She looked up at the window, the clouds behind the building were of charcoal black, chimney sweeper's black. The moon barely making its way through gave a little light left on the stage for her to make final adjustments. She turned on the camera and looked through the lens. There it is. The window, she thought; now all she needed was a man, standing there behind it.

She looked up one more time at the clouds before picking up the bag, an ominous warning she thought to herself. Chubby Rain, and with that thought she jogged back to the front door, with a little more trepidation than a hurry in her step. The wind greeted her at the door, as if to say not just yet. She looked back over her shoulder, wondering if someone was there. There wasn't, just the wind with a few words before the overture. Thunder bashed the front lawn, and Kate could almost here the wind laugh. Other forces she thought, the great illusion that we are alone. She swung the door open and briskly closed it behind her. Oliver was at the computer desk. As soon as she entered he got back up and walked towards the window.

"Good job, looks like you got it in a good place."

"It's picking up the rain out there." Kate says, putting down the red bag next to the piano bench. "What next Captain?"

"We need some camera's upstairs. Two of them, one in the hallway, and one in the room. Come on, I want to go upstairs with you. Get a good look at what we're dealing with." Oliver grabs the bag with the video camera's as Kate takes a tripod out of the red bag. They both look up, at the ceiling, as if a cue came to them to answer.

"Sounds quiet up there," Kate whispers.

"Yes it does, maybe too quiet. Come on."

Creaky old wood with splintering memories gave path to their ascent onto the second floor of the Day House. The hall greeted them at the top of the stairs; to the left were two rooms, and to the right was another stairway up into the attic, and the library which was across the way from the attic door.

Oliver and Kate made a left and walked in silence for a long second or two. They came to the door to the room where they wanted to be. The room with the window. The room Kate just saw from the front lawn. The room with the man. Oliver reached for the handle, and put his hand on the knob. Immediately he retrieved it and hid it behind his back.

"What is it?" Kate asked trepidatiously.

"It's cold. The knob is ice cold." Oliver tucked his hand underneath the cloth of his sweatshirt and touched the knob again. "Better, still cold." He turned the knob, and opened the door. "There, here it is."

Kate stands at the door, looking in the room. Gray walls of lonely days draped obvious memories of desolation and loneliness. An old desk with paperwork on it was the most modern piece of furniture in the room. Two old chairs sat in the corners furthest from the door, one in each. Old times, old memories of sorrow, and sadness sat there once, thought Oliver.

"Ladies first." Oliver suggested.

"Oh thanks, don't do me any favors." Kate laughs, jabs Oliver in the ribs.

"OK, I'll go in first." Oliver more than suggests.

"Now you're talking." Kate steps back a little while watching Oliver make a move into the room. Kate is right behind him. Their over zealous fears quickly subside when Oliver turns on the light switch. "It's not that bad in here."

"No, not now. Not too bad. Cold, though. It's gotten colder all of a sudden too. You feel that?" Oliver looks around, at the desk, the chairs, the few boxes on the ground. "OK, we'll need a camera in here, obviously. I'll set up an EVP too."

Kate walks over to the window and looks out. The rain is coming down harder than before. Slow drips of Chubby Rain slid down, wiping thoughts. This is where he stands, she thought to herself. "What about this place? So many rumors over the years, tales and ghost stories. Strange place. I've been here at night, but it's spookier tonight for some reason. I don't know why."

"Maybe because we're looking, and it knows we're looking. Maybe that's it. Come on, let's put some cameras up."

"Sounds good." Kate looks at Oliver, she smiles. There for a second she thought she knew him from somewhere, somewhere long ago.

After silence and screwing in cameras into lifeless pods, snapping chords like wild wild west gunslingers, on a mission the two carried out their part. The rain was hitting the two windows in the room. An eerie cascaded shadow of the tree on the window loomed over them, as if it wanted to be alive, belong to this old broken house.

"Something just occurred to me," Oliver stopped what he was thinking, stopped his director's cut.

"What's that?"

"We have no food."

"I took care of that," Kate laughs. "I have sandwiches and Cokes. I have water, cookies."

"Cookies?"

"Cookies. Homemade cookies. Chocolate chip cookies. Yum!" Kate laughs again. So does Oliver. The two of them look at each other. A sense of friendship was growing, but a frightening thing about it as well. It was an odd feeling between them that was being kept silent for what ever reason the two had on their mind. The feeling that they knew each other. Strangers who connect often feel a sense that they've known each other. Some will even go as far as convincing they've known them their whole lives.

"Come on, let's go back downstairs and see if this works up here. I think we've got every thing in place." Oliver walks awkwardly towards the door. Kate walks towards the window, and looks out at the tree. She can see the video camera tripod taped to the waist of the oak. It's trunk grew into something strong, her eyes turned to the over-reaching branches. Like arms and hands reaching out for help.

"OK, I'm right behind you." Kate turns her back on the tree and follows Oliver out the door. The hall looked less intimidating and the steps weren't as loud going down them as coming up. "I'll grab the sandwiches, and the Cokes."

"And the cookies."

"And the cookies. Of course."

Oliver stepped down off the last step and headed straight for his computer. Kate was right behind him, her head over his shoulder.

"Looks like a go right?" Kate said to Oliver.

"Yeah, I think we have it up. Here," he points at the screen image. Upstairs is clear and present. "Looks good right?"

"Yeah, looks great. Great angle too. If something moves up there, or anything I'm sure we'll get it."

"That's right we'll get it. I've got that camera running on separate infrared, low frequency spectrum, and ultra high range. It records in 55 frames a second so what ever comes in a flash, I'll catch it."

"Wow. Those are nice cameras. He is paying you right?" Kate laughs.

"He is actually. But it's something else. I have a hunch there's more to it. I think genius breaks through its epiphany during the process, not before."

"Hmm, I've never heard that before." Kate idles over to the window, looks outside at the tree in the front yard. "Do you have a screen shot from the tree?"

"Yeah, hold on. I've got it. Right here."

A screen shot of the outside upstairs window came full frontal before him. Oliver looked closely at it. Right then, he thought he saw something. But it was just a shadow on the wall of the building. The tree was swaying in the hellish wind. There was fog alluding up the side of the screen. Kate was still by the window.

"How does it look?" she asks. As if suddenly half hypnotized, under the spell of the rolling thunder. "What time is it?" she asks.

"It's dinner time."

"OK OK, I'll be right back." Kate snaps out of her blank stare, as if the air had a moment with her. She looked down at the floor, dead nail wood, she thought to herself. Yes, dinner. It's dinner time. She grabbed her red rain parka and swung it on herself. Looking at Oliver, "it is kinda raining out there."

"Take no chances scout."

"Aye aye Captain."

She was out the door before he could lift his head back up from the screen. He didn't give it thought, as much, but eyed the packages sitting there, next to him left of the computer. Two packages unopened just sitting there, calling; open us, open us.

He must have stared a long time. A feeling he was getting here in the house. Time. As if time was warped in a way. The hall way. Where Edgar saw the boy or whoever saw him. The kitchen, it looked scarier than maybe it was. But he said there was something odd about it. And

24

the door to the basement, he didn't even mention it. Oliver looked at the clock, six-fifteen. It was early still. The magic number was ten after one. It was like new years plus an hour or so. He could wait, usually, but there was another problem creeping up. An itch. A psychic itch he couldn't quite get a finger on. The hallway, the kitchen, the basement. The man in the window. Time. An itch.

What seemed like ten minutes was only a quick five. Oliver gazed into his computer screen, looking at the video from the room upstairs, getting lost in the stillness, the black and white. He was suddenly a-jared by the sound of the door. Kate was standing in the foyer. Something wasn't right.

"Someone took our dinner." Kate belted out, dispensing the air, slicing it in half.

"What?" Oliver turned, a little frozen a little knocked off his chair. "Are you kidding?"

"No, when I went out there, the trunk was open, and the dinner was gone. I don't know. What the hell, who would steal someone's food out of their trunk?"

"Are you kidding? Someone took the food?"

"I'm not kidding. I searched everywhere. I stood out there, wondering. It's baffling me. You want to have a see?" Kate's eyes opened wider, her hands clutching the wet coat she was wearing.

"Yes I want to see, let's have a look. I can't believe this. I was hungry too." Oliver got up from his seat and followed Kate. They almost walked through the door, but obviously swung it open as they headed out. A bolt of lightening hit the lawn. The rain was coming down. The two of them bolted down the stoop, and walkway, crossing the small cross street into the lot.

Kate took her keys from her coat and opened the trunk. Nothing. "See? I put it in here just after I bought it at Kings. This is really strange."

Oliver looked into the trunk, a faint attempt to reach his hand inside, to see maybe, but no. Nothing inside the trunk. "It's crazy is right. Who would do this? College kids? No, someone knowing we're here? Maybe. But who would even care? Stumped." The clouds rolled over, it was getting darker. Oliver looked up at the house, at the window. Nothing but darkness and clouds behind the house. The rain wasn't letting up. Strips of lightening came striking across the sky, followed by pounding sounds of creeping thunder. "Come on let's go back inside. I'll call for a pizza. And a liter of Coke."

"Sounds good." Kate scratches her head. They run across the street and up the path and stoop. Perplexed and ducking from the rain.

Oliver got to the door first, Kate was right behind him with the top of her coat over her head. Oliver turned around. His face took a smile off of it and gave Kate a look, one maybe that wasn't expected.

"What is it? Are you kidding?"

"No, I'm not. It's locked. The door is locked." Oliver jiggled the handle, nothing. He pushed on the door. Nothing. His brain was beginning to feel itself in a state of disbelief. Panic. "Now what? Our phones are inside."

"Well, thank God I work here. Come on, around the back, the cellar hatch. It was open yesterday. Edgar only locks it up at night. I don't think he got to it today."

"Worth a try. Who did this. Are they inside?"

"Come on. One way to find out." Kate leads. Oliver follows. The two jet back down the path, and around the back of the house to where the cellar hatch was. A few dark steps down and two iron doors lay clad shut.

"I got this." Kate walked down the steps. There were six of them. She reached her hand down and pulled the handle up. It opened. They were in.

They stood in a large room, red poles that were obvious support beams for the house divided the open area into smaller claustrophobic spaces to ween through. It was black as dark gets, Oliver reached into his pocket. "Here." He pulled out a Bic and lit it up. A small light gave depth to the basement. They could see where they were.

"Their must be a light somewhere." Oliver said.

"Yes, at the top of the stairs." Kate amused.

"I'm guessing that's on the other side of the basement." Oliver quivered, shook off the rain.

"You guessed correct. Come on, it's not far. It's just around that bend." The two walked a few feet, here and few feet there, kicking paint jars, and cobwebs, pushing away vacant broomsticks and soiled wood pieces.

"This place is creepy down here." Oliver holding out his Bic, occasionally letting the flame go, so it wouldn't burn his thumb.

"There, around that bend, right above us is the kitchen. See those steps lead to the kitchen." Kate points at the steps not twenty feet away.

"Oh good. I don't like it down here." Oliver whispered it again to himself, as if trying to convince himself not to think otherwise. The stairs came up on his right, holding a red pole he let the lighter breathe one more time.

Kate, behind him, put her hand on his shoulder. It wasn't the fact that she did that that startled him. It was the feeling again. That touch, he knew that touch. He wanted to say it too. Some oddity he didn't, and kept it to himself. The two of them started their ascent up the stairs. One step at a time. It was still dark, with only the Bic lighter to guide them. Oliver could see the light from underneath the door at the top of the stairs. "Look, the kitchen."

"I told you." Kate pushes Oliver in jest. He laughs and they reach the top of the stairs. A breath of relief hits them both. Oliver turns the handle. Nothing.

"Are you kidding me?" Oliver laughs, then stops abruptly.

"Don't tell me it won't open." Kate reaches for Oliver's arm, behind him, two steps below. The darkness closed in, the walkway felt smaller. Oliver panicked and turned around, then back at the door. Turning the knob, pushing the door. Nothing. "Fuck! The damn thing is locked!"

"That's crazy, why would that door be locked. It wasn't locked before. I don't think it was." Kate sounded frustrated. The two of them felt helpless. For a second, completely helpless.

"Hello!? Is someone behind this door?" Oliver pushed the door again, twisting the handle. "Come on. We have to go back down. There's got to be another way in. And I'm hungry."

"I'm hungry too." Kate turned around and started the descent back down the stairs. "Here, give me the Bic. I'll light the way."

Oliver hands the Bic to Kate. She lights it. Both in silence. Both beginning to question what was going on. All they could hear was the rolling thunder outside. Two minutes later, through the maze of red poles and branded dead memories, they reached the steps to the hatch and back up and out they went. The rain was still coming down. Only harder. Strips of lightening lit up the sky.

"Thank God, we're out of that."

"I have an idea." Kate stood beside him, outside the hatch in the back of the Day House, holding her hood on her head. Oliver right beside her, thinking thoughts unlike none she's thought of in a while. Who locked them out? Or what did? Or did they do it themselves.

"What's on your mind?" Oliver asked.

"You're hungry, I'm hungry. Let's go into town and grab some pizza and a beer. I can call Laura, she's the weekday clerk. She has a key. She can meet us at the bar and give me the key."

Oliver scratched his head nervously, but after a few seconds he felt a sense of relief. A plan, at least it was a plan, and it sounded better than standing in the rain. "OK, Let's go. You have your keys?"

"Yes. I still do."

"Don't you have a key to the place?" Oliver asks inquisitively.

"It's behind the door."

"Oh, okay, makes sense I guess; but it would help."

"Come on, let's go. This rain sucks."

The two ran back across the lawn and over towards Oliver's Charger. They got in and without further rain. That was that, the car wouldn't start.

"Oh well, so much for that. Can you believe this? I can't believe this." Oliver slightly pretended to pound his wheel in sudden frustration.

"I figure it's my car now." Kate looked at Oliver, almost about to burst. They both got out of the Charger and walked to Kate's car. When they got to it, immediately Kate saw another skew in the situation. She didn't leave her trunk open. She shut it the moment the two left for the front door, to find it locked. She knew, and there it was; open. Her face flared up, and she began to walk towards the back of the car. Oliver was right behind her.

"I don't fucking believe it," said Kate. And there they were, in the trunk, as if before them, the sandwiches, looking right back up at her, laughing, alive, and breathing; the sandwiches and soda. And on the left next to the tire were the cookies. Just where she had left them. The two of them stood there, looking at each other and then back into the back of the trunk, in some kind of still shock. Disbelief. "Insane." Kate said one more time.

"I agree," responded Oliver. "I was starting to think Edgar snatched the grub before he took off."

"That's funny." They both laughed.

The rain came down.

"Come on. I want to see something." Oliver had a look of peculiarity on his face, his eyes wide with epiphany. "Come on. I want to see something." He waved Kate over with him on the quick stride away from the car, and back towards the house. He ran up the path and stoop and right to the door. He put his hand on the knob, and turned it. What he thought may have been a fluke, turned out against his hunch. The door remained locked.

Kate came running up behind him. "It's locked isn't it."

Oliver turned his body around, and looked at his new friend. "It is. Damn, I thought maybe since the sandwiches came back, well, maybe the door would open up. Plan A after all. We have food, but no key."

"Come on, let's sit in my car and eat. You're hungry, and so am I."

"Sounds good."

The two ran back down the stoop and across the street into the small lot. The red Volkswagen sat next to the black Charger, the only two cars in the lot. Kate grabbed her keys and opened the door. She unlocked the passenger door and Oliver climbed in. Kate ran to the back of the car and grabbed the food out of the trunk. Still there, a silent second of fear grabbed her, but not enough to jolt her like the first time. She was still in control of her emotions, for now.

The clouds outside grew ever so black. Rain tattered on the windshield, leaving marks of buddhist remnants of passing moments. Oliver couldn't care any less. The storm was to be a bad one. That was the consensus all evening. But the oddities surrounding their unexplained circumstances were beginning to pry worms into Oliver's tiny brain as it was, and he wasn't so sure how much he could take. He had experienced things in the past like this before; and it didn't quite end up all that good then either.

The storm was moving in. The wind was picking up. The trees were swaying. Kate could see the video tripod hanging on the tree. The camera wrapped in a plastic bag on top, with water proof lenses, the fear of losing the camera to weather hadn't crossed her mind. The two of them downed their subs. Drank a coke from a paper cup and called it a full stomach. Kate looked at Oliver, sitting in the driver's seat. "Well? What do you think?"

"I'm game."

"Good." Kate stuck her car key into the ignition and started the engine. She turned on the lights and wipers and skidded her self backwards in the lot, then into drive spitting dirt behind her from tired wet wheels.

"Where to?"

A moment of thought. "The Shady Eye? We can grab a cold one while I get in touch with Laura. Let's leave it there, don't want to invite any more misfortune."

"I understand that." Oliver looked out the window, rain coming down like cats. Black little cats. "I hope she's home."

"She's home, little nerd reading a book or something. I'm sure she's not up to much." Kate tightened her grip on the wheel, incoming cars projected their lights harshly on her eyes. The car tugged the road, feeling the tires through her cold hands. "It's getting chilly outside."

"It seems to be. You're right." Oliver turned his head, to look at Kate's face driving behind the wheel. Like an old friend she looked like; but again, he kept it to himself. The rain bashed against the windshield. Gray fog cascaded across Main Street. The lights were long across the aves. Somehow the red bled into the rain and became hypnotic. Oliver tried to imagine when the red light would change to green, but it wouldn't; it felt forever for a minute. A minute light felt like five. And then to the next. The Hollow 8 was on the left. Next to that on the end corner was the Shady Eye.

Kate pulled up next to an open meter. The meters run long and all night till three. No one gets by on Main Street. They start right back up at eight. Kate saw a spot and parallel parked like it was riding a bike. Easy. Oliver patted her on the shoulder. "Good job."

"Hope the phone works in there." Kate shut the engine off, and unleashed her belt, opening the door and out of the car. A date in the night for two, with a rare hoping for a third wheel. Borderline desperate for a third wheel.

"Damn those skies," said Oliver as he stretched outside the Shady Eye, in front of the door. Looking up, he felt he couldn't bring his eyes off the sky. "The way those clouds are just gliding across the sky. The rain has settled down."

"I know. It's not raining up here. Strange, not much. Looks like those clouds are going to break open though, darkest clouds I've ever seen."

"Me too. Reminds me of a Spielberg movie."

"Poltergeist." Kate takes her head off of the sky and grabs Oliver's arm. "Come on. I've got to make a call inside." She lets go and leads the way to the door, opening it first, for Oliver. "Ladies first," she humors.

"You're hysterical." Oliver walks in. "I thought it was cowards second." He holds his hand up for an invisible high five. The inside of the Eye was dark, and gloomy. No one was in there except a pair of ratted out students, and three girls in a booth. And the barkeep.

The two walked in. Stranger Than Fiction was on a video feed, and the Replacements' Alex Chilton was blurring between audible for a dog or deaf for a Man. It was low. Just tweaking the air, splitting molecules of oxogen, thoughts between gods.

"Kind of dead in here, but I wasn't expecting a lot of people until ten. It's barely 8:30. Oliver walked up to the bartender.

A tall woman in a White Sox hat came out of the shadows and walked herself over to help. "How you guys doin' tonight? Wet out there huh? What do you have'n?"

"Two Guinness's sounds about right by now."

"Two Fluffy Irishmen." Kate said behind Oliver, "my Dad would say that in the bar when we were together golfing at the Put in the

Hole. They had a bar in the snack house, and that's the only reason my dad would take me there on Saturdays." Kate laughs. The bar keep pours two Fluffy Irishmen and hands them to Kate.

"Just don't call them that to him, you might get an Irish slap, or you might not get your beer." Oliver takes his beer, nods himself to the bartender as she walks back towards the other end. Where's the Orchestra by Billy Joel just came on, rather an odd song for this place, he thought to himself. "The beer is good here." He sips.

Kate wipes the white mustache of beer foam from her upper lip and smiles. "It is." She looks around the room. "Plenty of places to sit, you want to sit in the booth."

"Sounds good to me." Oliver follows Kate's lead to a turquoise booth, black table top. "It's dark in here too." He says while taking a seat.

"It is. Here, wait here, I'll call Laura, see if she's home."

"OK. I have my Guinness. I'm sure I'll be able to handle it." Oliver smiles. She smiles back, gets up without first taking a nice sip.

"I'll be right back." And into the back darkness she faded. There was a room in the back where bands played. A large curtain divided the two rooms. Oliver could see the curtain, but no more Kate.

He sat there, in the turquoise booth, thinking of the color, thinking of the first time he had liked that color. It reminded him of water, as a child, water was magical, and the way it appeared to him, gazing off a pool, or off an ocean, beams from the sunlight; well, it was all magical.

He looked up, at first it was the feeling, the space between; a woman was coming out of the bathroom. Immediately he felt it again, the deja vu. It hit him like smack off a villainous woman on a noir movie set. There she was, the girl smoking the cigarette with the yellow coat. Ever so noticing him, she glanced for a second as well, returning his attention that was on her to start. She walked, closely up towards, him, as if she had no control. She stood there.

"I know you. Don't I know you?" she asked. But it was more than that, more than just asking someone that they saw if they remembered them or not. It was a connection, immediate. He knew why, or he didn't.

32

"I saw you before, from my car window, outside smoking a cigarette." Oliver, poker face, as if he knew the answer to the mysterious riddle, and all the air went out of the balloon.

"Oh, that must be it. I don't remember seeing anyone. But I kind of do, I look at cars on the strip when I smoke outside. I see so many people. But I think I remember now. I think I do, you were stopped at the light."

"Yes, I was." Oliver said enthusiastically. "I felt a deja vu when I saw you. It was very strange."

"Oh my God, Laura!" Kate came flying from the back room. "I can't believe your here!"

"Oh my God, Kate! How funny is this." Laura looks at Oliver, and then at Kate, then back at Oliver. "You two know each other?"

Kate laughs. "Oh my God, this is Oliver. He's working up at the Day House, and I'm there as his assistant. You won't believe it, but someone has locked us out of the house." Kate looks at her friend.

"What do you mean? Someone locked you out of the house?"

Oliver reached out, took his beer from the table and started drinking it. "Someone is playing tricks on us over there or something weird is happening. The door of the house is locked, when we went outside it was open, and when we returned it was locked from the inside."

"And someone took our food." Kate almost belted. "It was really weird." Kate takes Laura's arm. 'Come on, sit down and have a drink with us. We need you to get your key."

"I have my key on me. It's on my key chain. Where's yours?"

"I lost mine at home and have been using the one behind the door. I take it with me, and then put it back." Kate looked guilty of irresponsibility, of crossing the line of employee delinquency, burning the hot dog at the Quicky Mart, or leaving the golf clubs out over night at the Pitch and Putt. "I'll get another one made. Just don't tell Edgar."

"Don't sweat it Katey Pie, it's no big deal. I can't believe you're here."

"I was just calling you too. I mean how weird is that?" Kate laughed, wiped off some nervous sweat from her brow and sat back down to rejoin her beer. She scooted over as Laura sat next to her.

Oliver waved the barkeep another round. Lightning from the outside cowered the darkness, lighting up the sky for a long three seconds. The thunder was louder than the music. The Smiths came on. Please, Please, Please Let Me Get What I Want. Oliver started to sing the lyrics. After that the conversation turned to a silent one. It was more sipping of the beer, listening to the music. The knowing that they had to get back to the house was of priority. They found the key. The beer was the icing on the cake. Why spoil the drink if you're hosting the party. The song finished, nods were given and just as they were about to walk out, there in front of them was a photo machine. Oliver thought about it for a second.

"Come on, really quick. Let's take a photo."

Kate amused him, "okay. Yes! Let's!"

"This will be fun!" Laura laughed as they all squeezed in.

Oliver put in his quarters and said cheese it. They all smiled and said cheese it. It happened so serendipitously that it almost took Oliver by surprise when he gathered the photos.

"Let's see, let's see." Kate wanted to see them.

"Oh I don't look too good." He showed Kate the photos, then Laura snagged them out of her hand. Oliver then snagged them out of Laura's and put them in his coat. "Another day."

The walked gracefully like rock stars out the door and into the breathtaking autumn air. They could reach the sky, and they felt of it. A curb away and into the car they were.

Ten minutes down Main Street they were back where they started. Day House, the now Historical Center of Pristol. The rain came down, and not much was said. A crazy version of Dear Prudence by Susie and the Banshees next to the Cure's Friday I'm in Love brought them home. It was on Kate's mix tape. The rain hadn't let up, it got stronger. By the time they pulled into the lot behind the house, large pools of rainwater puddled the remaining concrete, almost causing the suspicion there may be a flood. All three got out of the car. Oliver first, then Laura from the back seat. Kate turned off the car and bolted from her side. All three in an English football triangle ran along the walkway and up the steps. Alas, the door.

Oliver stood before it, he didn't even want to put his hand on the knob. Kate stood behind him, holding her hood, wiping off rain. Laura was next to Oliver holding the key in her hand. "Try it first." Laura said.

"Without the key?"

"Yeah, without the key." Kate chimed in.

Oliver stood before the tall dark door. Two hunches couldn't be wrong, he thought to himself. He put his hand on the knob and turned it. The door swung open.

"What do you know. Just like that." Oliver turned to Kate and then Laura, they laughed in unison knowing their chills, feeling them together, smiles lifted. Then in a way it got spooky, dark. The clouds, the assumptions, the mystery.

"Now I'm freaked out someone is inside." Kate stepped back.

"Yes," Oliver agreed, walking in a foot then two. "The thought just occurred to me."

They all walked in together. Everything was the same, the lights, the computer still on. Nothing looked touched. "Come on, lets' take a quick tour." Oliver walked around the living room and then headed up the steps.

"I'll come with you," Laura said, and followed him up.

"Well, then I'm coming too." Kate tore off her coat and joined the party. Halfway up the stairs, a charge of lightning came bolting down, hitting the lawn. The sound was deafening and shook the house. The lights flickered on and off for a brief few seconds.

"We may be in for a black out as well. Come on." He waved them along, they reached the top of the steps, then stopped. They heard a sound, all of them. It was coming from the room, the one with the man in the window.

"I"m not going in there," Kate whispered.

"I'll go." Oliver walked fast, pushed the door open. No one. Nothing in the room. Not a trace. Two chairs, a desk, and the camera. "It's safe. You can come in. There's no one in the room."

Laura and Kate stood at the door, looking in, concurring his observation. Dead quiet. Laura looked out the window. "That's where the man is? The man in the window they all talk about?"

"Yeah, that's the window." Kate paced the room with her eyes. Still weary of walking any closer.

Oliver turned and recalled everyone back downstairs. "Come on. Let's check out the rest of the house." They did. Basement, a dose of courage and all. No one, nothing in the house looked touched. The kitchen, the halls, the back room. The office, the study. Nothing.

The three of them came to a circle in the living room, the rug, red with silver diamond patterns comforted their feet from the old wood floors. "What do you think. I think it's clear."

"I think so too," Kate agreed.

Laura nodded her head. "Me too. I think it's weird, but I don't know. Ghosts? Has anyone brought up that this place is a renowned haunted site that exists on most Haunted House maps."

"Maybe, maybe so. Maybe not." Oliver walked over to his computer and sat down at the desk. "These packages." He picked one up and opened it. He reached in and pulled out a piece of paper. It looked like an ad for a rock band. Charlie at the Clash Bar. October 28th, 2006. Five dollars. 420 Hauton Ave, Pristol. He looked at it, and then looked back in the package. There was a photograph, a polaroid. He looked at it. A woman with long brown hair and a blonde, wearing a black hat. It was a strange photograph, as though it didn't look right, like it was a little warped. The two of them were smiling, posing for the photo. They had their arms at their side, and looked happy. Just staring at the camera. A different time, though the stamp was marked a week ago. An old photograph just over a decade ago? Maybe, Oliver thought to himself. He opened another package. Again a photograph, and a cassette tape. He looked at the photograph, studied, fell again in to that place. This photo was normal, like it was developed at a Walgreens. But again, it looked different, warped, slightly blurry in places. Again it were the two people that were in the other photograph.

"Look at this, come here." He spoke out to Kate and Laura behind him.

They walked over to the desk. "What you got?" Kate stands over his shoulder.

"The packages. They're not from that long ago. These two in the photo. Who are they, do you know?"

Kate looks, Laura peers in on them as well, "no, no, I haven't seen them before." Kate turns her head, walks into the living room. Laura overlooks the photos.

"What is it? Have you seen them before Kate?" Laura asks. Oliver stands up from the desk and walks over into the circle again, next to the piano.

"Strange, I just had another deja vu, looking at those photos. It was strange, like I've seen them, but not really. More like I was feeling what they were feeling at that moment. That was it. But not like I knew them. They were happy. I felt their happiness. But then I felt something happened."

"So you walked in here." Oliver looked at Kate, then outside. The rain patted against the window. The outside moon was lighting the edge of the glass. He glanced up, but then back at Kate.

"Yes, it was weird. The feeling I had was weird. Kind of spooked me." Kate said. She got up and sat at the piano, lifted the lid and started to play the first notes of Moonlight Sonata.

"Strange night," Laura said.

"It is," Kate said. She continued to play, hitting the notes solemnly, delicately.

"Where did you learn that?" Oliver asked, coming closer to the piano, a yard stick away.

Kate stopped, but not abruptly. She pushed the lid back down and sat before the old beast of a late 18th Century Steinway. "I took lessons, as a kid. My mom played, and I played her piano. She gave me lessons all through grade school, from Mrs. Gowan. She was a creepy old lady. I hated going. It's why I stopped."

"You play really nice." Laura said.

"You do," Oliver agreed, "really well. You should have stuck with it."

"I should have, but I didn't, so that's that. But thanks." She got up from the bench. And walked back into the circle. "You have anything on the computer? she asked. Maybe to break the somber mood she set.

"Yeah, the screens are up. We got what we wanted, back inside. Let's get back to work." Oliver walked back over to the desk, hit the space bar on his laptop and the screen came back up. All three rooms were in each corner on the screen, the top right was a shot of the window, from the tree. He could click on any box to catch audio. The recorders were on; it all looked good. Except for one thing. There was a mist coming from the window shot, a cloud. Not from the room upstairs, but from the video camera attached to the tree. It could be rain on the window, or rain on the lens.

"You want to check on the camera outside, Laura can go with you."

"What is it?"

"It's a little fuzzy, maybe the camera is wet. I'm not sure. You want to take a look?"

Kate walked back over to the screen. She nodded her head. "I see. Aye aye Captain." She walked over to her coat and put it on. She looked at Laura. She was already in suit. The two walked into the foyer and opened the old bulky red door, first almost questioning if the knob would turn, Kate turned it. It opened. Outside was a different world. Immediately showers of pouring rain came violently pounding up the steps and onto the porch. They both put their hoods on, looked at each other and gave each other a nod of mutual agreement that maybe together they could get through this, alone; not so much. On two, they ran down the steps, and into the yard. Like two shadows running into the powers of the dark screaming sky.

They got to the tree and felt somewhat relief underneath its looming branches. The camera looked ok. The plastic was still covering the lens. It didn't appear wet. "Looks good," Kate says.

"It's getting cold outside." Laura looked up at the window, the one in suspicion. "That's where he's been seen. The man."

"Yeah." Kate said, looking through the video viewer. "I've never seen him. I thought I did one night coming back from a party. I thought I left the door unlocked so I came back to check and I saw a shadow in the window. But it wasn't there when I glanced closer."

"Really? I bet you saw him." Laura laughed a little. "I bet you did."

"I"m not sure. It's a creepy window. All alone up there in the corner. Kinda freaks me out sometimes; so I'd rather just work and show tourists around."

The thunder rolled over above their heads. Streaks of lightning strips ripped through the black clouds, leaving the lawn a bright yellow and green for a brief second or so, and then back to darkness.

"You think he'll show up?" Laura asked.

"I don't know. I've been to a few ghost hunting events and stayed up all night at one of them. We didn't catch anything on film. We did get some audio once. A ghost telling us to get out. Just like in the Amityville Horror. I believe they're there, but I don't know. I mean who locked us out right? Somebody is playing with us."

A bolt of lightning came right out of the sky, hitting the ground about forty yards away. A giant explosion sound, louder than any other bolt that evening hit the ground like it was personal.

"OK, I'll take that as a sign to go back in. That was crazy." Kate scared, then laughed.

"I'm with you girl." Laura grabbed Kate's coat and pulled her out from under the tree. "Come on, this tree is next."

"I agree."

The two ran across the lawn and back onto the path and up the steps. The porch, the door, turning the knob; a trepidatious click on the second hand and they were inside. Lights, warmth, and Oliver at his desk looking back, over his shoulder, staring at the two of them, with a look they weren't expecting.

"Did you see him? Just now! did you see him in the window?"

"What, you saw him?" Kate shouted, excited. Briskly ripping her coat off and throwing it on the piano bench.

"Yes, and I have it recorded." Oliver smiles a grin, wide and beautiful. "I was sitting here watching the video feed off the tree, and there he was. Right in the middle of the window looking out, as if he was looking at the two of you."

"Really! Show me," Kate almost yelling across the room as she paced across it.

"This is crazy, I can't believe you got a look at the man in the window." Laura looked at Kate. "This is so exciting!"

Oliver sitting at his desk, in front of the laptop clicked on the space bar and alas a video began. The window from the outside stood lonely against a brick wall, and the rain splashing up on it. "Okay, this is from the outside camera." Oliver informed. Then there he was, on the screen, a boy, a young man. Black hair, and a coat. A white shirt and black eyebrows. He was looking out the window, down at the ground. Slowly he turned and walked towards the door. Then he was gone.

"That's spooky." Laura stepped back. It was fun, it was all fun and games she thought. It was a ride on a coaster or a theme park spook-house. But it got close, and she stepped back. She saw something she didn't quite know for sure whether or not she wanted to see.

"It is kinda spooky." Oliver agreed. "Now see this. This is the same shot from upstairs." He clicked on a few buttons on the keyboard and another shot of the room upstairs appeared on the screen. The room was in black and white, the desk was there, the two chairs and there at the window, standing, was a man, looking out onto the lawn. He had a long black coat, and black hair.

"Oh my god. Is he a ghost?" Kate shrieked, stepping back herself.

"I don't know. He doesn't look like a ghost does he?" Laura said.

"No he doesn't. But he must be because I ran upstairs to look, and he wasn't there. And then I came down to check the screen, if it was recorded. And it was. And that's when the two of you walked in."

"Oh lord. That's crazy." Laura started pacing, then looking at the screen.

Kate walked over to the piano. Do you think he's in the house?"

Oliver sat up from his chair. "Whatever he is, or who he is, he was there. I don't know if it's an intelligent haunting or it's residual; it could be an image frozen in time. It looks that way. But then again, he kind of looks real. Not a ghost at all."

"He looks like a ghost." Laura creeps towards the kitchen hallway. "He looks like a fucking ghost. I'm spooked out."

"Well, we're here to catch a ghost, and we just did. So maybe we'll see more. Supposedly the magic number isn't 1:10 after all. But it will come too. So we wait till then."

"Oh I don't know if I can quite handle this" I have to go, get back to the bar or something." Laura fearfully spoke, but in a relieving tone, as if it were the right thing to do and was on her mind, and now was the right time to say so.

"I'll drive you if you really want to leave," said Kate.

"I do, I sorta need to. Really, I was just hoping to let you in. You're sure you can drive me over?" Laura asked. "You know if you guys need me, I'll be right around the corner. And you know where I live."

"I know, thanks for rescuing us from the evil door knob." Kate laughs. Laura joins her.

"Thanks Laura. You did save us." Oliver leans over shakes her hand, then patting her on the shoulder. "Nice to meet you too."

"Good luck with that ghost. I'm sure you haven't seen the last of him, by the way of it all."

"Thanks, we'll keep you on the line. Posted and informed."

"Just not at three in the morning." Laura laughs, puts on her coat and nods to Kate. "Time?"

"Time." The two walk back outside and into the night air. On the way to the car, Kate looked up at the window, just a curiosity killing another cat. He wasn't there. Laura took a peek as well. But it was a peek or a glance, and not so much a stare. The fanfare was over. The party was over. And the afterglow wasn't so much lit as it was a remanence of an oder, a memory, a rising mist, maybe something they all wanted to forget. Something they all wanted to go away.

Kate drove and Laura sat there in her seat in silence, stupefied and baffled by pure adrenaline and fear. She leaned in and turned up the radio. An old classical song was etching its way through. It was a sad violin, and a piano. She couldn't quite make out the composer, nor wanted to ask. Kate drove, silent as well. Neither of them wanted to talk about much. The clouds, the rain, the wipers. The view through the windows, people walking on the street with umbrellas in their hands, strangers. She watched them as the car drove smoothly down

Main Street, the bars lighting up signs of beer bottles and beer companies. Newspapers flailing, flying by passersby in the unforgiving storm. The lights flickered yellow to red, to green, all in a haze of rain, wind and mist. The car was coming to its stop. The Shady Eye. They were there.

"Hey good luck with all that tonight. Spooked me out you know, but it's ok. It's thrilling, but I've had enough of ghosts. Knowing I have to open on Tuesday is creeping me out too." Laura by then had herself out of the car with the door open.

"Don't be too scared, hey I'm the one that has to go back there. Oliver is there, and I feel safe around him, so it's all good." Kate grabbed the vinyl on the wheel and started to grip it hard, almost too hard. "Well, I'll call you tomorrow or the next day and let you know. Thanks though, for letting us in. That place is crazy."

"You're telling me?" Laura laughed. "Good night my friend."

"Good night Laura." Kate blew her a kiss and waved. Laura shut the passenger door and turned herself to the bar door. Her yellow coat matched the rain, it was perfect New England garb for the weather. And it seemed fitting for a Chapman painting, or something you'd see on a salt container. But there was something else. It wasn't Laura so much as it was the Shady Eye. Like she's been there in some other time. A long time ago, or not so long ago. She wasn't sure. But the feeling of deja vu crept up her chilling spine quickly, hair stood up on her arm, the cold came in like brisk wake up calls in the middle of the night.

She drove off. Not far down the road, her suspicion was frightening. These deja vu's all frequent and sudden. Oliver was having them as well, and she was aware of it. She looked in the rearview, as if the answers were there. Out of sight she saw an upcoming park on her right, next to the Hardware store, and in-between the Coffee Rooster. Anderson Park, the sign read, and she pulled into it. She was no stranger to Anderson Park, it served many a purpose for quick get aways, and midnight walks during school. She parked the car. In front of her lit up was a twelve foot clock. It read 12:30. She wasn't sure it was right, but her thoughts were. She wasn't all there, at least not this evening. She was somewhere adrift through

42

warps of time, rain and fatigue. The man in the window was furthest from her mind, yet he was forefront in her brain's frontal. He was there, whether she liked it or not. She shut the car off and opened the window. A miracle or somewhat of one was taking place. The rain had suddenly stopped. Like the drop of a dime, the rain had stopped.

Kate got out of her car, and looked up at the sky. There for the first time all day, blue in the night sky was peering through by the color of the moonlight. She felt a sense of hope. A sense of ease. No matter where she was, or what she was thinking; as long as the moon lit her night, there were stars to sleep under. There was still meaning in life.

She walked down the path, little shrubberies sparkled under the lamplights guiding her. Empty benches with wet rain dew sat lonely on the black concrete; where tomorrow, lovers would sit and kiss, or argue over little things years later they'd question, maybe regret. Kate thought of a man, she once loved or thought she did. She thought of her school life if there ever was going to be one, or that maybe she wasn't a career woman but rather an artist instead, not as interested in money as much as being enlightened through art. She thought of Oliver, she thought of where she knew him. And why he was popping up in her head like an image on a piece of paper. Where did she see him before. It was getting late; and she knew she had to get back to the house. Oliver was there waiting, working, waiting for zero hour 1:10 am. She walked back in the direction from which she came and back to her car. Opened it, started it and back out of the lot like a kid girl getting dumped on prom night. She didn't quite care that much, but more or less had to. Planning it would only fudge it up, listening to what was happening around her was more in the journey, than the destination, more in spontaneity than a plan.

Oliver sat at the desk, looking at the tape; but more often than not, looking himself at the packages. He picked up the flyer. Charlie written across the top, a Pear was in the middle of the page, in the background. He wondered about it. He thought about the name, it sounded familiar. He couldn't remember the band. He took out the photo of the guy and the girl, her hair flowing brown and curly. She looked really familiar. He studied the photo and something odd was happening. He couldn't quite make it out but there were flashing images of things going through his head. He was seeing a stage, or feeling he was on one, and looking out seeing the people in the audience. He could sense the feeling, though it was more than deja vu, it was as if he were there. Actually seeing it from the epicenter, the heart and eyes of a place, rather than mere memory.

Fifteen minutes until show time. He was wondering where Kate was. It was coincidental as he looked at the clock and heard the door open from behind.

"Hey Oliver, you still breathing?"

"I"m here. Just looking at these photos. How'd it go. You were gone a little while."

"I stopped by the park and had a walk around. Needed a breath of fresh air. Had you noticed the rain stopped outside." Kate took off her jacket and walked towards Oliver. "Anything new on the camera?"

"No, nothing new. It's almost showtime, five to one. I want to check the hallway too. Where Edgar said he felt activity, near the kitchen. I've been seeing some mist appear and then go, but I don't know if that's just the residue from the rain, and humidity. Probably."

"Yeah, it probably is that." Kate looked over Oliver's shoulder, seeing the photo of the man and woman smiling for the camera. They looked eerily spooky, like they were trapped in time, ghosts of another era. "Are they Charlie?"

"Oliver picked up the photo. "I don't know. Good question. They could be."

The clock struck one. A bird came puzzling out of the door at the top of the clock and kookoo'd once for the time, and once more for good luck. It then went back into its little hole. Neither of them quite paid much attention. Kate walked back over to the piano. "They look like they're somebody. I don't know who, but somebody." She sat at it, started to play a church cantata by Bach.

"Man, where did you learn to play that stuff? That sounds great?" Oliver shifting his body around the desk to face Kate. He listened, he loved that piece. He always had loved that piece.

"I told you, I took lessons as a kid. She taught me all kinds of classical pieces. Five Easy Pieces, remember that movie? With Jack Nicholson?"

"Yes, I did see that. That was a crazy movie, with that crazy girl with the eyes. And he leaves her at the hotel. That was sad." Oliver laughs.

Kate giggles as well, still playing, soft in her own sphere. "I was a church organist in another life." She attempts to laugh more.

"You must have been. Maybe you were Bach in another life?"

"Maybe or maybe Anne Frank, all curled up scared half to death in some small room hiding from the world."

"No, no, you weren't. You were probably a beautiful gardner taking care of the farm somewhere in Norway."

"That sounds better." Kate picks herself up from the bench and walks towards the window. The clouds were dispersing and the moon was shining through. It was full, and big as a lover's pie. She felt warm next to Oliver, for some reason. Safe. She was also getting that feeling again. The one she had in the car, the one that made her think there was more to the story than was letting on.

"It's almost that time. Let's check the cables, wires, and cross the t's." Oliver picks himself up from a daze, wakes up from the melancholy of the piano, walks over to his lap top and sits back at the desk. A minute and a half till the infamous 1:10, when the man in the window would appear. Not that they were counting on a second show, or an encore, because what they had on tape would suffice anyone's speculations.

They waited and watched the clock. It was reading ten after. The digital clock on the computer was at 1:10. It was the hour of the witch, at least in this case. They scrambled impatiently, Kate pulling up a chair, sitting herself next to Oliver. "This is creepy."

"He won't show up. It was a residual thing, it came and left already. He did, or whatever he was." Oliver looked at the screens, shifting his eyes from left to right, up and down, scanning all the cameras in the rooms, and the one outside. Nothing, no one.

Oliver stared back at the screen. He thought he saw a shadow. Something move in the kitchen area. A shadow across the floor.

Kate sat there next to him. "Anything?"

"I don't know. The kitchen area. Maybe mist from the rain."

Kate got up, and walked back towards the piano, then turned towards the window, looking out. The moon still bright, shown the colors of the front lawn a forest green, on a dark blanket. "How lovely it turned out to be tonight. After all that storm."

Oliver turned from the desk. "You're right. I'm glad it stopped raining. Play some more. It was nice."

"OK." She turned back around to sit at the piano, only there was a space in the corner of her eye, a black space; she could see immediately. It grew into a shape, then a shape of a person, a man, dressed in black. Someone was in the room, and she felt it before she could look up, and as she did, a man was standing in the foyer, out of the hallway from the kitchen. It was the same man in the window.

Kate screamed. Oliver shook. The room shrank, then grew, it got dizzy. She screamed again. She went for her coat.

"No, wait." The man said. "Don't be frightened. I'm not a ghost. I can't explain it until you calm down, but I'm not a ghost."

"Who are you," Oliver stood up. He could see the man looked human. Tired maybe but human and alive. "Who are you and where did you come from."

"I've been watching you from somewhere I can't say, but I came from that room in the back. It connects to somewhere. I can show you, but you wouldn't believe me."

Kate stepped back, her fear was subsiding. She could see it too, but she wasn't quite sure he wasn't a ghost. He was talking of coming from a place in the kitchen and that wasn't right, red lights go off when people immediately talk nonsense. "What do you mean you came from the kitchen and it connects to somewhere?"

"It connects to 2006. I was at a party a month ago, and there's a basement in a bar in town, and I'm from then. And I went into the basement and there was a boarded up room, and something glowing behind it; so I went and dug thinking it was money because it was glowing gold. But as soon as I crawled back there, I snapped here. I thought it was the same year, but I walked around outside and picked up a paper. And I saw the date and the cars looked different too, that's how I could tell. I almost felt it right away."

Oliver walked over, closer to the man. "You're trying to get us to believe this? Are you drunk?"

"No, I'm not drunk, I'm not high. I'm telling you the truth. My name Mike Taber and I live off of Werth Ave. I drink at the Shady Eye. But it was a different place over there, it's just called the Eye. And the furniture is different. The bartenders are different people. It looks like a different place."

"OK, I believe you. For some sick reason, I believe you." Oliver looked at Kate, she looked scared, but she looked better than a minute ago.

"How is it you're not some thief, did you lock us out? Were you the one who stole my food then put it back?"

"No, that wasn't me, but I saw who did it. They came from the same place. I think the hole was discovered after I found it." I saw some kids hanging out with a secret on their minds back there."

"Back where, in 2006?"

"Yeah. If you're not careful you may go back further, but I usually show up then. I once went to 1982. I was there a day, then I went back to 2006. But what I'm not getting, is that it was different looking then too. Like it was a different town almost."

"Show me where you came from." Oliver dared up, spoke, looked outside. The moon lay a dead eye circle in the middle of the window. He looked back up at Mike. "I want to see, it's okay, I believe you. I want to see where you came from."

"Okay," said the man. "I'll show you. It's out of the kitchen. In the pantry closet there's a room." He walked over the rug, and back towards the kitchen. There was still something wrong, something different. Not of this world. They followed him anyway.

They walked through the old hallway and down towards the kitchen. It was old, but well kept. Black and white tiles checkered the walls. They reached the pantry. Mike pointed. "Here, in there." He opened the door and a seven foot or so little room hid. White shelves with a few books and a couple tins sat on them. In the back, at the wall was a small box like hole. Small, but large enough for someone to crawl into. There were a few boards around it, but obviously they were broken, and on the floor. Someone had gotten through, maybe it was Mike. Maybe it were the others he spoke of. Maybe it was all a joke and it was a dog. But it didn't look like much of joke, or a dog.

"How come you're famous here a long time, up in the window. People talk about a man in the window."

"Time stretches." Mike said. "Before I say anything more, I need to tell you something."

"What is it," Oliver asked. Something itched, he could'n't quite make it out. He looked at Kate, she looked back. They both appeared frazzled, and couldn't make checkers from chess.

"Is it bad?" Kate asked, for some reason I don't like what you're about to say.

"Well, it's different. It's not bad. It's different." Mike looked down at the wood floor. He could see the spaces between the boards, showing the basement. For a second he got lost there, not quite knowing what to say or how to respond. "Well, I'll just say that the two of you aren't who you think you are."

"What do you mean by that." Kate, blood pressure rising, sounding a bit scared. "Tell us what you're saying, in English."

"The two of you are already there, in the past. But you are going under different names, or known by different names, and you look a little different too. But when you go back you'll see. I figured it out. I've been following it. It's not like it's the past. It is and it isn't. It's still there. How can I explain this, it's in another dimension, or world. But it's the same life, only you guys were expelled into another world, and wound up here."

Oliver laughs. "You're kidding right?" He laughs more. "That sounds ludicrous."

"It is. But it's not. It's real. It's like a dream. In a dream you are somewhere else, sometimes you can't see yourself, but you see through your eyes, yet you can feel a person there. And you know you're there, but then you wake up. It's like that."

"Why are you telling us this?" Kate asks, tremors building in her hands.

"Because the two of you are a couple there. You're also famous musicians. But something happened and a schism in the life stream of the universe created a false world and you fell into it."

"But I remember my whole life as me, Oliver, me. I grew up in Pristol, I remember everything, my schools, my friends. I don't get it."

"No, you lived that life here. In a way. It was a shift in time, like you were watching a movie. It seems like you're watching a lifetime in a movie, but it's still only two hours. You do live here, but you don't belong here. As soon as you go there, you'll be in that world and you'll know, you'll see. You'll notice the time line too, how it's more real. Here is a fabrication. It's almost not real. You're in a trap of sorts."

"Who sent those packages?"

"You did. When you will have returned, which will be soon, you will send those packages, to tell yourselves to avoid the trap, and believe me. The two of you were special and were meant to help that world, but others got in between the two of you. And something happened." Mike walked over towards the back of the kitchen, stepping out of the pantry. He stood at the window. His profile looked like that of which they were watching when they first saw him on the video. His strange erect posture, his hair almost perfectly combed, all neat and clean, yet you could feel the cold on his face, the distance he traveled in his life.

"What if you're a crazy person, who broke in here and stole our food, and then put it back, and locked the doors?" Kate was staring at him, as he gazed out into the night through the crossed window.

He turned around. "I know you'd like to think that, but it isn't the case. The truth is in the hole."

Kate looked at him, wondered who he was. "Why us? Because you think we're two rock stars from a decade ago, or more than a decade ago? Wouldn't we know who we were?" She looked flustered, confused, tired. It was past bedtime.

"Yes, it's hard to believe, but not really. You may have to take my word for it." Mike took a glass out of the cabinet and filled it with some water from under the sink. "You see, I'm not a ghost, I still drink water."

Oliver laughed.

Kate looked half amused. "That doesn't prove anything. In heaven you can eat all you want."

"Well, does this look like heaven to you?" Mike smirked, Kate stepped back a foot.

"No, not really. But it's earth. And I know my life, and because some hoodlum from the other side of the tracks all blacked out in goth tells me this isn't, well I'm not so sure I want to accept my transfer right now and follow you into some black hole." She walked out of the kitchen and back into the living room. "Why the hell did I come here? This is crazy!" she screamed and sat herself down at the piano. "Meet Joe Black. No thanks!" She lifted the guard and started playing Beethoven. She thought how old Ludwig was deaf, poor guy, she said to herself. Poor guy. Her fingers hurt a little from being cold. She played anyway. The sound of the piano reverberated through the hallowed halls of the bleak house, engulfing the echoes of her maddening dilemma, leaving a peace and calm only Beethoven could resolve for her. It was deep, and an underlying scar brought her to a place she felt safe, to a place only she knew.

Oliver stood there, in the foyer out of the hall. Michael was behind him as if both were in awe of the stillness, the sound of enchantment. The life hidden now brought back.

Kate finished the notes of a lonely Moonlight Sonata, fitting as she loomed out at the real thing, casting it's bright light through the window. She looked up at Oliver, then Mike behind him. "Just don't ask me where I learned how to play."

"I won't, but you play beautifully." Mike said.

She got up and walked over to them, looking at Mike. "Thank you. I'll take your Magic Toad's Wild Ride."

"Why the sudden change?" He jests.

"It's hell here. Something's wrong too. And if I drink the cool-aid I won't die, right?"

"That's right. We'll be back here tonight if you'd like, but at least see for yourself. And if you go nowhere, then you're just in a hole in the pantry right?"

"That's right. I mean, it sounds like something out of a sci-fi movie, but we're here hunting you, and here you are, and the whole thing isn't normal."

"It's not normal," Oliver butted in. "It's true, but I've been having funny feelings all day. And it's been raining all day, and maybe there's more to life than just working, maybe there's a supernatural part that no one would like to admit."

"What like fairies in Druid Land?" Kate laughs. They all laugh.

"Yeah, like fairies and Leprechauns."

Mike steps up, rubs his hair. "You know, I never thought I'd be here, but here I am. I wouldn't be taking the chance if I weren't telling you good people the truth."

"Then where are we?" Kate asked, hesitantly, as if she didn't want to know.

"I told you, you're in the future, but there was a lapse in the time, and a warp and it changed things. It creates it as it goes along. I can't explain it. It's like asking me to drink a glass of milk out of a carton and then having me fetch the cow it came from. It doesn't work like that."

"Why not? Get the cow."

"I thought you were in. I'll bring you to the milk, you can drink all you want. We can be back here in an hour. Like I said, what's the worst that could happen? You crawled through a hole."

"Okay, I believe you. Let's do it." Kate looked at Oliver. They both nod and agree in solid conjecture.

"It's not rocket science, you just crawl in the back, it's hard to explain."

"Does it hurt? Will it fry my brain?" Kate asking behind herself, working herself through it, laughing a little.

"No, it won't hurt. It won't fry your brain either. A little dizzy for three seconds, but that's it. You won't pass out or anything. You just crawl and until you're there, on the other side."

"That's it?" Oliver said. "Crawl until you're there? What, is there more hole behind that thing that we're not aware of?"

"Just a few yards, ten yards or so. Nothing to be frightened of. You can take the flashlight, but it won't work with light. I tried it once.

You have to go through in the dark." Mike scratched his head. "Trust me."

"Trust you? You scared the crap out of us and now you want us to crawl through a hole into another dimension. Trust you. That's funny. OK, I trust you." Kate walked towards the pantry door, opened it. "OK, that's it. I'm done talking about it. You want to go first honcho?"

"No, you go first, I'll be right behind the two of you. Oliver can go after you. We have to move quickly too. There's a time limit on the opening. It's why I only show up at certain times, like one in the morning. There's a reason behind that." Mike scratched his head more, pulling his hair back. He looked nervous, panicky. "Let's go. I can't explain it any longer."

"OK, OK, I'll go!" She walked into the pantry, it wasn't much, a little creepy but she could deal. She walked to the far end and bent down, towards the hole. She looked into it, pushing away some frail boards at her fingertips. Nothing but dark, a few feet she could see easily, but it was dark after that. "No problem, here I go." She put her hands forward with her arms and squeezed through. "I'm in. I'm crawling."

"How is it? Can you feel anything, see anything?" Oliver yells through the hole, standing at the head of the pantry. Mike behind him.

"Just dirt. I'm crawling."

"Tell me when you hit the end." Oliver yelled again.

"OK, I'm still crawling."

"OK, just keep talking so I know."

"I'm almost there. I'm just about there." "
Oliver breathes a sigh, almost laughs to himself.

"Okay, I'm there."

"Okay Good," Oliver yells out. "Anything?"

She waits a few seconds. "Nothing. No change. I'm still here. Now what?"

Mike stood at the head next to Oliver, scratching his head. "I hope we didn't miss it."

"Is this some kind of game you're playing? Are you mad or something? A town junkie maybe." Oliver looked at Mike, saw him in his hair. Brightened his eyes.

"No, no game. Like I said. She can come back out."

"Kate!" Oliver yelled back through the hole. "OK, you can come back out now. I think we've all had enough."

There wasn't an answer.

"Kate? Can you hear me? You can come back out."

No answer.

Oliver stretched down, put his hands on the wooden floor and reached his head into the hole. "Kate, you there? You OK?"

"Boo!" Kate's face appeared right in front of Oliver's, in the dirt, one on each side of the boarding. Oliver bounced backwards, hitting his head and then landing on the floor of the pantry.

"Jesus, you scared the crap out of me."

Kate laughed a little, pulled herself back into the pantry and got up on her knees. "Nothing back there boss. Nothing back there at all." She looked up. Oliver was on his hind holding his head.

"Ouch that hurt, mother." Oliver looked up to see what Mike was thinking about all this. He wasn't there. "Fucking shit, where did he go. Mike? Mike!"

"What, he was here with you? Mike you in the kitchen?" They both got up and walked out of the pantry and into the kitchen. It was bare.

"Mike!" Oliver cried out.

No answer.

"Hey weirdo!" Kate cried out walking into the living room. It was empty. Nowhere. Nothing. Oliver followed her and looked around the room as well. No one. He dove for the stairs and ran up them. No one was around. He called out, Mike, Mike. No answer. Mike was gone.

Oliver walked back down the stairs, his head somewhat down and disillusioned. He couldn't quite spell it out. Kate was at the bottom of the stairs.

"He's not up there, is he?" she said.

"No, he's not. He was standing next to me, and then he wasn't. I bent down to see where you went, and then I hit my head, and then you came through. Strange. He just vanished." Oliver stood there at the bottom of the stairs, not knowing what to think. It was late. The clock was ticking, and somehow they both felt had. Oliver walked over to the computer, looked at the screen and shut it down. "I quit. My head hurts and it's late." He said. "I've had quite enough, really. Let's pack it up. What do you say?"

"I agree. We got what we came for." Kate laughed.

"I don't know, did we sign up for this?" Oliver had to chuckle and nod his own head in agreement. Kate nodded too. A good laugh was in hand like a bird, and they took it.

They took their things and put them in the bag. Oliver went upstairs and grabbed the camera out of the room, somewhat in anger, somewhat in appeasement. Kate grabbed the cameras downstairs. After putting everything in the bags, they thought it a good time to put the key back to use and lock up.

"Crazy night." Oliver said zipping the bags. Zipping them up good.

"You think he is a ghost or something like that?" Kate leaned down and put the rest of the chords in the orange duffle bag.

"I don't know. Maybe he is. Creeped me out too." Oliver reached down as well, grabbed a tote and put his laptop in it. "Got everything?"

"Yeah, but the camera outside on the tree." Kate took her coat off the piano. "Really nice piano too. Shame we weren't really stars back there in that place stuck in time."

"Yeah, sounded nice, didn't it?" Oli laughed.

Kate laughed back. "It did. It sounded awesome in a way, like it gave me reason or a purpose. Just for moment. I felt it. Did you feel it?"

"I felt it." Oliver nodded as well, a warm comfort hug people give with their eyes and face. They were enjoying the break, the release, getting along like old camp buddies back from the haunted woods, all ready to feel real life again.

"Well, I'm glad we're leaving here. We have everything?" Kate asked one more time. They headed towards the door. Turned off the lights, looked around and walked outside. It was beautiful out. The moon, the stars in the sky. The thoughts about life, and the love of it. It whistled in the air.

"Such a nice night." Kate said, she turned around and locked the door, putting her hand on it strong, giving it a good shake. "Locked to me."

"Good." Oliver briskly jolted forward. "Then into the night we go!"

"The camera, on the tree." Kate said, as if she felt Oliver forgot about it.

"I didn't forget. I'll get it now, meet me by the car."

"Okay."

Oliver walked down the steps and onto the lawn, and headed towards the tree. The grass was wet, and he could feel it on his shoes. Skipping past little puddles he walked carefully along the least pooled areas on the grass. He came to the tree. The camera was there. It was still on. He turned it off and took it off the tripod. He turned to see Kate getting to her car. She was opening her door. He thought she may have looked up to see him, but it was still past midnight and dark, so he couldn't quite make out the details on her face, just a figure past the light in the lot.

For a second he couldn't tell if he had tripped first or glanced, but the camera slipped out of his hand and fell to the ground. When he went to reach down for it, he lost his balance and fell hands first on the wet dirt. Whether he cursed, or didn't he wasn't sure, but he was sure of the feeling he had, freezing there in a second or two to make sense of it. He glanced up when he felt he shouldn't have, or maybe it was fate that made him do it. The window, he had to look at the window, the window made him fall; he thought. And when he did glance up, his suspicions were correct. The man was back, looking out, looking down. There he was standing in the shadow of the moon, behind the glass of a vacant room at the infamous Day House.

Oliver felt the wet in his hand, wondering if it were the wet from the ground, or sweat coming from his body. He picked himself up, took his sight off the window and shoved the camera in the bag, leaving the tripod on the grass just sitting there. He paced fast, carried himself clear across the lawn, away from the tree. Away from the window. Away from this house.

He paced straight over to Kate's car sitting next to his, opened the passenger's side and got in. "Drive." He said.

And that was it.

She felt something. Maybe he saw something. Maybe they both have really had enough. She did just that. Drove. Oliver reached over and turned up the radio. Your Song by Elton John was on, "moss on the roof", a sense of relief came over and he leaned back in the chair. He looked over at Kate. She looked at him back. Drive, she could hear him say. Drive.

She sped out of the lot, drove down onto Main Street, passed the Old Fire Station, The Library, Barbie's Barbershop, and the Eatery. They were coming down to the Eye. The light crossing was blinking yellow.

Just ahead Oliver could see a figure on the side of the road, it was right at the upcoming light. In front of the Shady Eye. "Slow down." He could see a person in a yellow rain coat. She had something in her hand. It was cigarette. Just like when he had seen her before, standing there alone at the light. "It's Laura."

Kate slowed down and pulled her red Volkswagen over coming to the curb. Oliver pulled down his window, letting the outside air in. Laura stood there, seeing them, happy. She came running over to the car, waving her hand, throwing the cigarette to the wet concrete. It was then that Oliver got that feeling again. That strange feeling he'd been having all day long. That feeling of deja vu. That feeling he'd been here before.

"You need a ride home?" Kate asked over Oliver's shoulder.

"I do." Laura said.

Oliver got out, lifted his seat up and Laura squeezed on into the backseat. Kate stepped on the gas and the little red car drove off down the mild cliche of Main Street. The moon lit over the telling sky, separating itself from the not-so-innocent clouds of 2018. 2006 wasn't far away. That's what Oliver was thinking. He reached into his pocket

56

and pulled out the photos taken earlier at the Shady Eye. He looked at them, rubbed his thumb up and down the black and white little mementos, wondering to himself if they all kind of looked like the people in the photo from the package or not. Not that much, he thought, maybe a little. Maybe enough to doubt himself, or believe that man in the window a little more than he'd like to credit him for. Just down that road, he thought. He'll send the photos off tomorrow maybe, put them in the mail, he told himself. Nothing left to lose was the old song. 2006, wasn't that far way at all. Through a little crawl hole in a pantry closet, right down that road. Not that far away at all.

"What you got there, Oli?" Kate looked over, turned down the radio."

"Nothing really, just the photos from the bar. That's all."

"Oh." Kate looked ahead. The street was barren. She looked through the review. Laura was passed out. For the better, Kate thought.

No one was on the road. Pristol was dead, even the parking meters have shut down for the night. Just three little indians in a little red Volkswagen heading north on Main Street. "Can I have them?"

Oliver looked down at the photos, thought about it for a long second. "Yeah, sure. Here you go." He handed them over to Kate. "Guess that's that."

"Guess it is." Kate put her foot down on the pedal. She then opened up her window and threw the photos out into the heaven's sky.

"Guess it is." Oliver looked at Kate, then Kate back at Oliver, her eyes right on his. That feeling again. Deja vu. She felt it. He said it. "Like we've been here before?"

"Exactly. You felt it too?"

"Yes, I did. That one hit me hard." Oliver looked at Kate. They didn't have to say anything else. At once, together they both just started cracking up laughter, loud and with due hysteria, knowing each other like a good old book, like school kid camping friends, lovers without the wounds, drama students, singers in a band. Both of them just laughed. And for once in a really long time, it felt like it was all they ever really needed. Like it was all they ever wanted. They laughed. And it felt good.

Pilate's Dilemma With a Witch

Berklee College sits on Boylston Street inside the outside of Boston Massachusetts. Just down the street on Symphony Road sat a string of beautiful brownstones, housing a good share of the South End of Boston. Berklee sat there like the kind of school it was in the eighties, before music faded out of society like the CD player left the laptop. Berklee housed the devout music diehards of the era. It was a well famed place where the good went and studied.

Oscar came to the school in 85, a time where Cadillac Sedan Devilles were the car in style, and only the very rich could afford a Jaguar. The iPod hadn't been invented, and the radio held the attention of the passersby and morning wake me up in Americas'. It was off to school, and work, and society had its work to do; it carried on with or without anyone. Oscar James Warhl, 19 years old, found his place along the right wing of building A, next to the freeway. Blank windows with real life, real world on the outside let the light in, on a long hallway filled with musical rooms, jazz players were rehearsing from the Fake Book. The yellow book that had the Roman Numerals for all the standards one may need to know, if they were to play out and make a living from it. Oscar billowed the scores, took them home to his one bedroom studio. He lived just above a bar called the Eye. He was a pianist, and when he saw the poster on the wall that morning, outside the Eye, he kind of stood back, took something in, and had hopes for a fresh start. Leaving his high school years behind him.

Harvard
-holding off campus open audition-
Jesus Christ Superstar Andrew Lloyd Webber
Musicians, Singers, Actors, Crew
October 4 Twelve to Three pm. Music Stage 2 Auditorium

Next to the Library on College Ave

Oscar James had this particular poster in his head all day long. That was it. His favorite musical, that and Godspell. Oscar had a large array of records in his collection of musical genres at his fingers. He lived for music. It was his obsession. Records. Vinyl records. Everyone around him, all they ever had were vinyl records. He wasn't much into social scenes or Bingo Night. Records were the magic of life. They made sound, and music possible to the masses.

Oscar took down the date. October 4th. He memorized it. And the time was more a visualization to a day's 'noon' and the few hours that followed. He ran back to his apartment. His neighbor was making noise above, a floor up. It bothered him, but there was nothing much he could do. Children growing into adulthood are always floored by new things, new perceptions, new ways of life. A kid from a well to do family life all of a sudden was thrown into the City. The ghetto was just outside the window. But he was none the less safe for the time being. He hadn't met the darkness yet.

His way home was a late September snow flurry. The cold all decked out for halls. Halloween wasn't even a month away and it started to feel ominously haunted of the new familiar. Oscar got to his flat, opened up the door with his silver key, etched with the number 9 on it. A number he was already afraid of, but when it comes to door numbers, you get what you get, and learn to live with it.

His flat was clean, nothing but a green couch, two red chairs, and a blue ottoman in the middle. Some piano keyboards and a tape deck. The place was warm inside, compared to outside. An unusual chill echoed outside the dirty windows, shaded by a more modern tapestry, of yellow and brown vertical stripes. Oscar James put down his school bag, and threw the books on his single bed. He then took off his coat, and pulled the paper out of his pocket. October 4th. Twelve to Three.

Marisa Sorcer was walking back towards her dorm at Harvard College. Her freshman year was lingering on into pure isolation, trying to gain head-ground. Trying to find comfort in school, leaving her family behind in the suburbs of Worchestor. She came from an upper middle class family, her father selling insurance and her mother a Librarian. Marisa, Mari as her friends liked to call her, tease her, make sisterly love gestures back and forth over cute boys in cafe sessions. It was okay then, but Harvard was a bit unyielding and nerve-wracking, too much studying already, and it's only been two weeks into semesters. Sorority row was everywhere. Mari wanted nothing of it. She had come to Boston thinking she could be an actress and study literature, art, music, maybe something with meaning other than her parents stuck in a town, same job same day after day routine. Five O' Clock came fast, and out of her own school Library, she found a bench, under the oak-woods scattered about. Leaves just turning color. She had loved this time of year, her entire life. She lived for Halloween. She was Jamie Lee Curtis, and Halloween was a small love affair. One she had left in high school, as her classmates and her rented old brownstone in the heart of Boston for three years. By orchestration from their principal, they got to rent out an old building, dress it up and put on a masterpiece of a wicked haunted house come October. This year the privilege conceded to the next grade in line to continue the Halloween tradition; by such a smashing success, they were to continue the scholarship in the school. Part of a Media Arts grant given by the state to excelling students and programs in schools within the New England Pristol area.

The night whispered, a breeze sang songs of the Halloween Tree next to her as she thought of Ray Bradbury's book. One of the best books she's ever read. She put her books to the side, on the marble stone bench she was sitting on. She reached into her coat pocket, and pulled out a small pack of Camel Lights. She took a cigarette out, lit it with her black Bic and stared into the beautiful orange and yellow sunset. A beautiful day to be alive. She said it again to herself, after hearing it in her head the first time. She had no idea at the moment what that meant.

A gentleman was coming down the pathway. Normally she wouldn't have minded, passersby and all; who looks? He had a black derby on and a Levi's jacket. She would've thought he may have been wearing a peace sign on the back, or Hell's Angels. She didn't care which one it was, because in the end that whole bunch were on the same team. The putouts, punks, dropouts, gang members, deadheads and soul seekers all road Harley's in the end, and lived in trailer parks in Florida. But he looked different. His eyes were crystal blue, shining wide and white. His cane he was carrying shifted fingers and hands as if he himself were in a play no one could see but her. He was as if dancing, in some moonlight that hasn't yet arrived, or in-between places, steps, he would show the real him. Something not quite right, but surreal enough to get into the best shows in the East Village.

He stopped, right there. And pulled his chin up from a downwards tuck. His lips together, yet not even a grin of unknowing, nothing opaque. There was no seeing through of any sort. He had his business, and he was going about it. Marisa sat mesmerized. Beginning to clutch onto the cigarette. Both their eyes locked. He could have told her the world's secrets just looking into them for a bit of two seconds. All the heavens of the sky could've opened up and no one could have seen it but the two of them. A sudden sense of confusion wrapped around Mari's senses, her eyes not feeling quite right, as if everything was all of a sudden a bit more three dimensional, yet slightly vertigo as well. He looked at her not a second longer without tipping his hat, his frail fingers gripping the brim. One cane stretch later and he was back in stride, passing Mari all together. She needed to get inside the Library. She needed to work on her English Comp paper. She needed to understand why she was sitting there, seeing this bit of an English Play unfold before her, messing up her calendar of particular thoughts, that liked to take dominance before a less rational or more vulnerable one. He was gone, out into the mist of the parking-lot that sat on the north end of the library. He wasn't gone from her mind. She called him Mr. Spook from that day forward, because he would always come into her mind like a black spot, dissolving into a metallic etched photograph, sitting behind her own beautiful eyes. In her case they weren't blue; they were brown, but in her mind, she was seeing blue all along.

Mari picked herself up, tossed the cigarette into the bush, not before stubbing it out with black steel tips. She had a paper to write. Her dorm-room was not a football field down the hill. It was as if it were waiting for her, as she walked inside the Library, sat down and wrote for the next hour. Her dorm building was old, built a century or more ago. People joked about it being haunted. The new freshman loved the lure of that, going along with ghosts, ghost hunting, haunted things come October. Colleges all over the county went an extra mile setting up decorations, welcoming the holiday in a way was borderline normal, a little more out in the moonlit rural to urban cities; Halloween made it's own mark on the Calendar.

Mari closed the door behind her as she left the Library. Made a right at the path and walked down the hill. Her dorm was at the bottom. There was Craigo, the security guard. He said hello to Mari on the way in. She smiled back and asked how he was doing. "Same old, same old," he'd say, and to the stairwell she walked. Away from Craigo. Not thinking about him at all for the rest of the night.

Across the pond, on the same campus, on the casings of Elf bridge, what the students call the bridge that takes students and walker-ons across the Charles River and into Cambridge, walked Christi Anne. Christi was from Missouri, Columbia Missouri right next to the Mizzou campus. Her party place at 18 was the dungeons of old punk rock clubs lingered in her clothes for the last two years. Her wish was to go to Harvard, become an English teacher when she left, move on from being the lone wolf in circles of wolves. It was a night and day persona problem. It was study study study, stand in front of punk rockers on the weekends smoking joints with the local hoodlums of the in-town kids. That was it. Nothing fancy, nothing out of the lines. It were the lines that got her in trouble in the first place, she wouldn't be where she was at otherwise. Christi looked up. On a pole standing in the frost dropping snow, as it was coming down harder now. She needed to get inside, but she could recognize it right away, the poster on the frozen steel pole. It was the shape of two angels standing head to head praying to each other. It was the cover of Jesus Christ Superstar. Christi walked up to it. Auditions. She read. October 4th. She tore it off the pole, looked around in an almost humorous suspicion, and quickly stuffed it into her pocket. Going back towards school, she stepped inside The Town Cryer, a bar on the south side, just over the bridge. She had a smile on her face, she couldn't do a thing that night to wipe it off.

Arthur Wirth. He was a different boy. Soul seed from the South side of Newark, moved to Pristol Falls when he was 12 and found himself walking the streets of the poor city until he found himself at William Paterson College, a four year school where a student could get a state education without the school population getting in the way.

Arthur was thinking of his hometown, staring outside the window as a kid, watching the snow fall. He had just arrived a few short days ago into Boston. Arthur disliked large cities, something he'd have in common with many freshman that come and go from the Irish meat-grind. He was in the home of the Celtics, the Red Sox, and Cheers. There had to be a little give and take. Coming from a small town, not much to do in Pristol Falls. He would soon find himself suited wrong for the color of Autumn in New York. It was Autumn in Boston.

Simmering through the comics on Newberry Street, inside his favorite little buy and sell comic shop, Arthur thought about what he heard on the train coming in. He was thinking about something someone told him once. Never let a girl ruin your career. Never let love ruin that. He had just broken up with his girlfriend from back at school in Pristol. It was a fresh start he thought. Then she started hanging around with some really bad folks, persuasive and shallow, nosey and opinionated, social butterflies from another era. Someone looked at Arthur in the subway, just looked at him. It was a cold day, even for September.

"You're not going to forget her you know." That's what the guy said. None of them would see any coincidence of Marisa walking past the two gentleman. She had no reason of being there just yet, in a play playing out, the beginnings.

"You're never going to forget her you know." And then the man walked away and up the T stairs and out onto the street. Holding his newspaper tight under his arm. The wind pounded on his face. Arthur wasn't going to pay much attention to it all, but for some reason the image of the man played on throughout the afternoon. Every twenty or
64

so minutes that passed. "You're not going to forget her you know." And a face attached to those words; a bad tape loop of words. "You're not going to forget her, you're not going to forget her."

Arthur Wirth, for everything he couldn't forget seemed to have vanished with a small epiphany before him, like a wisp of air, a small world before him. He had walked all the way down Newberry Street, and headed towards the Eye Bar. His apartment house was just above the Eye Bar on NE Main Street. A comic strip of the latest Batman was in a plastic bag, with a velcro seal for comic diehards, for days like this. Snow in Boston. And it was coming down. When he got to the Eye, he poked in, no one there. Not yet anyway. Maybe a pint later he thought, and then proceeded up the stairs.

His small one bedroom was sitting as the first apartment at the top of the stairs. Two others were on one more floor above, and one down the hall from himself. A woman, early thirties, quiet and polite lives right next door. Arthur doesn't talk much to her, but feels one of the neighbor attractions between them, but they leave it at that. She was nice and attractive, there wasn't a crime in that, Arthur would tell himself, and get on with the day. She wasn't there this evening. He turned the key and let himself in, the room was lightly coated with fresh paint, an off white with light blonde drapes. Art turned on the light. It flashed momentarily, then came to a brighter homeostasis. Five seconds or so, maybe a short minute, not long enough to put his coat down, the phone rang. The five pound hard plastic red phone rang. Arthur put down the coat and walked over to the wall next to the sink. He picked up the phone on the silver hook. A sticker of Goofy stuck to the side of the red painted phone.

Arthur wasn't in time. The caller had hung up by the time he had gotten to it. Short ring too, it left him perplexed. He looked at his coat, then outside his window. He went for the phone.

"Oscar. Did you just call?" Arthur wrapped his puny little fingers around the dirty red wire. "Someone called. Was it you?"

"No it wasn't me. We still on at the Eye tomorrow? I'm looking forward to it."

"Yeah, we're on. Ten O Clock. Don't show up earlier."

"Cool. I won't. Ten O Clock." Oscar hung up.

Arthur put the phone on the hook. Opened up the fridge, saw a half-eaten, half-not cheese sandwich. There was a yogurt, some milk, some Oreo cookies. He went for the cookies. Ate two of them and put them back in the refrigerator and replaced them with the cheese sandwich. Arthur ate it and looked outside his window. The clouds came rolling in off the bay, the lights in the high-rises shined bright against the monstrous moon hanging over no weak city. Art turned and walked over to the shelf, took Danny Elfman's Batman out of its sleeve, and put it on the turntable. AJ often felt like Wayne, the underdog misfit from town who hung out in the cemented underground clubs, where everyone made their mark at least once in their days there. The years piled up for AJ, Arthur James, in his young 20 year old life. But as a kid, time runs slow. Everyday is an opportunity to go somewhere, do something while you're there. Take a picture, the flower isn't permanent. Parks are to walk through, the forest is there to explore. Camping trips, outings, tailgates, all designed to slow down time. And succeeded.

Craigo wasn't there that morning. There was a sky of fresh air blaring down, greeting her to a morning not to forget. The pavement was brisk and sound under her new Converse Chuck Taylors. Her sweater was red, like the scope of her lips, her knit hat, red and orange stripes, holding her brownish hair tight around her face. It was a beautiful morning, and not as cold as the day before. The snow wasn't as bad around, only on the green. It had faded away as fast as it would come. It was early yet in the season, and the warm Indian Summer hadn't quite wanted to leave town just yet. The snow the day before had come from a Midwestern front coming down from Canada mixed with some warm weather from the south. It created a mist in the air, almost tangible. Mari walked further down the road that took her to her English Comp class. Today's topic was about the 'hysteria' in Salem, that may or may not have taken them a bit far. Or, it could also may have been an evil in the woods so unspeakable, noted and remembered that it became an issue for the girls. None the less, it was up for debate in the class. She arrived, like a small gathering of dogs, all knowing the rules of class, came in, became quiet, and sat down;

waiting for the teacher to speak first. In a way all school was about was learning; the more you listened and learned, the better you did, hence the better your life would turn out to be.

Halfway through class, the cute boy Alex Grother, turned around and stared at her for an innocent second. But long enough to let on he may have had a crush on her. Mari looked back in a blank stare as well.

A bug of mistaken identity flew by, from desk to desk. Miss White took out a fly killer and splatted it on Tommy Wolfson's desk. It died right there. Everyone started to laugh. Then the buzzer rang and the class walked out of the building. Not before each student in the class lined up to hand in their papers. Not exactly sure anyone felt good about theirs, how the night before they invested hours on at least two references and a good conflict between sides. Mari found herself captivated by the subject.

Mr. Spook was waiting outside just as she was leaving the door. For an odd reason she was going to meet Christi out behind the school gym, she made a left in the hall, rather than a usual right. Not that Mr. Spook was waiting for her intentionally, he wasn't. It was more of being in the circle of the loop they were now penetrating that mattered. If for some reason, Christi didn't call her that morning, there probably would have been a meeting of the seconds. There probably would have been another locking of eyes. Love wasn't what she would be thinking either. But it wouldn't matter all too much right there any way. She made a left. And Christi was on the stairs just outside the far end of the hall. Mr. Spook on the other end of the building, outside in front of a dead oak tree, putting out his cigarette. Something should have told her parallel universes exist. But it didn't that day. That day, the two would have lunch and talk about an audition for their favorite play. So happens Mr. Spook was now on the other side of the campus by then, carving wooden animals where he liked to hangout and unwind, in the Friarton Hall, where the art students hung out, making monkeys out of clay and birds out of silk-wood. Irie, the main schoolgirl freak always hung out there late. It was a place to escape the need not even mentioning. One of those girls, one of those situations.

Ten O Clock and the doorbell wasn't working since 1975, when Scary Eddie smashed it in in some profound frustration against the one who was behind the door, obviously refusing to answer, so he broke it and bragged he broke it. And since then, no one wanted to bother and fix it. Arthur was setting up. His drums were fine Slingerland Western European, imported from London in 67 and bought by AJ when he was fourteen, having his first crush on an instrument, and star lust. Kids fell in love with instruments then, when they were young.

Oscar looked up from his shoes and gritted the doorway, walking past the bar. He took off his hat and put it on the rack next to the stage.

"Keep it on," AJ muttered, pointing to the hat. "It's groovy, looks good on you too."

Oscar reached for the hat and put it back on, climbed up on the stage. "No one's here yet. Dead tonight. Slim Jimmy is behind the bar again."

"Yeah, I know. That dude can be a little less creepy." Arthur reached into his pocket, picked himself out a cigarette, "It'll pack itself in in a little while. The game is on and people are watching that. They'll be out. You'll see." Tossed the cigarette around his fingers like a magician from the London Square Carnival Series. "That hat looks good on you. You should model bro." Arthur working on the set up, wires, chrome ware, snare adjustments, cymbals. "You got your keyboards?"

"Yeah, they're upstairs in the room. I'll go get them. Just wanted to see if we were on." Oscar turns towards Slim Jimmy, then back at Arthur, "alright, I'll be right back. Hold down the fort."

"I'll do that. Gonna be rock'n tonight, you'll see. You watch fella." Arthur tightening the knob to his Zildian ride. "Ahh, gonna be a rock'n night tonight."

On the way through the bar, Oscar gave Slim Jimmy a nod, Slim Jimmy responded with a creepy nod of his own. Then as if thinking about angels, for some peculiar diversion, angels came into Oscar's mind. The opposite of Jimmy's grin, innocent angels, powerful angels. Whether he saw the poster first, or thought of the angels second, he wasn't sure, nor ever will be.

Jesus Christ Superstar
Open Auditions October 4th
Harvard Theatre Presents 12-3 pm

Oscar looked at the poster. For a minute almost, staring at it. Seeing a different color of black on white. Wondering if the angels were gold, surrounding the text in the middle of the page. They were an off gold color, almost brownish gold. None the less his brain fused, and there was an abundance of lightbulbs arising in his head. He marched out the front door and on up the steps in the hallway. His studio place none the less was above the bar, not minding he had worked out a payment with the owner that he would help get the music scene going again downstairs in the pub. The Eye was always a predominantly deadhead scene left over from the early eighties, but the clientele began vanishing, and quickly; so Arthur and Oscar began a series of talented guests sitting in with them as they experimented on jazz, rock, or whatever was catching their fancy. Arthur came back down ten minutes lately with two different keyboards- an Arp Electric Piano and a Korg Poly Six synthesizer. Mick was by the side curtain, playing with the lights. Arthur had to step over Mick's wires to hop on from the stage's left stairs. There was a nice little corner set up with a rug, a seat a boom and a microphone sat there as well. All he needed to do was put the keyboards out on the stands and crunch himself into a comfortable seating. The rest of the night goes like magic.

Christi was across the Charles, sitting on the lawn of Cambridge campus. Her cigarette was in her hand. The moon was above her. Thoughts of a man in her head, she getting him out of it. She grabbed the joint in her flannel shirt pocket, and lit it up. Looking at the sky, the purple blue sky, little dots for stars poking through, as if a threat. She couldn't give a damn about much. The smoke from her lips flume'd outward and into the brisk night. Away, she couldn't scream it as much whisper it to the night gods. She debated going out, further into the darkness that spread like a virus in this city at night. Birds flock together, so do blackbirds, birds of the night time, bats. She took a few more drags, walked closer to the Charles river, put her boots in for nothing to do but a mindless experiment, just a moment to see if the water could penetrate her shoe or not. It didn't. She stepped back up the small inclination. Back up next to the bench. The walkway had lights every hundred feet or so, one bright makeshift lamp that was supposed to emulate a similar from the eighteen hundreds. But it wasn't the eighteen hundreds. It was the nineteen eighties.

Oscar finished up Take 5, Arthur was uncanny on the kit. Fills and smiles, all through some serious improv on Oscar's part. "Take twenty, back in a drink." Oscar walked off the stage. Arthur put down his sticks on the white of the snare, and followed suit.

"Good set." Oscar said, his eyes a little red, wide. "Smoke a little outside?"

"Yeah, sounds good." Arthur and Oscar walked like young sound new talent on the fickle scene. The red door almost opened for them as he glided their pale hands across the threshold. Two young women caught the play early and followed them out the door as well. In all retrospect the door could be said to have been left open for them. The wind from September, the last days of September always called in October like the dead stare of a lion. Beasts always stood tall before the winter, as if kings of the winter. October was the lion at Winter's door.

"It's cold tonight." One of the girls says. "I'm Valley. This is Osbrin."

"Hi." The four nodded, shivered a little in their coats.

"It's nice though," Valley would say. "This stuff is good."

"It is." Arthur took a long deep hit off the joint. "You gals are new here, students?"

"Yeah," Valley laughed. Osbrin followed. Then they all laughed. "The whole town is a bunch of students, and the people who work for the student's money. I don't know what's left here. I mean there are a lot of bars."

"You're right. Lots of good bars. I love this city." Oscar belted out some smoke, laughing his way through the sentence.

"You guys seniors?" Valley asked.

"No we're juniors," music majors. Oscar goes to Berklee and I go to the Conservatory." Arthur passed the joint to Osbrin. Her eyes
70

looked at Arthur's with a moment of surreal gratitude. The night was going well. The energy between the four was innocent and meaningful.

"You guys are really good up there." Osbrin lays in. Her hands pushing back her hair a little. A moment to say so. "I really like the drummer keyboard duo. It's an interesting sound. You guys should come to our production audition this next Saturday. We're putting on Jesus Christ Superstar. Just a two night showing, and a rather B-production. But we're doing it to raise some money for the homeless over winter. Really we could use some musicians. It's kind of an experiment."

"Wow. I just saw that poster," Oscar says. "I was curious about it."

"Well, you should come by, the both of you." Osbrin quietly flirts out.

"Maybe we will." Arthur replies. "Maybe we will."

"Yeah, we'll see..," Oscar tails.

"Yeah, we'll see what...?" Osbrin follows. They all laugh. And talk about dreamers in the dank dark September night.

The beers went down, and a few shots of memoryless moments later enclosed the long, yet joyful evening. Sometimes feelings don't get etched into a moment. Sometimes they are stained in like a painting someone sees in a museum and never forgets it. But the feeling is gone, it's the feeling that can't be transported through time, only a still photo of it there lacking in the big regretful mind. Arthur and Oscar walked up on stage one last time and played a ragtime bit, before busting into a mad version of Beethoven's Moonlight Sonata. And then everyone went dark. Last shots, last goodnights, last rides home with classic rock FM on the radio thinking it'll be ok, getting through the youth of life, doing what has to be done. It's a madness later on, but today it'll be ok. That was the modo of the eighties. Everyone felt old, older than they actually were.

Christi walked all the way down to the Commons, took the T over a few blocks, and wound up at the Beer Garden just across Harvard Square. She went around the back, there were more than a few people hanging out, talking at their tables, exchanging school campus banter. Teachers out of class with students exchanging ideas, tourists walking past on the cobble stones, workers heading in out of the pink doors leading to the kitchen. It was a scene for discussion. No one will quite remember that night for a long time, maybe never again. But the vortex, once gone into, puts that etching into print; and there it will store itself into the back of the mind, presumedly forever. Christi walked into the back and sat down in the corner where three chairs remained unused next to the cigarette standing ashtray and the fake Honolulu lamps hanging from strings around her head. Mari showed up ten minutes later.

"Hi honey. How are you sweetheart. I'm sorry I'm late." Mari leans over and kisses her friend, holding a red bag in her hand. Looking to the left. How are you holding up."

"I'm doing well. Okay, I guess. Don't know where I am much anymore. The city is so slick, you know, it's famous for everything, yet I don't know. I feel so alone here."

"Shut up and sit down. Listen I have to tell you something." Mari leans in. "Jesus Christ Superstar is coming to town. Don't freak out but I think I want to try out for it."

Christi leans back in, almost jokingly close, "that's it; that's what you want to tell me. Jesus, I thought you got yourself pregnant. Lord, who cares what you do. That's great. Really. I'm happy for you." Christi laughs

Mari laughs back. "You're a fucker. You know that? Oh Lord. Nice night, I have to say. It's beautiful outside."

Christi leans back, dusts off her light blue cardigan, "it's gorgeous. Charlie is playing this week at the Eye, aren't they?"

"Hmm, I don't know, not sure. Thought I heard they broke up." Mari takes out a cigarette. Lights it. "Yeah I don't know with that group. One day they're the biggest thing, the next day they're quitting and becoming Tibetan monks, then they're doing a reunion tour. Then..."

"Alright alright, I get your point." Christi kicks her friend under the table. "Where can I get a good pint. Over there, gotta get up and go to the bar, what you're saying?"

"Yeah, got to get up, walk over there and order a beer. That's what you have to do. Try not to hurt yourself or talk to strangers." Mari laughs.

"Yeah yeah. Boston is a stranger in a strange land, I'll try to keep my eyes down." Christi picks herself up, gives her friend the stupid finger and walks towards the bar.

Mari leaned down, felt something braze her leg, like a flying bug. Then looked up and out in front of her, thirty feet from the table, a man, dark in spirit and reflection, a man who can freeze time was standing at the door.

"Jesus Christ! That took forever." Christi was back. "What, who are you looking at?" Christi pales over her shoulder. "Oh him."

"You know him? You know Mr. Spook?"

"Yeah. I do. I met him a couple times at the Eye. He's a strange Willy. I got to give it to him. Caught my goat the first time I met him. Just a couple weeks ago. Strange right?"

Mari looked at Christi. "Then you don't know him, you're saying."

"You call him Mr. Spook? That's funny." Christi picks up her beer and guzzles. Doesn't even stop for air, one after the next, about five or six, maybe seven straight guzzles. Then she stops. Laughs. "Mr. Spook! That's great!"

"Shut up, he'll hear you." Mari throws her hand in the air towards Christi's mouth. "Shhh."

"Okay, okay. I'll be quiet about it. Jeez. Drink your beer."

Mari looks up. Mr. Spook was gone. She then picked up her beer and began drinking her first pint of the night. "That's why I call him Mr. Spook," she leaned over and told her girlfriend.

Arthur woke up like a sprite ghost who had just seen himself in the mirror. An image of a woman. She had on a turquoise and orange scarf. And long brown hair. Her eyes were deep brown, haunting. And then that was it. The pale white crackling ceiling. He reached over, turned on the light. Got himself up and looked outside his window. It had started falling again, the snow. It was quiet and comforting. He stared outside his window thinking of as much life a twenty year old can think about. The stillness outside breathing in like a child, as if happy it too is alive, sharing the evening. Arthur's black hair could be reflected in the white cold frost, snowflakes, all around the window. He noticed the contrast, then saw his own reflection. For a second he could recognize who was there, looking back at himself. Then for a brief instance, he could see someone else. Someone who was like a stranger, even to himself. The thought didn't stay, and he glazed forward out into the night, the mist, the lonely snowflakes falling to a melting pavement below. It was a lonely night. A lonely night in a lonely town. Even the snowflakes felt it.

Mari was tucked in, into her purple down comforter, her down pillows and soft teddy bear clutched between her fingers. It was three o' clock in the morning, no one had noticed but Oscar across the river, almost in eye to eye distance; no, it was the numbers on her clock. Glowing. 3:00. Her eyes just opened up, wide awake in Seattle, but this was Boston. Her dream was taking place in a theatre. She was part of a play, her role wasn't as important to her director as she was trying to tell him. She felt ostracized, and controlled by someone. She felt a presence in the room that threatened her, made her feel the fear she was experiencing. She didn't like it. For a second as she was walking away in her dream, a man on a passing trolly train came off his steps, saying "you won't forget me will you? You're not going to forget me, are you?" Then she woke up, staring chin up into her alarm clock, digital green spraying the time. She thought of calling Christi, but it was too late. Too much alcohol she thought, maybe that was it. She rubbered eyes, downed a pint of coconut water and planted herself on the couch. Squiggles the Hug Bunny was there next to her. A pink super comfortable stuffed thing she had won at Pristol Beach one day with her friends back home. She leaned over, grabbed it by its arm, with a smile of relief, and gave it a big hug. "I miss you Squiggles." She told him. "I miss you too," she would say back pretending, knowing too much Mr. Squiggles couldn't talk. But maybe he could, maybe on nights like this. He could.

The next day, the end of September, it was freezing. The day after that, October 1st, it was freezing. October 2nd was a beautiful day in its high fifties. Harvard Square was filled with young fresh minded students, all looking for a unique recollection why they were there, their thoughts intently on their subjects, the faces, the new people everywhere. It was exhilarating. Christi found her seat next to the Sigma Tao Delta bake stand. There were a number of groups and fraternal houses having bake sales. Anything to make a buck. There was a small group of marble benches next to the water fountain. The circle attracted the hippies of the bunch, the ones who might study a little less and party a little more. A tall oak tree hung over and the leaves began to turn into their infamous autumn selves. She lit a cigarette and shook her head, her hair, getting a grip.

It was roughly eleven o' clock. Most classes change shifts at eleven. Her eleven o' five was on English Comp. She waited outside the Library, ready to walk over to the Barker building. Her argument against the hysteria vs evil witches of Salem were a fresh and unique look at evil in modern society as opposed to what it was like then in the seventeen hundreds. They weren't electricity efficient, and the woods were something always dark and mysterious, throughout the entire history of mankind. It may be due to the fact the animals who could attack in the dark, live in the woods, away from humans. Bats live in the woods, bears and wolves. When people started seeing ghosts, and banshees in the woods, that somehow intertwined with the initial fear of them. The forest is a frightening place to be at night, and what happened in Salem happened because of a woman in the woods who initially meant no harm. But she had a Southern Haitian Voodoo background and a practicing ritual type thing going on that she was showing these girls. It scared the girls, something happened to stir up the air as well. There was a magic only the few understood, mindful alchemists and healers. Her roots were unlike anything the young women of hysteria were to admit in the courthouse. Their youthful acceleration into a frenzy of fear and excitement boiled up against the curse of the witch in the woods. The strange woman all mixed up in a voodoo none the likes had been seen in Puritan Country. No man or woman for that matter didn't forget the roots of Pristol Falls either. There were tales of witchcraft mingling in, rituals, sacrifices, missing people, shape shifters, and so many strange things happening. Christi thought of her home town, and saw the correlations between Boston and Pristol, how alike they really were in so many ways. The darkness too. It carries on and down the road with you unless you shake the boots off pretty good. Like marijuana, it lingers. Things as innocent as attending a Wicca meeting or ritual can have strange and unapologetic consequences years later. Doors can open. And they're not so easy to shut once they open up too. She waited not a minute more in her thoughts. Put the cigarette out and walked over to Barker Hall.

The students in her classroom were as still as the snow that morning. Half melted by now, the warm 50 degree morning was full of wonderment and a solaced reflection of how the students presented themselves, together, eager, passionate. Everyone was in their seats except for her teacher. The class waited, as the class usually waits. The basic rule is the teacher gets 15-20 minutes to be late, then it's a free for all. No one gets penalized for leaving. But she came in. Not 15 minutes late on the clock.

"Damn Yard Birds in town kept me up late last night. Sorry class. As we were saying." Dr. Yasman Hwan shuffled through her book-pack, reaching for a piece of chalk, or something to write with on the board. "OK, OK, here we are. You bright young pieces of mindful creations do your homework? Pass them up, you little witches, wizards for the boys."

The class laughed and every one passed up their papers, in an archaic fashion, something no one forgets since first day of school, grade one- how to pass up papers, from the back of the row up to the front, from leaning behind you, grabbing the person's paper and then relaying it up. It was Pavlov's Dog right from the start of one's academic career.

"Witches in the woods, OK. How is everyone holding up on that subject. Witches in the woods." Dr. Yasman puts on her cat glasses, makes herself looked less disheveled and more into the role of a paid professional academic scholar. "Little shits in the woods. OK OK. What do we have here?" She rolls up and down the isles taking the papers from the front row victims, who have in changed handed them along to Dr Yasman.

"Okay, let's see. 'The Witch From Outer Space' OK, not sure yet where that is going. What else." She picks through, putting some down, rolling her eyes at others. 'Framed, Hanged, Sold. A Witch of a Deal Real Estate Scam.' OK OK, that one is pretty good. Glad people are seeing there was a political stake at the time for the landowners of Salem. Okay, what else. 'Quicksand Witch.' "Witch Way Did She Go?" Very good, she throws the rest on the desk. "Nice, good job." She shivers her hands together. "Okay, warming up. A few days under the radar, it was frick'n cold."

"Colder than a witch's tit" some anonymous student yells out from the back. The class laughs, silences up.

"Yeah, that cold." Yasman says.

They all weigh in. giggling, feeling the freedom of a classroom. "Fucking cold outside. I hate the winter."

"Why do you think these kids went hysterical?" Dr. Yasman cuts off the banter. "Was it the woods, was there an evil in the woods that influenced their thinking?

Tom Hardle raised his hand.

"Tom."

"I think that lady Tituba, in the woods started making fires, and conjuring up all sorts of crazy stuff. Talker of animals. I think there was an evil laying dormant maybe. And she let it through, and the young kids saw it happen. Scared the hell out them."

"I think the girls coerced it, the evil, fed into it," Laura in the front row said. "I think what most people don't realize is that we're all supernatural creatures. And we can conjure up neighboring spirits." She puts her pencil in the little pencil holder on the desk. "You know, most people don't know how much power they actually hold."

"Good point Laura. Why is that? Is it modern day mass hypnotism by phones and media and tv? It is true the woods must have had more power then, without the interference of the television and radio. Good point Laura." Dr. Yasman looks around the room.

"Burn her, she's a witch." Someone in the back row yelps to a half expecting class.

"Who said that? Richard Tower, why do you say that. Don't you think burning the witch is only going to increase the evil of the supernatural? Or do you think the evil goes away with the witch?

Hmm," Dr. Yasman looks around the room. "What do you think class? Burn the witch?"

The class laughed, chimed in. Weighed their opinions. "Mass hysteria, contagious evil. A witch hunt. No, don't burn the witch!"

The clouds outside looked ominous and big. Christi took a breath in. Dr Yasman's words faded from her hearing, her face from her optics. The outside, she looked out the window. Outside was filled with many mysteries she thought. There are many things unknown in the woods. Past the buildings. People are visitors here in the darkness. The walk into the woods at night.

"I think there is an evil," Christi blurted out. "But I think once you start the match, the fuse is lit. And it's just a matter of time. Evil is a concentrated diamond, and once it is let loose, the energy escaped is too much." She got quiet again, as if she never said a word.

"It is." Dr. Yasman said. "It is just that. Where does it come from? Where is the epicenter of the energy, and is it a different kind of energy? And who controls the energy? It's an interesting thought. Good Christi, good."

Christi didn't quite even hear her response. The wind outside started blowing and the trees started the wave dance. The sky was dark and gray. There is something out there. And it wasn't or was that October had begun, or that maybe Halloween has shown its face, she just sensed something, and it wasn't good.

Coming outside after class, which was exciting and meaningful, Christi had her first moment of melancholy. She will always have a pin-pointed moment in her memories of school. The gray sky all around her, engulfed her; as if she had taken her first hit of marijuana, or dosed on her first mushroom trip, it looked different outside. Her skin began wrapping itself up, the cold pounding occasionally of spirits who've yet to arrive. Tomorrow was a day she wasn't quite sure of. "Jesus Christ Superstar, what a genius whoever thought up that play. What a fucking genius." She walked back over the front lawn, crossing the street and into her dorm. The lights were all out on the first floor. She didn't give it much thought.

Across the river, Arthur was in his solitary room of self induced confinement. The walls were looking like they've been plastered with news paper headlines, models from New Look Magazine and post it notes mixed in with flash cards. This day is important, this day is more important than that day. Phone numbers in pencil, pen, magic marker. He's only been back at school a month, but his room hadn't changed a bit. No one moves out during their entire stay on campus. The month break at the end of Spring Term quickly bleeds into the Summer Session; before you know it, it's Fall all over again. Arthur trying to get his thoughts on school began pounding lead on his head, his ability to organize himself was feigning. The phone rang. "Not now. I'm not home. Not now." He walked over to the phone, picked it up. It was Oscar.

"You want to go tomorrow to those auditions? I don't know, she didn't mention it was a paid gig, plus those songs aren't easy to learn."

"I don't know. We should go. I have a strange feeling I should go. I'm buried deep in too much and I need to unwind." Arthur picks up a baseball mitt lying on the couch. A half bruised beat up ball was already waiting for him in the pocket. He gripped the ball, held it like a kid who just won the Little League World Series.

"Let's go, just for tomorrow, forget it if it sucks. We won't even bring our instruments, we'll just check it out." Oscar could be heard chewing on Pringles or something, opening up a can of Tab.

"OK, I'll meet you on the north end of the square. High noon. On the button."

"Got it."

They both hung up as if clones of each other, one then the next, on cue like blood brothers. Their obsession to play out all the time, their passion for the music became an excuse after a while. Could music be just that to someone. Someone who may not be able to sustain the purity and beauty of life, and the need to constantly escape it by the phenomena of music and being in a band or along that end. One cat only killing the other on their way down. But singing all the way, maybe. Everyone goes down in the end. Arthur stood there a foot away from the phone. "Everyone goes down in the end. Do they," he said to the phone. "Does everyone really go down in the end?"

Arthur looked over. He had two posters that were legit, as in they were bought in the mall at a Spencer's Gifts. One was of Rocky, and the other was of Dirty Harry. One of Oscar's favorite sayings. "Not sure if I fired 5 shots, or six..., you feel lucky?" Does anyone feel lucky, he says to himself. Or is luck just a random act of plotted placement.

It was 12:00 and Oscar was crossing the yard. Arthur James was on the other side. They met almost in the middle, Arthur walking four steps or so meeting him as Oscar panted lightly. It was cold outside again, a little breezy but doable. "You're on time rugrat. Awesome. Beautiful outside isn't it?"

"Yeah." Oscar wiped down his face, sweating a little from the walk. It is a little cold out today."

"Nah, it ain't cold. Just wait till Halloween. You'll know cold."

"You're right, still a little cold." Oscar smiled, genuinely. And the both walked up Peabody street towards the theatre. There were little flakes of snow just beginning to fall.

"Look it's snowing again." Oscar alerted.

"It is. Good sign my friend. Good sign. Let's go, the door is right over there." He points to a group of students and friends hanging outside a door. A little snow and ice are scraped around it. They're all gathered around it like animals wanting to come back inside. Arthur immediately saw Osbrin, in a long red coat. Her black hair glistening against the autumn colors and the trees that give them life.

Valley came running over. "Oh you made it, you made it! I'm so glad! Hey listen, listen, Joey never came over to open up the auditorium." She looked around, panicky, a little too much energy in the hands. "Listen. We're going to do this again. I can't believe Joey hasn't gotten here yet. He said he was coming right over. It's been twenty minutes and he lives three minutes away. He'll be here."

Arthur looks over at Osbrin. She's smiling drinking her coffee.

Kids in coats were shivering off the cold, standing laughing in the background. Cups of regular coffees seemed to be product placement, as they glowed with the snow coming down. Uncle Pete's Coffee Truck was on the corner so it wasn't difficult for Arthur to make the correlation between how so many hot cups of Joe were floating around when they got there. There were twenty or so kids just hanging out, all drinking coffee. It was weird.

Oscar walked up on over after dusting dirt off his shoe. "What do you mean you can't get in?"

"Wait, there he his. Hold on." Valley runs across the lot. A man is walking up the wayward. His head is up, then its down at his feet as he walked faster to the demand to resolve the matter, and do it rather quickly.

"Oh God, where have you been! No worries no worries, thank God you are here!

Joey holds up his keys to Valley's face. "I'm here." He walks over, no one needed to be excused as they stepped aside to his unique command. There were those people you know or met in life who've figured it out. And there was a keen sense that others recognized this. It was like that. Joey, or Joey B. That was all. No one had to be fancy about it. He had other names. He knew that too. But today was to open the door to the theatre, it wasn't carving out Mount Rushmore. But it had its need.

"OK, OK, sorry about that." Valley gathers the students and whereabouts like cattle, and herds them in like sheep. "OK, OK, everyone take a seat. We'll start in a moment."

Arthur and Oscar aren't far behind, though presumedly Mari and Christi came in, not a minute later. The light from the outside day was beaming through the doorway, lighting up half the theatre. The Music Hall Theatre was unique that it was small and meant for small productions. It held two hundred seats, that fit nicely into the floors with amble room to move the feet.

"I don't know. We'll see," says Arthur to Oscar. "We'll see about this." They both give a little laugh under their breath.

"OK, OK. Thanks for coming out today. Sign the sheet I sent around. Hi, Hi, what's your name sweetheart?" She leans over to a cute blonde girl in a deep blue navy coat.

"It's Laura."

"OK, nice to meet you Laura, you're friends with Osbrin, I know." Valley looks around, nervous. "OK, Let's have someone up here shall we. If you're a musician and trying out for a music role, than let us know.

Oscar and Arthur give each other another look. And a brief chuckle, as uncomfortable as it was.

"Who's first? Laura, how about you?"

"OK." Laura gets up from her seat. Stands on the stage center mark, lights coming down on her.

"Do you need music?"

"No I think I'm OK." She stands there, takes a breath in. She starts to sing I Don't Know How To Love Him. It's beautiful. Magical. She took the room over. There was silence when she finished, silence she earned, she felt maybe.

"Very nice. Very nice." Valley said. "The role of Mary Magdalene. I presume. Well done. Make a note of that Osbrin. OK. Who's next."

Arthur looked at Oscar, both agreeing to give it a shot. They walked to the center of the stage, hands down, relaxed and started to sing. They sang the words to a familiar song, an old forties diddy, and smiled in laughter a little, wondering what was going on, really. But they went on anyway. All bashful and maybe too silly for such a an audition.

"OK, Oscar, you play Jesus, and Arthur I want you to play Judas. Can you do that for me? Just a few words.

Oscar knelt down like a chivalrous knight. The small awkward audience chuckled in a moment of questionable reactions. Oscar wasn't sure what to do or what he thought of singing when he had arrived. People never arrive, or they arrive every day they kiss it. It was a moment, maybe not his. But like later when he'd be in his fifties, kicking out Frank Sinatra's "My Way" on a Karaoke machine at someone's lame fiftieth anniversary. God bless him, fuck them. He took in a breath. "Then I was inspired. Now I'm sad and tired. After all I've tried for three years, feels like thirty." He knelt again, his head in his arm, holding out notes he thought he'd never hit. Touching feeling he'd never feel again. He finished. He'd die if he had to, like the song. As if why it was even the slightest bit personal. He'd maybe know someday. Most people wouldn't want to know the day they were to
82

die. When most are asked if they'd like to know the day they were to die, they almost all don't want to know. "All right I'll die, if you want me to." Christ had three days to think about it. Oscar had his senior year to forget he ever sang it that day.

Arthur came in. Almost unapologetically, as if Phineas on the limb of a tree, "I can see clearer now, at last all to well, I can see where we all soon will be..." the group gasps, holds their breath at the authenticity of the sounds of Judas, coming at them, like in a surround theatre, at last it had some aspects of design by the sound it was creating for the voice as it sang.

And then there was an "OK".

"Very good. OK. Absolutely fantastic. From the music schools?"

"Yeah, he's from the Conservatory, I go to Berklee." Oscar holding off a little sweat.

"Well, you were fantastic. You two can have a seat now. Very good." She looks down at her list, thumbing through. "OK, Christi, your turn."

Christi stands up and swindles on over, sings another song the same song Laura sang, though a little rougher. A little more punk rock sounding, less giving a shit, maybe. It took a minute then she stopped and walked fervently towards her seat.

"Very good. Thank you for that. We have two Marys'. Let's figure what we can do and maybe you could switch off, or one will be happy in the choir. OK, OK, I'm sending another sheet around. It's just that we need a signature saying we aren't responsible if any of you get hurt or something during the play. Just precaution." Valley passed the flier to the first row. The students sat there, took the pamphlet, signed it and passed it along.

Mari, sitting next to Christi looked up and then at Christi's purse on her chair. Holding it up for her when she hurried down. "Three Marys' actually. But I don't count." She leaned over, took her friend's hand. "You were great."

"God it was awful." They both laughed.

"OK, next we have Jarral." Valleys points to a man in the back. Mari didn't see him earlier, seemed to her he came out of nowhere. "OK, what song is it you're singing? She laughs, and looks at her sign in sheet which was given back. "OK, good everyone signed it. We can move on now."

Mari looks up. She starts jabbing Christi's thigh with her keys.

"What the fuck are you doing."

"It's Mr. Spook. It's the dude I saw the other day. I saw him again at the beer garden."

He nods yes. "Yes it is. Jarral Silling. I'll be trying out for Pontius Pilate." Jarral looks over at Mari, she wasn't far away, just sitting there in the second row. Then he looks down. He kicks his sneakers. "Ready to get on with it Mam if you don't mind."

"Go ahead the stage is yours."

"I met a Galilean. The most amazing man. He had that look you rarely ever find. The haunted hunted kind." There was a pause in reality. The temple split in two for Mary's eyes. She was locked in. It was beyond surreal, she thought to herself. Only for a second. But it felt like an endless worm hole. Mari could hear him. Loud in her ear, as if she were next to him, inches close, singing softly in her ear. "Then I heard them mentioning my name and leaving me the blame."

"It's fucking Mr. Spook" she whispers to her friend. "OK, that's really fucked up." Mari jumps a little out of her seat, looks at the door, the light now just shining through the long crack through the middle. The rest of the room was dark, except for the few lights shining on the actors. "We have to get out of here. I'm telling you. This doesn't feel right anymore."

Mari pulls Christi's hand. "Come on. Let's go." The two leave abruptly in a frantic hurry. Valley looks their way, the doors opening, two shadows leaving. "What was all that about," she thought aloud. Never mind. Jarral Silling was putting on the performance of his life, inside a small theatre with 15 or so students hanging around. The lights dimmed, he sang. And the place went dark for the next four months.

"Mari what was all that about? Why did you pull me out of there?" Christi is trying to keep up with Mari's arm still tugging at her sleeve.

"That my dear Watson was Mr. Spook. I'm telling you, something is quite not right about that guy. Never have eyes on me had such a creepy affect. He scared the crap out of me just now. I can't explain it. He was at the school the other day, and then the other night in the beer garden." She slowed herself down. The both came to a stop when hitting Cambridge Street. Mari breathing heavy, trying to talk but giving it a break.

"That's it? We left for that?"

"Yes! We left for that! Who else is going to come along and creep me out more? Anyone in line you may know of? My, the whole thing about it. Those flyers on the pole. That lady running it. It was worse than a makeshift sophomore year high school smoking session. Someone thought of putting on a show, and then it looks like that. People could do better. I mean It's Jesus Christ Superstar. You know?" Mari starts brushing off dirt that isn't there on her blue overcoat.

"I know what you're saying Mari, I just don't know why we left. I was enjoying that too. And it looked like fun. I don't know. Everyone just hangs out in their dorms, smokes a shit load of pot, crams in their studying at eleven. I mean people study, but this place doesn't do much. Oh you know what I mean. And the two guys were cute too, who sang. I mean you can't find that anywhere in Newark can you?"

"Newark New Jersey? Are you kidding me. I know where I am right now. I know what you're saying. But that Valley chick was a bit off the cusp flakey borderline certifiable too. And then Mr. Spook shows up. I'm not going back there. I'm going to class and going to study and going to pass this semester with flying A holes if I have to give up my fucking Halloween candy to do it!"

"No there will be no giving up of Halloween candy, don't you worry." Christi throws in a smirk of comfort, lightening it up a little. "It's okay, I know what your saying. We need to buckle down. I have a lot of papers due already, and my periods in Lit are getting overwhelming. I mean Romantic alone I have four books to read this semester. In Early Brit I have like six books. And then there's History, and then Environmental Science. I have four books in Critical Writing we're reading too. I'm surprised my gym coach doesn't just give out random books for us to read too. Here's the answer, read some more books, read read read. Till your lips fall off and your eyes fall out.

Ever meet a teacher who doesn't want you to read? No never. I never met one."

"I thought you liked to read?" Mari laughs.

"I do! That's the funny thing. I love to read. It's just that when you're forced to read twenty books a semester it's rather difficult. And it's not that I don't like to, I do; it's just that twenty things are planned along with it, and Mom and Dad are already planning their alma mater back for Thanksgiving, and then you have to go to a fucking Jesus Christ Superstar that is giving open auditions." Christi laughs, kicks the dead leaves off the gutter as she puts her Docs meat to the concrete. "I don't know."

"You're right. What they tell you at the first day of class right? You could either party, study, or sleep. You can only choose two out of the three. Chose wisely. Remember?" Mari looks ahead. Some revolutionary war soldier cascaded in iron was tooting some horn. "I mean for real. Is life a party or are they trying to teach us that in order to survive, we must put priorities first. We won't make it if we just party all night with the Shim Shams on the third floor. Right? They won't get through, or maybe they will, and their all genius's up there. I don't know. But they're not us, and we have to study."

"Yeah, but it wouldn't be an ism if it weren't true. Either you party and sleep, no school; or you sleep and go to school and not party. Or you party and go to school and get no sleep, which you can't do. So they already made the choice for us, didn't they." Christi lets it breathe. They get to the other side of the lawn. Across the way is Jim's Donuts. Just passed it is a small cafe The Willow Cafe. They go inside and have a seat.

Arthur and Oscar walk across the street. The auditions were a joke, on Oscar's mind. There wasn't even a piano, not that he'd play it; but the probabilities increased the odds. But where there is no magician, there is no magic.

"In here. Let's go in here. I haven't been here in a long while. I need a cup of coffee." The day was getting warmer as he waved his friend into the red plastic door to the Willow Cafe. "Se la vi my friend."

"I know. It was kind of funny. That guy at the end there, doing Pontius Pilate, he was great. But creepy too. Funny gathering of people."

They both walked into the cafe and sat down.

By shear coincidence they happened upon familiar strangers; Mari and Christi were smack dead center in the cafe. Another unreal coincidence.

"Hey you were the guys in the theatre. You guys were great! Pretty lame director huh?"

"Yeah," said Arthur. Pretty lame. I don't know. We got our own gig going. At the Eye, downtown. Near Cheers."

"Oh cool. I haven't been there."

"Cheers?

"No the Eye." Christi smiles. "Join us, will you?"

"Yeah sure. This is Oscar."

"Hi Oscar." Mari and Christi stand briefly and then sit down.

"Hi. Ladies, and this is Arthur." Oscar plays on the play they just came from, being overly dramatic, as if still on the stage.

Everyone laughs for a brief allowed second or so. They sit down. A woman comes up to them wearing a fair pair of worn out denims. Her shirt was a new maroon and gray checkered flannel. Her hair was waved back, and her demeanor was one that came with a chip, a side of humor. "OK, you guys can cut it out. What can I get you?" The waitress, Winter, gave everyone a moment to gather their thoughts. Everyone kind of tried to throw a laugh.

"Four coffees?" Arthur looks around for everyone's nod of approval. "Yes?" Everyone nods in agreement.

"Four coffees it is. Pie?" She picks up the menus, holds them back out. "Pie?"

"No thank you, no Pie." Arthur braves.

"No pie," the others chime in.

"No pie then." Winter taps the menus on the table lightly. "No pie." She turns her back like a boomerang, bad performance of a slow military salute. "Suit yourselves. Four coffees it is." And walks back towards the kitchen.

"How did you hear about it?" Arthur asks his new friends.

"I saw a poster on a pole." Christi says.

"That's what I saw too." Mari buts in. Feeling a bit of a third wheel on a four wheel carriage. "I mean. Hey, what was it with that guy. Who sang the Pilate Dream song. Do you guys know him?"

"No, I don't know him. He did seem a bit of a Frankenstein, and with that hat."

"Yeah, Mari calls him Mr. Spook." Christi bursts out laughing.

"That's funny," Oscar says. Looking at Christi, almost with a familiar tone, a sense of knowing a person just as you meet them.

"What did you think of the girl running it. Valley?" Arthur asks. "We met her the other night at the Eye. She came over to us. A little drunk maybe I couldn't tell. She was with another girl, Osbrin."

"Hmm Osbrin." Mari thought aloud. "I heard of that name before. I don't know where. But I could swear I've heard someone talking about an Osbrin the other day in the dorm. Weird."

"I don't know. Are you guys going to do the play?" Oscar looks at Mari, wondering for sway.

"I'm not sure," Mari says. "Maybe we'll just go back there to see if we made the list or not." She laughs.

"We're all on the list." Oscar remarks humorously. They all laugh.

Winter comes walking back over to refill their coffees. As if she wasn't noticed, or maybe as if she were. Only for a second in time. That long second like at the audition, when Pilate paused, Mr. Spook. There was a fear right then, it could be felt from the back curtain to the front of the theatre. It vibrated against the steel that held up the rafters. But it was silent, and quiet. Like all calming before the storm.

Oscar picked up the tab. He found himself taking Mari to the side just as they were heading out. He bashfully folded.

"Can I get your number, call you?"

Mari laughed a little, "Yeah, sure." She pulled out a pen from her purse and wrote on the back of an ice-cream coupon.

"Thanks Mari, Oscar looked up slowly, after staring at the numbers on the old coupon, "Great, I'll call you. Come by the Eye on Friday if you find yourself in the itch to get out. We'll be playing."

"Sounds fun. I probably will. Maybe we'll both come down."

The four walk out the red plastic flab door. Oscar holding it for them as they all slipped on through, giving quiet gestures of friendly gratitude as they passed. The day was getting warmer out. The cold had lulled into a fair breeze of the familiar recent Indian Summer.

"Well you ladies have a good day!" Arthur curtailed.

"Thank you, you two as well." Christi renounced back. "Maybe we'll see you Friday."

"Maybe we'll see YOU!" Arthur laughed himself for the last. The girls giggled, as the cobblestones never count footsteps. The old oil lamps would flicker to begin coming on around five. It was yet around two. In all, there would be a lazy boy session for Oscar and the Red Sox, playing the Yankees. There will be an all out war for finding a lost first draft on Mari's next English Comp Paper Modern Witchcraft and Hysteria. Arthur played his drums for the next couple hours, and Christi went down to the river, and looked at crewmen practice their sport just as the sun was going down.

It was a cool day in Boston. Newberry Street was crowded as crowds emerged out of the hallows, and up into the sunlight. Oscar was thumbing his way through Batman comic books in his second home, Newberry Comics. It was kind of bizarre how things were happening. Strange coincidences were happening, like meeting those girls at the cafe. It's really rare when it happens back to back though. That means you should be playing the lottery. Mari, or a woman who looked like Mary came down the stairs. Always go with your instinct. Advice well adhered as he walked over to her, confirming his affirmations. "It is you, my, how weird that is!" Oscar laughed, rubbed the hair under his cotton hat. "If I'd of known I would have called! How funny is that?"

"Oscar, wow I can't believe it. Do you come here a lot?" She took off her gloves.

"Yes, I'm always here! Crazy, I can't believe it."

"It's beautiful outside. What you got there?" She pointed down at the comic in his hand. "Oh this, Batman Goes Nuts and Beats Everybody Up." It's a spoof, It's a side illustrator, someone I know. He had an idea to continue the series on a more comical tone behind

Batman. Almost like the series on TV. I mean I'm not sure. I like Mad too. I always pick up Mad when I'm here."

"That's so cool! I'm impressed. So many people don't get culture, you know? I mean what's the point if you're not going to shake a leg once in while. You know? Get drunk. Everyone else did." She laughs.

Oscar laughs. Then he looked over towards the steps, and could see the sidewalk just above and people walking past, going hither and thither about. Why he looked, he wasn't sure. Then a man bent down, maybe to pick something up he had dropped. But then the man looked inside the store, with his head to the pavement. Oscar caught his eyes, glaring through, making a vacuum or wormhole strait to the heart.

"You're not going to forget her." the man says. Beaming, and shining through, radiant. Oscar stepped back and looked at Mari.

"What is it?" she asked, and turned her shoulder towards the steps. Someone was coming down. Another student, a kid with headphones on his head and his Walkman in his hand. Mari turns back around. "You OK? Oscar?"

"Yeah I'm OK." He looked quickly back towards the steps, but the man was gone. He had walked past. Now all he could see were more legs. "Yeah, I'm OK." He shakes his head, a little. "You coming by Friday?" As if he were intentionally changing the subject.

"I have a better idea. Let's go for a walk. I have a paper due on witches and I want to visit the courthouse downtown, and see the tree where they hung that witch."

"OK, let me pay for these." He points down, the Mad magazine dangling from his hand. "See I'm a Mad fan. I get it every month."

"You're funny. OK, I'll be outside." Mari first walks then runs up the steps and outside onto the sidewalk. She takes out a cigarette and lights it. A crowd of people walked in all kinds of speeds, passing her as they went their way. She kicked a stone that was next to a Coca Cola can, then she kicked the can into the street.

"OK, I'm ready." Oscar shows out his Newberry Comics bag and points in various directions. "Downtown? Uptown?"

"Downtown Salem. The courthouse silly. You know where it is." Mari smiles. A cool breeze flows through her light hair. She feels she's on a date. Boston was a lonely city. How some did take that for granted not caring for the really lovely feeling a couple can feel just walking down a path together. It was nothing serious. She was thinking that as she walked silently. Just going down to the courthouse was all, where they condemned a witch in the late 1600's. They grabbed a slice of pizza, non-withstanding, and then jumped on the T to Salem. When they arrived, they hopped off the T and looked around. Mari was waving her arms around, like the Sound of Music and Oscar felt like he did when he was young holding a balloon. Light as the air it hung by, lighter than the air, and that is the point of a balloon.

Tell me something, what is it that got them where there is a courthouse, here on Washington Street. Right here, that someone had built a museum about a group of women who conjured up a story so horrific, and so full of hysteria that people were innocently killed; without the remission of any of the girls involved in their accusations." Mari stood there. Looked at the place.

"OK, I know in a way the evil is evil, and that was the other side of the television for them. They didn't have TV or media then, so it was the evil in the woods that gave them goosebumps, or the odd rattlings in the house. The dark. But they were afraid of something, to the point it drove the women mad." Oscar saw a bird, flying, up ahead there on the roof of the courthouse. It was black, and belonged near a hallowed tree, one without leaves or birth.

Mari walked a good ten feet and then twirled again, as if she were in love this time. She idled, and stopped. Walked again. Stopped. "So they were afraid of evil. And then the only people who were able to battle against evil were warlocks and the Church."

"Yes, that's true. The Church was for a reason, not like today. Now it's a fear of not getting into heaven as its main sale's pitch. What would be the point. I thought Jesus was the king of dispensing evil, from people, from sick people. He projected evil into a herd of pigs, that were demonizing a poor man. He rose Lazarus from the dead. Dead can't be good, and he rose him from the dead, you know?"

Mari agreed, now they were walking side by side. "I know. It's true. Jesus was like a magician. He warded off evil, he multiplied food by looking at it. He walked on water. These are magician tricks. But they weren't tricks, you know? They were more than miracles. Miracles displayed something to be mystical, like it could never happen again, or set in stained glass. They're for those who pray Hail Mary's and play the lottery tickets, then they win and it's a miracle. But then, it must have been prime time dinners that gave them their fix, and wine, and conversations in the clay huts for houses."

They both laughed. They walked into the courthouse. There were a few benches and a table in the front. A long red velvet rope alluding to the fact that no one can go any further. Oscar walked up to the table, the rope at his knees. He leaned over a little and looked at the wood. It was ordinary. There was nothing special about the wood, or the two hundred year old desk. Or the pews, or the antique windows, or the candle holder. It was what happened here that mattered.

"Jesus was the one for some reason to figure out the powers he had learned in the east. And fighting evil was one of the disciplines of a yogi or buddha of his day. Evil is all over the history books, the scriptures, the artwork dating back three, five thousand years. It's been around forever. Stephen King dedicates his life to fighting it, though he brings out more evil than good I believe sometimes. We put it everywhere in everything, ghost movies, Halloween."

"Halloween was awesome. I love Jamie Lee Curtis. I always wanted to be Jamie Lee Curtis." Mari laughs. Oscar laughs with her.

"I think Jesus was onto something when he returned back from the East and saw what was going on in Jerusalem. It was a slum lord filled with dirty profit minded people. There were the Jewish, and the Romans. He came back to a moment when sacrificing a lamb on a holiday pleases God. I mean the idea of that is insane to begin with, and he was supposedly a vegetarian! He came back to a bloodbath. At the end of all he did, all the miracles, he fought the establishment. He rebelled against religion. He flipped out at the end, turning over the tables at the temple. He tipped his lid." Oscar gave a flip to his imaginary hat.

Mari listened, seeing Jesus's ghost hat fly off his head.

Oscar took a breath. Feeling fervor. "And now ironically all we have is religious sects all over the globe fighting with each other. Jesus didn't want that. He didn't say, OK, in two thousand years, you will all fight over me, and kill over me and turn on each other in families over me. No! he told us to love one another. And that was all he said. Some other stuff, he said tons of stuff that is relevant, but no one listens to it. They have to go out and come home and make the bed and feed the dogs, and survive. They can't ask the Church to feed them."

They now both stood there, in the empty room. No one was even guarding it. It was just this wooden room the size of a nursery. And 17 people were killed for witchcraft. "What do you think happened. Was it evil that got into the girls, and just went amok? Frenzy, pulling out the hair kind of mad crazy hysteria?" Oscar leans over.

"I've seen girls like that today, lose their shit over nothing. So heaven knows what the woods did to people then. I mean, are the woods the problem? Does something live in the woods. I mean they're not far from here. Salem is built on a small hill and farmland around a wooded area. And these woods are said to be haunted. So what came first the haunted woods? Or the witches of Salem? Guilty by association." Mari skipped her shoe on the wooden floor. "Come on let's get out of here. There's nothing in here."

The two walked out. The bag started weighing heavy on Oscar. They walked toward the Salem Inn, there was a cafe next to it. The Mole. They sat down in the quaint inviting chairs, took a breath and gazed around. "You want a cup of coffee? It's getting cold out." Oscar asked Mari.

Mari smiled. "Maybe a cup. A small cup." She looked at him as he graciously got up from his chair to get them both a cup of coffee. He came back not a minute later. He handed her her cup and sat down. They didn't say much. The sky was gray and silent, taking the words from them. A peaceful wave of wind would come around every so or so often and lift the leaves around the bottoms of the cafe tables. There was no one outside but the two of them. A tall couple came walking by them, nodded and then walked inside. A man on a bicycle passed them and waved. But other than that, it was a silent place they were in, and maybe for the brief time in their lives, they would enjoy it. They left twenty minutes or so later. Walked across the street and went into the T station, waited not two minutes for a train to take them back into

Boston. They both laughed over frivolous things, smiled at each other's smile.

Mari brought up that tomorrow they would be posting the parts outside the theatre. Oscar didn't quite burden his mind. He was already hoping he wouldn't get the part. There was something too makeshift about it all, it didn't feel right. The T was making a strange sound. It got real loud in the car for a second or so, but it became quiet again, real quiet. The subway flew out of Salem on a true man's whistle. Oscar had already left his thoughts on the play back at the stop. He had to get back home and practice his Bach. The train arrived on the North End not before a traveler could stop time himself. The two of them said their goodbyes. Oscar watched the train leave his station and into a black tunnel. He walked up the subway stairs and out into the street. It was colder than before. The sun was beginning to set. And Oscar had Bach to rehearse.

The woods were long and wide through the college campuses along the river's side, east of Boston, in the Cambridge traditions. Houses of the wealthy after wealthy skated a long line down the realities of Skull and Bones, The Illuminati, the wealth of the Masons, all in Club Row. Drinking their expensive wines, their wives in cahoots, seeing the detail in the art displayed in galleries downtown. There's no discourse, it's all organized like the golf game. It's all planned out, generation to generation. Someone came to America years ago, and put a stake in the land. And there it stayed, and the lawmakers would bind their titles. What the pioneers weren't expecting were not the Indians, but the woods, the enchanted evil woods.

Arthur was stricken by them as a child. He remembers seeing a figure in his home town of Pristol, where he grew up. He saw someone there about 50 feet or so in front of him, like a shadow, someone not in focus. He frightened Arthur, for one of the first times in his life he was frightened so. The man was standing there, two trees beside him about ten feet on each side. He was there, and then he wasn't. Nothing or no one moved. He just vanished. He was thinking of this by the great pool in Boston, outside the Christian Science Center, in front of the giant
94

glass globe. The night was calm, a slight wind once in a while blew by and gave him a sense of being someone, existing in time. He came here a lot. To spill out his thoughts in the pond, to empty his fears in the Churchyard.

There were a group of mimes just across the way, on the other-side of the pool; they looked as though they were practicing for something. A man was with him with a camera taking photos of them. It was odd and a little funny. Arthur smiled after dazing off in their choreography, and vulnerable serendipity of the night.

As he got up, he turned around. And started walking away from the pool, away from the mimes. As if exiting church. The sun was going down fast now. For some reason homework wasn't on his mind. Although he had to do some. He felt hungry. Hungry for something real, more than food. Something in life. He thought of the musical he tried out for. That first girl who got up there. Laura was her name. She looked like a witch, he thought to himself, and laughed. The thought came and went like a hippy bus on a milk farm when asked to leave.

The sky was down, and he didn't feel the greatest in the world. He thought of her, who she was, why she looked different than the others. Who was she? Arthur looked up at the sky, then down at the ground, and noticed his legs striding in uncanny rhythm, as if he was part of the little ball, rolling an inch off a glass floor. The night was beyond sacred, he thought. He was asking himself why he chose to play Judas. Why he had picked that song? When did the fight for the side of Judas emerge? Why did the two of them, both Jesus and Judas wind up on the wrong end of a stick. Jesus was hung on a cross, and Judas hung himself from a tree. What in the vaults of heaven happened that day. The day it all fell apart and turned on Jesus and his clan. People talk of it, how Jesus hung around the sinners. What did that mean? Arthur thought about it. The sinners were obviously the ones engulfed in lust and wine and laughter and hangovers, and sin. What sin was then. He thought about it, at one point he even turned back around to look at the pool just before losing it to a right angle intersection with the street and the Christian Science Church. The mimes were still there in the far distance. He heard something or didn't. None the less, he was home fifteen minutes later. There was a blinking light going off on his answering machine, which meant he had messages.

"Hey it's me. I forgot to tell you that I'm going over to the yard to see if we're on the list. I heard they're posting it by eight. I'll let you know. See you tomorrow." Arthur opened up his refrigerator. Pulled out some milk, and grabbed the Froot Loops sitting there on the counter. Poured himself a bowl, grabbed a spoon and sat down at the kitchen table. There wasn't much of one, it was a studio tucked in together with a gazillion other studios that inhabited the apartment building. He sat there and ate, and wondered who gets the job of drawing the stupidest things on the backs of cereal boxes. Certainly not him. He ate the Froot Loops, and the Froot Loops were good. And it's all he really cared about at the moment. Tomorrow would be another day.

Mari walked across the garden and into the yard. She was excited to see if she had gotten the part or not. A little nervous, but not as nervous as maybe she should have been. The air outside was refreshing. The Autumn was slowly creeping in. Behind her, about a half a mile or so, Oscar was walking across the bridge. He was thinking about something he could kind of care less about as well. This play. When Oscar crossed the lawn, over Cambridge Street and up to the gate, he thought of something weird. This has been happening a lot in his life lately. He kept thinking of things and then it would happen. He walked up to the theatre walkway. There were a few kids, say five or so hanging out there. Mari was one of them. His suspicions would be correct. Mari walked up to him.

"Hi Oscar, looks like they closed down the play. They said they couldn't say why just yet but will let the people who tried out know at a further date. I can't believe it. I walked all this way."

Oscar laughed. "Are you kidding me? They closed the play. That's crazy. I had a strange feeling that would happen. Just now, as I was crossing the street I thought that the play was going to be cancelled. Isn't that weird?" Oscar buttoned up his coat, looked at Christi's pretty blonde hair, and watched her turn towards the theatre door and then back at Oscar. "I think it's nuts. Those two girls, Valley and Osbrin. I don't know who they were. They looked like they had ulterior motives, like there wasn't going to be a play, like it was a project or something. Like hippie stoners sitting in their living room thinking of how they were going to put on a play without putting on the play!" Oscar laughed.

"Or something like that," Mari laughed back. "What happened you think?" Mari looked confused.

"I don't know." Oscar scratches his head, puckers up his lips and lets out a breath. "I really don't. I wish I did. I just walked two miles."

"Man, that sucks." Mari catches Oscar's eyes. "Don't worry about it. One less distraction. You know? They were wackos in there. And the theatre could use a makeover. Where's Arthur?"

"Oh he's at his pad. Or I don't know. Man, this does suck. You guys coming tonight to the Eye? It's going to be a good show. We have a group from New Jersey coming out to play a set. The Bitter Chills. I hear it gets cold every time they perform, weird thing about them. It should be cool."

"Yeah I'll be there, come on. I'll walk you back to the bridge." Mari and Oscar walked, talked a little about squirrels and how beautiful the leaves were. Arthur was a mile away in his studio apartment, looking out a window of someone trying to dismantle a bookshelf on the curb eight floors below him. The guy had a saw just going ape on this bookshelf. He thought to himself how bizarre it was to be witnessing. That sound of a saw gnawing through wood. Who does that? he thought. He would never be doing that. If he had to throw out a bookshelf he would just drag it to the curb and leave it there. Oscar and Mari walked to the bridge. They waved goodbye and Oscar crossed the bridge, back to his place.

Three miles up the river sat Boston College, just above that the Eastern Woods. Laura sat in the middle of a circle. She had made it herself with some sea salt and a rock to make her mark. She didn't believe in those sort of things. But yet she found herself there. Minutes later, Osbrin came walking through to the site. As if expected she had gotten into the circle. She pulled out a Colt 45 beer can and tapped the lid. She started to chug it. Taking down the night with five gulps and on the ground an empty tin can found itself. Howls in the woods. Howling and beer. The two girls looked at each other, even wrestled in laughter all in the fallen leaves. "We're crazy!" Osbrin said. "We're batshit crazy is what we are!"

"What a night. We met a few people though. What do you think? I liked the boys, they were cool. We're still going to the Eye? Right?"

"Yeah late though. We'll get there." Osbrin told Laura. "You sounded great the other night though. It's a drag there will be no show." An owl hooted half a football field away. They sat there on the dirt, quiet, listening if it had anything to say. The woods were dark except for the one beam of light from the moon breaking through the tree-branches above. Irie gave them a book to say out loud. She said it was important. Laura and Osbrin didn't quite know what to make of it, but they said the few lines near the fire. And then laughed, almost mocking it, and threw the book in the fire itself. One more beer each and they began walking back to the car, which was parked in a small dirt lot which led to the path.

Walking into the Eye an hour later, the two of them felt lightheaded and both had a good buzz on. Magic Man was on the stereo, there seemed to have been a band change they walked into. Laura sat down at the bar first, as Osbrin sat next to her.

Oscar and Arthur were on the stage looking to set up, moving around keyboards, and fixing drum hardware. Another man was fixing the microphones and testing them. He gave a thumbs up to the soundman in the back of the room.

"Looks like we'll catch them."

The lights went low. The stereo went silent, and people watched with slight anticipation. Arthur and Oscar starting jamming, a simple slow blues jam. Arthur brushed his keyboard with light and simple melodies. Arthur sat on the beat, just gliding along, going with the flow. The sound of the snare off a light stick, his keeping a steady measure with his foot on the base-drum.

The set was an hour into no recorded time. Osbrin and Laura still sat in a silent blur, started to talk a small conversation between them. Arthur saw Osbrin from on the stage earlier, so he walked down and over to her sitting at the bar.

"Hey, Osbrin. How ya been?" Arthur asks. He looks at Laura, "hi I'm Arthur, you sang at the auditions right?"

Laura sits up in her bar stool, "yeah I did. Nice to meet you too. I'm Laura Park." She holds out her hand to shake. Arthur shakes, and Oscar right behind him leans his hand in as well.

"Where's Valley?" Oscar asks.

"She had something to do tonight." Osbrin shy's backward, twitching an eye lash. "Yeah, things haven't been as good with her lately. I mean it's OK."

Arthur looks around, Slim Jimmy is behind the bar, gives Arthur a small nod, fingers to the head. Arthur pale faced and expressionless looks back at the girls. "Why did the show get canceled?" he asks.

"Oh that was because Valley couldn't do it anymore. So she called me last minute to put up a flier." Osbrin starts biting her nails. "Anyone want another beer? Arthur, Oscar would you like a beer?"

"No thanks, I have one over there on the stage. I'll grab it." Oscar stands there a moment or so, before heading back towards the stage.

"It just seemed real weird," Arthur said. "I don't know why anyone would just abandon something like that. I felt bad for all the people who had to stand there, and go through auditions. Kind of a little flakey if you asked me." Arthur didn't know what quite to say.

"Well I have some more music to play. Catch you girls later." He walked towards the stage, picked up his beer he left on the bar on the other end, lifted himself on the stage and got behind the kit.

A minute later the two were back in the groove, people were talking everywhere again, but somehow a sound within the entire place could not be heard.

Osbrin and Laura were outside taking a cigarette break from the monotony, both in a stupor of silence. Laura lights her cigarette, and then Osbrin's. Ten seconds later, on the door of serendipity, Arthur and Oscar come out, joining the small circle by the side entrance to the Eye.

"How are you girls, it's getting colder outside at night. Arthur says. Arthur pulls out a joint, they light it up. Cars flew past, sounds of tires, and the wind took over. Osbrin pulled back her hair a bit, then opening up her hands to whatever comes next. Arthur takes a hit and passes it to Osbrin.

"You ever wonder why we do this?" Laura says, I mean smoke and hang out, listening to Jam night?"

Osbrin passes the joint to Laura. She thinks about what she just asked and took a hit. Coughing on it she quickly passed it to Oscar. "What do you mean? Why aren't we home tonight studying?"

"You can say that." Laura adds. "Why are we all a bunch of hippies today. There's nothing to do. I mean, we have school, and people at school."

Oscar takes a good hit and passes it back to Arthur. "Drugs. Some people will just one day say, oh, he had a problem with drugs. Or he died from drugs. They don't get it those people. It wasn't the drugs that killed him usually. Alcohol maybe, heartache, bad times, too much conflict. The only drugs you're allowed to die from are heroin, alcohol, cocaine, and pain killers. If you die and you smoked pot, it wasn't the pot. The rules with bad drugs are you never ever do them."

"No one ever sees what we see or hear. I don't know. Who cares." Osbrin laughs, takes the joint from Oscar. "You know what, we all took too much shit from just liking to smoke joints. And for too long too. It's about time hippies are kind of respected a little. They're just a bunch of kids who liked music and liked going to shows. Walking around, meeting people, having a buzz going on. What's wrong with that?"

"People are legally allowed to get drunk," Laura says, "and drink at bars. No one has a say against that? Yet it makes so many people really really sick the next day. The hangovers get worse and worse. Who does that? I mean why do I even drink! I love it that's why."

They all laugh, passing around the joint. The air outside was brisk. The scent of Autumn was about, showing its pride a little.

Oscar took a hit. "Where's Valley?" he asked the girls. As if the wind was taken in from an invisible vacuum, as if the silence decided to speak.

"Yeah where's Valley? She didn't come with you tonight?"

Again. A dead silence, dead air on the radio. Osbrin put her finger in her hair, twirled it a little. Looked at both Oscar and Arthur. But that was it. Laura just dropped her chin, looked at her shoes.

"Is she OK?" Oscar asks.

Osbrin turns to Laura, looks into her eyes, and then at Arthur and Oscar. Seconds seemed like minutes, ticking, feeling the air on the back of your neck. "Yeah she's okay, she just didn't want to come out tonight. That's all." Osbrin looked again at Laura. And then to Arthur. "Thanks for the smoke. You guys have a good night."

And then they walked back down Boylston.

"What was all that about?" Oscar James Warhl said.

"I haven't a clue." Arthur dead handedly responded.

Harvard was playing Yale. Oscar was always a Harvard fan, he always dreamed of going to Harvard, but his music managed to take center stage. Being in musicals, and playing at the local Church when he was young, he didn't quite believe he would go to Berklee. Music was his second choice in life, though it was what he felt most comfortable with. He was at the game, sitting in the 200's, one level up. Arthur was going to meet him, but he hadn't shown up quite just yet. Mari had mentioned that Christi and herself were going to go to the game as well. So Oscar's eyes kept looking through the stadium, as if he were actually going to see her.

Behind Oscar's shoulder Arthur was walking down the steps, an older couple was in front of him. He had to wait a hair for them to move in order to get to his seat. He spotted Oscar, waved and walked into his isle, crossing the legs and bodies of two complete strangers, giving a nod as he over stepped them. Then he came to his seat. "Hey Champ! How you doin. You here long?" Arthur took off his coat, it was getting warm outside.

"I'm OK, Harvard is about to score. They better fucking score. Seven to nothing, Harvard."

"I'm OK, shit awesome. I heard from Christi last night. When I got home. There was an answering machine message. Her and Mari are coming to the game. They said to meet them at the Beer Hall right after the first quarter." Arthur leans in, gives Oscar a hug. "Good to see you Bro. We're winnin' huh? Awesome!"

"Totally awesome. You want a beer, I'm going to head on up for a beer."

"Wait till the quarter's done. We'll meet Christi and Mari up there in a second. It's almost finished." Oscar taps on Arthur's shoulder, "give it a second, you just got here. Harvard is about to score."

The crowd is up on its feet. Loud cheers and hollers, the stadium was in high decibels, and could almost excuse ear plugs, or a headset. The two of them stood just inside their perimeter. Quarterback Jeff Witter fakes the hand off and runs into the end-zone. No contestant! Oscar high fives Arthur, "all right, let's get there before the rush."

The two walk up there via the concrete steps, passing a few people on their way up. They got to the top and the stadium opened up into the causeway. The Beer Hall was right around the bend. The two of them walked as the people began flooding out into the mezzanine. They spotted the Beer Hall and walked in. The line was not very long; they walked up to it and got behind two men who appeared to be in some frat. They were loud and happy about the finish of the first quarter. Arthur and Oscar soon came to the concession stand and asked for two beers. They got their beer and sat at one of the tables specifically there for the beer drinkers. Arthur as well as Oscar looked around for the whereabouts of either Mari or Christi. Out of nowhere they could see a shadow, racing towards them. They weren't sure at first, it was all fuzzy and everyone was cascading every which way. But sure enough it was Mari. She looked more and more frantic the closer she got to the boys. She finally crashed her hands on their table.

"I can't find Christi." That was it. She looked at the two of them. "She was with me and then she said she had to use the restroom, and now I can't find her."

"Maybe she's talking to someone. Chill out, she'll be here in a second. You told her where you were going right?" Arthur tries to calm down Mari.

"No seriously, I can't find her. I've been looking everywhere for her." Mari pulls up a seat. "Oscar, you want to get me a beer. I can't stand in line right now. Maybe if I drink a beer she'll come back. Oscar, can you grab me one. Here's five bucks." She hands the money to Oscar. Oscar doesn't take it.

"No this one I got. Hang in there. I'll be right back." He nods his head towards Arthur and then at Mari. "Hang in there, she'll show up." He jumped out of his chair and walked back to the counter. He didn't have long to wait. Dropped a ten on the counter, "three beers." A man behind the counter, a bit older than the students who were working the Beer Hall, gave the beers and two quarters change. Oscar dropped the quarters in the tip bowl. He arrived at the table before he could even think about it.

"What did you get me a beer for. I have one already." Arthur holds up a half filled beer.

"Well, you're almost done. You're a half-empty kind of guy anyway. Drink up. Here." He hands a beer to Mari. "Drink up."

Arthur looks up at Oscar and gives him a look.

"I wonder where she went. Do you have a quarter?" Mari asks Oscar.

Thinking fast, "I can't believe it, I just gave my quarters away as a tip."

"OK, I'll wait for her. She knows we're meeting here. I just have to give it a little time. She's probably flirting with a professor somewhere is all."

The three of them drank their beers, just sitting there. People were scattering about, getting beer, getting hot dogs.

"I can't take it. I have to go look for her." Mari downed her beer and then got up from her seat. Oscar joined her, not before chugging his last four gulps.

"Come on. Let's go," Oscar said, as if deciding to lead the way. "We'll find her."

"You're right about that," Author exclaimed. "She's just talking to someone."

They took the stairs down to the main floor, field level. Mari's head was moving left and right, her body following. Oscar was following Mari, and Arthur in the back. They walked outside the gate and onto the back lawn. People were everywhere. The three decided to disperse just a bit, and watch from a close distance.

As Arthur eyed the west side of the Stadium he saw something on a pole, about ten meters from where he was standing. There was a man next to the pole selling cotton candy and hot dogs. Arthur walked up to the man. "What's that?"

"What's what?" said the man. Now beginning to blow up some balloons. "What's what kid?"

"That behind you, on that pole." A missing persons photo was taped to the pole. "Can I see that. Can you take that down so I can look at that?"

"Sure," said the man, assuming Arthur knew his business by asking. The man took it down, ripping a little of the lower right edge. "Here you go, kid."

Arthur took the poster from the man. His eyes widened. His jaw dropped. "How would anyone know this already? Who put this up?"

Have You Seen Me?
Christi White
Reported Missing
Last seen at the Willow Cafe

"This is crazy," Arthur exhumed. "She wasn't missing until ten minutes ago. Who put this here?" Arthur looked at the guy. "You, who put this up there?"

"I don't know guy, Some other guy I think. Not long ago, about fifteen minutes or so."

"Thanks. Where did he go? Which way?" Arthur pressing.

"Oh man, I don't know man. That way." He points south. "Towards downtown. I think I saw him."

Oscar and Mari come immediately over to Arthur. Spotting him from across the way, they looked as though they had seen or heard something. Attracting attention, they quickly walked over and inquired. "What's going on?" Oscar asks Arthur. He sees the paper in Arthur's hand, as does Mari. Mari snags it from Arthurs clenched grip. Stupefied he half gives it over with ease. Mari's reaction wasn't complimentary. "Jesus Christ. What the fuck is this? Who gave this to you?" She looks at the man behind the kiosk. "What the fuck, how did someone already print this up?" She looks at Arthur and then Oscar. "Come on. I have to leave this place. It's making me ill."

As they walked past Stadium Boulevard and onto Peabody Street, leaning against a pole, holding a duffle bag, or a very large knapsack, she spotted him first, then Oscar, and then Arthur. "What the fuck is he doing here? Mr. Spook pays a visit. On all days of days."

"Maybe he's looking for Christi too." Oscar shies by, clenching his fists. "It's getting cold again."

"Maybe he knows more than we know. Come on. Let's go." Mari pulls Oscar's arm, and they tread across the yard. Mr. Spook is still standing against the pole. His bag on his shoulder.

"What the fuck do you know? Mr. Spook. Where's Christi?" She holds out the flier. Gives it to him. Jarral looks at the flier, and nods.

"Yeah, I've seen her. She was at the tryouts. I remember her." He picks at his hair, long black and greasy. "She's missing?"

"Yes she's missing! Are you as dumb as you are one creepy mother fucker." Mari looks as angry as she sounds."

"Listen lady, if you think I have something to do with it, you're nuts." Mr. Spook opens up his duffle-bag and hands her a sheet of paper. "I have my own mission I'm on." Mari takes the paper from Mr. Spook. It's another missing persons flier. This one is of Valley, the girl who was organizing the play. I've been given a job to put these up, that's all I know. I can't say names to protect the victim's identity. It's all I can say."

She pulled back and looked harder at the flier. "What the fuck? What the fuck is going on here? Someone explain what the flying fuck is going on here!" As if a train-wreck of a cartoon character, Mari walked away, threw the paper in the air flailing her arms. "What the fuck." She could be heard as she walked aimlessly down the path leading to the south side of campus.

"Do you know what's going on Art?" Oscar looks dimly at his fingers, rubs them on his coat.

"I have no idea what's going on my friend," Arthur responded while looking at Mari disappearing into a fog of fellow students and delirium.

Mari went straight to Christi's dorm. Walking in madness, bewildered by the insanity. No one answered her door. It was locked from the inside. "Damn it!" she cried. She stormed out, pounding the doors she walked through, swinging them open like they had no weight. She almost hit a girl coming in as she was flying out.

"Damn it!" the girl said. "Slow down!"

"Fuck you! I'm busy!" Mari threw back. She then went straight back to her dorm. She looked for a note, nothing, no one. No one was around. She didn't want to go to the police. That was her last resort. But it began creeping into reality's choice by the minute. Twenty minutes later she was at the doors to the Cambridge Police Department.

They said it was too early to file a missing person's report. They said to give it 24 hours, but if they heard anything they'd be in touch, and that they'd keep an eye out. Mari ran out into the street, again throwing her arms into the mocking air, breaking down into the concrete below. "That fucking play!" Mari looked up over at the doors she just came out of. Her face was pale and pink, a high temper'd color of blush and sweat. Her hair was slightly greasy and wet. The snow was falling at an indifferent pace, not caring who it fell on. It fell on both the poor and rich, the innocent and the guilty. The snow didn't choose favorites.

Oscar went to Mari's thinking she'd gone there, and then thought maybe she'd be at Christi's so she went there. All in all, he was tipped off by a neighbor she had gone to the police; and if anyone came by, they should be directed there. The neighbor was a punk'd out geek in his thirties who fixed televisions and computers for a living. He wasn't much a sight, so he kept to himself mostly, occasionally bumping into Mari in the hall, but it was rare they would. Oscar though would run into Mari just outside the police station downtown. She was crying in her gloves. She looked like she was going through something more than just a missing friend. It was all breaking down inside her. Nothing made sense to her. She wasn't sure about the poster, what it meant, and why Valley was also on a poster. It freaked her out. And Mr. Spook being there at the play. He was the devil, she thought, and picked herself up off the ground. Oscar was there to greet her just as she arose.

"My God it's you. Thank you Oscar, you're a sweetheart."

He took her arm as she fumbled to balance herself.

"Thank you love." She embraced the moment of friendship between two people. She was glad he was there.

"Yeah, no problem. You OK?"

"Yeah I'm OK. Thanks. Who put her on a poster? I was with her just prior to it, I mean not ten minutes go by and she's on a flyer? Doesn't make sense Dr. Watson." She laughs in a burst of a hysterical laughter. "I mean who does that? And Mr. Spook had a flier too. That Valley girl, funny right? Her name is Valley. Who names their kid Valley? I need water. Come on, let's grab a drink. I need a drink. Water then beer."

"I don't know who would do that Mari. It's really odd. I don't know. Is it a mindfuck? Do you think someone is messing with us?"

"Those fuckers inside said to give it 24 hours. She might be in eight different pieces by then, in eight different bags, in eight different states. She better be baby sitting her brat nephew, I swear."

"Calm down. We'll find her. It's a trick, I'm telling you. Some one knows where she is and printed those fliers as a trick or something." Oscar scratches his head. "Oh, I don't know. Come on, let's grab a beer. I need one too."

"Where're we going? Cheers?"

"Yeah 'where everybody knows your name'."

They both laugh.

"Maybe she's there. That little fuck. I'm going to strangle that girl when I see her." Mari laughs. Oscar laughs. The distance to the pub was less than a quarter mile. They found it in good time. Went in and sat themselves at the bar. The Harvard game was over. They beat Yale. Everyone seemed to be in an overly festive mood. It was as if it were Saint Patty's day or something, except people wore deep red instead of green.

"What about that Osbrin chick? Where's she been hanging out. Haven't seen her in a couple days."

"I don't know," Oscar said. He flagged the bartender. "Two pints of Guinness."

The barkeep nodded his head and began pouring right before their eyes.

"I don't know. They were at the Eye the other night, but really weird about stuff, about how they knew and didn't know. It was all really weird. And the way that play opened up, and how much of a flim flam it was, and then it being shut down like that. There was a poster for that too. And there were posters for the play, that's how I found out about it."

"That's crazy. I mean, posters are what people use, but that is a good observation." Oscar nods to the barkeep, hands him a five-spot, thanks him and again a nod. "I mean where do we begin? We have to find out who made those fliers."

"Who gave the fliers to Mr. Spook? We should've asked him that. Do you know where Mr. Spook lives?" Mari looks at Oscar. "Oh, forget it." She laughs and drinks her beer. "We have to find Spooky."

"Sounds like we do." Oscar sips his beer.

"I have a paper due tomorrow. I don't know how I'm going to do it." Mari sips her beer.

Oscar nodded. "More witchcraft?" He laughed

"Yeah." Mari laughed. "It's all anyone cares about in this town." He looks up, over Oscar's shoulder. A painting was on the wall of Babe Ruth in a Red Sox uniform. He was in a pose, as if just hitting a ball that smashed all records. His face was solemn and glum. As if he'd nothing left to prove.

"I don't know. Maybe there is an evil. Maybe people are at the mercy of something darker in their lives than they'd like to admit. Those girls in Salem were obviously affected by something, it's just that premature hysteria, a girl's hysteria had something to enable, and throw it out of control. No one could handle it."

"Other shit too. Secrets. the kind of secrets girls keep in their diaries. The kind of secrets girls keep in the dorms. It's dangerous. And they could create the play of plays with that."

"I wonder. You have a good point. Women are different than men. The obvious signs no one likes to talk about, like lipstick and make-up, and earrings and hair products." It's not like that is wrong, but men don't do that, or very few men. I mean, I don't want to sound sexist." Oscar sips his beer, thinking if he'd gone over the line.

"No you're not. I know what you're saying." Mari smiles. "It is different with women, and girls. We had this Prince Charming and Cinderella's Ball growing up in Disney and we had all these great expectations to follow."

"Ah yes, but there was also the witch in all those tales. Disney has more witches than any other movie studio."

They both laugh. Drink their beer. Mari nods to herself. "You do have a point. That you do. Why is that you think? I mean Sleeping Beauty. 101 Dalmatians. Snow White and Seven Dwarves."

"Bednobs and Broomsticks," Oscar smiles. Now seeing a cute game of it.

"Escape to Witch Mountain." Mari smiles back. They both laugh.

"There are so many! Oscar muses.

"Tells you something, right? I mean there are more witches in Disney than there are prophets in the Bible."

"Maybe, maybe not." Oscar sips his beer. "There are witches in the Bible too. 'Though shalt not suffer a witch'."

"That's a good one. Where the fuck is Christi!?" Mari yells out, almost a bit too loud. A few of the bar-standers looked back and around. The music became noticeable, almost everyone in the back bar silenced backward, something hit a nerve, and it was coming from Mari.

"I don't know. I really don't. Come on, let's get out of here." Oscar pulled Mari by the invisible arm and suggested he come with her. They both put on their coats, Oscar lead, as Marisa followed him an elbow's length away. The bar began to chatter again, the music faded into a shelter for beer consumption, Cheers was back to normal.

When they got outside, they stood there, thinking where to go. They walked together not saying a word for the next ten minutes. Just enjoying the wind, and the lights against the mist. Sounds, cars, people passing them by. They came to the T and that was where they were about to part.

"What are you going to do?" Oscar asked.

"I'm not sure, I guess I'll head back to the dorm and start that paper." Mari pulled in her coat. The cold air pressing on her face.

"Sounds like a plan. Call me if you need anything." Oscar offered and then gave Mari a hug.

"I will, thanks." Mari hugged him back and got on the T towards Harvard. Oscar turned back around and starting walking towards Berklee.

He took in the night, not believing what was unfolding. Kicking a can halfway down the street he saw a light coming from one of the apartments. A window was open three flights up. A stereo was cranking which sounded like some acid jazz out of the sixties. Oscar stopped there, stared at the paper before him, taped to the light pole.

Have you seen me?
Missing
Christi Anne
Last seen at The Willow Cafe
Call 511-553

Oscar dropped the coin he was somehow finding himself twirling. It fell to his feet. His eyes wouldn't come off the poster. A faint mist of light snow was coming down from the gray sky. The pole was touched with melted flakes. The poster had marks of ink bleed from the melted snowflakes that landed on it. Oscar began to think about the snowflakes, how good it must feel not to be involved in such madness, but yet they were. Yet another poster, another signature on a pole. He couldn't figure it out. Not tonight. He walked another block coming up to his building. From a closer distance he could make out another poster on the light pole in front of his house.

Have you seen me?
Missing
Vally Summer

Last seen on Harvard Campus
Call 511-553

Oscar stood there, alone, in front of the pole. Looking at the familiarity. The sky was silent, little flakes of snow were falling on this poster too. Freezing the event in time. "Is it Halloween yet?" He took the poster halfway off the pole, then decided against it, leaving it there half dangling in the moonlight. "Who the fuck is doing this?" He walked up his stairs and into the marble floor foyer. He pulled out his keys and opened the door. The lights were out. He took off his coat, threw it on the couch, and turned on the lights.

It was seven thirty. He looked on the ground. There was a flier folded in half, on the floor at his feet. He didn't see it coming in, but someone put it under his door. At first he assumed a poster for another missing person, but it looked a little different, it was the color of a pale orange. He leaned down and picked up the piece of paper. It was an advertisement.

Halloween Spookhouse
October 10 - 31 Seven O' Clock - Midnight
Salem Witches Fairgrounds
(the woods behind the old firehouse on Willow Lane)
You've been warned

Oscar looked at the flier, in a low tone. "Is everyone mad on a poster child case? Jesus. Nothing but posters. Who the fuck is doing this?" He brought the flier over to the kitchen and stuck it on the fridge, with his favorite magnet. "How'd he get in the building?" He walked over to the tv, picked up the clicker and turned it on. "I give up." He sat down, and was curious why he hadn't heard from Arthur.

Oscar went to the phone, picked it up and dialed Arthur's number. No answer. He thought of it for a minute, even with the phone back on the hook. He wanted to call the front desk over at his place, but decided to take a walk instead. He grabbed a bowl of Apple Jacks, put the bowl in the sink after he finished, looked around his place for no stones turned and out the door he went.

"Halloween Spookhouse." He closed the door, keyed the lock, and walked down a thin three flight of stairs, and out into the world of the unforgiving moon. Around the immediate left was the pub. Oscar walked down the stairs and through the front door of the Eye. There weren't any bands going on right now, in an hour or two. But his amusement was correct. Laura and Osbrin were in there, drinking pints, sitting at the bar. Oscar walked over as if on their cue. He sat down next to Laura. The girls smiled and asked how he was.

"Have you heard that Christi is missing?" Oscar said to the two of them.

"Yes we know. We also know that Valley Summer is as well." Osbrin said. "What do you know?"

"Nothing, people are making posters." Oscar took off his coat, deciding to stay for a pint. "What do you know?"

Laura leaning forward. "Less then you." She reaches into her pocket and hands Oscar a flier.

"No thanks, I have one already." Oscar pushed the flier back towards Laura's pocket.

Laura looks Oscar in the eye, "take it, it's not what you think."

Oscar squares back,"Really?"

Laura hands the poster over to Oscar, he takes it.

Have you seen me?
Missing Person
Arthur Wirth
Last seen Harvard Yale Game
Report Locally if seen
551-553

"Who's making these posters?" Oscar opens up, sounding like he's railing the two. Beginning to sound angrier than sarcastic. "Who's joke is this?"

"It isn't a joke. We found it on a pole coming over here, and we know you hang out so we were going to give it to the bartender Jimmy, to give to you. That's if we didn't see you. But we have to go now."

"OK, I have to go try and find him." Oscar looks at the girls and then his head eyeing the pub. "This place is dead tonight huh? I gotta run. If you hear of anything. Just leave a note on my door. I live on the third floor."

"We will. Good luck out there."

Oscar walks to the door, the two girls behind them putting on their coats. He's putting his coat on as he walks. He felt a feeling about those two. But they were images in his head, rather than specific feelings. He wasn't exactly sure what to make of them.

Oscar walked over to the Conservatory, and went up into the dorm wing. Straight up to Arthur's dorm. He knocked, no one answered. Oscar knocked again. No one answered. Oscar began getting frustrated, there wasn't much to go on, but a couple fliers. "Mr. Spook." Oscar turned away from the door and started trotting down the hall towards the stairs. "Mr. Spook. Where did Mr. Spook get those fliers he was giving away?" Down the stairs and flying outside, Oscar took a break. The cold air surrounded his lungs now, as sweat started creeping up on his forehead, and hair. "Who is that guy, comes in and sings Pontius Pilate, creeped us all out." He heads down the street, again light snow crippled down on its vulnerable victims.

Three miles up and into the woods Laura and Osbrin pulled over. Osbrin got out first from the passenger side. Laura took the keys out, grabbed the six pack in the back seat and got out. It was just a quarter mile walk to the camp. Osbrin led, Laura walked behind, eventually catching up. They didn't say a word, nor could they see a thing if not for Osbrin's flashlight. It took roughly ten minutes on the path, to the left was a wicket of trees and some chalk on a stump. Six foot rock mounts gouged over and opened up for a great camp site. The two found it years ago in high school. Laura walked over towards one of the sitting stones, sat down.

"We forgot the salt," Laura said with slight regret.

"It's OK, we'll draw a circle," said Osbrin.

"I hear that doesn't work. We need salt. What if we start something." Laura got up and started looking around the camp.

"We already did start something." Osbrin took up a stick and started patting it on the ground, sitting on a stone.

"We didn't start it. Valley started it. Now she's gone. And some of Oscar's friends. Do you know what we should do because I don't." Laura walked over to the cooler stone, pulled a beer from the fish-killer plastic holder and cracked it open. "Here, drink this. It'll help." Laura cracks open another and hands it to her friend.

"What if someone finds out?" Osbrin taunts.

"No one will find out. They had it coming to them." Laura chugs.

The moon was up above in the mast of the trees, blinking stars occasionally shone through. The sound of wolves could be heard close by. The two girls looked at each other. Should they be scared, they thought. Laura walked back to the sitting rock and sat down. Osbrin finished gathering twigs and got the fire started. Together they finished the six pack. Laughing, crying, singing things, they couldn't even hear themselves, not giving a damn. They eventually circled themselves in with rocks carving into the dirt. They began chanting, all in a foreign language, all in a stupor or space not even they were all that familiar with. It started as a schoolgirl crush on the paranormal boys in high school. It turned into something they weren't expecting. They stopped at one point crashing to the ground, falling on their own young bones. Not before a voice from the forest yelled out to them. It was also in a different language. When they woke up four hours later, it was five in the morning. They crawled out of their own mess, picked themselves up and walked back towards the car.

That morning Mari walked back over to the Police station. She gave them the flier of a missing person she had on her friend Christi. It wasn't official they said, but took the report none the less. After much dissatisfaction and lack of interest in her story, she left half heartedly and walked back out into the street. There was nothing. She thought of going over to Oscars, if he were't knee deep with his own stuff. She needed all of this like a whole in the head. She walked, and as she walked she noticed having a keener sense towards fliers and telephone poles.

Mari arrived at Oscar's by ten. He was practicing fugues. She knocked on his door. Oscar stopped what he was doing and answered it.

"You busy?"

"Yes, I'm very busy. Come in." Oscar kissed Mari on the cheek and let her inside. She took off her coat and put it on the couch.

"I don't know what to do. Where to go? Who to talk to?" Mari started to cry. Oscar puts an arm on her shoulder. "I mean who is doing this?"

"Arthur is missing too. Here look at this." Oscar hands the flier to Mari.

"Are you kidding me? Oh my lord. This is all too much! What the devil is going on?"

"Do you think the posters are real?"

"I don't know. There's a spookhouse in Salem tonight. I think we should go. A flier came to me last night from under my door and I think it's related." Oscar got up, "would you like anything to drink?"

"OK, a glass of water would be good. Thanks." Mari looked over her shoulder out the window. It was gorgeous and sunny outside.

"When is your paper due?" Oscar looks out the window. "You know, Jesus was a magician. Doesn't mean he was God."

"True. Was he God?" Marisa answered almost as if in a daze. Waking up. Turning her head back around from the window.

"I think he tapped into the eastern magic while studying with buddhist monks and who knows what he saw. I mean give the man his due. He was really good at figuring out the powers, walking on water, multiplying fish."

"Who was he and why all this. I mean no one has had that much power in the sense of worshiping someone. I think sometimes God got the short end of the stick." Mari took a sip of her water. Looked over her shoulder.

"He tapped into God so much, more than any other. If God made Jesus as a literal son unto him, and if Jesus thought this, than who are we to argue. But I don't think it's what Jesus meant. Were all children of God, that was his point. We all have the ability to tap in but we're weighed down by superstition, guilt, idolatry, and the rules of religion and especially the rules of society."

And now its mass media, mankind's greatest distractions. Back then it was wizardry, and seeing things happen from the hands of a person. People are unique, we dismiss anything of the abilities a human is capable of. If you claim you talk to God you may find yourself in an institution."

"It's true. A lot of talented people wind up there." Oscar walked towards the window. It looked beautiful outside. A man was raking his front stoop below across the street. It gained Oscars attention.

"Where do you think everyone is? And why don't the police care?"

"I don't know," shrugged Oscar. "I don't know. We'll find out something tonight."

"Meet you after class? By the T?"

"Sounds good."

Mari got up and put her coat back on. "Why has everything gone mad?"

"Don't think too long on that one, but you're on the right track." Oscar opened the door for Mary. She kissed him on the cheek.

"OK I'll see you later. I can't believe it. Arthur? Should you call someone?"

"I will. I'll see you later."

"Sounds good. Good luck." And out the door she went.

Mari thought about evil and why the church was around to begin with. It was to protect people from evil, the evil in the woods. Woman have other talents. In the beginning of mankind, hunters and gatherers-women were the gatherers. They had a mind of insight and a gift to heal, find medicine, mix and try out their experiments, these things exasperated over time throughout the genes of womenkind. They have spiritual powers as well. They learned very early on to keep these powers from others. Witchcraft was one of them. It protected them from spirits, especially evil in the woods, unforgiven territory.

Class came and she handed in her paper. Halfway through, Mari excused herself from feeling a bit dizzy. She walked out of the building and to a small garden across from the music building and sat there, catching her self and her breath. She thought of witches, and their impact on society, dark women that project with sexual lusts, hysteria, and magic, but magic none the less. Whether it came from the side of light or dark, it was magic. The manifestation of something into the form of another. Was Jesus a magician? she wondered. What happened to Arthur was her next thought.

Mari and Oscar met up at the T and subbed into Salem. It was dusk, and there were signs of Halloween approaching everywhere. Pumpkins on porches, paper witches on doors, creepy makeshift graveyards on front lawns, skeletons hanging from trees. Salem appeared to have their hammer on the season. These were the days of Poe, and Bradbury, Stephen King and John Carpenter. Michael Myers on the front porch creeping his way over towards Jamie Lee Curtis. It was Halloween. Every year Pristol Falls High school is awarded money for a haunted house. They are awarded because of their outstanding theatre department and high school band which comes in first in show every year during the football games. Their theatre puts on shows that are so remarkable they are asked to tour. They compete with Broadway, they are that good. So every year the theatre hosts a haunted house to bring in money for the homeless. This year it was in Salem, the Spookhouse. The winters are cold in Boston, and many people help out when they can. The haunted house was a well known way of giving back to what can be a nightmare for some as soon as the temperatures begin to drop below freezing.

When they arrived at the house, a line came around the block. Children, parents, students, artists, everyone wanted their fill. The pathway to get in was scattered with leaves and small rocks, trees leaned over as if each one had its moment in a Fellini still-frame. Laughter is the best medicine was the prescribed dose as everyone in line chattered to stay warm, and in good spirit.

Mari and Oscar got to the back of the row. Oscar pulled out the sheet of paper, the one with Arthur missing on the front. Then he pulled out the ad for the Halloween Spookhouse. They were both on the same paper. Or as much as he could see. The line inched forward, couples and students came and stood behind them.

"They're from the same place," Oscar assumed out loud. "I think the body thief has something to do with this place."

"Because it's on the same paper? How could you be so sure?" Marisa questioned lightly.

"Because the timing, and the paper. Only different colors. But the same paper company logo etched in at the bottom." The line moved forward. The two inched their way closer.

"There is something creepy about how everyone missing is from that play, I mean there may be more that we don't know about, but still." Mari put her hands in her pocket. "It's getting chilly." She looked at the ground, at her feet, watching them inch closer and closer as the line moved onward. "It looks pretty cool."

"It does, it looks really cool." Oscar pointed up at a window on the second floor. There were screaming sounds and organ music coming from it. A woman kept coming to the window looking outside from it, at the line below. She'd come close and then back away. Her hair was all white and gray like her face. She was dressed all up in black, with white make up on her face, like she were a ghost, a dead woman.

The night came glaring in with whispering black clouds against a long navy sky. Speckles of stars intermittently shone through. Screams and feet moved the line. A woman was at the front dressed in victorian white, her hair the same color, red lipstick replaced her smile for a grin. Mari and Oscar could see her now as they rounded the corner for the last stretch. The woman was waving people in, as if floating, her arms as light as the joyful mood. The organ above gave heed a second glance down on the passersby. Dark opera music sang for the lady in the second window, still occasionally peering out below.

As they came closer, Mari pointed to the woman in white. "She looks familiar," pointing to Oscar.

"She does. Is that Laura from the other night, the play?" Oscar looked as though he may have literally seen a ghost.

"It is, it's Laura. I didn't know she was a part of this." Mari looked closer. The woman's arms still dangling about, waving people in, giving them fliers. It was just a matter of unspecified time that it would be Mari and Oscar's turn to greet the woman. They both ran in their own space, took shelter in their own coats, and reached out for each other's hand.

"Laura? Is that you?"

"Ah you two. Happy Halloween! Yes of course it's me sillies. Here." Laura hands Oscar a piece of paper. "That one is specifically for you." She cuts back on her syllable, as if a vacuum took the breath out of her words."

"Thank you. I guess we'll go in now." Oscar looks at Laura, her face malformed and looking demented for a second, her lipstick all covering a facade he wasn't quite sure about.

"Come on, let's go in," Mari said, and pulled Oscar's arm into the spookhouse. Together they entered, like that Bruce Springsteen song 'into that tunnel of love.'

The first room was the foyer of the house. Just old furniture lying around, a funky blue color paint on the wall. Nothing or no one would have made a deal of anything or anyone, except for the man in the hat standing in the corner, his back to everywhere. "Move on! Move on!" he screamed. He said it again. "Move on!" Mari and Oscar, and everyone in the foyer got the point and did just that. The arrows on the wall pointed towards the stairs. Where everyone went. Up the stairs.

Upstairs contained of a long hallway. There were rooms, and it was quickly brought to everyone's attention that it was the wish of the house for them to enter them. A long red tape was gliding itself down the hall. It was sort of a guide. The hall was dark, creepy, but more empty and silent. There was a chair at the end of the hall. It was red, and there looked like someone was in it when everyone gathered, when Mari took a second look, the person was gone.

Mari and Oscar, without a smile walked into the first room on the right, they inched their way in. There was a person playing a piano, and a woman next to him, standing there. Then the piano stopped, and the duo turned around and looked at everyone. Especially at Oscar. "Oh we know why you're here. We know a lot of things you don't." Then they laughed. Everyone in the room felt nervous, didn't know where to go, so they turned around. The duo at the piano kept laughing, wearing white make up, laughing like an old talkie from the

1920's. There was a hallway next to the room, at the other end, the red tape guided everyone there. Mari and Oscar walked in the dark hallway. They could hear sounds, everyone was quiet; yet they could hear screams from within the house, just not in the hallway. A sound came from inside the room. It was of a lady whispering. It must have been from a recorder, and from hidden speakers. There were fake spider webs in the corners, occasional old chairs leaning on its sides. Old photographs of slaves and young poor girls were hanging from the walls. At the end of the hall a woman was standing there.

"You can't come through here, you must go back," she said, like a banshee, like someone who is there one minute and gone the next.

Everyone was confused, they didn't know what to do. Mari looked at Oscar, it's all been so confusing. They walked towards the banshee. A man was standing at the other end calling everyone to come his way. But this time he pointed out towards the room to the right, this room was a different room. There were different furniture pieces and a different color paint. There were paintings on the walls of dogs playing poker, women holding pets, and old soldier photos. "Come this way," the man said. "If you know what's good for you. Follow me." Everyone followed him.

They were all whisk-fully pushed through the room and back into the hall, where they were originally, just a little further downward. They walked past and into another room. It was dark, and a strobe light was pounding. A man appeared behind the door. "Why did you go further than you were allowed? Why did you do such a thing?" He stood there. "You don't even know you're the star of the show!" He laughed. Everyone just stood in the room. A woman from the same attached hallway that came from the other room was standing at the other end of the room, next to the passageway. The people were waved through. Images of horror and fear passed through Mari, 'this isn't right', she thought to herself.

Attached to the room was a smaller door, as if for elves or dwarfs or just plain old short folk. The little red tape brought the people to the door. It was open, and everyone slipped and tucked on through. It led to a huge back room, its size could hold a ball given the night. The floor was marble. There were more dead folk, this time they were all over the floor, just lying there. A woman came running up to everyone coming in, at the patrons. "Can you help me?" she said. "I have a small problem, they all just fell, and now they won't get up." She ran up to another, "oh you don't believe me, OK, well, they stepped over the line. Do you believe that one?" The woman laughed. The little red tape sashed across the middle of the room. Some held onto it as they walked, others didn't. They just knew the direction it intended, and that was straight forward.

Another opening from the room loomed a stairwell back downstairs. Everyone was pretty much thrown out that way, so down everyone went. Through mazes of confusion, the steps were nothing different than ordinary steps, but at the bottom they found themselves no longer inside the house, but now outside, in the back yard. People were hanging out drinking. As if it were a party, a Halloween bash, ghosts and ghouls and witches all holding glasses of beer. There was a vampire at the keg. Fairly large slabs of concrete created a path to the keg. The vampire was pouring beer for a group of college frat boys. Their hats on backwards, all happy about the beer. It all looked like any other Halloween party, anyone's backyard bash, except for the 5 holes all in a row at the back of the yard, with grave stones sticking up from each one.

Osbrin holding a beer came up to Mari and Oscar. "Hi guys, how are you? How did you like the haunted house?"

"That was it? We didn't see anything." Mari looked at Osbrin.

"No? I'm sorry about that." Osbrin looked cynical and smirkish, she took a swig of her beer. "Have you seen those?" She points at the holes in the ground towards the back of the yard. "Go, have a look."

Mari and Oscar don't even excuse themselves. They walked thirty yards or so and reached the fence. There were five holes in the ground, graves. There was a coffin at the bottom of each hole, and a poster on top of each coffin. Gone Missing was written in big black letters. Mari looked at Oscar.

"What the fuck? I mean that's a little close to home." She turned around, looked at all the students coming out of the house and into the yard. There was a man standing there next to the keg now. By this time it didn't surprise Mari, nor Oscar for the matter. Mr. Spook was having his mug poured from a young lad at the keg. Mr. Spook could tell Mari was staring at him by now, as he looked his creepy eyes over and into the questionable soul of Mari. "What the fuck! Mr. Spook. I'm going to talk to him. Come on, let's talk to him."

They both walked over to Mr. Spook. "Hey, you. Are you part of this too?"

"Hello. No I just hand out fliers. Did you get your flier this evening?"

Oscar thought of the flier he was given at the door stuffed in his pocket. He took it out and unfolded it. ARE YOU NEXT? HAPPY HALLOWEEN!

"What is this?" Oscar half said aloud, half to himself. "Who made these fliers?"

"Pristol High. The girl at the theatre department, the girl who works there. She's part of the theatre department. I don't know her name. It's too much, and I shouldn't be saying this to you."

"Do they know that there are missing students?" Mari looked at Spook, her eyes intent on his.

"I don't know. I don't know. I really can't say. Lives are at stake. The girl who made these, well I met her a couple weeks ago. Her name is Irie; well she ain't right. There's something up with her, her eyes, the way she talks. Something ain't right upstairs is all."

"You're talking?" Mari half joked. "Well this Irie girl, do you have her address or number?"

"No," said Spook. "I don't. I met her and was given a mindful schedule to pass out fliers. They said they heard of missing students and we're told to hand out fliers. It's all I know. It's all I can say. You should go, before it's too late. I am treading lines."

"Who handed me the flier under my door?" Oscar continued, though would rather leave it in it's own.

"It wasn't me. I just passed them around on campus. You saw me." Mr. Spook replied.

"Everyone missing was at the tryouts for that play. That's kind of strange don't you think?"

"Yeah," said Spooky. "I do think of it."

"Oh fuck it," Mari said. "Come on Oscar. I had enough of this." She pulled Oscar's arm and they walked out into the street, under an exit sign next to a sad dead oak tree. They both didn't say much walking to the T. It was all too much, Oscar thought. He had some gigs coming up he needed to pay some attention to. Mari had her classes to worry about, not missing friends.

"I'll see you soon. I'll give you a call if anyone shows up or I hear of anything." Oscar reassures Mari. She nods, gives Oscar a kiss and gets on the train.

Later that dismal evening, Mari tucked herself in the books. She studied her Art Appreciation, read a short story for Critical Thinking and jotted down some notes for a paper in her Comp class. After the notes rang sharp on her telephone, thinking it was Oscar, she was found unanswered when she held it to her ear. It wasn't a prank; there was also no one on the other end of the phone. She decided to take a break and grab a cup of coffee down at The Willow Cafe.

No one was in her dorm, it was oddly empty. Everyone was out, and there was also some big thing going on down at the student center. She walked down the stark concreted hill and onto the main path, passing Peabody and onto the sidewalk. The lighting was luminous, and surreal. There was a dampness in the air, giving her recollection of what it must feel like in San Francisco. Autumn was Mari's favorite time of year. The leaves, the mystery that surrounds the season, Halloween, everything. The moon above lit her way for the last stretch. She walked into the Willow not a minute later.

She sat down at a table. Someone had left a book on the table. Mari got up and returned it to the barista behind the counter, ordered herself a cafe late, and then sat herself back down. She reached into her pocket, pulled out a half eaten container of PEZ and starting chewing down a forgotten meal. The girl behind the counter came over with Mari's drink.

"Thank you," Mari said, and looked out the main glass window, coffee and a view, it couldn't be better. Some liked clustering away in their novels, or typing away on their typewriters, but there will always be the ones who just love drinking coffee and looking out the window.

"You're welcome, sweetheart." The girl walked back to the counter.

Mari sat there in her chair, scooting herself to feel more comfortable. She was thinking of her assignment; witchcraft and religion. It was a broad topic; there were many places one can go on it. Religion, she thought was based on a man God left behind. Most religions, Buddhism is about meditation, and awakening. Christianity was about a man rising from the dead promising eternal life. Christ represented the truth. It was the way, as in Buddhism. She sat thinking, her coffee on her chin, hot and satisfying. Who was Jesus she thought to herself? Who were the witches God warned against in the book of Exodus, and why were they considered dangerous to men. Mari thought about it. She thought of the theory about Christ, who this man was. What fascinated her was trying out for Jesus Christ Superstar. Oscar was mentioning that Jesus was given a potion just before he died, and this made the appearance that he had died. This way they could take him down from the cross, and take him to his tomb. Were the clouds and thunder that came in circumstantial? We're the rollers of the dice for his clothing curious on who this man was. They took Christ down three hours afterwards, at his appearance of death. Joseph took him to his tomb. Three days later, he rose again. Joseph was a known alchemist in the area, the study of potions and transformation from different elements into compounds. Wizardry must have been prevalent, there was a keen suspicion that most Kings of the old days spoke to God, or a God, and wielded powers to convince the people this king was sent. This happened over and over in civilization of mankind as time elapsed. When did the witch come onto the scene? Was she the one who made the potions too? Is witchcraft a mental illness or just another religion with different variables on the table. A way for women to pass secrets, both good and bad, a way to figure out meaning behind life, and to help contour its path. She looked around in a heavy witch populated area on the globe. Boston Massachusetts was famous for a few things, and witchcraft was one of them.

She drank up her coffee, put her coat back on, and placed a dollar on the table. On her way out she had a gut punching feeling something had happened, something bad. It was a feeling. She looked to the left, there was an old Picasso print in an old frame. Its worth of two dollars came to her mind, a throw away. She pressed for the steps. When she climbed the stairs and up onto the street, she combed down her coat as if it were infiltrated with hair and dustballs, even though it wasn't. Something was wrong, she could feel it growing. Mari looked around, down the street, to her left and up at the windows from the building where the Willow sat. Then she looked ahead, her suspicions immediately coming true. On the light pole just in front of her was another poster.

Have you seen me?
Missing
Oscar Warhl
Last seen at the Spookhouse in Salem
Call 511-553

Mari walked up to the poster, read it like she was seeing things in Kansas; nope, she wasn't in Kansas and the name was correct. "What the fuck?" She tore it off the pole, got a second look, looked around her, then back at the paper. Oscar Warhl. She tried to think if that wasn't his last name or someone may have made a mistake. "Jesus Lunatic! Who's doing this?" She looked again, frustrated not knowing what to do. She decided to head back to the dorm. "This is insane," she said over and over. "Who the hell is doing this." It was getting late, and she wasn't expecting anything new that would pile on complications, it was bad enough. There really is a limit a man can handle, a woman too.

Mari's plans were simple, go back to the Spookhouse. First, she walked over the English Department, through the glass doors and down the hall. Dr. Yasman's door was the last door on the left. She came to it and knocked.

The door opened, Dr. Yasman immediately surprised. "Mari, hi Mari, come in. What is it? Please come in and have a seat. Are you OK?"

"It's weird Dr. I'm sorry to disturb you, but I'm having problems. Have you heard of missing students on campus, and around town?" Mari looked at her fingers, noticed there was a little dirt underneath her nail. "Here, look at this." She handed the good doctor a poster of Oscar being missing.

"This is your friend?"

"Yes, my friend Oscar, and his friend Arthur is missing, and my friend Christi. They all wound up on these fliers, but it's weird. They're not official fliers. I went to the police.

"What did they say?" Dr. Yasman asked.

"They said it wasn't official but to come back, but it's all been happening so fast. You talk a lot about witchcraft, and it feels like that. Something evil, and some supernatural force related to it all."

"Interesting. Why do you say that?"

Discarding the dirt underneath her nail, Mari came back to full attention, in shock, "I don't know, it's really weird. Everyone who tried out for this play we saw advertised, Jesus Christ Superstar, well, we tried out for it, but it closed down right away. People started to disappear. It was all really weird." Mari looked out the office window for a second, thought she saw a shadow, but then came back to Dr. Yasman's face. "It's really weird Dr. Yasman."

"Well I would say go back to the police. Do you feel threatened?"

"I don't know, maybe a little. There's this creepy guy. I've been seeing him around, and he was at the spookhouse, and they had all these coffins in graves that said something, I forget." Mari reached for a cup of coffee that was on Dr. Yasman's desk, then realized it wasn't hers. "Dr. I don't get it. I'm sorry to bother you. I should go."

"Well, if you need to go to the police, go there. But stay safe. Don't be alone." Dr. Yasman stood up, walking Mari to the door. "And don't worry about this week's paper, I know you have a lot to deal with. Just get your self together and do what you have to do."

"Thanks Dr. Yasman. Thank you." Mari walked out the door. As she was just a few steps away, she could hear the door close behind her, but it was a quiet sound, as if it were all fragile territory, and Dr. Yasman had more than an inclination; there was that fear she remembered as a child, walking into the Eastern Woods above Pristol. It had returned like a puff of smoke leaving a visual memory, and the harrowing feeling that accompanied it. Mari continued walking down the hall, feeling the residue the closer she got to the main door, the moment she stepped outside, it had gone.

Mari walked down the main path that passed both the science building and the music building, when she got to the theatre, she paused. "This is where it all started. Who began this play?" Mari looked at the door. There was snow on the ground the day she had found out the play had been canceled, but there was no snow today. The lights were going down in and around her, coinciding with the coincidental sun. The darkness was coming in, to engulf. She looked up, the clouds were silent and no more judgmental than a daisy farm. They could care less. She walked down across Peabody and towards the T. When she arrived she saw another poster of Oscar. How bizarre she thought, not giving it twice the look it asked for, half of what it deserved. She got on the T. The train pounded into the ground, shifting speeds going around bends, solid like a moving six inch thick bullet of steel. People holding on to the rail, looking aimlessly through the black window, occasionally seeing lights flicker as the railcar passed.

"Who could be up to this?" Mari asked herself. She thought of it. That girl Irie, and Laura and even Osbrin. She thought of them, how they appeared to be innocent through it all, yet remained unscathed by the recent rumblings about. Her station arrived and Mari got off, her backpack still on her shoulder, a few important things inside but nothing too heavy she couldn't carry around. She walked a few blocks and over towards the old witch courthouse, and the Salem Inn. Just down the road was the spookhouse. The leaves were coming down in a fierce voice, the wind howling with laughter and mischievous joy.

When she came to the house, again there was a line, but not as long as it was before. Again there was a woman in the window, but not the same woman as before. The line inched but at a faster rate. The leaves were all over the ground draping a horizontal curtain for the great below. Concrete slabs still lay ground for her to walk over. She was in a place, in a time, but not out of reality. This is all make-believe she would tell herself. This is just a play. So was Jesus Christ Superstar, that was supposed to be a play as well. She inched forward, the girls in front of her were in anticipation for what was ahead. There was an older mid-forties couple in front of them. And then there looked like a bunch of high school kids. After that it began to blend with the shoes all gathered below the coats.

Mari got a good look at the front as she turned the corner, the last leg of the line. There was a woman in white, painted face and white hair, waving, waving people in, but she wasn't sure if it were Laura or not. Marisa got frantic, impatient, couldn't wait any longer. She budged herself upward in line, people got all loud about it. "Hey you can't cut! Hey! What are you doing Lady? You can't cut!" Mari pushed her way up the line.

When she got to the front a woman in white was standing there, but it wasn't Laura. It was Irie. Mari could tell. She was young, black hair, black eyes, a quaint taste of complete control over the situation.

"Oh honey, slow down. I'll let you in." Irie said. "In fact you've been expected."

"Who me? What do you mean by that? Who's expecting me? You?" Mari tilted her head to the side, to see if there were any others standing near. It was just Irie. "You going to take me too? Is that it?"

"Oh honey, what fairy tales. Go in. Have a good time, take a load off yourself. Oh baby, really, go on in."

As if Mary had no control, as if all her brain functioning went on some odd default, like a child seeing a toy for the first time and all he or she does is want it. There is no thinking, just instinct and attraction, lots of colors and amazement over what is happening. "Yes, of course, I'll go in," she said in a mindless daze. "Yes, OK, I'll go in." She walked up the steps and entered the house.

Laura was on the side of the house, coming around the front. Irie grabbed hold of Laura's eye, and head as she nodded a wicked grin amongst certain clicks.

Mari walked into the familiar foyer. The dead gray walls seethed down in old mildew and dreams long gone. It wasn't though a familiar story, as she crept along the red rope, like sheep with the others whom she followed.

There was a man in the corner with his back to the wall. He turned around as if on cue. "Hey you," he said, looking strait at Mari. Mari walked on, her head shrinking, her arms closer to her ribs. It was

128

cold inside the house, and the group stayed close like everyone does when it's cold. They got to a place where the stairs went upstairs, and not down. She knew the floor-plan, but something was different. She could feel the ghosts, she could hear the walls scream. She wanted to cry back, holler and say she too exists like these ghosts, buried in the walls. Buried in the backyard cemetery. Mari flew down the hall, through the rooms, hand on the red tape. She knew the drill. She ran down the steps and pushed open the door. There were twenty or so scrabblers and beer downers loping about. Everyone noticed. The door slammed behind her, and there was silence. Even the upstairs music coming from the second floor ceased on the lift of a finger.

"Ah look what we have here." Osbrin walks from the keg. Almost laughing. "What have we done now? Are we being little detective woman, bit of a Nancy Drew?"

Mari stood there, her coat all vulnerable and used. She felt alone and without her friends to help her. She was the strong one not that long ago. The world was a different place back home in high school, she thought.

Laura and Irie came round the bend, from the path that led to the front of the house. "I see the mouse gets the cheese after all."

"Oh what are you creep'n about." Mari stands up a little, shakes it off a little. "What the fuck is going on around here?"

"Everyone wants to be a star, Marisa. Haven't you heard, it's the thing, its what society sold their soul for, to be on TV, or to be on stage in front of fifty thousand. Wasn't that the number, fifty thousand? Wasn't that the number Mari?"

"What number? What fucking number are you talking about?"

"Have you any idea what is going on here? Sweet Mari? I'm sorry it has to be like this, but you are in the north now, in the woods of the Eastern God. Did you read the Lottery? Shirley Jackson, it was a classic Mari, come on! It was a classic. No one had regrets the day after, they all got on with their lives and didn't think once about their contribution to the stoning of a woman chosen of nothing but ill luck. Poor lady! You know the rules here, Mari."

"What the fuck are you talking about? The lottery, this is some kind of sacrifice?" Mari looked around her, saw the gathering of fake ghouls with white on their faces, and saliva running from their mouths. "What the hell are you all doing? What have you done to my friends?"

"We didn't do it, Mari," said Osbrin.

"Then who did it? You tell me Osbrin, you tell me Laura who did this? Oh fuck you." She bent over, looked for a rock to hold on the dirt. But there wasn't one there, just dirt and dirty grass, the kind that has been walked on. When she got up, her nerve hit a bell, like going back to the second grade on the first day of school. "Mr. Fucking Spook!" A man was behind a tree, not halfway the distance between the graves and the keg. He came out of the darkness even more to show his face. "Mr. Spook, say something. You know what's going on."

"Throw her in, throw her in." Some college brat came staggering out the door, as if it was his time to greet the keg at the end of the tunnel. Unfortunately for Mari, they all began following suit. "Throw her in! Throw her in!"

Mari didn't know what they were talking about, but they were leaving the pathway to the graves open, encircling around it towards, her. "Throw her in! Throw her in!" They chanted, over and over.

"You can't do this! This is insane! Aren't there guards here? Where's the cop at the door? Who the fuck are you!" Mari ranted, she waved her arms, threw her bag at the first dawn of the dead character that came on her. "Get away from me. Get the fuck away!"

A bandit of humans, brainwashed, disillusioned, and against their behalf; too young to know, all gathered around Mari. They lifted her up by her feet as she screamed.

"Throw her in! Throw her in!" was all they could say. It sounded like the play, she thought of it. "Crucify Him, crucify Him. But that's not what they were saying. They got underneath her, almost pathetic on their good treatment towards her, and lifted her along the path.

"Put me down, mother fuckers! Put me down! Put me down!" Mari chanted back. She laughed, this was hysterical, how could people get away with this madness she thought. "Put me down mother fuckers, I'm going to have all of you expelled, arrested and your broomsticks taken away, mother fuckers, put me down!"

They lifted and carried, above the small row of carnations planted at the end of the field, and then they stopped. Five open holes lay before them, like planted little pods, one after the next.

"Fucking shit, you mothers."

They lifted her down onto the ground as they all surrounded the empty grave, the one with the coffin lid open. Then someone heard something, something different sounding. It was a cry, a loud cry in the night, a hollering, a howl for life on no extension, nor exaggeration. And it was coming from the grave just next to the open coffin. Mari looked down at it, hearing it, recognizing the sound of a familiar soul. The door of the coffin came flying open, and behind the lid was Oscar, all covered in a white powder, his mouth all covered in dirt. His eyes wide as the clouds breaking on a very windy day. His scare was beyond comprehensible. Mari was in shock, so was everyone else. Something had gone wrong.

"What the hell did you put in his drink Laura? Laura, did you mess this up Laura?" Irie came flailing in, making a scene.

"Osbrin made the drinks, I didn't make any of the drinks, I swear it." Osbrin's eyes opened up as wide as Oscars.

Oscar sat up, screamed one last time, faulting in his vocal chords. Then he looked up, he looked around, where he was at. He saw it quickly and jumped up, put his hand on top of the edge and helped himself out of the hole. "Mari, it's them! Get away from them!"

"I know it's them. We need help."

"No we don't," Oscar picked up a shovel on the dirt next to the grave, fortunately a prop came along at the right time. "Get back all of you!" He then went to each coffin, starting from the first, climbed down into the ditch, and opened it. Arthur was in there. "Wake up, my friend wake up!" Oscar pulled him by his shoulders. A second later, there was a cough. Arthur began to resuscitate, spitting out dirt. Then there was a scream. So loud it shook the hole he was in. Arthur, all tucked in his autumn coat came revived sitting straight up.

"Oh my God! What the hell just happened!" He came to, looked around, saw his friend Oscar staring down at him.

"Good, Buddy, good, just breathe." Oscar grabbed him by the arm and pulled him up out of the ditch. Everyone standing around looked as though they were in shock. People were either dead silent, or just plain dumbstruck to know what to do. "Everyone stand back!" Oscar turned to the crowd of nitwits and faux ghouls. He jumped over and landed himself in another ditch.

Mari stood numb and in surprised horror as she watched what was unfolding. She looked over her shoulder by the tree. There he was Mr. Spook coming out of the shadows. He caught Mari's eye and walked towards her. Mari stepped back, but she had no choice but to confront the fear itself straight on.

Mr. Spook stood there, almost speechless. "Let me help," he said to Mari. He turned to the right and saw Irie standing there, as well not knowing what to do, how far this charade has landed itself. "It's your fault," Spook said to Irie. And with that he jumped into the fourth pit. He opened it up and there was Valley lying in the box. She looked comfortable and sleeping as if she WERE drugged. "Wake up," Spook said. "Wake up Valley."

A small cough came from the edge of Valley's throat. Spook took her by the upper body and tried to hug her. "It's OK, you can wake up now." Another cough came from her throat. It was dry and filled with dirt and dust.

"Oh my, what just happened," Valley said to herself. "I was in the woods, and then I started to dream, and I remember knowing I was dreaming. Where am I?" She looked around, realized she was in a dark place, inside a dark coffin outside? She began to panic, lifted herself up.

"It's OK now, you were poisoned, but with a sleeping drug." Spook held her up and rubbed her back.

Oscar came back over and went to the last hole. He jumped inside of it and flew the lid open. Christi was lying there, not even asleep any longer, but awake. She was in a state of shock. Her eyes were split open and white as the moon. Glistening with real fear and horror. She felt better the moment she came upon Oscar's face, a clarity began to settle in Christi's eyes, she began to feel a sudden sense of calm, and rescue.

"Oscar, oh my Lord. Where am I? I am OK, right? I didn't die, did I?"

132

Oscar leaned over and hugged his friend. Mari came up to the edge. My God, Christi, are you OK? Mari started to cry. She looked over at the girls, Laura and Irie, and Osbrin, "you'll pay for this, you will. It's all fun and games in your world." Mari then jumped in the ditch to help her friend out. Both Oscar and Mari pulled her up and out of the hole while Arthur drew his hand in.

Mr. Spook stood there, tall and giantlike. His hand was also in the muck helping the poor girl to her feet. "I know I should have said something. I had no idea it would go this far." Spook told Mari. "I'm really sorry." He looked over at Laura and Osbrin, "the three of you. You went too far."

Valley walked up to her friend Laura, "I can't believe you tried to kill me."

"I didn't try to kill you, it was a sleeping potion. You were going to wake up three days after you took it. You knew about it. You said you wanted to try it."

"Not like this," Valley said. "I swear you're all nuts."

Christi brushed herself off, taking in breaths, Arthur was aimless walking around trying to reconnect with his balance.

A shadow of authority came into the back of the house, he was looking around. He had someone with him, Dr. Yasman. Dr Yasman had pointed to Mary and the two of them walked over towards the makeshift graves.

The officer reached out his hand, Oscar shook it. The officer than looked at Mari, "are you OK? Are the two of you OK?"

"Yes, I believe it was a prank gone too far, or they didn't know what they gave us, and we wound up in these coffins."

"Don't go light on them," Mari ousted. "They tried to kill you in plain sight."

"Is it true?" said the officer. "You were all in those graves? How long?"

"I don't know, a couple days the others; me, I was just put in there." Oscar brushed off more dirt. Wiped some from his face and hair.

The officer picked up his talkie, "we have a circus over here at the spookhouse, a poisoning incident, possible attempted murder. I don't know, need some back up. Send two cars." He looked around, "OK, everyone has to stay right here, you cannot leave. This is now a crime scene."

Cars showed up with flashing lights and loud sirens. Yellow tape ran itself around the perimeters of the entire back yard. A slew of detectives came pouring through the back yard like adults breaking up a high school underaged drinking party. They began questioning the girls. What was the motive, who was involved. It took its sweet time as well, as Oscar and Mari, Christi and Arthur circled themselves in their own friendship ring, their own way of saying life is stranger than fiction. There was no karma here, no one deserved it.

"Come on you guys. You've had enough for tonight," the officer spoke. "Looks like the high school kids took a little too much artistic liberty with this year's show. We'll be in contact over the next few days if we have any more questions."

The officer looked at Oscar and Mari, "the two of you can go." He nodded his head towards Arthur and Christi relaying the same. The four of them hugged, thanking their God that it wasn't as bad as it could've been. Mari and Oscar then walked to the front of the house, somewhat in shock and disbelief, somewhat just being part of a really bad nightmare.

Oscar took Mari's hand and headed themselves back around to the front of the house. "They're going to be in trouble, and that will be that. People are crazy today. They love getting themselves into this kind of stuff. They love the sound of a cult, witches, ghosts and spook jobs." He let go of Mari's hand. He turned to her. "I'm really happy I'm alive. Let's just say that."

Mari looked back at Oscar, "I'm glad you're alive too."

The two of them, fragile, just people walked themselves down the lonely road. Their boney skeleton'd shadows accompanied them close, with only a coat to cover their lonely young souls. Their thoughts on strange happenings and wonderments, birds flying by, swarming out of the gray sky added a keen sense of surrealism to the evening, putting a film on their mind they would never forget. Mari and Oscar each found a friend that night, love even. Through the dark tunnel of love, an adventure within an instant, time would go by. And
134

they would rather forget more than remember that night, no matter how much they sometimes wanted to. Two souls walking together, with a piece of time and an image attached to it would only give them some sort of meaning of what love meant between people later on. Two frail people in a city of so many, trying to blend in, make sense of what they couldn't understand. They would shine on. Half way back to the T, Mari took Oscar's hand and said to him, in the most endearing way that Oscar would never forget for the rest of his life. "Everything is going to be alright," Mari said. "Never forget that. Every thing is going to be alright. Don't you worry about a thing."

Catcherman and the Great Madness

Is it my fault, I asked myself. Or is it his, that man. I awoke this morning into, or better yet out of a great madness. I went insane. The reasons were everywhere, like a whipped butter gone real sour, yet the skies somehow remained blue through it all. My village was unscathed by the appearance of something gone terribly wrong. Just the opposite, it was a billboard or an advertisement for something that was supposed to look right, but under the ugly underneath, it was just like all the others. The shops downtown haven't been occupied in over a decade. The few that remain somehow must have been handed down, like a chimney. From the old coal to the new gold. In a town like mine, the shops are owned by the few rich, everyone else is in crammed up apartments trying to pay the rent. In this town, a cop on every corner or behind every mirror. In this town, far from St. Louis. They burned buildings down in that town. They lit it up like a candle. Wave the fucking candle. This is fiction. Those fuckers took something, lugged themselves down the street, stole from store owners over there. Who does that and then screams justice? I know evil. I've seen it face to face. A long time ago a man came into a dream of mine and just stood there, below the wooded awning. In the door way, and there was nothing to my soul of this day that seemed as horrifying as that dream.

The coffee was good this morning. It was delight. The line wasn't out the door like it usually is. But the television spoke to me differently. I guess it was my time I thought to say something. If someone can scream on the maddening television that it's okay to burn down a town over a court decision, well then I guess what can a poor white guy from Bullshit Town New Jersey lose by speaking his mind. I really thought I was going to go silent. I saw the madness not long ago come from somewhere I never saw before. Some guy a few years ago gets on a bus, sits next to some stranger and then cuts his head off with a fishing knife. That story hit me then. I was going to begin this tale with that happening. But then a movie came out and some guy goes apeshit killing half the theatre. Then some school shootings. Kids going into schools with semi automatic rifles and just fucking firing away into their kin, their friends and teachers. What's wrong with everyone today, is it just a few, or are we as a society squeezing this product out of the top of a cake decorating cone of chaos and karma. I awoke today feeling better than I've felt in a long time. I think I realized I was given a key, out of all of this. The deal, it was more simple than I thought. No soul was going to be sold, or deal with those in which we do not speak of. No deal with the devil. I was asked to write it down. That was all. But I had to call it fiction. Because all of this is fiction. And for that reason, it should be as believable as life itself.

To know madness, you have to know its opposite. The calm, the beauty, the serene. One's self looking inward, throwing what is around you away from you. If you're a Christian, than you are a Taoist, or a Buddhist. Jesus was. But drift away we did. The madness on the Television. Is it in my town. I will tell you about my town, but I have to go inward, more, more inside the depth of fiction. There is no nonfiction now. There is only the made believed. Like a fire you can put it all out. Like a darkness; just light the match. It all glows. Four rabbis were murdered in a temple, praying. What is the sense of that? What war has gone on, that hasn't been inside our minds, the apples don't fight with each other. Nor do they fight with the peaches, and the bananas. Nuts are more sane than the human race, and they are nuts. I don't know. I woke up today. It happened yesterday, a long time ago, the day I was born. They asked me for my birthdate today at the pharmacy. I had to pick up some pills to prevent a nervous breakdown. I guess they don't know it's me. They always ask me for my name and birthday. It used to be your social security number that gave off the 1984 stigma of the great New World Order. Now, it's your birthday. None the less, the day you are born, you're looking for a way out.

The riots today on the TV. They say it's unlike the LA Riots. 100 people were killed in the LA riots. I have to say I find no sense in the racial dispute. It's an eerie thing to say, but I think it's deeper. I think it

137

has to do with weed. Marijuana. I think that the people who like to smoke it in this country can't; and that's the problem. The police become spies on those looking for the weed on the streets. They call this a crime, so they lock up anyone they can find in these cities that is breaking this law. Travon was killed because he went around the corner to buy a twenty bag or something. Whats his name goes after him because he's the great almighty security guard of the West Hills Falls community, and needs to protect itself from people doing dime bag drop offs and the what not. It's all insane you see. The people then have a reason to back the race card. There is a race card, people play it all the time. But before there was MTV, and before African American men wore their pants half down their ass, well, there was a peace and respect in this country. You saw it on the ivory walls of the great colleges and institutions, where race wasn't an issue, your grades were. People wore fine clothing and nothing rude was tolerated. They, or we all had a job to do. It was our destiny inside our minds speaking. Homelessness couldn't break us. Being broke was just a phase. Times got tough. I remember. They said come on in, here's a bed, have a good sleep and we'll convince you it all didn't happen. That's right, here's a pill, it will forget it all for you. Here's the internet to forever prevent you from having a real friend again. Here's the rest of your life in a room staring out a window watching twenty year olds down kegs and twist off each other's bra straps. I don't know. Insanity, do you think about it? Like mentioning those in which we do not speak of? Faucault says it's folly. There's a lot to be said about it. But there was a time when hooking up didn't mean having a good love life. We all stood for something then. There were barriers. There were boundaries, and separation from each other. We weren't sheep, but I don't know if the metaphor of people being sheep is a pejorative statement or not. Sheep are pretty nice creatures. They don't make bombs and blow up people with them. They're a well nourished in their soul, a tame and happy little bunch. Now the people here are wolves in bad clothing. The sheep are dead, and the planet shrivels. The land is drying up, and a great cry can be heard. Fuck it, and that's the point. If you can't say fuck it, then you can't build your house. If you can't separate yourself from the cause on the TV, you can't get back home. When we were in

138

college it were the books that interested us, it were the stories that old of yesterday authors wrote. Today, it's fear and more fear, and an empire built on it. After 9/11. Fear. The next decade, fear and war. War on the TV, war over seas. War next door and war in the bedroom. War and no water to extinguish it. Star Wars was dead, and Yoda couldn't win in time trying to get the audience to believe in the Tao, the stupid light sabers always got in the way and fucked it all up, or a quest for a mask that somehow told society that aliens looked like muppets. No, an entire civilization is going down before our eyes, and anger isn't just a word in a Yoda script. It has somehow given itself life again, and when I watch it on the glory box, I humble myself before a God of my own understanding, and hopefully yours that something has seriously gone awry. Something has gone wrong. And Houston we do have a problem.

I told the class that day, because in this fiction world, I'm a teacher at Harvard, a professor with a doctorate in English, if I don't sound as though I am, well; there have been worse that have gone down these hallowed halls of weeping, crying in the dark till your eyes bleed, red blood, down the fucking cheek. I told the class that day that the towers came down, and everything after was a bi-product of a mask called fear and more fear, through intimidation and uniforms. The police backing, retreating from a culture that has given into pure evil. What fool steals a tv and then cries innocence. I don't know. The powers rose when the towers fell. Sadness matched the clothing that sagged off the tired faces for an explanation. I told the dumb idiots, and I told the genius's that day. The day it came to me. Like when we were young, and a surprise hits you. You're ten and something happens. Like landing on the moon or a new technology like cable TV that brought you HBO. Someone invents a Walkman and the world looks different. Analog was taken over by Digital media and technology. It failed miserably. It helped fuel the disillusionment of the people. It helped brainwash friends into thinking social media was a substitute for friendship. Emails were easier than a visit or a letter if it were so important. I find it disheartening that the send button is the 'return button'. There should be a red button in its place that says

Warning Panic. Sometimes, of course it's good to get mail from my old friends at the Harvard Yard, but it's a mess everywhere. And to have them try and enforce all this media and email and Spacebook; well, I have to begin to disagree. Walden was written for a reason. To relax in the woods and contemplate how much MTV went the wrong fucking way and brought in negative music with violent themes and graffiti for DaVinci. It's not art when its fame. It's not Walden when it's some AUTHOR trying to scare someone to death in a HORROR novel. I tell the kids this shit, in the class room, behind closed doors, in temple corridors, bedsheets and broomsticks. I remember a day when I could walk outside and know that everything was OK, everything was calm. Jimmy Carter was president and no one really gave a shit enough to create an argument that brought on a violent altercation. The news is an evil thing these days. God bless them all, but it's fucking depressing. The violence on the television has spawned from the depths of the Horror genre in the movie industry. Kill. What part of though shall not kill didn't we understand? I got along with everyone twenty years ago. We all walked in the deli and ordered subs and were quite content at jobs that had meaning. If you ask me, it was the computer and the virus that came with it. The doors it opened for suspicion, crushing marriages through old contacts that came forward who you'd never think you'd hear from after 1982. It's beyond comprehension that something more malevolent was at hand. Kids didn't go into high schools every fucking other day and shoot off rounds on their school mates. It was unheard of. If there was a war, it was Vietnam. A darkness came over the eighties. But the 90's got even more Dark with Cobain and all that underground shit I was so in love with. The Smiths, and Depeche Mode. INXS, the guy kills himself. Kurt kills himself. The 27 club increases it's members. People now, now. Now I say, not five years ago, or twenty. People are dropping down, to the floor, like flies and squid. No one cares. They got their Moon Man award from MTV. Ripping rhymes, faking songs. Lip synching to Jan and Dean. Whatever the case, we're always back here at the beginning of this mystery. It's bad out there now. 6 Feet of Snow in Buffalo over night. It's bad out there now. Ferguson is up on fire making the Occupy Wallstreeters look like they should learn
140

something from Mr. Rogers. It's bad out there now. No one can afford the rent if they're in the bottom 99 percent. They're losing their minds thinking how they're going to pay back tuition in a market that was taken from them. There are no store fronts like there used to be. They're all vacant here in Bullshit Town. Let's give this a name, because it's all connected anyway. The name of this town is Madness. Madness town. And I think God agrees that after Reagan came Bush, then came Clinton, then Bush and somewhere in there wars happened over oil distribution and valuable land. "In the name of God" became a catch phrase to kill without guilt or remorse or even the slightest notion that that statement in itself is the furthest from anything God has said. In any scripture where God is spoken of, it's usually something divine, kind and glorious. There is no glory in war. It's the oldest mistake in the books. The only ones who ever spoke the truth of war were the dead, and they're no longer here to listen to. Society and the great madness that arose somewhere between borders and boundaries came to us. It's speaking. The students left for the day, because this is fiction and we're supposed to learn something from fiction. The students left for the day and began marching downtown. I went home and fixed myself a peanut butter sandwich. I threw it up an hour later because the peanut butter was over a year old, according to the date on the side of the plastic container. I didn't watch the news that night. I crawled into bed and prayed to God so that living another day meant more than the cause. It's a difficult balance to maintain. But when it comes to sanity, insanity is it's looming shadow. In a fragile way.

I began teaching this year at Silent University, named after Jeffery Silent, or Jeffery Maxwell, a boy who was silenced after a small crime against the University. He wouldn't give up the name of a black list for an underground ring of poets, dreamers and communist party want-to-be's. He was ordered that no one speak to him on or off campus. Jeffery went mad, but maintained A's throughout his stay. He earned his Masters and Doctorate at Princeton. He teaches, wrote a shit load of books and preaches the holy mantra of knowledge every chance he gets. The school recoiled on their hasty and severe judgement that the students and faculty took it upon themselves to metaphorically rename the college Silent University. To a group of students who took their lives a little more seriously, without a need as much for a large focus on social groups and societies, breading candidates of a blind country, nothing like that. It was about individuality, and by this they all got along better. They were there for the knowledge, not the keg parties and naked swimming pool parties, but for something different. All though something happened there. Not that some didn't stray and smoke marijuana in the woods, or hide a flask in their upper coat pocket, that shit didn't matter. Maybe it was a specific decision not to have a football team, or a basketball team. They just had a baseball team. Been around since the founding day when Louis Arthur cut the felt ribbon in front of the University Library. 1802 was a long time ago. But something happened later on, after the great silencing. Long after. Two years ago, or was it three. Dimensions of time shifted on a bus that goes only one way. Where there is nothing but one way tickets down a long lonely hard hearted life, nothing but misery and the anguishing panic that comes of it, down that line. Walden. A book about settling down, taking notice of the pond, the ducks in it. The sun coming streaming and divinely down on its household of nothing but goodness, made of good God given wood, and pottery of labor, silverware of pride, and a hard mattress that carried the broken bones of old men who move there with their old and tired wives. Stop the clock.

Someone was murdered on campus. A note was left behind. I was called in. Shown the note. It said. There will be more. But in a black itched pen, scratched into the diamond edged paper, a gathering of letters spelled out a master's plan, an epitaph, there in cold words "silencing ghosts always leave behind traces of unwritten history'. Meant nothing, is what I thought. They asked me what it meant. I didn't know, I told them that. I didn't know anything that was going on. The missing students were my students. I had to tell them that, but I didn't pry into their personal lives. I moved on with my own, a long time ago. But something did come back. A little, like Cohen's "crack in everything, that's how the light gets in." It hit me. It wasn't real. The students aren't missing. It was a faux, a hoax. Students have it out on Mr. Yeller. That's what it is. A hoax, a paper trail, a fake paper note. Wasn't real, is what I thought. None of it was real any more.

The militant police gathered on the west side of the school. There were to be more protests downtown of more angry African American, and poor White Folk who didn't have any identity any longer left for a cause to carry. It was all a mess. More buildings on fire in Ferguson. The couch looked lonely and the fridge was empty when I came back to my apartment. Walden. I was so hungry I went for the peanut butter, then put it quickly back down and picked up the phone. I ordered a pizza and a couple cokes. Put the phone down and moved over to my window looking out at an empty street. Why would any one play such a prank, I thought to myself. Why risk your education and all that. What if it weren't a prank. What if it were real. No, was my hunch. It was a prank, but there was a motive. Had to do with something.

I turned on the TV. Someone was throwing bricks through the windshield of a police car in Missouri. I got back up off the couch and turned it back off. I then went to my bedroom and passed out. Who gives a fuck about some school that doesn't want to talk about it, I thought. I was out right about after that.

The morning came, went. I didn't notice; though I began to think. More rational about the matter at hand. There were three kids missing, and I didn't know where to begin to look for them. The coffee was hot; leave it at that. The bagel down the street on College Ave hit me the wrong way and I felt ill from 4:00 that late mid-afternoon to about 6. Then the stomach wrench went away. I began to frill, hither and thither my way across what looked like images in my mind. I picked up my keys and headed to Morrison Dorm. I got there. They didn't recognize that I was a professor at the school, so they let me through on me telling me who I was and what I was doing there. There were a couple more guards around than usually posted. The note was correct, no one was in their dorms. Three of them back to back in a coed dorm and no one saw anything.

"Hey you, kid, come here. Ryerson right?"

"Yeah," he said. "I have you in lecture."

"I know," I said. "What's the deal here. Where did everyone go, where did those fuckers go? You know anything?"

"Don't know a thing." Ryerson looked frantic and began to pace inside his own head, back and forth, back and forth."

I looked at him. For a minute. One long fucking minute. "If this is a joke, I'll have who ever is behind it, well, it ain't going to look good on their fucking resume! Let's put it that way."

Kids were standing around now. The dorm was cold orange with a black line going down the walls. The rug was maroon with purple box patterns all over it. Thank God I didn't live there. That's all I thought. "All right. Get back to it. Sorry I got carried away." I said. No one believed me. They knew I had a temper. Didn't like kids who didn't do their homework. It's all teachers ask of their students. Do the homework and you get an A, because you can't forget this shit. This shit stays with you long after the initial imprint. Paste it and hang it up, like clues in a box. Take them out of the box and put them up on the wall. That's all I was thinking. The kids aren't in the dorm. I said goodbye on the way out. There was neon light hanging from the Art building. It made me want to puke in a way, though it made me want to be back in college again, as a student. We had a ghost on the Yard, where I went. We all gathered in Anne Cotter's dorm house and looked for her on Halloween. I knew every campus had its legend. I knew people disappeared here and there, but you never thought it was going to be on your own campus. I left the walking green and up to the lot, my car was sitting underneath an out of dated lamp-post. This place needs work, is what I thought.

Class began Tuesday. Monday was a day of rest and respect for the missing. Class wasn't imperative; if you were going mad over the missing you can skip class, but you had to make up the work over Thanksgiving break.

I got home and opened the fridge. Empty again. I picked up the phone and ordered another pizza from Bachagalloops. It came an hour past with a couple root-beers instead of cokes. I sat there an hour after that, dumb to the television and facing the window. People were turning over cars in Ferguson now, still setting them ablaze. Outside the apartment window, below was a cat scurrying at the garbage cans on the curb, yelping and crying like a hungry cat does. I turned to the television again. What's with you all, I said to myself. Gone fucking mad. Gone fucking mad. That was it, and I knew it. Even if it were a hoax on campus and everyone comes out alright, well that would be enough to take and leave where I stand, I thought. It was late and that cat wouldn't shut up until the wee hours of the witch's hour. I can hear it try and get into my dreams. I had two guards standing in gray, long spears against the crest of their breastbone. There was no way the cat was getting in, or anyone else. I slept like a baby, and everything was fine. Fine like a word in a lyric.

The next day was horrifying. The anguish of high-blood pressure. The future of uncertainty, vulnerable to defeat. Three knocks at the door before the clock hit noon. Two by detectives, one by the Sheriff. I put my gloves on because it was cold outside, and I didn't want to face the freezing rain and cold, slush and snow hands naked. It's gotten colder out there, and we all kind of fell into a mind that's really not ours; or is, but thinking things we'd never think about. I don't understand what happened to Michael Brown. Stole some shit, knocked over someone in a food mart. Don't go and steal from a store, knock the owner over, charge out the door, jay walk with false pride and esteem. A crime was done. Someone chased the crime, an officer. The two weren't playing bingo. No one rarely ever dies in bingo, or at church. No one ever really dies taking the bus to school, or in a classroom, unless a raving lunatic comes in with a gun and guns down everyone.

The Winchester House in California is a good example; the wife of Mr. Winchester made and mass marketed the Winchester Rifle. Mrs. Winchester felt that she enabled the killing that took place after the Civil War, her husband invented something that could kill easier. It entered the museum of something to be revered, instead of feared. But she felt the fear, Mrs. Winchester; she felt it after her husband died and started hearing ghosts in her house. They were telling her that they died because of her husband. The ghosts were growing too. Mrs. Winchester had no recon except to see someone who dealt with such paranormal oddities, ghosts and shadows. The psychic was later proclaimed to be a fraud, but still the experiences were real for her. He advised her during a seance that she should start building, to add additions to the house, to build with hammers and nails, and that the banging and noise would cease the ghosts from haunting her. She believed him and began additions on the house. She would still hear and see ghosts so she would build more and more onto the house. She would build stairways to nowhere, doors that opened to brick walls, doors that if you took another step, you would find yourself falling three stories to the ground outside in the open air. She kept the building until the day she died. They say the workers just left the scene the moment they heard of her death. Nails were half driven into the wood in places. The workers officially turned the house into an exhibit of fear and freakdom. It's now a popular tourist site in California. But then, the ghosts were real. They drove her mad, which makes me wonder if the madness ever left, if it has been around for a long time. But it pushed me to the point of trying to remember when it got so bad that millions took to the streets. It was 1969 all over again. No one can ever recall the decade that followed 9/11. They can't even name it. We had the Eighties, the Nineties, then what? 9/11, that's what.

I picked up a notebook from the coffee table. I looked inside. Romantic English in the 21st Century. A play on words I thought. I skimmed through. Notes on Shelly, Frankenstein. Amid a pod of nothing in the brain, I glanced deeper, past the page. The kids I were thinking about. They took a trip all three of them. Didn't seem like hard drug kids. A prank, but the note. I skimmed through the notebook some more. Students, lists of student's sign in sheets, a grouping of them. One after the next, about nine days worth, nine or ten. I looked at the sheets, then the names. Then I saw Kate.

She was standing in the corner of my office. It was seven at night. The lights were dim. There was an ugly green in the corner. It was glowing witchcraft. The darkness had a shape, of a shadow. It somehow morphed into the shape and looks of Kate, whatever her

146

name is. She stood there, her eyes milky white. Her grin was red. Staring at me. Standing there. Five seconds or so and then gone, fading into a mist just an inch off the ground, then completely gone, as if never a trace. Playing tricks on my mind, is all it was. I moved on. Went back over and got ready for lecture. I was just going with it. When I got to the lecture hall, three people were inside. I laughed and said the two most wanted words in the great halls of a higher education; which would be class dismissed. But soon after, I noticed Melonie Barns in the back row just sitting there.

"Class dismissed, you can go" I said.

"Can I talk to you Professor?"

"Sure," I walked on down the platform and over to a seat in the front row of the auditorium. "What is it, the missing students?"

"I know where they are, or where they went."

"Where? How do you know this? Where are they, tell me, I'm listening," I said without anything hesitant in my tone.

The world stopped in the auditorium. The lights dimmed without anyone touching a lever. There was a war brimming with anger everywhere. A local strip mall was vandalized over night, as I rode by in slow motion this morning. Now a young woman was telling me where the kids were.

"They're alive. They're playing a trick on you, that's all I can say. I needed to tell you," she said.

"What do you mean?"

"I can't say anymore. I can't. I have to go. I've said too much."

She then got up and left. I walked back to my desk, not even questioning my lack of enthusiasm. The world was up in arms, the school was eighty percent dismissed. There was a failing of the Great University. There was a falling of arms. The guard at the door fell asleep somewhere between here and there. Prayers seemed fruitless, silence appeared apropos. There was the sound of birds outside coming through the door as she opened it and left. The sound-waves came in like air trapped in a small box and the lid suddenly lifted.

The hallway was glittered in gloom as I walked past pictures of prior inhabitants of these swollen institutions. Helter Skelter came and went. The great race war Charles Manson tried to ignite was bridging on reality, and happening. But below in the ghettos of the mind. We as a culture have created an obscene representation of what we stand for. The gun has empowered the empty spaces in our hearts. The religions are dead, I thought to myself as I can hear the rubber on my shoe touch the tile stones of Hallowed Hall, mysteries seemed to be more tangible. "A hoax." I knew that, but why would she say that. And why the ghost, unless the ghost is someone else. That was another possible scenario. There are ghosts in England. And this was a fact I didn't hesitate on. Boston had always called. Crying in the night, wailing it's desires and emotions all over the place. Ghosts or no ghosts, I sure as hell felt like one. 2015 wasn't what they said it was going to be. It got worse. Something shut itself out, after all, after the dead took in the great fall, after the only occupations left were gun holders and sickness healers. The law, after the great fall of the mind you really don't mind abiding the law, it works in your favor the more insane you get, the further down Hickory road you travel. You start picking berries instead of keeping the news on. It's always someone shooting someone.

Yesterday a man took an ax and killed two police men in Bryant City. It was a tragic happening. I could only hear the dead if I could only stop myself long enough to listen. But I didn't even have the time for that any longer. No one was playing a trick on me. They were gone, the kids. And it came to me as soon as I felt the autumn breeze on me, leaving the great Hall of Kin, and on to the great lawn of the chosen kindred. She was a ghost too. That girl, I just talked to; was a ghost.

I found myself walking down the side wall of the administrative building, a slow tepid walk, a thick drizzle beginning to accompany me. I thought of the girl. I thought of where I needed to be, because life wasn't going as I'd thought it would. There were protests beginning to gather downtown. The news was flashing red, yellow and blue. Teargas was going off somewhere in America. The great meltdown had fallen upon us and we were all a little too numb to even notice. Death was a threat from so many angles, but we dodge bullets and stay away from fire. Buildings were being burnt to the ground, police were mounting up for another night of protests. Across seas,

Embassy buildings were being attacked as death tolls rose. Puppets for presidents would pass like fleeting images across a screen. Faces of the brave embroidered in holy fabric were only replaced by the next face, and down the line of countries we proudly exhaled as the rising Arabic Spring. Now it's murder again in the name of God. Millions of weapons tortured the minds of the hands that held them. It was a gruesome act; to kill. It was the furthest thing from God's envision for us all. We were supposed to sit around camp fires and sing songs, roasting marshmallows. Instead there is a war going on, and it's not inside my head.

The rain picked up, and for a second I could see the same girl inside a coffee house across the street from the main bike rack. There was a mist and a haze shadowing Karl's Coffee and Diner. There was a man across the street in a rain coat. I thought of Eyes Wide Shut. He was just standing there, like the character in the movie, or any other spy thriller of the Fifties. But he walked away, unlike in the movie. I paid no more attention to him as I would anyone. But it was how he disappeared I guess that moved me peculiarly. There was a bus, it drove on by, and when it did, he was gone. And that was that. I walked to my car and thought of quickly calling it an evening. There were to be services tomorrow for the missing. Prayer services. No one was calling anyone dead just yet, but they were itching to get there. Little mosquitoes biting at their necks holding tiny hour glasses against their conscience. The door was unlocked and I got in. Drove right home, without looking at a light. Just obeyed and played the part of acting citizen in this cold horrible place. I got to my apartment complex, pulled into a spot. A dangling branch snagged me as I opened the car door. I slammed it shut like putting out a fire, one big bucket of water. I pulled my brief case beside me and walked like an old man. Getting too old for this, I thought. I grabbed my keys for the front door. It was open. I walked in and said hello, any one here? But no one was. I must have left it open, I reckoned. Never a chance. Someone opened the door for me, but didn't come in. That was the feeling I was getting. I pulled the covers down on the bed, threw off my clothes and plopped myself in. I pulled the covers over myself. The lights were on. I'd turn them off around two in the morning, but for then I just passed out and recited mantras in my dreams, reaching places where I'd never thought I'd be, in thousands of years. Amongst all this chaos, ghosts and goblins, disappearing students, I was somewhat happy. I couldn't quite explain it, but the more the insanity rose around me, the more content I was actually becoming. At least for the moment; and that alone allowed me to sleep better than I've slept in years. The following morning would be different, and of course it would be. Who bets on the day. No one. There isn't a weatherman who knows the fortune and outcomes of the following day. The lottery doesn't even post such odds. But sleeping doesn't calculate the odds. You just go with it. One enormous hologram of thoughts, visions, suppressed desires- they all come out.

The television was screaming college walkouts across the country when I got up. Thirty six were killed in a stone mine by Islamic extremists. I was trying to keep my head about. I've been passing out on the couch, the bed, not of my own mind, but their's. I was twisted up inside of all the doing upon's of others. These kids missing. There was something to it. So I saw a ghost, people come up to me and say they've seen ghosts, and I always just shrugged it off. This time the notion was festering. There was an irritation, bites on the neck from invisible bugs.

The class was for eight in Morris Hall. I had the slide show prepared by the skin of my own midnight oil. Veneers were apparent on my immediate surface, of what I looked like and what I've become. The podium was taller than I. I found that disheartening. I put the notes on the desk. There were fifteen in the auditorium after I called roster. Most students skipped last week, so they were beginning to show up again in fear it might affect their grade.

"What were the main reasons for the fall of humanity, if it were to fall tomorrow. What, in your own words, what would be your answer." I looked around, the class was looking more attentive. "Write down your answer in a paragraph or two. You have ten minutes." I walked off the stage and sat in the first row all the way to the left side of the room. I took the attendance sheet and looked at who was absent. Ryerson was not on the list. That would make it two strait. The missing kids came to mind, but I didn't start thinking he would be one of them on that list. Not yet. I was trying to concentrate of the failings and fallings of mankind, the subject at hand. What really was on my mind was something incredibly different. Never give yourself to someone telling them you're nothing. The loneliness of man, that was the subject.

We talked of how the armies in the Middle East and the countries attached to them were the cause of modern day civilization, the wars brought upon ourselves through oil ownership, the fact that it sits on the site of the Holy Land, doesn't help matters much; but none the less, the wars are a fear. Isis is real, it's a thought and a manifestation of power against us Western folk. Here people are oblivious. They sit in their room, stare out the window, give up on working because it costs too much to live in such small places. Either you're making so much you can afford a house, or you're renting a shit hole for 1500 dollars a month. Inside the heart of its owner sits misery and emptiness. The students could obviously see this on me. They handed in their paper and returned to their desks, we talked more on racial division in America. But the subject wasn't as sincere as it could have been. Skin color? Really? Possible candy coated yelps from tired and angry mouths who can't feed themselves because welfare just doesn't cut it. They're gone, cousins, uncles, mothers, fathers, sons, and sisters of the great mental breakdown. Society can't keep up with over brimming jails filled with people who just couldn't cut it was all. They stole or dealt small deal drugs, or big deal drugs, because they couldn't cut being Mr. Smith with a suit and forever look like Brad Pitt. That man with the golden voice, won a spot on a tv show because he was holding up a sign. The man with the golden voice got some one's attention. They signed him, with or without the fear that he was a recovering alcoholic and that he would stay away from the booze if some one would just give him a chance. They did. They watched him drown in three weeks flat. Back to the booze, back to the bars. He's no longer remembered by the general public, the vulgar. But the weird thing is that that guy thinks about his chance and his golden voice every day, I bet. He's the one that has to live with his pain, every day-day in and day out. That alcohol, that poison that leaves such good memories there in the caboose. But it never lets you remember the pain, the suffering that went with hangovers and the loss of broken marriages that came soon after. The TV never lets you in on all that stuff. They just show you the pretty skirts and the fast cars, the guys hanging out smashing beer mugs together. They never show you the lonely man in the window looking down on the streets. Filling his half cracked glass with broken ice and frozen cold eyes. They never show the shaking hand as the body screams for hydration. They never show you life.

Broken at 50 is what the man calls himself, is what I've called myself. It all came up too quickly for me to handle. There I was, alone again. The students had left. A piece of paper was left behind, on the floor where Elizabeth Jewels sits. I walked over to it and picked it up. Notes on nothing. Well I thought that at first, but I put it in my breast pocket for safe keeping, none the less. I felt a fear beside me as I did; it came quickly too. I looked to the side of the auditorium; I thought I saw something or someone there move. It took me back. I gathered my things and found myself walking down the west corridor and out onto the great lawn. A light off the main columns reflected onto the lawn, I walked straight for it. When I got to them, I paused and looked back. No one was in there with me, I kept that mantra going over and over in my head. There are no ghosts on campus, I wanted to put that up on a pole or a tree, let the young minds that ghosts are just in people's heads; like Molder's poster stated, "I want to believe", but not sure I do, or maybe I really don't want to believe, don't want to face it.

After I caught my breath, I began walking past the great lawn and past the History Department building, Hoverton. Just past that was my car. I shuffled for my keys as I didn't even look back. I wanted to, believe me; I wanted to enjoy the night. I wanted peace, real peace- the kind of peace that you can walk outside into your yard and hear the mosquitos choir in and pacify the night with its orchestral lullaby. It's peace when you can hear the frogs over in Acker's Pond. It's peaceful when there are no serious problems, like heavy war or terrorist attacks on the homeland, where there is no fear of them either. We don't know peace, as a people. There have always been an overdramatic display of non-peace, whether it's on the news or in the movies. A serious sense of the amount of peace that was lost was the day the towers fell. Well, without overstating it, or beating a dead horse to death. We kind of always have to go back there. Kind of like the 5th of November. It's difficult to be heard when the majority of the people are screaming the same words. They get lost in a sea of metaphor and allegory. Voices get lost like beating a blanket of dust off a rug with a baseball bat. Revolutions in the street can't change the minds of people. How many times they've tried and just more and more revolutions follow. Funny how the gun wasn't mentioned in class as a major factor in the falling of our nation. War was written all over the walls, but the gun. That always somehow squeezes through the cracks.

Walking down the street the air felt fresh, and a breeze was blowing through my unspoken hair. The air alone on my face felt nice, to spite the feelings inside my heavy and broken heart. Shallow words for a man in his mid century crisis. Midlife horror. People don't know it, unless a person writes it down. He's broken. Tired. There was a party at the Friar's Hall. Bring your own buds, beers and maybe you find yourself a conversation. I was thinking of going. The weather was nice for this time of year. Early winter. Early biting beginning. The teeth are sharp come January. You can't breathe in that kind of air. So the best is stay indoors and cuddle up with a book you can't stand. Or it's too long, or the author doesn't seem relevant; whatever the case, better to read something than nothing. I was working on this book, more of a journal than a book. But that's up to me, the character in this opus. Bugwit. More shit piles up, and the worse you feel. Too weeks from last week, too old from last year. The rain was beginning to come down even more. I had a class to teach and I didn't want to teach it. I didn't want to join society any longer. I didn't want to have to be someone's savior through this mad world. It's their lives, another teacher can show them the ropes. I thought, picked up an imaginary snowball and threw it at the Hughs Hall. I continued walking towards the parking lot. It was another day, and it felt like I had just done this specific thing. Like bad deja vu. Like bad Chinese. I was a vegetarian for ten years or so a long time ago. I had dreams of playing in the wings of theatre. I remember when there was a choice in life, a choice of car, home, career, dream. Something came along and wrecked all that. The desert attracts all kinds. I was trying to listen, but couldn't. I couldn't pick up the phone if I tried. There was that too. The frequencies in the new phones. The airwaves were filled with electromagnetic fields. The missing kids had me thinking they went somewhere. I wouldn't think portals, unless I was into portals. Magnetic frequencies, portals, missing kids- my ears couldn't stand the sound of it. But the ringing in my ears; well, that just keeps you thinking on. That just keeps you thinking that there is something out there. That was my last thought before I got to the lecture hall. More protests last night. Lots of walk-outs. I was wondering how many were coming to class. I opened the door. Mrs. Hawk, Dean of the English Department was standing there, leaving the hall as I was entering. I said hello. She returned by saying that she had to talk to a student who was in my class. I nodded in confirmation and acknowledgment. There were ten or so sitting down in the chairs facing the stage, where the desk was. The desk itself could be a character for all it's been through and seen. I threw my briefcase on top and sat down. The students were dead silent. I didn't open my mouth for the next four minutes or so. I just stared at the ground, the floor, the wood on the stage and wondered what led me to this point in life that the wings were no longer filled with wonder and anticipation for something exciting. I wondered in the deadness of it all; the words before me for todays lesson shook my hands until the piece of paper fell out from under me, and onto the floor. I reached for the paper, the words shined themselves blindly in my memory; I'm coming for you Mr Peters. And that was that.

I walked outside and took a deep breath. Ten, thirty seconds later I walked back into the lecture hall. "Why is everyone so silent, seems like someone died or something."

Everyone laughed.

"Well, thanks to those who came to class. Obviously come grade time, it weighs heavy, but you don't need to know that. Good you come to class. It's always good when you come to class." That was all I needed to say that wasn't coinciding with the rest of the group, and how they were feeling.

"Feels like society is tearing a hole out of the sky." A kid in the back row yelled out. "Feels like a giant vacuum is up there sucking all our air. That's what it feels like. This place *is* a police state. They're everywhere. Can't take driving to school no more, they're around every corner. It's Nazi Germany all over again.

"It's true", yelled Melonie McGuire. "Prisons are all filled up, like little cities. They're the new concentration camps. They just want to put you in there. It's a business, the system is a business. It's sad, you know professor."

"Yeah, I know," I said. "It ain't easy being green."

"Who's green here?" Yelled Bobby D in the back.

"I'm green with envy I'm not you." I said. "Wicked world for you all, so enjoy your comfy stay here at winter wonderland. Read the next three chapters in The Shining. We're going to compare plots with the movies next time around." I looked around. All their innocent faces were beaming back at me, waiting for me to part the Red Sea or something. It wasn't going to happen. No frogs were going to fall from the sky today. Just another in-between from here to there. That's all it was.

The day flew by. In the rain, without rain. The skies were dark, a slight light from the moon was lighting the front of the courtyard. I was sitting in its light, just inside the bay window, just sitting there, contemplating on sins and the blocking of life. I was hoping that life lasted forever and that Jesus was real, and would someday come flying out of the sky, trumpets angels and all. There had to be more to it than this, ghosts and things that go bump in the night. I had feelings, feelings in my legs and head that had to come attention to. I picked up a book. There was a boy on it holding a bucket as if he had been from 1901, stuck in some dumb ended job, doing a job his parents should be doing, or he shouldn't be doing at all. Kids then were slaves. Huckleberry Finn wasn't a book on slavery as it was a book on finding individuality and freedom within yourself. Gurus, Authors, Magic Men, the whole slew can't find healing by having congregations around them, in a way it works. People are healed by healers all over the place. But they have to face the music somewhere. The music was like the same song going over and over in one's head. It never stops and people get brainwashed by the Philadelphia Experiment. The Manchurian Candidate was a reality based film on the notion that this stuff was happening. The television, and then the internet just kept people tuned into the frequency the Power of Man had over them. Whatever power is controlling the force, whether it be the government, the schools, the jails, the system..., it grabs you and doesn't let you go. You have to remain sovereign to yourself. You have to see yourself as a powerful entity unto itself.

But no man is an island, no one can survive in society alone. But they do. The hologram was real. It was more than bits and bites, more than digital. If it were all digital and an analog tape was born of it, than what would that be then? Analog or digital? We are more than digital, there is matter and atoms, and cells. There is intelligent life out there.

I walked outside and towards the car. The annual Halloween Party was going on in the basement of Morris Hall. I was a little tired, but wanted to go. I wanted to see Miss Jay. She was this magnificent personality and friend. But over the years, the work got more loading on and no one really got to see each other unless it's this time or Christmas. The Howard Hall, just across from Morris sits on the river and over looks Pristol. Technically I'm in Pristol here at Silent U, but that's never the matter. The point that it's always beautiful, but there is something more to the landscape and environment of Pristol. It's poetic, and kind. It's dangerous in the way that nature can be dangerous. People set their own traps. Then they step in them. I walked down to the river and waited a minute or so to begin the tradition back up in Morris Hall. But the water was gleaming like a Monet or Van Gogh. Huge blocks of liquid life flowed on and over each other underneath the merciful sky. I sat there and thought of Jay. She was probably already there. I was dressed as a skeleton. I had a black shirt and pants I painted bones on, then made up my face all white. I raccoon'd my eyes with black eye shadow. I looked more creepy than anything you'd want to hang out with. I wanted to be Dracula, but I didn't have the cape, or teeth. They were all out of teeth and everything when I stopped by the pharmacy, where I get my costumes every year. So I settled on the skeleton. I turned around and there was a girl, standing there in front of me.

"Can I help you?" I asked.

"Can you show me to Peter Helsh's room? I'm lost and it's Halloween. I missed his room last year and I can't find it again this year." She got all twirky and shadow like, she looked like she was dressed like a ghost too, all white make up and all. A trend between us I wasn't aware of at the time.

"I'm sorry, I'm not sure if he's still here, I've heard of the name somewhere. But maybe you can ask someone in the student center." I was getting a bit scared, in a way that wasn't natural. "It's over there, you know where it is, over the hill there and down the walkway. You'll find it."

"Thank you, I'll find it, thank you."

"It's OK, you have a good night. Happy Halloween."

She didn't answer back, she just walked into the dismal air, into the abandoning fog, the timeless and desperate night.

"How did she know my name. Peter Welsher, came close anyway." That much I thought aloud into the cold air. Snow soon? Or some more rain. There was a poor sickened sycamore standing over. A shadow cautiously paved a path for me to take. One ghost was enough to follow this evening. I walked up towards Morris Hall. About now, ghosts were adding up, taking space. I didn't want them there, fiddling around with what was upstairs.

"Peter! So good to see you!," Says Ms. Jay. She was wearing a blue scarf and her hair was gleaming in the moonlight. I thought a car was going to come around and illuminate the ad. "You're all dressed up, I have a mask." She reaches into her purse and puts on a blue mask that covers only around the eyes. It has little arrows pointing upwards at each end. She looks rather stunning and it's been a while since we've talked, so I opened up slower than needed be.

"You look magnificent. Are you ready for a really boring party?" I say with trepidation. I didn't like these things much. But I was happy to get out and see someone. Being alone and at home wasn't as thrilling as people thought. There always comes that time when you're a bit needy and a person isn't around. Panic and fear begin to dwell.

It's good to get out. And Ms. Jay was perfect company. Always happy and smiling. Couldn't bring down the party tonight. I went with it. We walked in and that was the end of the last half hour down by the river. That was the end of the ghost for now. They were beginning to appear as if I'm being played. Like the girl was saying, they were playing a joke on me. We walked in, and we both took a seat by the end of the stage, where the DJ was hanging out. Kill the DJ was playing. Faculty and students both mingled together or just really sat at the tables. Some of them talking, some of them not. Mr. Crasser, head of the English Department, Sigma Tau Delta, and the school paper was standing there talking to Erin Glouster. I had her in Dynamics and Semantics. They looked like they were getting along, laughing. Little Edward Anderson was holding a girl's hand I couldn't put a name to, but a face, yes. Dan McLory was talking to Mrs. Devonstaff, she was head of internal affairs on campus, and Dan is the leading scorer on the campus faculty rugby team. I don't play because of my knees. The place is dead other than that. Not as many people as I thought.

"Want something to drink?" I asked.

"Sure, whatever. Beer, Jungle Juice, Big Jim's Kool-Aid."

"Yeah, I'll take the Kool-Aid about now too."

She laughs it off. And I got up from my seat and towards the drinking table. Really bad banjo music is playing now. Couldn't tell if I were in a ho-down, or Whoville.

Morris Hall was an old Victorian castle-like brick building built back in the early eighteen hundreds, 1801, when the school began growing ivy down its minded dream. At the birth of all things, movement and progression, determination and persistence, to be taken for a folly minded fellow, or to be taken seriously; it all sprang from these walls. Intelligence isn't knowledge, though commonly confused. Intelligence is the ability to hold information as data in the brain to come to conclusions based on the data. Knowledge is what we put there. Certain data takes, and certain data is discarded. Tonight was of nothing of these things.

A bright ball of disco breath silenced the room, dancing corpses smiled to everyone as they left the dance floor, and over to the punchbowl. Sweet Home Alabama came on over the speakers. Then it stopped. The music died suddenly. The lights flickered a bit. The bowl of juice on the table shook like a small yet awakened ocean. The lights were now out. It was pitch black inside the Hall. A few lighters came out. Erin Glouster came over to me and Jay. She was trying to say something. That she saw a ghost or something outside on the deck. It was dark. The only light was coming from the emergency glow spot light in the corner of the room. Someone I didn't know lit a candle right next to me. There were already candles around, so it was easier for the man to just grab one of the lit ones, but he insisted on lighting this particular one.

The lights then came on, almost as soon as they went out. They flickered at first, a few flashes of splattered color and costume gave the scene a more eerie feeling, as if they knew they weren't in control. The lights going out also took their power. But them coming back on, well that gave it back. There was a sense of relief, and no longer a stranglehold on their psyche. They were at ease to go back to Halloween and be themselves. It was easy as everyone laughed around the room, letting the immediate past go. Music came back on, but it was a different tune. Odd tubas and clarinets at a slow pace accompanied by small horns and depressing sound clouded even the obscure and skeptical. There were ghosts around, everywhere. And no one should doubt the living when they go. Sometimes the spirit is all anyone has. And the throat is no longer strong enough to voice the broken spirit; so it comes back. And sometimes it isn't as pretty and poignant as people would like to think it is. Most times its different. The maze is big, and though the rooms all look the same, different monsters and ghosts live in different rooms. Not every snow flake looks the same. Not here, not on this campus anyways.

I found that love hides behind every door. In the rooms there are entities, people. Love is a warm card. Lovely speaking. It came into life and left as though it left a mark there on the wall beside my desk. It was where I spent most of my time, writing and going over papers. Papers stacked on the right side, and the left side was reserved for what I've read and what needed to be given back to students. Students know love before the hurt, before the pain and sickness it can cause. Big problems with the in-laws when I was married. Found it more sabotaging than not. But I left it there. Bittersweet shit, marriage. I have my love, Jay. She knows, I know, but we keep it there. We meet when we can, say hello at the cafe shop over coffee and conversation. Love is pealing the veneers away, holding the person when they fall. Love is everything. It's God, and that in itself is a tall order. God is a lot more than just love, though I do think God is love. With a mind to think and create at free will. Words out of God's mouth became physical and manifested into reality at the instant they were spoken. "And God said animals and birds, and there were animals and birds." Just like that. Instant coffee for God. It was Saturday and the party was nice. But I wasn't thinking of Halloween any longer. It was November 1st, All Souls Day., holy, yet ominous and quite spooky to think about. We are all souls, with bodies outside and controlled by light and sound and voice and will. We move as if a miracle occurs every second. A million different messages go out all over the body every single second. Who does that? What does that? The Razor's Edge. Great movie after a great book, about love and loss and finding yourself. In the movie, Bill Murray goes up to the top of holy mountain to find a monastery. He is cold and is carrying Holy books of wisdom and knowledge. He becomes so cold in the snow that he decides to burn the pages to stay warm. The wisdom I thought to myself. I lived in quite a few states. Experienced quite a bit of heartache and loss myself so related with the man on the mountain. The cold is always cold. And the colder it gets, the more the warmth is all you really seek. The peace and comfort of the warmth and what it brings. That's what it is.

I was at the office by the time any thoughts of notes came upstairs. I was fine, as it's comforting in its own sick way to be fine with just about anything when your whole world is collapsing before your eyes. The desk in my room faced the courtyard adjacent to the Hugh Building. It was a large yard and they would sometimes have quartets from the Classical Department play for the students and faculty, when spring came and the air got nicer. The winters are hard and difficult to get through on campus. This season has been increasingly chaotic. The protests have been out of hand. There were about twenty students outside the gate holding signs for the underprivileged, tuition hikes, police brutality and high rent. They all had their gripes, but mine were more private. I didn't like to go out there and hold signs in the air. I enjoyed being a part of the background. I didn't like being sought after. I usually am quite content, but the letter underneath my door did give me a slight panic attack after throwing my coat on the side chair. It was just sitting there on the gray cement floor. A carpet covered most of the floor, but some of it was left open. I used to think it made the building look old, like they should put some new hardwood floors down, but that never happened. The letter sat three-folded on the old beat up rug. I leaned down and picked it up. The letter was typed in old school typewriter face, not from a computer. It said:

meet me at the bell tower the witches hour

That was all it said. The witches hour was at three in the morning. God forbid I have to be anywhere at three in the morning. Who would write such a thing. What ghost leaves fingerprints? What hoax leaves a trail? It was all alarming and quite disturbing for me. I folded the note up, like the way it came, and sat down at the chair. The room was dark, allowing only the day's light through the high windows. A knock on the door interrupted a much needed daydream. I was looking outside and saw a circus of sorts doing all kinds of back flips and cartwheels on the front lawn. I wasn't sure what brought me to think of it. But it was a fall festival inside my head and I was kind of playing along. Even after the knock, I was playing along. The knock took about four seconds to sink in and realize someone was at the door.

"Come in," I said. "It's open."

It was Ryerson.

"What's up Carl? What you got there in your hand? Books? You studying while everyone is playing 'hands up' out there?" I poked fun, it was easy to poke fun at Ryerson. His red fro hair and goofy smile, like he was always innocent as a fucking fly. "What you go for me kid, I'm all ears?

"Well, it's about the students sir, the missing students."

"Yeah, what is it? They showed themselves up, and it's a hoax, right? Is that it? I kind of looked half-ass in the mirror on that one. But

161

I shuffled the situation into control. "What is it. You haven't been in class. I thought you were missing."

"Yeah, I've been walking around. I saw one of them. I saw Jerry. Then I saw Kate. They were next to me in my room, both of them just standing at my bed. I didn't know what to do. I got so fucking scared. Excuse my language. I saw them Mr. Peters. I saw Elizabeth Jewels too, in the Library. Last night. That's what started fucking with me hard core. I was so scared I ran out and to my car. I drove right to the dorm and sat with my friend Harry and we played video games until our friend Jill came over. We were up until one in the morning. Then I saw the other two hovering over my bed. I had to come and talk to you or someone, a guidance counselor or somebody." He looked around. He looked spooked, and white and lifeless.

"Listen, you just hang in there. I'm sure you're overstressed with homework and midterms. Just take it a day at a time, and hang in there; even when the wire gets tight and you feel you got nowhere to go."

"I have nowhere to go now!" Ryerson raised his voice this time, getting loud in a small room.

"Listen, I have to be somewhere." I didn't, I just said I did.

"Okay, I'll take it easy. These ghosts. I don't know what to do. I never thought I'd believe in them. You think they'll catch the guy. I mean I think they're trying to tell us something. Communicating or something."

I felt the same. Ryerson put his knapsack to his back and said goodbye. I reckoned he never stepped through that door, even though he did. I just had my mind on that note.

I taught class. The routine was beginning to grow fatigue on my mind and still had another six weeks to go before the end of the semester. I got to my car and stopped. I wasn't going to stay on campus until three in the morning. The odds that I wasn't even going to go to the bell tower at that time. Sounded like a hoax to me. I got in my car and drove the hills of Pristol back to my apartment in the same old town I've been in some time now. It was getting dark as the popcorn sun came down over my windshield, as I pulled into my spot. Alone, even my girlfriend was somewhat imaginary. I can taste kisses

162

on my face that weren't there. I opened the door to my apartment. The lights were out, all but the small light above the stove in the kitchen. I turned on the lamp with a quick flick to the switch on the right of my entrance. I threw down a pullover with my laptop inside and plotted myself down on the couch. It was somewhere around six-thirty or seven. My clock was stalled at three. The batteries must have gone out. I got up and checked the kitchen drawer for some AA batteries and found them tucked behind two hot gloves. I took the clock down and unlocked the pocket where the batteries go. I put them both in, fixed the time to my phone and put the clock back up on the wall. I felt a whole lot better. Clouds and fog filled my mind with mindless thoughts, a breeze coming through the window screen. I laid down on the couch and didn't even notice myself falling asleep. I was out for a while. Long enough for the clock to turn midnight and push itself a little past. I got up at 2:35. I thought of the note. I thought of the bell tower. But I didn't think of getting in the car, driving across town to campus. No, that thought barely stood a chance.

Somewhere some author out there sneaks in a dream and meets you half way. You dream as the protests get worse, as the presidents blame each other. Torture is on the new list of items going to plague the United States and stain itself of blood, insanity, and Godlessness. I didn't start this war. I just had bad in-laws. That was all. I had a few words and a dream.

Sick what brought my attention somewhere between sleep and the next afternoon. Somewhere between the coffee no longer a luxury, but as necessary as the next coming. You kind of wish for the Gods to come out of the sky and take order of this place, give us all a beautiful cleansing. Robin Williams dies and you're not much yourself for a while. Killing himself. Like that movie the Happening. The hopeless. Good Will Hunting. "It's not your fault. It's not your fault. People who run and lead the flock jumping off cliffs and hanging themselves, taking pills and overdosing. It's not for a teacher to witness. And I wonder why we read this shit people write, call them books on the way to something literate, without being obtuse.

I got to the office the next day, the one after that one. I parked the car to Phish blaring my speakers. The day was gorgeous. I drank coffee worth mentioning. Magic highlighted the aftertaste. I was on a mission of sorts, like I said.

I said damned if I do, damned if I don't. There was another letter laying on the floor as I opened the door to my office. I was going down the hallway, the paintings of dead presidents lined the peripheral. I wasn't a second late or early- just doing my thing. Words piled up, papers remained constant, yet a moment of silence for that that shouldn't be there. A letter on the floor. This time I wasn't sure; who was this one from? I didn't want to think too long about it. The letter was in my hand before I could give myself time to look at myself picking it up. It weighed differently than the last one. A little heavier, a little older. I opened the three sided fold and looked onward, with as much of an open mind allowed.

Meet me at the bell tower at three.
Meet me at the bell tower at three o clock.

That's all it said. Two lines made it heavier, my first thought came and left. No, it was dropped recently, that's what made it heavier. The soul of the child was still close. I could feel its presence. It was a girl, a young woman. I sensed her standing there beside me. I sensed her shadow crawl up the bookcase. I wanted to look, but couldn't. I was somehow frozen. The letter was staring at me, getting its grip. What did she want? What the devil did the poor girl want? And why was she leaving these for me? There could be anyone out there that could replace me for her liaison. I stepped forward, without taking off my coat I plopped down on my chair. The letter sat between my two hands in front of me. Why me?

No knock this time to save me from the loneliness the situation was beginning to create. If it's lonely out there in the shed, above the bricks we build here, why tell us. Why tell me you don't like it there in the afterlife. We all find out some day, they tell us that anyway. Why come back and even think to pretend that I'm going to meet. Three in the morning, again. Three, that number. I always hated that number and for good reasons be. It's a witch's number. It's the devil. It's magic and I've had quite my grueling share of it. Weighs a heavy burden,

164

magic. It sure does. Three o clock in the morning, reminded me of Jodi the Pig from the Amityville Horror. The pig shows up at that time. 3:15. Glad the girl in the tower isn't synching watches. Alright, I thought. I'll meet you. I'll meet you in your tower. Hoax or no hoax. Halloween came and left without much of a storm. Nothing stirring up except missing students and protests, and a few misplaced letters without envelopes. Nothing a middle aged professor couldn't handle. Nothing at all.

I have class in ten minutes. The thought knocked my coffee over. I picked it up, grabbed a paper towel and cleaned up a slight mess. Music hit my ears. I looked up at the turntable over in the corner begin to spin a record, late forties. Beethoven, piano sonatas. I was getting itched and creeped out. It wasn't playing before the spill, but somehow began as it was happening. A doorway. Somewhere in this place spelled passageway. It was how the person girl ghost was getting in, leaving messages. It's where the others went, the missing. The gone.

The music increased in volume as I got up to turn it back off. I picked up the wet paper towel from my desk and threw that in the garbage. Class. I had class.

A tower of a building stood tall inside the east end of Campus Square. It was where I taught this class. The Hughs Building had been a pillar of a think tank club after think tank club. It had housed and taught the brightest and most brilliant that have ever come down this way, this path of nothing but a head to rely on; and when that goes, it all goes. Enter Dementia. Instant coffee is much nicer sounding than instant karma, I went with the coffee and hoped for the best in the karma department. We all run a little shy of our sins sometimes. We all fall when the chips are up. We fall when they're down too. The odds break even in life, as we do reap what we sow. Storms all over the world. Bunch of protestors blocked the main artery into Pristol. But I knew they'd soon be done with and gone come winter. Just had to get through a few days. I wasn't against them. They stood for a good thing, my opinion doesn't matter much more than these words will be remembered next week. I walked into the building that housed the bells. That tower, the Hughs Tower, or better known as the Hughs Building had a calling attached to it in the form of a letter. I pushed the doors open and walked three flights of stairs. I didn't account for the missing and protesting. I just walked up to the third floor into room 304, again scoping the courtyard.

"Hello everyone."

"Hello Professor." They all choir'd in.

"Your October was good I suspect?"

A nod of acknowledgement and approval swept the room like a wave at a football game in some large stadium, only without the fanfare. To the lions, I thought. We feed them all to the lions. These poor kids stand no chance. We throw all this knowledge at them so fast they can't even digest it, let alone barely learn it.

"Stephen King. What do you think of this fucker? Is he any good? And why are we watching Eyes Wide Shut today, instead of Kubrick's Shining." I looked around the room. Dead stares for a slow second, then one by one souls appeared behind tired eyes, confusion and fatigue began to fade. Awakening students was a nice sign. Fresh and hopeful.

"Stephen King sucks, period," yelled out someone in the back. Simmons. "Stephen King is nothing but someone who has dedicated themselves to an hour glass, punches in and punches out. Whether it's a good day of writing or a bad day, we have to deal with it. Nothing is taken out, we just read a thousand pages of insanity." Simmons got lost and shut his mouth.

"I just read Under the Dome. I liked it. But it had a hundred characters and it drove me crazy." Teresa Malcom spoke up. "He's OK."

"You didn't answer my question. And we're reading the Shinning, not Under the Dome. Though we should've been reading Bag of Bones. A better novel, it's just I want to make some points." I took a swagger of Smart Water that I brought in with me and put it back down on the desk.

"Someone broke into a cafe and killed someone in France today," Kelly Moter said from the back. I think Stephen King creates violent scenarios so that when people read them, they become what he's reading to them. Words are powerful."

"They are," I said.

"Words are flesh manifesting themselves into reality."

"So," I said. "If we write horror, our world becomes horror? Or is Stephen King gifted with a sense of darkness that we can't see, and unfortunately people are literally eating his darkness? It's a good question. But why Eyes Wide Shut. Who's seen it, probably everyone." I looked around the room.

"I saw it."

"Yeah, I saw it."

Almost everyone in the room. About twenty of them scattered about. Missing ten or so, maybe fifteen. The three kids, and some protesters. No one was thinking about the missing kids. No one, not even me. I wanted to blot it out, make no sense of it on purpose. For a second I looked at the desks, to see if they'd show up. I looked for Kate and Liz. And I looked for Eric. No one to be present. Just young faces looking at me, as I had answers for them. Maybe I did, maybe I didn't. But I was being paid to have answers. There are no tricks in the teaching profession. Keep them all guessing with questions, love your art, know your passion. Love blank stares looking back at you and keep wondering why they look so blank in a world that's literally gone over its edge. Keep the questions coming, the answers always show up. Like actors who want the job.

"OK," I said. "Let's all just have a few seconds, some deep breaths, and watch the movie. Somebody turn out the lights. Oh, and count how many Christmas trees there are in the movie. Jot them down." I finished and sat down. The screen was a nice size for a class room. Watching movies on this particular screen was always a bonus teaching this course. Need a lesson plan? Watch a movie. Even better, emerge the two.

"Is this Eyes Wide Shut?" someone asked, quietly.

"Yes, Kubrick's last film. We'll talk about it later. Watch carefully, for things out of the ordinary. And take notes." I shuffled around my seat. The class room was like a mini amphitheater, the rows of chairs all climbing up as you walk to the back row; like a movie theatre, but smaller-enough to keep it intimate, yet large enough to hold about one hundred people. Something was scratching my back. I was getting relaxed and excited about the film. Something was itching

167

my back. I thought it was an itch until I reached behind me and found a piece of paper was the culprit. Nothing meant anything but to extinguish the itch. I didn't think of it then, but I crumpled it up and threw it towards the wastebasket next to the door. I missed; so I got up to be PC about it, and just as I got out of the chair, lights down and all, a moment hit me. It was no ordinary piece of paper. No, that fucker was meant for me. That little bastard there on the ground had my name written all over it. I picked it up. Froze. Opened it. Froze. Read it to myself. The students were already into the opening credits. I was on the sidelines reading from the day's playbook. Oh, it's ordinary. Laugh who ever this is, I said to myself. Say something other than meet you at the fucking bell.

meet me tonight bell tower midnight

That's all I needed to see. I felt weak, and confused; a sudden pulse ran up my arms and through my legs. My blood pressure was going up. Nicole Kidman was getting naked on the screen in the open, for all to see. A ghost was screaming for a meeting with me. I was trying to listen. The borders were blurring. I wasn't so sure it was a hoax any longer. I was getting a curiosity to follow through, a maybe. Leaning more than maybe. Kind of an obligation from somewhere knocking on your door, saying whatever is going on in life can go on just as it is. But this was important. This had to have an ending; because- this had meaning.

Outside, the wind howled against the lonely cold bricks of Hugh Hall. The paths of laid slate and memories cast a shadow, almost welcoming. Names were being silenced, apropos of my walk, hither and thither across an empty and sullen existence. A shallow life has awakened somehow. I didn't want to adhere to the calling, but choices really aren't given a choice. It's always do the right thing or pay the consequence. It's always one way on the path. Feet walk the path. The leaves on the trees just collect the memories, like puffs of nothingness from those who walk underneath them on their way to early morning class. Inside I was staring at a screen made of silicon and vinyl. I was thinking how Tom Cruise and Nicole Kidman were married during the
168

filming of this movie, and how they both divorced soon after. Yes, we're watching Eyes Wide Shut, I muttered to myself. The rest was me and the movie, and the lost kids in the rows of broken futures, miserable diseases and pure chaos. But for now; it's just us and the screen. That did just fine. The piece of paper was in my pocket, already fading into the obscurity of defining film noir. I was frightened, but didn't quite know it yet.

The movie ended. I got up. I noticed everything again, like viewing a news reel playing scenes in your head, in your mind. The lights were out. Jeffery Cone turned the lights back on.

"We'll discuss it next week. I want a comparison paper. I want you to compare Eyes Wide shut and Stephen King's the Shining. And I want you to throw in the Shining by Kubrick and tell me if there are any other comparisons there. Have a good weekend." I picked myself up and packed my things. Jenny Hart came down from the top row. At first I was praying it wasn't another ghost. It wasn't. I knew Jenny.

"I saw things in that film, professor," she said. Then she walked out of the room, like a dead zombie. As if completely mesmerized by the film. I looked that way, and as she passed the gateway to the hall, I could've sworn I saw a shadow follow her. I thought about it enough to make a distinctive correlation. I picked up my things and walked out of the room. I turned the lights out and shut the door. The hallway was dark, and smelled of a freshly bleached floor. I walked down the hall as if there were someone with me, I don't know why, but I did. The bar handles on the door represented a sense of freedom as I pushed, excessive force propelled me into the open autumn air. There was a lamp-post just outside the building lighting the walkway. I would think the outside was the same as the inside, but it clearly wasn't. I decided to take a walk towards the pillars in the courtyard. There were people over there hanging out and about. I needed company. Jay hadn't been around much this week. Neither have I; that needed to change. Isolation is a disease. Books add to the disease. Explaining that Eyes Wide Shut is The Shining; well, that was the least of my worries. Time was moving on a line, inside and out of barriers I continued to cross. I didn't mind. It was my life, and rule or no rule, I pretty much stood by my convictions. I wasn't exactly going to stop now.

The students stood around Monument Court, where four giant pillars stood tall, old remnants of a building that stood there two hundred years ago, and was since burned down. The only remains were these pillars. The students had bags and tents, food and backpacks, wine, beer and joints. Protestors, or what was left of them come last week's sleep in. Some were still hanging out, it appeared. It was a party of sorts, only no music. The silence played loud over the crickets, and other bugs that sounded their moonlight complaints. Signs and broken bottles were everywhere. It reminded me I had a date; midnight, at the bell tower. And how this was going to be different from the last two appointments I was supposed to keep.

I walked past the pillars, got some creepy looks from burnt out students as my ghost dribbled along the stone pathway that lead to the parking lot. I grabbed my phone out of my coat pocket and called Jay. She answered and agreed to meet me at the Cold Horse for some coffee and maybe a donut or something. But mostly she had agreed to come along for the midnight ride of Paul Revere. Screaming that the British are all Zombies now and that Elvis had officially left the building. Paper cuts from magazines, illusions of grandeur. I may be in this alone, but I had at least one person. I looked down at the sad school magazine rack where they kept the school paper for dispensing. There were a couple of them around campus. The last one was near the parking lot where my car was. I happened to peek down at it as I was walking. The paper glowed new fresh ink, still wet from the press. And as I looked down it wasn't that easy to ignore the headlines.

STUDENT MISSING AFTER HALLOWEEN BALL
ROOMMATES IN GRIEF-PANIC ON CAMPUS

I picked up a copy and walked towards my car. It was dark; and I looked behind me, I heard a sound, a crumpling in the leaves. The dark branches hung over and scratched the roof of my car- maybe that was it.

I heard it again. I got in the car with a quick turn of my key. The tin confinements drew into a near state of claustrophobia and panic. I started the piece of shit up and pulled back out. I stopped halfway, and thought about returning to campus for an odd reason. It looked fun on the square. But fun is something not worth exploring twice. I balked but moved on, put the car in drive and moved forward. I had to be back there at midnight. I wondered why the time changed. First it was three in the morning, now it's midnight. We have an impatient ghost is what we have. Yeah. That's what I said. I drove off into the falling woods that dwelled the Cold Horse to meet up with Jay. It was that time, and I was on some line, some lazar beam that bent and stretched its way along this hallucinogenic hologram, some makeshift dream of substance I could never quite get a grip on. So I went with it. I drove and slept, ate and fucked. I just went with it like a wave on some birthday ocean, never knowing it was alive yesterday; and whether it did or not, it didn't matter. Just surfing on waves of oceans being born every second, somewhere in this infinite universe. And of all things I had a meeting with a ghost. Peculiar how this universe works after all.

I showed up early. But so did Jay. She was sitting in the back, in a light blue booth. She was wearing a dark blue sweater, her brown hair came over her ears like a puppy dog, all wet from the rain outside. It had just started pouring. I tucked in. We said hello and talked about nothing, until my ghosts made us speak of those we don't like to.

"I get these letters. They're lying on the floor of my office, and today I got one behind my seat at the auditorium. I thought someone was playing a trick on me. I'm supposed to meet them at the Bell Tower at midnight tonight."

"That sounds like a joke. Who writes out letters and say they're from ghosts. I don't know Peter, I think it's a bit fishy."

"But I get stuff and feelings, and see things when I shouldn't be seeing them. It gets scary. You know?" I picked up the salt shaker. Think I'll have a burger. You want a burger?"

"Yeah, I'll have one. So you want me to go with you tonight there."

"Yeah, I want you to. If you want, you don't have to," I said.

We both didn't say much for the next minute. Then she spoke up. "Yeah, I'll go along with you. It doesn't sound that scary."

"I know. That's what frightens me. You hear they killed a hundred and twenty students, kids in Afghanistan? Terrorists. This world is coming to some strange places. It almost sounds silly chasing ghosts when times are as bad as they are."

"What are we supposed to do, chase terrorists? That's not our job. We're here to sing life along and try and skip to it."

"Yeah, I guess you're right," I said.

A woman came up to us dressed in red checkers with a white apron. We ordered two burgers, fries and a root beer. We ate, drank our root beers, talked some more than headed back outside to our cars. It stopped raining. But thoughts about impending doom and rainy day ghosts still drizzled in the forefront of our minds, they were as blank and naive as the sheets to the imagination- dressing up specters in our finest linen cloth, poking holes in the middle for our shallow scared eyes.

Then it hit me- this was a story about love. And the fear of losing it. It's why people recluse themselves from the world, hide away from their soulmates. The darkness is deep and the wounds and scars hurt too much to think about these days. Lovers cry and scream in the night. Night terrors shake their bed. They are tired of the daily grind, we are tired of burning the oil without choice of what we want. Authors like King write, and fiction raises itself from the dead and paints images in our minds, forever more; like Poe and his black cat.That guy in that fucking wall getting all bricked up. It's sadness, love. It's breaking down barriers constantly, only to meddle into new ones, and over some really crazy shit. Fights and arguments tear the fabric of the skin, and paint textures of what pain looks like on canvas. School is an alibi. Teachers and students hide there. It's easy to hold a sign up and say 'don't shoot'. I didn't rob that quicky mart. Lot of love gone is what I say. I try to find it, but it hides. Love is scared. The church is on the brink of understanding what it means to be a human being. I just feel bad for these kids and the woman next to me. As I drove towards campus. It was only ten at night, but I was thinking all sorts of strange anomalies on why the world was the way it was, and why it should matter more to me than it did. Though it did. It mattered because love was involved. Love drove the engine. And not necessarily the love for a woman, (though that may almost always be the case), but a love for life. Like the old movie with Kurt Douglas, A Lust for Life.

We walked across the path that lead to the library, and down a steep slope around back to another courtyard. This one was behind the Morris Building. The courtyard was effervescent, glowing in psychedelic greens and purples. There was music coming from an open window in the dorms above the woods, that acted both as a wall of privacy and a hiding place for those who liked to sneak into them, whether to smoke a quick pinner before class, or to just hang out with your someone. It was the other side of the Hugh Building, and that's why we were going this way. I wanted to avoid the scene in the main yard, all the tents. It's a nice walk this way behind the buildings. It made me think of childhood, and how the woods were our playground. How we built forts and guarded them with all our strength. Those days are always back in our mind, bleeding through our skin to come out and show itself, how we once felt. We were young once and did feel a certain way about things. Life was different. 9/11 changed all that. It was just too much of an advertisement of red white and blue revenge against those who took down the towers to make any real progress for individual freedom in the setting of social chaos.

We sat down on a log just a yard or two into the woods. Maybe ten yards really. An open patch bestowed a nice place to sit down and relax. Not as many drinkers on campus as there are pot smokers, but that was all for the better as society was shifting its gears on the benefits of legalizing. The air was nice and fresh, brisk against our bodies as we were both wearing winter coats. I had a date; we had a date with a ghost come midnight. The leaves on the ground were of New England or Northern Jersey, temperate trees leaving memories of too many seasons come and gone. We had a date with a ghost, and time was neither on nor off our mind. Silence screamed through our lack of conversation. We were prepping up for the moment, straitening our ties, pulling up our sour disposition. We sat on the log, and heard owls, and deer pass, birds skitter across branches as wild mushrooms grew slowly around our feet. Dead hour time was what it had become. Dead hour and it was time to get up from the ground and walk towards the tower. There were staircases inside the Hughs Building, one of them led to the bell. And the ghost there awaiting us.

It looked different late at night. We opened the doors where we had class many times before; though now, this time of night it was dead and empty. Darkness engulfed the situation. Even the rows of lockers running down the hallowed halls of Hughs came screaming in dead silence. We walked down the hallway that was about a few and some. Long enough. The yellow walls were dark manilla with banners that said "Go Knights" and "Crush Them Tigers" beckoned attention from weary students. They got very little of mine, and Jay's. Time to climb steps, I thought.

I opened up the door that spelled the words Stairwell on it. It led straight to where we needed to be. We had five minutes to spare. We climbed, still silent, making small sounds of noise attached to our fingers. Our feet stepped onto the marble flab of the over-walked and over-used stairwell. Seven flights to the top. Three and a half floors. Not very high up you would think, but they were tall floors, with high ceilings. And the tower was almost three stories in its own right. So a little walking was entailed. We stopped for a second to look through the brick open window facing the courtyard. When we got to the top, we were stopped by a door. On the door stenciled a sign that said 'Personnel Only in Bell Chamber.' I looked at Jay, and she looked at me. At that, I turned the knob. The door was open, so we walked ourselves in.

The floor and room were dusty and had a strange wood smell to it. The air outside gushed through empty pockets leaving shrills and feelings of frailty. The door slammed itself behind leaving us there feeling even more alone then we felt before. We were talking, saying minimal things. Things we wouldn't remember anyhow. I looked down again, as I did when I first entered. There was a piece of paper that looked out of place, newer than the other objects or surroundings would gather. I picked it up.

"A note. I wonder," I said. I looked at Jay; she looked back at me as she took my hand.

"Open it, what does it say?"

"Thank you. That's all it says. It just says thank you. What kind of trick is someone playing on me. I don't understand it." I crumpled the note up and threw it against the side of the wall. Not seeing it at first, the bell, the giant bell in the middle of the small tower room ceased to be invisible any longer as it woke from its cold slumber. A giant ring, or gong sound bowled us both to our knees. We quickly covered our ears. It was midnight exactly on the dot, and we were both victim of circumstance, calling this one out.

We picked up ourselves thirty seconds later. Twelve gongs counted. Twelve miserable soul piercing sounds, decibels not well to mankind. That is why it stood high above those down below. We weren't meant to be up here, and the bell was letting us know it. When I looked back where I threw the paper, it wasn't there. It had gone. I looked for it.

"Where did that note go?" I said.

"I don't know. Over there?" Jay pointed in the corner. A small piece of paper gleamed from the light coming through the cracks in the wooden steeple. I walked a few paces, leaned down and picked it up.

I had flown in from Boston last week, and tonight I'm in a bell tower looking for a ghost that was just a piece of paper. What did cops and race have to do with an education. When did protesting begin for a cop out, or a way out. I can't make it on the streets, no one can. So I stayed in school and got a job of some sort. Taught my own ghosts. Bled my own wounds, and paid dearly for my own little meaningless dream.

We walked down the street and to the car where we parked it. The sounds of bells shook me from the inside. I was delivered from something mysterious, something dark; I came out of something. We, Jay and I, were holding hands. We were both frightened and yet relieved. The bell. The calling. That sound you hear in life where you wan't to break through all walls, you want to scream through all ears. Ghosts do that. They try really hard to get their points across, like leaving notes and letters at your feet, under your door. They like to scare you while they can; it's their job. Because it's not the fear they want from you, you create the fear out of naivety, the ghost just wants to be heard, like everybody else screaming their fucking head off.

We walked back to the cars, and I kissed Jay goodnight, watching her drive off. I stood at the edge of the courtyard looking up, up at the inquisitive night sky, and all so knowing moon.

"I'll find him, but there's a price. I'll find him." A man came out of the shadows, in the courtyard. There was snow on the ground. He looked older than a student, younger than a grown man. In-between. He had dark hair and a smooth pale face. His hair was cut short and had a black hat on. His coat was also black, as were his shoes. Black soul, was my first thought.

"I'll catch the guy who took those students."

"Who are you?" I said.

"I'm the Catcherman. It's what I do. I catch people in my dreams, I lock them up when they aren't looking. I see them catch people and cage them in my dreams, and I find them. I don't do it much, but when I do, I succeed. Caught about twenty five people. It's what I do. I can find these folks, these kids."

"How," I said. "How you going to find these kids."

He came out of the shadows, the light was sprinkling snowflakes of innocence and purity- things evidently gone in this world. "I'll catch them, but I told you there's a price."

"What's the price?"

"Can't tell you now. It's not much, it's just an exchange of sorts, a shift in energy. If you do it right, no one can get hurt."

"What do you mean get hurt."

"Someone can die, or lose an arm. An Aunt or something. I find people and then that energy built up seems to pop up close around them. They lose someone. I have a remedy. I have something if you wear it, nothing will happen to you. And you must say these three things, before you go to bed at night. Thank you, God for today. Forgive me for my transgressions, protect me and those around me through this. That's it, say those three things."

"Thank you God for today. Forgive me for my transgressions, protect me and those around me through this."

"Good. Now..., who am I?"

"I don't know, you didn't say your name. The Catcherman."

"That's right, the Catcherman. Meet me tomorrow at the Smaller Cafe on Bleak Street. Across from the campus museum. You have good privacy back there. We can talk about things. I need to know things about these kids. You have any papers by them?"

"Yeah, I do. But why should I trust you with this. You call yourself the Catcherman."

"Yeah, I do. We all need protection. My real name isn't important. I'm an orphan of sorts, lost my parents when I was three."

"Okay, if I show, I show. I already got stood up by a bunch of ghosts."

"You'll see them again." He looked at me with large white eyes, giant black dots infiltrated the spectrum. Snow screamed behind them.

"Why do you say such things, especially to a stranger."

"Because I know these things. I may be one of them for all you know, or don't.

"I have to go." I said. "I have to meet a friend. Tomorrow's another day," I said.

"Yes, I know it is. Meet me at the Smaller Coffee House. Noon."

"I'm not going to be there, you know that right?" I thought I heard someone behind me, the snow was coming down heavier. I looked behind, towards the Hughs building, through the trees. I thought I heard someone say my name, something close to it. No one was there. The yard was empty all of a sudden. I turned back around. "Hmm, thought I heard something," I said.

But I said it to the air and wind, Catcherman was gone. In my hand I was holding a crystal amulet, a talisman. And I was supposed to know that all this was OK, that all of this was some how a little normal. It wasn't. And I had to believe that.

The next three days were grueling. The aftermath Thanksgiving, and Christmas creeping up was like an unremovable tic. I couldn't get release from the stress. Finals were too soon ahead, papers to grade were invaluable to each and every student. I had to prevail somehow. Missing students, protesters everywhere I went. It was madness in the streets, and the cliche wore its badge with bot pride and prejudice.

I was sitting in my apartment. Christmas was a cold and lonely thought I didn't want to think about. I looked outside into the abyss of ice and memories. Jay was on my mind. We were close, like lovers, like friends. But like a brother and a sister relating to one another. She knew a few things, how to bake wasn't one of them; but she knew how to add and subtract, find ways through mazes and out of hells. These were dark times; I knew this more than most. It's a stone's throw away from homelessness and everyone quite knew it. I couldn't understand the wars between people. Most people just talk. No one can afford to live. The banks keep it that way, the minimum wage is too low, the average wage is too low. The rent is too high. My salary barely kept me afloat. I was lost, and this book, like I said in the beginning was the only way through a maze I one day found myself in. I wasn't a lost individual all my life. It just happened one day. And now these ghosts, and these missing kids on a fairly small campus. To me, seemed like everyone was missing. Seemed like everyone just disappeared. Isn't that the life of the author, and the teacher? I had to ask myself.

Imaginary snow fell fast, gripping the ground as it touched. Like the man who wants to go to Mars all his life, never steps his feet on earth. What a beautiful place and no one gets to touch it. The flowers, the people, and their lovely faces. I sat there still on the stoop overlooking a dull pale day, overlooking thoughts that come and go, in and out of my musical mind. It's own enigma. I had to follow it. I had to follow the signs that people were leaving. I had to listen to the Catcherman, whoever he was. I had to meet him. That was today. At the cafe down the street. Fear wasn't an option in life, although it showed itself in many ways, it had to leave.

I got to Old Maria's, that was the old name of the cafe. The place was dead. I had a note in my hand. It said Thank You. There were missing kids, and this man, Catcherman said he could catch the guy who was behind it. I hadn't many options left in life, so I pretty much had to go with the gut feeling he was right, and I was in the dark. But noon came and no one showed up in its place. I was fooled again. I got out my cell phone and texted Jay. A failed response came back saying that the message hadn't gone through. I had to change my service was my first thought, but that wasn't going to happen; so I just sweated it out. The coffee came after the waitress paid me a cold nod of approval. The sun was down or behind clouds because it was unusually dark outside. My car looked like a prune sitting there outside the glass. I could see it from where I was sitting. It looked lonely, screaming in silence there, like myself. Catcherman wasn't coming, and I had to get some kind of grip on the particular belief system attached to my peculiar situation. Again, I had ghosts dropping notes and shadow people playing no shows. I tried Jay again, this time I called direct on her number. She picked up in two rings.

"Hey Peter, where you at?"

"I'm at Old Maria's." I picked up the coffee. "I was supposed to meet someone here. He didn't show."

"Really? Who were you going to meet."

"Well, no one, really," I said. "Someone said they knew something about the missing kids. So I came here to meet him." I put the coffee down; after I realized I was staring helplessly into it, as if I needed it to hold me up. Anyhow, I put it down. "You want to go to the tower. I have the suspicion something will happen, or someone will talk to us if we go."

"Again, we just went there a couple days ago." There was a pause. "OK, but only if you read me some poetry while we're up there."

"I'm thinking of just sitting up there with the great shutters open, we can feel the wind."

"Read me something." She began to sound impatient, wanting more than acceptance.

"I need to see something up there. I need to feel around again. We left too soon."

A woman, the waitress came by with a check, and placed it down on my table.

"I need you to come along," I said.

"OK, I'll meet you at the bottom in twenty minutes. I'm all dressed, and was going to buy a book at Barnes and Noble; but I'll come down."

"They closed down Borders by you, that's right."

"Yup, they did. I'll see you in twenty minutes. I have to mail something before I meet you. I'll be there in no time." She hung up the phone before I could finish my agreeing verbally. And that was OK, for now it had to be.

After I paid the bill, I walked through the dirty glass doors and outside onto the open sidewalk. There was a girl, across the street. She was staring at me. A bus came by, the sound I could hear like a lion moving down the block, it passed me with a roar. When the street cleared of tin and metal, the bus left me for sight; she was gone. There was no one across the street. The girl had disappeared, vanished into the fog and smog the bus left behind. It was an old bus, green and yellow trim. Big window in the back. Didn't even know why something like that would be on the road. When I turned to watch it go, away from me, there she was, standing in the back of the bus, watching me, staring at me. I couldn't help but get spooked, kind of scared for a little bit. One second she was there, wearing a yellow dress, looking gray in the face. Ten seconds later, it was but the size of a bug in my view running down 7th Ave. I was still standing there, trying to slap my face back into reality, but that didn't work. Nothing was working. No one was working. The whole idea of a dream of what I learned in college was turning out to be nothing but a list of papers I needed to grade and hand back.

Why the tower, I thought to myself, why is there this intrigue with the mystery of that old fucking tower? Have to sit there, in an empty box shaped bat house. The air was cold, and I had my P-coat on. Jay was going to meet me there. I stopped myself short, not a thing in hand. I just stood there and looked at it. Ten yards from the base, cold doors with old cold knobs allowing entrance to such minds who stand for its meaning. The tower. Why a tower, three stories tall, holding a bell and ten classrooms hold such magnetism for every student. The building itself was magnificent in its own outstanding right. The bricks were solid and made by the finest of Masons. Secrets of hard labor and love went into the Hughs Building. Memories of so much cried for snow, cried for something. The saddest conclusion was that there were only a few that ever got the meaning of this building, and why I was here. It wasn't the note. I had come here long before the
180

letter from the ghost. He was a no-show. I was here, and had something to say about it. I looked back into the yard, no one was coming. There was no sign of Jay, and I hadn't much space left in my mind for anything other than her. I turned back around, looked up at the steeple which raised itself so high that I couldn't quite make the top out clearly. The day was gray and had a cold mist about it. Either it were my eyes that wouldn't give me the site of the bell, or the rainy mist. I couldn't care; I just had to get up there. I stepped forward for what seemed eternity and reached for the door handle. It open, and for a Sunday, that was good news.

"What took you, I've been up here an hour. I thought you saw me." Jay said.

I couldn't believe what I was hearing and seeing. The walk up wasn't as difficult as it was easy and soft as a bird taking wing, or like a bat knowing its way to a bell tower. It was a feeling like all the songs were crashing down on you. Jay was standing behind the bell, coming out as soon as I showed my face above the hole in the floor, the door to the bell tower.

"What do you mean, an hour?" I was taken back, but I asked.

"I saw you looking at the tower, outside, up at the bell. Your head was up looking at the bell. I yelled your name. You didn't answer. You just walked in, but I couldn't find you. I looked in all the class rooms and been to the top three times. I don't understand. Where were you?" Jay looked at me, confused.

"I don't know. I guess I got lost in my head. I go places maybe. I don't know. Really? I was gone an hour?" I don't know where I was. A classroom. A picture of a basement came to my mind. A lot of whicker wire, fencing. I looked at Jay, more confused. "I thought I got here first. I just got here. I was outside looking up, yeah; you're right about that. But not an hour. I definitely got here about five minutes ago. I just came in and up the ladder when I got to the top. Tell me you're joking Jay Bird."

"I'm not joking. I got here over an hour ago, pacing, walking everywhere. I thought you had a seizure. So I stayed, thinking you'll show up, or I'll find you. You weren't in a classroom?"

"I don't know, maybe a basement. But I don't know. Just a picture of it. This is so strange. Today has been so weird. I don't know but it all feels real strange right now. Come on, let's get out of here. I need lunch. I'm hungry."

"OK, but get that checked." She was half-kidding, following me as I took my hand and legs forward, climbing back down the ladder.

Jay was a close two feet behind me, placing one foot on each wooden beam. There were twelve. I would count. We walked down the stairway. The marble walls were a safe haven for thoughts. Thoughts bounce off of marble, flutter themselves out the door. We got there too, and out into the open courtyard, main lawn of the Pristol campus. The sun was just coming out; that was a good sign. We walked over towards the pillars.

"That was a little jaunting; I think I need to lie down. I feel dizzy." Jay got a hold of one of the stone pillars, than she tethered her way towards the grass at the base. "I don't know what got hold of me. I feel so dizzy."

"Here, put your head on this." I took off my coat and tucked it under her head. It wasn't as cold with the sun out now. I took myself a glimpse of the white Hughs bell tower. It stood there, against the backdrop of a dripping yellow sun. I could hear angels from here if I wanted to. Instead the bell above decided to ring itself a few times. I couldn't count. I stopped after four, but it must have been eighteen or twenty. But over it, over the sound of clanking bell tones, I could hear small beautiful angels sing. They were singing Jay to sleep, on the nicely dewed grass. There was a feeling that everything was going to be alright. Jay's eyes were closed. She was probably dreaming of something comforting, as a slight smile dressed her lips. I waited patiently, for her to wake back up, for her to come through, for life to say that everything was just a passing phase, that trials and ghosts were something that we were going to talk about when we were old and gray, tell our grandkids- that kind of thing. Truth was, I was already getting that old, and Jay- I felt bad for the girl. She was lost, as much as me. I was grateful for her company. I wanted her to know. Especially as she lay quiet on the ground, breathing in miraculous thoughts, and quiet meaningless dreams of what it was like a long time

182

ago, when innocence wasn't something so easily lost, nor something that could be recalled at the drop of a note. But maybe a bell. Maybe the sound of a bell could cure the sick. Many ceremonies use bells, to heal. Maybe this was one of those times. I looked back up at the tower. The blue sky exhaled in the background. A tower and a bell; whose idea was to dream that up? I didn't care. She, Jay was asleep in my arms. I was beginning to drift myself. We dream big here, or we don't dream at all, I told myself. A few seconds later, I could barely hear the echo.

I broke down in my mind. I couldn't stand it any much longer. Winter break was almost here. What was happening was a dream, it had to be; like one of those dream within a dream things. My mind wondered as I had Jay's head in my hands. Her legs hugging down under her plaid skirt, black socks and sandal shoes. Cute as a button, I thought. I looked up, saw something. As my eyes feared their way into the dark ally between the Hughs building and the student center, I saw something, someone. A man was standing there in a dark outfit, a hat, something, a shadow.

"Wake up, are you awake, Jay, wake up." I shook her a little.

"What is it? Where are we?" She started to wake up.

"Do you see someone? Someone over there? I see someone. Look over there."

"I don't see anyone." She hadn't moved from where she lay.

"Sit up, look. Over there." I pointed.

"I don't..., yeah. I see someone. Who is that?"

"It's the Catcherman."

"Who's that?"

"Someone I just met."

"Why is he standing there?" She pulled herself up, as did I.

The man just stood there, fifty yards away, tucked into the bushes. Now assuming to blend with the bushes that carved their way upwards the student center side bricks. Then he disappeared. Gone.

"Where did he go? Did you see him leave?"

"No, I didn't see him leave, but he's not there is he?" I said.

"Was he ever there to begin with?" She had me questioning.

"I saw someone, you saw him too, didn't you?"

"I don't know. Let's get going."

"Yes, let's get going. A long day. Jesus I don't know what's going on. I'm hungry. Dinner?"

"Where would you like to go?" she asked.

"Anything but Italian." I said.

"Wine and cheese. Like in the movies." She drifted off into amnesia as she lifted herself all the way up, brushing the stray grass off her flannel plaid skirt. "This school, I don't know why I ever came to this school."

"One of the best," I said.

"Yeah, so what."

"Yeah, true. So true. Imagine all the stuff that went on in that building." I barely pointed at the tower, got a finger in its direction. "Crazy stuff. Crazy secret meetings and stuff, orgies in the basement."

"Oh, is that what's on your mind?"

"No, you're funny. I was thinking of a movie we're studying in class. Eyes Wide Shut."

"I love that movie."

"You should sit in on my class. That movie is Stephen King's The Shining. In the book, there is a scene where there is a gold room, and a lot happens in it, where Jack talks to Lloyd, the night he drinks?"

"Yes, I remember."

"Eyes Wide Shut is that night from the book. First tip off from the movie is that the first twenty minutes take place in a very large shiny gold room. That's the ball room in the Shining. It's almost exaggerated in Eyes Wide Shut to get the point across. What's interesting in the book, it takes place on Christmas Eve, so does Eyes wide Shut. In fact there is a Christmas tree in every scene. Also in the book it's creepy, and there are a lot of dead people around. If you look closely at the scenes, in Eyes Wide Shut, they all look dead, in the rooms he visits."

"Wow! That's crazy."

"It is. The whole set takes place in a very artistically fake world. I mean there's a lot more than just that. The coincidences pile up rather quickly if you compare the two." Peter looks up at Jay, wondering
184

what she's thinking. "Oh I'm boring you. It's the professor in me. "I smiled at her, cheering her up a bit. "Come on let's get something to eat."

"Sounds interesting, it does; and dinner sounds deliciously appetizing. I'm starving." Jay smiles back, laughs. "No more ghosts for this evening. Promise me."

"No more ghosts. Not for tonight, nor tomorrow if I can help it."

"Good."

After we ate and parted ways, I went back to my apartment. Quickly I got tired so drifted to my bed. I fell asleep rather fast. I dreamt of horror. I dreamt of nightmares and panic, and ghosts. I woke up to a light coming through the window. It was early morning and a light had pulled me from something. I needed to live. My room, small and impact, I needed to get out of here. I needed a life and more than a roomful of students, a life. What was a life. The news wasn't even on, and I knew what was going to happen. Another fallen plane, another one missing and taking two months to search for it, until the public has had more than they can bear any longer. The news, people killing each other all over the place, bullets and bombs. And when the news is good, like winning a gold metal or some guy healing a few sick people, well; you just can't seem to touch with it. Two minutes ago they were giving you the most negative brainwashing you could imagine, now they want to cover it up with 'hero of the month'. I don't know any more. It's not like it used to be. Too many people who can't speak English in America. Too many hiding in the closet from the Immigration department. They can't move; they wish they could, but they can't. People came here thinking there would be gold in the streets, that there is money if you work for it. True, very true- there is money out there. It's just in bloodless veins now. Working for the man, working for someone. I always told myself I wouldn't work for the man. I always said I was going to be someone on my own. I was going to be a writer of some kind. I don't know how that worked out. Frick'n ghosts were always on my mind these days. And television. That tv in the corner. That old couch smitten with cigarette smoke and imprints of depression. I'd seep into it late at night and stare at that fucking thing. I wish they'd put something on it like the old days. Like Starsky and Hutch or Happy Days. Dallas, Twin Peaks, X-Files, anything. It's all Seinfeld forever. It's insane, the thing. I don't understand let alone find the need to indulge my day with it. Shit does change. I just never saw it all coming.

I pedaled myself over to the dresser, pulled out some socks and what not. I undressed myself and ran into the shower. The heat was low so I felt cold. I felt happy in a way too. The water was frozen water, ice coming out of a steel tube. It warmed up in about four seconds or so, but the initial cold woke me up. Gave me somewhat of an epiphany, a jolt into somewhere I wasn't. I was suddenly floating, in my mind above the ground. I was drifting forward into a space that had both structure and meaning to it. I was alone, and outside was far away. My thoughts were breaking cascades, cathedrals of stoneless imagination. I was free, and the water on my face knew 'forever' itself wouldn't last, but yet somehow it does. People will always come in and out of your life, and you'll always remember the special ones. In the future, it will be like that. Everyone you ever loved in a room, smoking a hookah, listening to strange and exotic music will be there. In the future there will no longer be as many words. I was drifting in and out of my own mind, my hands scrubbing my scalp. Listening to the water rap upon my head, my skin feeling alive. I was free. Like I said; I was free.

I got out of the shower to the sound of a whisper. Something I heard, all of a sudden. The music stopped in my head. The colors went gray again. I grabbed the towel.

"Hello? Is anyone in here with me?" I asked the whisper. "Hello?"

No one answered. I walked into the bedroom. No one was there. "Hello? Is anyone here?" No one.

Ghosts, I thought. Ghosts again. I couldn't take it. The world was a lonely place and I was in it. The air beckoned to be heard. It called from the space between the space. I didn't want it any longer. I wanted a friend. I thought of Ryerson, what he was up to. I thought of the missing kids. I cared more for the missing than the cause. All my life I stayed away from t-shirts with a cause attached. I meant to keep it that

186

way. My heart bled enough as it was. I was crying inside, and I needed a solution.

I looked over at the cigarette pack. No good, I thought, but reached for one anyhow. I looked out the window, imagining a deer pass below through the crooked pathways the courtyard complex was made of. One more time, "hello?"

I couldn't speak to them any longer. Why were they chasing me down. What angel spread his wings of knowledge to gain the power of feet? Where is this Dickens's ghost?

I took a drag. The clock on the wall was its own entity. I was drifting in and out of time, so the clock wasn't quite making sense. The phone rang. The clock all of sudden was the only other living entity in the room with me. The ghosts felt suddenly gone. I reached for the phone. I did this with no contempt. Speaking into the hard cold plastic piece I asked who was on the other end, but no one answered. Just blank space into more space, leaving me more and more empty. I couldn't deal with it, my blood pressure rose and I began to panic more. This constant nightmare was unnerving. I had to balk, take a pause. Give up. I had to see the light coming through the window. I had to forget the people in the courtyard, and the ghosts in the tower.

I was ready for class. The door was a slice of standing wood, easily passible. There was no turning back, I couldn't, just a few more classes and it was winter break. We were going to talk about Eyes Wide Shut, we were going to talk about a lot of things, and probably still will, but something at the foot of the door on my way out that morning had me thinking differently about a lot of things. Who guesses when a surprise shows up. At the foot of my door, in the midst of an open dark hallway, sat a book. It was on the downside so I couldn't quite make out what the book was; I leaned downward and picked it up. Immediately it began to breed familiarity. Orange, a drawing of a horse..., of course. It drew me back immediately. Fear took over and pushed me somewhat back inside my apartment, which I haven't yet locked. Catcher in the Rye was in my hands. I couldn't quite catch the coincidence, but yet couldn't help grip on noticing. Catcherman, that's who dropped it there. Strange that book, always linked to murderers who were obsessed with it. Son of Sam, the

Boston Strangler, Ted Bundy. Who ever, chills spilled over and took me on like a shadow in a dark cold pool. Catcherman, the book fell from my hands and onto the floor. I quickly ran myself back inside of my apartment to give me some reason, a way out. Leaving books now, I thought. They're leaving me fucking literature.

Class was beginning in an hour. I thought about that. I thought of not even going to a class I was teaching. That came across my mind as well. I wound up walking through the grounds, the courtyard. No one was there, or they were all sleeping in their tents. Protesting signs and beer cans splattered all over the grounds. I walked through, all the way past the columns, past the student center and to the door of the tower. Above it was the bell. I wanted to scream, do something. Scream really loud at it and tell it to go away. Ring itself and all of its ghosts into fucking oblivion and forever wish it away. That's what I wanted to say, something like that. But it wasn't going to happen, and I somehow knew it.

I taught class; it went by effortlessly, or I'd like to to at least think it did. I then met up with Jay, where we got a bite to eat at an old Italian restaurant on the North End. Afterwards we drove over to the apple farm and got some ice cream. It felt right, that's all I can really say about it. Love is something you really can't describe in a book; maybe you can, if you're a good author, maybe you have a shot at it. Love for us was the absence of fear, or I'd like to think; the comfort, taking the nails and thorns out each other's sides. Being there through the thick and thin. The joy and the bleak. The laughter and the floods of sorrow. Love let all the problems in the world let be for the brief time it allowed. What are ghosts, but memories, old long lost love screaming to be heard. Love was all that there really was, in the end. It's how I was feeling, under the blue sky and cloudless evening that night. I wasn't thinking about missing kids, the notes, Catcherman, the ghosts, nor the bell-tower. Just my girl Jay, and the love I was feeling at that moment. It was like the vanilla ice cream, and how it made me shiver in the cold Autumn air. All it took was her warm arm over my shoulder, and a comforting smile to make it humorously bearable.

The Vanishing Tree

Chapter One
Bugwit Hampsterfur The Blessed King

The blessed king picked himself up, off of the velveteen comforter, cotton pillows and blinked into the forgiving sun. "I am happy", he said to himself and looked out into the vacant courtyard.

"Dementia, they say I have. Fooy. Never. Crackers all of them. Dementia, early settings in of insanity. I have to laugh at them all. All crooked and demented themselves. Gambling thieves run amuck."

King Bugwit looked over the cold brick windowsill, and out where the morning crooned old wit with the air that takes half of it.

"Alas! Autumn my friends, it's what winter dreads most of all, and tales of tangerine skies, and walks among the apple trees. Ah tis what I yearn, for." Bugwit picked himself up, off of the ledge and walked himself into the main stay attached to his sleeping courters. This too had a large balcony overlooking the garden, east, where the sun comes up as well. Bugwit's cloak soaked his pajama's in no soothing manner, but it wasn't a thing of match as it was a matter of being, in the clothed gown, as opposed to wearing it. He reached to the ground, picked up a piece of paper that had scribbles on it, threw it aside and thought of an itch he had beneath his hair, beneath the skin on his head. He scratched with a sound that blew cricket whistles half mast, and thought nothing of what the future day lay ahead for him. Not even the loud knock at the door christened acknowledgement to anything stupor, unforeseen, or clouds. It was as if puffs of white smoke riddled the room of questions unanswered, chaos wasn't in the King's vocabulary, he appeared to have somehow accepted the oddness of his own ways. King Bugwit. William Bugwit Hampsterfur. There was a crown. There was an oddity amongst men, a man that didn't fit in, bumped his head too many times. Hit the square peg with his circular shape. Not at the first leap, jump, bridge crossing. Not at the first words spoken, or the first sight of something passed did he come face to face with what he had been hoping to attain. Drifter King, William the drifter, the school master's worst horror. Asleep when a man walked in wearing a full red squire dress, wearing a mitten and holding a cricket paddle.

"Breakfast, your majesty. Breakfast is ready and the dogs are out back for todays hunt. Wise to wear something a bit warm-steady, bit frisky on the hills. Won't be warm till the sun starts beating on the cherry trees."

"Good morning Squire, thank you. Tell madam Jay that I will be down in a moment, and look forward to her ravishing blueberry pancakes. Mighty day Autumn, is here, alas. Squire. Go now. Let me attire."

"The blessed pigeon came to my window this morning. I've seen him three times this week, pass the syrup my beautiful love. Pass the sugar. The coffee is sublime this morning. I want to taste the honey of life. What a beautiful day!" Buwit took the cup of sugar and syrup from his wife- the Queen of the forest, and beyond, if not her home where her dreams come from. Queen Jayleene, strong in will, powerful in her own femininity. She smiled gently across the table as the sun sang through the stained glass window. The fraternal wood, beams of the Victorians kept the house up on a tilt, the castle outside the house surrounded the courtyard, lifting all that resided inside to a merely gleeful elevation. Two hundred feet above what lay below was of no concern, as the jelly and fruit passed from hand to hand. The coffee was strong, freshly picked beans from their own private farm of coffee beans as if whipped to special delicacies and delights.

"Yes, my dear, a beautiful morn. God bless, you know. Why doesn't anyone say God bless, and good morning any longer. Oh a pitiful world out there, I saw it on my way into the village. We give them everything. We give them homes and peace and food, and they all just wander around at night, blasted off their rockers from too many bar runs around town, is what it is."

"Oh what do you want them to do, dear. My Las, ah the air, it's thick in oxygen and spirits. Beautiful Fall." Bugwit looked around. There was no one but a silent squire at the door, "Forget the dogs, I want to go and smell the orchard on my walk into town this morning."
190

"Looks like rain, sir King, well to come mid day sir."

"Nonsense. I hear no such thing. I want to go and find me some love among the dirt road where all eyes lead to the left or to the right."

Queen Jayleene looked at her husband with disbelief and utter confused posture, "pass me some nickerdoodle cake, I want me some of that. That sure does look good."

"You're right, this does look good. You hear me Squire, no dogs today. In fact no dogs again. Those dogs look tired and need to lie in the fields for a few weeks. We've been running them too long."

"Absolutely correct King Bugwit," the squire nodded, then went back to his focused stare into the garden, a pictorial view from where he was standing. The sun screamed outside as it was unusually warm for this time of year.

The road was long beyond the driveway, which also was long. In retrospect, Bugwit remembered going down that dirt driveway thousands of times and it always took forever. And now that he was in forever-land he thought it best to slow down, take in the flowers, breathe the air.

Bugwit stepped without knowing, his nose, eyes, soul leading his tired old person along. He cheerfully clasped onto the notion that today was no different than any other day. Be back early, they would say. Be back by supper and don't stray from the road. It's been some time, they would say. He listened, or didn't. Was that kind of man. Kind of out grew himself over the years. Memories weren't thought of as they were instantly placed inside the visual cortex of his brain. Bugwit didn't much care for a lot, and there wasn't much to consider as his loftiness kept taking the pounds off his shoes. Only opium addicts know a better high. They lived not far from the King, but far enough he didn't worry much about them, or give their existence much thought. He carried on like they did, had to do what they had to do. In the end they both saw as many sunsets. In the end they both fertilized the land with their tears. But before he could set his mind on the frailties of existence, he saw a man up ahead. Not a mile down the road. He looked small but could recognize color and objects of notice. Bugwit walked the little he had to; and by no time at all, he came to a man standing in the middle of the road. Just beyond the man, the road had its own thoughts; it had appeared to have divided itself into two roads: one leading left, west; and one leading east, to the right.

"You can only ask one question. Ask me the question. You want to go to the good village. I can see. I lie or may tell the truth. Ask me and I'll show you the way to the good village. But remember the lying man will point to the opposite in which you ask, and the good man will always tell the truth. To get to the good village, you must ask me where you want to go." The man hadn't seen anyone in some time, so he looked excited and plum. He mumbled on, "ask me, ask me."

Bugwit took his hat from his head and put it before the man's feet. "If it's money you need, here's my hat so you can beg gracefully, your sir knight of the wandering hills."

"I am no knight, Sir King. I am your servant, and you need to get to the truth village, the good village. I will show you."

"But what if you are evil and sinister in intent, and wish me to drown in the marshes north. What will I do then? Trust you with this, I can't. I have to decide on my own." Bugwit scratched his head where his hat had been. If you are from the good village, you only speak good, correct?"

"Correct," the man said.

"If you are evil, you only speak evil?"

The man didn't answer.

"Hmmm, allow me to think about this momentarily. You jesters on the path to paradise had me confused before, you won't bide my time further. Which way to your village?"

"Ah, you got it Sir Master."

"It's why I am King, and you are the jester. Point me to your village, and we'll call it yet a more blessed day than it was before."

The man pointed to the left of his own face, right to the King. Bugwit put his hat back on and walked away with a smile. Funny fellow, he thought to himself. There were a group of clouds westward creeping his way. They were white as cotton, but behind that particular set creeped another that were a bit darker. The King paid no mind and kept walking down the path. It's been some time since he'd walk to the village. He knew the way, of course, but the jester's card had to be
192

played. He would have picked right at the fork. It's not as if he didn't know his own road. But the story says that sometimes many get lost on the one road, and wish for a fork to add to its contempt and misery. One road to paradise and no one is ever on it. A map shows many roads, many many roads. Do they all lead to paradise? No, but to most they lead to home. William Bugwit Hampsterfur was heading in the opposite direction.

Bugwit walked for a mile or two, as the skies darkened around him. There was a stadium of weeds and grass built high into the air just to the left about a hundred or two feet in. Bugwit thought of the days when he was a young player himself, kicking the ball around the field hoping to score a goal for the classmates. He thought how much school meant to him when he was a young lad, what the day felt like around the classroom. It was different; it wasn't all in the mind. Nowadays, it is.

The ground became more corse and tiresome to walk on, pebbles every which way. His wife surly must be wondering where he had walk'n off too. Surly she wandered off from time to time herself, but this wasn't one of those times. Bugwit looked lost. The road was getting thinner, indeed the road he thought he'd walked a hundred times before when he was that classmate kicking that ball around. But it was different, his head was higher above the weeds, he could see; and it looked unlike that of his childhood memories. There was a block of houses coming up on the right. They looked abandoned and dark themselves, but he paid not as much attention to them as he did to the forest just past the houses. A forest that didn't seem familiar to him. There was a sign hanging on the dirt path. An old tinkering dinky thing. Appleton Way. Harry thought about it for a minute, feeling less drunk and delightfully glee than he had when he woke up. His walk amongst the apple trees and the delicious snugberries; well, there wasn't going to be much debate on the matter. He had to look back. He wasn't going to turn into stone and he knew it well haste the misguidance of bad superstition. Pace me once this way and turn it all around, he thought as he did. His left leg completing now facing hindsight, his back twisting the ceremony and old saying into what lay squid in his unfathomable quest to begin with. He was now facing home, and walking back towards the castle. No time, no day for kings to stray from the path. No day for kings not to remember verse. No day for kings not to remember love. His fumbling fingers picked up dead stones, reciting these words over and over as he did. He managed to collect three or four good ones by the time he came to the gate of his own home. A bridge crossing was easy this time of year, as delightful to see the trees spring with color. Bugwit walked on in. The guard at the gate opened the door. It was a pleasant day for Bugwit, he had thought to himself. But Appleton Way was something he didn't see before on earlier walks. And the man in the middle of the road pointing him to the direction of the strange forest wasn't there on his way back. He had thought of this but nodded against paying it much attention at the time. By the crossing of the bridge it gave him wonder. When his wife Jay came up to kiss him on the cheek, the man in the middle of the road was completely wiped fresh and clean of his mind. He could smell the pot pie on the iron stove. The sun was coming down. How he had been outside all day and not given it much thought upon his hungry stomach was beside itself.

Bugwit stood up from the table. A lull light was coming through the sky, leaving a trail of wonderful thoughts about the day's journey. His wife's eyes too tall behind her loveliness. There was something to be said of the two. He gave it thought, as she replied the same in minor gestures least forbearance. Mind his frailty, she thought. Mind his mild temper and fantastic illusions for dreams.

"Are you full?" Jayleene asked her overgrown husband.

"Yes, I think I am. And I'm heading to my quarters. I want to return to the place where I read a sign upon its entrance." He now spoke with a whispered fog, knocking. "I saw a sign leading to the Enchanted Woods of Essex. It was a map on a post board past the stadium. That's all, I just feel a feeling to return there."

"You have too much time on your hands, and where do you see such ridiculous things on sign posts. All that is out there is the village, and the idiots who run them. Regular town folk. There's nothing beyond; because if we haven't gone there already, well, it's just not there!" The Queen sat back down throwing her napkin on the table.

"Squire, get me a glass of red wine. No make it white. The finest in the cellar."

"Yes, me lady," the Squire returned and then left the room. There was silence for a minute or two. The sun radiantly was going down, and the sky was magnificent purple and blues, reddish squinting through. Yellow beamed a ray of epiphany into the ordains of their marriage.

Bugwit was suppliantly adding to the confusion, as if a musk scent over-ruled, and nothing but the scent could attain the acquired attention; there was a nose sniffing, and he needed to bush out the whacker. "Rather queer of them all, gathering nuts about. Love this and love that. I'll find this new place if I have to. Under the nose of my squirrel! That's what I'll do. The treasure is underneath the rock, and all I have to do is lift it. There are dreams about, and mad misfortune gathers moss. I shall find a way, and have my fortune too. By hook or by crook, do not underestimate the power of an empty stomach. Instinct had long been a word forgotten. Love was a second place land owner in comparison to instinct. Love gnawed and scratched. Instinct leaped, ate then slept. Yet love in the end conquered all things. It were as though instinct was love's greatest mistake. "Goodnight!" yelled Bug through the walls, down the stairs. The empty hallways shred shrills of sound hither and thither, this way and that, inevitably into the ears of his dearest wife.

"Goodnight, love." Jayleene sipped her wine and followed suit. She tucked herself into the bed next to her husband. She felt the love, the warmth, the time between them. Drifting in and out of spirit and body, she felt something stronger- like age from wine. Thoughts of delusion and small frights whispered through the cold of the night's moon. Cold and lavender, frailty spoke silently as she tucked her arm around Bugwit's waist. He tucked himself in towards her. They were happy. And that was a place to be in this town. Happy was a place well deserved, and well earned. As they both knew, it was a gift too. From somewhere, it was a gift well long written in the stars above, as below they slept under a forgotten moon. Dreams too well forgotten in the future, silent beetles, and grasshoppers, humming birds and dragonflies.

Bugwit crossed the bridge and looked back at the castle. It glimmered in fantastical light. Clouds glistened in gold over head. The bright sun beat down, beamed through horizontal shades of gray. He wanted to go back to the road where he was before. He saw something in a dream, and wanted to follow it. The road had a calling; it always did. And love was usually there guiding it. Whether a great love of a kind and beautiful woman, like his wife, Queen Jay. But there was something else the road caught attention to. It were a painter's dream, the colors and sights, the endless array of life peeking in, making itself known. Not all dreams come true. Bugwit walked on. And that he did.

There was a man at the end of the road. He was pointing. It was the man of truth. As he came closer, he was the same man as he saw the day before. The man pointed towards the right of Bugwit. No words were exchanged, only a smile of a gesture, and Bugwit walked on. Towards the houses. There was another man standing on the side of the road as he came closer to the suburban folklore. He was selling apples.

"Pleasant day," he said to me.

"Indeed it is. How about it? What do you have for sale there Chap?"

The man looked at Bugwit, into his eyes and outside onto the fields that lie abyss before him. "I have apples. Apples and more apples. Would you like a delicious apple to quench your quest Sir Knight?"

"I'm not a Knight, I'm your King. But that doesn't matter does it much. I'll take an apple. Here is a piece for it." Bigwit handed him a 10 gold piece and watched the man's smile come to life.

"Thank you your Majesty."

"Not to mention it, this road. Where does it go?"

"This will take you along for a little while, but of course you must know, being King and all."

"Not really. I don't travel much, and my brain isn't as sharp as it used to be. I saw a sign for an Enchanted Woods." Bugwit took a bite out of the apple. "This is good. You don't lie sire."

"The Woods of Essex, is where it will take you. The Enchanted Woods of Essex. But don't go in there. People go in there, and well, they don't come back out."

"Sure they do, they just come out the other side."

"Well, yes, sure some do. Well, you take your chances your Majesty. We all take our chances. Don't we?"

"Some do, and some don't. It really doesn't matter too much. But I guess I will. It looks like a nice enough day, so the sun will be on my side through as far as it takes me. Thank you Sire." The King took another bite and headed towards the general direction hence he was proceeding.

There before him stood a dark and intruding entrance to a mysterious forest. Two tall trees divided worlds, and wonders before him. He thought of his wife, he thought of his friends whom have all gone astray into their own worlds. Sire would be pleased, he thought to the sky. He gave it ominous direction and wondrous thought to what was inside the forest. Was there more to worlds than they appear. It was then he heard a tree fall not far inside. There was no path, only two tall cedar trees drifting their light headed leaves in the clouds of heavens above.

Bugwit glanced himself another second guess, another question. But that was it, he knew what was on his mind, and how it could help the situation. Dreams are people's thoughts, and what they work out. The real thing is different than the image in the mind. He's heard many accounting of horrible things inside where he would soon enter. None the less; he thought it deserving of a dream or two to venture hence where he sought. Where he heard the bell go off inside the courtyard of the Church. Inside the hallways of his castle. One last look back, and he was in.

The day flew past the further he stepped. Mixed branches with dirt soil, wet from the yesterday's rain. As he walked, he thought of his wife, and by now reading the note; the one he had left for her on the kitchen table. "I went for a walk, love. Won't be gone too long. I love you and you are the dearest." That was enough, Bugwit had thought. By this time a great light came out of the sky, shined brightly lighting the bottom of the grassy twigged ground. A great oak tree stood mightily tall, again into the heavens. This one felt the stars under his arrow head, leaves cascading their way touching sensations no one has ever quite felt. At the bottom of the tree Bugwit stood staring, piercing his way into the barked wood.

The tree then turned a different color, an orange, a yellow than a glowing white. The sun beamed its way down onto it, it all happened so quickly, Bugwit didn't quite know what to do. It was then a door appeared in the center of the trunk. The tree was enormous, the trunk could fit a horse and buggy; it was that thick. Bugwit walked in. When he got in, he could sense, yet not see a door close behind him. He was now inside something different. It got white, all white, glowing rainbow white. Then Bugwit felt something in his head; then fainted on the ground of his newly discovered cove, one that happens to be inside a tree.

He woke up a little bit after, and the glowing had gone away. There was no bright light mist or flashing colors. He was about ten feet from the trunk of the tree, and the lights had gone down. As did the sun. He was alone in the enchanted woods of Essex. For the very first time, or so he thought.

He could hear an owl when he awoke, it had flown away now. He stood up and looked up at the the tree he was just inside of, or at least felt as though he were. There weren't any doubts, only skeptics from the outside. Peering in at mere speculation. His thoughts were solid, and he felt confident what had just happened. Though it may have been a dream. or hallucination, he still felt a sense of confidence and security. Love was something he felt before, but this felt a lot like the feeling love gives you. Bugwit began to walk away now, away from the tree. There was a stream below, not far from where he was. He got on a path, the first he had seen since being in the forest. He began to walk along it. Thinking majestic thoughts, and claiming all kinds of victory. You can't buy experience. It's something that happens. He didn't think to look up or behind, the shrubbery was thick and maze-like. He had to maneuver through it. He had to think about what just happened to him. He came to a rock; it overlooked a road. Though this road was different than the roads he was on all his life. He thought where his castle was, he wanted to return, but somehow had the suspicion that he had gone somewhere back there in that tree.

Something happened to him. He felt younger, his hands looked younger. He looked down at the road and decided to leap down the hill and get on it. It was made of rock, a solid kind of rock. Like melted rock. There was a yellow line down the middle of it. He looked at the sun and thought to go the way where the sun would be going down. West, that would be. "I'll go west", he thought aloud. And so there, he began to walk.

Where was he? This was strange to him, he thought. The road doesn't look like a road. It's been played with, or hardened with hot sand. The sun was strong. The tree didn't seem right either, he had remembered being trapped inside of it; but then he was outside of it. And a strange sun to pass out to. All that light, and then waking up floored out on the ground. It all didn't make much sense.

Bugwit walked a while. He must have walked the other way, because he still could not find his castle, or have the looks of it. But he could see something, or somethings ahead in the distance. The sun was beginning to go down. But there were odd shapes of really tall buildings in the distance. Shadows of large blocks of black coming out of the ground, something Bugwit had never seen before. He continued to walk, the sun beat down. And he began to think. First this strange road, then these things in the distance. He was wondering if he had woken up in heaven, a different world, or a different time. No matter, the sun was still there, and going down as well.

It must be just about dinner time, Bugwit thought to himself. He was beginning to miss his wife, and thinking about her, wondering if he had made the right choice running off the way he did. He hadn't seen or heard anyone in hours. Just this road, not even a horse or buggy to come by and give him some water, or food.

Just as he was thinking it, it may have occurred simultaneously or not, but the thought of seeking help brought attention. There ahead of him, he could see a light, and it appeared to be coming his way. With that he could hear animals, roaring in the distance. He ran to the side of the road, into a wooded area behind a tree. The light was coming faster and he couldn't quite believe what he was seeing. Just as his premonitions paid tribute to the unheard, it passed, and with wicked speed. He could barely see it, but it looked like a horse and buggy, without the horse. He wondered where he was; was he in the future, or some strange land. Bugwit Hampsterfur came out of the trees and back onto the road. He could see in the distance a small bug of something on the road he was on. That was it, he thought. Next time he wondered whether he should stay on the road or not. If there was to be a second chance. But he thought that the road was made for vehicles, and there was bound to come another.

In his mind he could hear his wife, "where did you go? Why did you get on that road? Why didn't you come back." He could hear her voice, the one he loved. "Hearts are made of stuff human beings do not understand until its too late." This is what she would say. He kept walking. Towards the big buildings in the sky. He was in a place he wasn't sure of, but he kept walking. It was his thing as a kid. The Walker, he may well have been named.

The yellow line kept his eyes peeled to an imaginary friend, someone to guide him. It was some sort of time travel he thought. He wasn't sure. But he had never seen buildings such as these, at least he thought this. He wasn't far from them. He could hear anther vehicle coming his way, back a hundred yards or so behind him. This time he stayed on the road. The car came to crawl the closer it got to Bugwit. It crawled even slower, and roared like a lion, then it stopped. It's bright lights blinding Bugwit to the point of near ecstasy. Glory be of goodness, he thought. What could it be? A car that roared. From a planet of other sorts, must be, his misguided kind head briefly thought.

Then the vehicle car stopped its mouth, and roared no more. Piles of smoked ghostlike figures came pouring out of the back, like putting out a fire at home, in the back courtyard, on a holiday. Its bright lights gleamed through the night sky, making the moon jealous. Then there was silence. The lights went out, and there was darkness. Bugwit stood there, complex in thought, gasping in suspense and anticipation. A sound, like a door opened up, and a what appeared to be a pair of boots got out of the box buggy. It was a man, and he was wearing a strange hat. He looked at Bugwit, then the ground. Bugwit didn't know what to do, just standing there.

"You okay, Buddy?" The man finally spoke.

"Yeah, I'm OK, what is that? A buggy? Without horses? Where am I?"

"What do you mean, you're in New Jersey, don't you know where you are?"

"Those cities I see ahead. What are those?"

"That's Newark my friend. Where you from?"

"Oxford, England. Around there. I'm, well King of the country. But I don't think I'm there any longer." Bugwit looked confused, standing there on a yellow line, in the middle of nowhere.

"You're in New Jersey now." Says the man. "Come on, get in, I'll give you a ride into the city. You can find some food and shelter. It gets cold here at night." The man opens the door for him, "come on, get in."

Butwit gets in and closes his door, after slight hesitation on how it works. "What year is this?"

"It's 2018. And you are right, you don't look like you're from around here. My name is Ned. Ned Willows. What's yours?"

Bugwit scratches his head. "It's Bill, I mean, King Bugwit Hampsterfur, the first."

"So you're a king, from England, and now you're here in Newark. God, bless you. Surprised to see you on the road, was going to pass you, but you looked like you needed some help." Ned pulls out a smoke from his upper pocket, "want one?"

"What is it?" asks Bugwit.

"It's a cigarette. You mean you've never seen a cigarette before?"

"No I haven't" responds Bugwit. "Where I come from those are called Toddtellers. But they don't look like that, much thicker."

"Well, you want one, or don't you?" Ned grabs the wheel while juggling tobacco. "Come on kid, take one."

"If you insist, never turn down an offer of hospitality and generosity. That's what my good lady says back home."

"You have a lady back home, why the hell aren't you with her?" Ned looks ahead, the road is thumping of new pavement, intermittent cascades of gravel hit the windshield causing Ned to be slightly alarmed.

"Yeah, my Queen Jay. She's there at the castle probably wondering where I am. Is this England?" Bugwit scratches his head again.

"No my friend, this is the United States of America. This isn't England, Jeez what did you drink and from what party did you come from? You smell a little like booze, but did you hop on a plane or something?"

"Whats a plane?" Bugwit looks even more confused.

"You're kidding, right?"

"No, I'm not kidding."

"OK, just hang in there. We'll get you into town, and some help right away. Just hang tight there, Buddy. Hang tight." Ned looks at the road, then his friend, who just seemed to have passed out in the passenger seat. "Hang tight, little fellow, hang tight."

And so he drove, into the city of lights, ambition, and failing dreams.

Butgwit woke up in a sleeping bag, in some kind of small tucked away room. There were flies, and sounds that flies make. There was a weird box in the corner which appeared to be bread and tomatoes on it. Where was he, thought Bugwit. Where could he be now. He was in a car, a buggy, without a horse, going very fast, but that was all he could remember. The room was tiny and had a door, nothing to it but melting paint and no firewood, or fireplace; he was thinking. The room was gray, and a small light hung from the ceiling. Nothing Bugwit had seen before, or so he thought, maybe a lantern that hangs. He's seen them. Bugwit picked himself up off the floor, and then brushed himself off. A long way from home, he thought. A long way indeed.

Bugwit stood tall, not too tall, because there was still some space between himself and the light above. He looked around the room and noticed the door almost right away. He walked over to it. It was fat and thick, tall and wide, a big door. He put his hand on the knob and turned it. The door opened He walked outside the room and looked around. There was an immediate sense of relief, yet hesitant on not rejoicing too soon. There was air, and a tree next to him about ten yards from the door. It looked like the same tree as before. He walked outside, because he could remember where he was. He ran, down the path. He looked back, not to see a house he had come out of, but a tree. He was back home. He didn't know if it were a dream, or if he'd gone

202

somewhere else. It didn't matter. He was close again. And not far from the castle. Just down that dirt road a bit. His wife would be wondering what had happened to him. Or she would trust his best judgment and say he had gotten lost. But he ran, all the way. Excited, confused, thinking about the man in the buggy. He must had brought him home, he thought. Who would believe it anyway, not Jaybird at home, making a pie. And not Squire, he'd be off hunting fowl. So many thoughts came and went, feelings of DeJa Vu passed, sending shivers along side himself. The feelings that he'd been there before ran though his mind. People and images and places, all like giant statues he once tried to recall. He brushed them off. He was back home, glad he made it back, he was glad about that.

Chapter Two

Bugwit Hampsterfur and the Vanishing Tree

Bugwit picked himself off the floor. He didn't even know he fell out of bed. He had a dream he was falling. But that was just a dream he thought to himself. Falling out of a tree. When he opened his eyes, the dead cold floorboard greeted himself to a good morning. Jay was downstairs, he could hear her yell his name.

"Bugwit! Get out of bed! Breakfast is ready." He felt a hangover. Too much mead the night before. And he could hear that rooster crow sometime in the middle of the night. Damn that rooster, he thought to himself. Then it hit him. The tree. Falling from a tree, landing somewhere. Seeing lights. A place, or a land he had gone. He had thought.

"Bugwit!"

King Bugwit Hampsterfur, King of England, King of places around the hills and folly amongst the town folks. He picked himself off the ground. "Damn this headache, ouch." The flooring was hard, and his hands hurt. He didn't feel the pain, until seconds later. But he now could feel it through his body, and it hurt.

Bugwit put on some clothes. Looked at himself in the mirror. Good enough, he thought, and then proceeded to walk himself down the stairs, passed the two mutts in the living room, and into the kitchen.

"There you are."

"Had the strangest dream. I dreamt of a tree, that I was falling from a tree."

"Good morning, oh really. It was no dream."

"No, I had a dream. I went somewhere, and there was this man in a flying machine, like a buggy. And then I came home."

"It was no dream sweetheart, you were gone for a while, maybe the part about the buggy. Maybe that was a dream."

"What do you mean? It was no dream?" Bugwit scratches his head, reaches for the bread, and grabs a flask of orange juice. "I was somewhere, I can feel it now. God, how much did I drink last night?"

"You drank a horse's share, and then some. Honestly, I don't know what got into you. You came home ranting about a tree, and a place where you went. And a man that took you for ride in a flying buggy."

"I said those things?"

"Yes, you said those things." His wife, Jay starts pouring them both coffee from the kettle. "Listen, you take it easy today. You had a rough night, and I know they come and they go. But you're home now, and safe. Away from the woods and the tricks that it reeks havoc on the defenseless brain."

"You must be right, Loueez, you usually are. I am hungry. That coffee smells so good too."

Bugwit takes in a breath. He looks outside the kitchen window, into the garden. The sun is beaming through the small narrow gate, opening the threshold of the aperture, creating a slight picture obscurer on the back side of his shadow.

Jay leans over and kisses his forehead, handing him a cup of coffee. "Here you go, you had a rough night."

"I must have," but it's not that bad, things happened I tell you. I know they did. I went somewhere in my dream too, it wasn't just yesterday, or maybe it was. I don't know much today for some reason, in-particular. I need to go to Pristol. And then to Forrester Hills. I need to see Father Brighten in Pristol. He said he knew someone in Forrester Hills that believed he went somewhere in time. To a place, where there was this mass gigantic city, buildings and castles of such that reached the sky."

"Oh Honey, eat, you're starving. I can see it."

"No, he went somewhere in time. He traveled through time!" A great wind came in through the foyer. The head on cat Frank kittened up and meowed at the fainting ghosts. A door slammed behind, and in walks Squire Otto. "You said quite a lot of things last night, there Bugwit. Good morning to you, and lovely Jay."

"Good Morning Otto," Jay responds, graciously, and without reservation to his always bright and sunny charm.

"Perfect Otto! You're coming with me today! We are going on an adventure. To Pristol, and then onward to Forrester Hills. It will be a grand time!" Bugwit bites his nails, takes a gulp of coffee, wipes his dirty hands on his plastering knickers. "Today is a perfect day."

"No, today you will rest; you had your adventure!" Jay looks at her husband. "Can't believe you are saying this. Today is no day. It's supposed to pour, according to my advisor, and we have barely enough for cover. No, you aren't going any where."

"Oh yes I am." Bugwit stands sternly. "Come here Squire, yesterday...,where did I go?"

"You went to a tree, like you said, and then you were gone for a minute, then you came back and we went home." Squire is now scratching his head. "You were gone a while."

"That's right! I was gone a while. But what if I told you I was gone for a whole day, and a whole night! Would you believe my skin then? Master child? Squire Otto, I went somewhere, and my dreams were trying to tell me that. When I woke up, I know I went somewhere."

"You drank a lot of mead last night, King." Otto looks at his Master, Bugwit. "I'd hate to be the one to damn you with such thoughts, that you might have been a little wee drunker than you might even know your own kinder thoughts!"

"Oh dilly. Drink me; shrink me. Let's go. Pack your things and meet me by the wolf shed in an hour." Bugwit turns to his wife. "Any other day sweet pea, I'm yours; but today I have to see a few things." He takes a few bites from his biscuit and feels relief, full. An egg and he's happy.

Otto disagreed, but then gave in. "In an hour. It's your court yard, and the ball is no longer on my side of the net. Too bad no courtiers are in witness to your serve. Ten O Clock. See you then King."

"Don't forget an extra pair and some socks, and a good shirt to tie you over a few. The weather is damp these parts and some of the ground is a bit tilted. We have a good chance to catch up on some good sun, seeing these rays come through the window such as they are. Agreed?"

"Agreed."

An hour later, nothing but a frog jumping off a stone, into Wolf Creek. A lonely gray shed, half falling apart, half bewildered into thinking itself awake, awaited two men unexpectedly. They arose to their calling. Jay, behind thought quickly, what to do. The frog was far upstream by the time any inkling of good merit came abiding. Her wishes for a husband were dear and to her heart. He could only calm half the way down to entertain her deepest night prayers. But there were other worlds, and other places. Places in his dreams. Places he needed to figure out the maps to. Places with hidden treasures, and fairies all giggling, throwing muses around like they are afternoon sugar cubes come tea.

They gathered underneath the willow tree, west of the sinking pond. They were old friends, in a world where peasants were vulgar, and common was borderline obscene. But the food was neither plentiful nor taken for granted over the hills. A bird falls from the tree.

"Bugwit, Sir. We're here, now where." Otto says.

"There!" Bugwit points. They were way past any path taken before, nor were they near the tree yet. The path that goes to the tree is East, and they are heading West. Into the town, the Gathering of Festivals is also going on, and being no one ever sees the king much, they could easily hide. Until they come across Father Brighten. At the Church of the Holy Blessed.

They began walking. "It's lovely out today, I seem to not be able to get enough of it. It reminds me of the days Jay and I would frolic around these parts, watch geese cackle the days away. We would chase squirrels around and imitate our favorite Globe Players, dance around, make complete fools of ourselves! Those were the days Otto!"

Otto listened, as they walked. Deeper down the road, deeper into the woods. The town was not far ahead. They had plenty to think about, their lives and dreams. But that was business elsewhere, maybe.

They got to the Festival of Harvest at noon. Merry children and content happy adults danced around to flutes and melodic lyres. Hands of circled groupings lifted the sky in praise of the yearly holiday. The townsfolk gleed in delight, food was devoured at every corner. Tents of marketers and cow-lenders, milk goats, and chickens. The sun too was happy above as no clouds of rain-dust dared to bleak out the day. Otto quickly raised his spirits as he and Bugwit walked down the dirt pathway, crowds of people every-which-way.

The church was on the other end of town, and as things appeared, it didn't look as though any one would be there. They would be here, at the festival.

"Let's have a drink Squire," Bugwit exclaimed. "I don't quite feel as if we're to leave here without a pint of good hearty mead, would you not agree?"

Otto shook his head, up and down. "Agreed! Agreed!"

They both sat down at a table. Children of ten and twelve, and fifteen, or so ran rapidly between their isle, singing "Maypole Maypole!" Laughing and giggling, there wasn't a drop of silence anywhere. Noise and laughter, that was today's news.

A lady, middle aged and robust came over, "hello there fine gentleman, can I get you a pint of our today's finest?"

"Please, me lady, as you are so kind to ask. Yes! We will have two pints of your harvest best!" He looked around, Bugwit. Swatting a fly, thinking of Jay, how much she would love this place. The sky was glorious blue above. The dancing couldn't move any much more in synch with the beautiful sway of the lock lilies. "Come on let's dance!" Bugwit belted aloud to his pal, "come on!"

"No Sire, I want to drink me a pound!"

"You're right, me too!" they both laughed.

The girl with the braids came back with their pints. They both gleefully accepted them, as she lay them down on the table.

"Good thank you Mad'm." Bugwit complimented.

"Yes, thank you kindly," says Otto.

They both drank strawberry ale, masqueraded under a fine Autumn's afternoon. It was time to breathe, take in the merry excitement of the town's people. Little younglings were cascading

208

through unmerited territory! It was a day to feast upon what they both do not see very often. Madness was not an ingredient in today's soup! It wasn't even considered. Happiness wrote its heart on every balloon, on every swollen face, blistering over with sheer joy. Indeed one might mistake joy for madness and madness for joy. They often blare a fine line, blinding eyes could see better. But they don't.

The sky above looked down for a second, as Bugwit caught a quick notice of fast change. They both were sipping their ale on a long narrow table, holding about fifty jolly town's keep. But there was something different all of a sudden. A shadow. Down at the far end of the table making its way up, towards Bugwit and Otto.

Clouds now engulfed the sky, quickly moving their way across the straw laced land. People dancing began to slow. People drinking began to think. Even Otto drew a face. "What is it?" He said to Bugwit.

"I don't know, something."

"I think we should move on," Otto muttered.

Then a man, out of nowhere, wearing a small tweed bowler, and holding a wooden cane, tapped Otto on the shoulder. Bugwit didn't even see him coming.

"Mind if I sit down here, chap?" The man said. He didn't even wait for an answer as he laid himself next to Otto. "You two, on a ways-ward something interesting?" The man took off his hat, breathed in a heavy sigh, and then looked at Bugwit. "I know you. I know who you are. The two of you aren't fooling anyone."

"What do you mean, wise man?" Bugwit asked.

"Well, to begin. You're the King. And you, are his servant. Actually, we all saw you coming our way, and it made us happy. So we danced. We even held a party in your name, but you wouldn't know that."

"Well, now. I wouldn't have a guess. I did think we were just strangers in a crowd, actually." The King spoke. "You most are a peculiar fellow. What is it your name Sir?" Bugwit drank his ale, speeding it down, wiping his lips with his old aged hand.

"I'm to point you to a tree," that's all.

"A tree. Well I've been thinking of a tree all day yesterday, and today, well the Sun brought me here. I'm supposed to be looking for a fellow."

Otto looked at Bugwit, thinking of who this man was. But it didn't matter. He kind of felt something off. But something he couldn't do a thing about. "What about a tree?" Otto says.

"Well first I want you to visit a house, there's a man there inside. He'll tell you about the tree, and where it is. I'll just point you in the right direction. Bugwit didn't know much what was going on. The man put his hat back on, and by the time he did that, Bugwit knew what they had coming for them. The clouds grew darker, and the people mysteriously began to disappear like a wicked side show vanishing act. There were only a few staggering along, dancing off kilter with the a-tonal lute. The folks at the table were no longer laughing, or jolly. One of them there was pulling out a tooth, while a woman had her baby girl by the hair telling her to hurry up, "places to be" she would say to herself. But then that was it. Just the two of them, and the man, who was now about to face bow and bid his way. "Well, then" he would say. "The house be that way, up there over that hill. Just follow the path. The man up there is Brighten. You can talk to him."

"Father Brighten," Bugwit tried to agree with the man.

"Yes, he used to be the priest of the Holy Orders, but now has retired into his home. He'll be there for you."

"How did you know I was looking for him."

"He sensed it, like you could sense the Autumn air coming its way first day of October. Now I've said too much already. You best be on your way. As you can see the party has ended, and now we bare you fair well on your journey. It should not take you long. Not long at all."

The man picked himself up and walked towards the pond. They both stared at him go, down the dirt road. A happy little puppy came jumping out of the high grass and joined. Bugwit could almost hear him.

"Come on, let's heed the mans vision. We are far from the tree, I thought it was the other side of the mountain, since that was the way we walked over just days ago. But I don't know. Maybe there is a different tree."

"What's up with trees?"

"I don't know." Bugwit responds to his friend. "But it's all a bit strange, you think. Come on. This place is creeping me out. Let's go."

They picked themselves up and left the vacant fairgrounds, and proceeded to walk up the dirt path where the man had pointed to. There was no house ahead. And no man. Brighten was still in his church back at Forrester Hills, but the two didn't know that. They didn't know much at all at this point.

The road was thick with bristles and overhanging dogwoods. All kinds of animals scurried in the woods that lay left and right of the path. They walked, and the longer they walked, the less they would say.

"Is the house near?" Otto asked.

"It must be, or we lay a trap for our own suspicions. Ah alas, my friend, I'm not sure there is even a house ahead. The birds keep flying south, and we are in the direction of those fearful inklings. We must keep walking. There must be something ahead or the man had no purpose back there."

"You are right, Sire." Otto shook his head. Thought for a questioning second, and then let it go. "What if it were a trap? What then Your Majesty?"

Bugwit Hampsterfur, quick in the past to fall for gullible insinuations of his character, thought there for a minute. And then proceeded to open his mouth. "No, it's not a trap. It's the tree. He couldn't help but point to the tree.

There before them, about a hundred yards or so just to the right of the path stood tall above the others. In a clearing up ahead. It was the tree. The man in the hat, Bugwit began to think of. He could not lie about the tree.

"There it is Your Majesty."

"Maybe it will be like the other tree. Maybe there is a door there in it, like the other one." They walked a little more, just a little it took. The mud cast ground sat aching for their tired feet. But they had come a distance, like the man did say. The tree was tall and stood there many years, it had appeared. When they got to it, they stood beneath it, looking up at it. They touched it like a baby's first born day into the world. They felt it like feeling for secret door knobs in a secret library. Nothing, no door. No lapse into time. No future world.

"What now?" Otto asked his King.

"I don't know. Sit beside it. Rest for a second or so." The King sat down, there below the branches hung over. Leaves scattered every which way on the crusted dirt. "I need to think."

"Me too." Otto put his hands on the ground and lowered himself, leaning his frail back to the tree. "Me too." They both drifted there on the ground, and fell asleep.

When they woke up, a rooster was crowing. They were both flat on their backs. Mystified. They reached to get up, maybe put there hands on the tree to help them to their feet, but something was wrong. There wasn't a tree there. It too had vanished into the mist. It too had something to leave them bewildered and confused. The tree was gone.

A woman, dressed in a white plain gown walked up to them. At first, Bugwit thought it was a ghost, then he thought it was Jay, but then got a better look at the figure. She was someone neither of them had seen before.

She looked at the two of them. "You took my tree. Where's my tree?" She screamed, loud. Their ears pierced. Their eyes opened. Glass broke. "Not today, who took my tree!" The lady flailed her arms, grabbed the wind by the throat and shook shivers down Bugwit and Otto.

"We didn't take your tree lady!" Otto yelled back.

"No Ma'am," said Bugwit. "We were just lying down, here for a quick nap. It was gone when we woke up. I tell you the truth, good lady."

"Hmm," said the lady. "You look honest." She calmed down. "Someone took it. Did anyone come by? No, you wouldn't know that. You were asleep. Oh Lord, who could have done this?" Her hands punched the air in anger. Her feet to have fallen way to the gravity of her legs, which were turning and twisting every which way. Her walking away was the only thing that began to make sense to Otto and

Bugwit. She laughed and cried simultaneously, her voice could be heard the further she was. She was gone before she ever got there.

"What a strange one," Bugwit responds, breaking the ever brief silence. "What the devil ever got into her?"

"I'm not sure Sire, but she was strange indeed. You've got that right for a whisper in a library. Scared the bejeebees out of me!"

"Well, I'm glad she's gone. We can get on with the day. Maybe say we've been had and head back where we came from. We never got to Brighten, nor did we even come close to Forrester Hills. I believe young Squire we may as well be lost, here in the hills of Dumphfry."

"Have you noticed something?" Bugwit asks.

Otto finds a branch, twitches it aside, "what's that Sire?"

"The tree, the other tree. Why didn't I go to that tree to begin with. I don't know now. It doesn't make sense. But now this tree has gone, and now we're left with two missing trees."

"You don't make sense. You kind of do, but you don't. I don't know. Maybe we should head back to the other tree." Otto scratches his head.

"I think we may want to. But from here, I'm not sure how to get there. Maybe we should go to Father Brighten first. If we're witnessing disappearing trees and ladies, maybe he might know a thing about that."

"Very well called Sire. I'm with you, lead the way." Otto points to a path that is barely there.

They walked for hours. Birds clawed the sky. Long gone bones of animal passersby shrieked in silent unison. They walked for more, and lost they were, sometimes thinking they knew just where they were, but they didn't know. The sun was beginning to go down. There was still some daylight left on the sun dial back at Homingworth Park, but they weren't there. They were somewhere else. And the blankets of wonder and whereabouts lay the advice of Father Brighten; well, neither of them could tell, any more than they could find their way home.

They walked more. Puzzled by the fact they haven't seen a soul on their walk back. But it was just when the sun was setting faster than they wanted, they saw someone or something coming their way. It was a boy. He had blond hair and was on something, like a mechanical horse. Coming closer he was, as the two seemed a bit prepared at this point for anything. The boy came their way fast and then a skid into the dirt as he and his mechanical machine came to a halt.

"Hey you two lost?" the boy said.

"Yes, how could you tell, and what is that you are on. Something with wheels I've never seen before." Bugwit wakes himself up, looks strong at the boy.

"It's my bike, you've never seen a bike? It's a bicycle. I got it for Christmas last year."

Otto scratches his head, notices the same color of hair on the boys head as that on his own. "A bicycle. I never seen one. Where you from boy?"

"I'm from Maywood. But we moved since my Daddy joined the Marines. You're in the Barrens in case you don't know. You must be lost looking the way you do." The boy has almost too much confidence, kicking his bike with the back of his burnt out Converse sneaker.

"I'm a king. King of England. I've been a King a while now."

"Well, that won't do you much good, I know a lot of people who say they're kings, they hang out with my Daddy at the soup kitchen, where we get our food."

"Where are we then?" Otto talks.

"New Jersey."

"New Jersey, like Jersey. Oh that's not far from us Sire." Otto looks happy, as if he'd found his home.

"Why do I get the sense that it is," said Bugwit. "Why do I get the sense it is."

"Well good luck fellows, like I said, you two looked like you could use some good food. It's about a half mile that way." The boy points back from which he came. "Just stay on this path. You'll run into a church. But I must be going. My Dad doesn't want me to talk to strangers much, but you two looked as though you might need some help."

"Thanks chap. Or is it Shwinn, is that your name? Shwinn?"

"No it's Simon actually. That's just the name of the bike. All the kids at school have Shwinns, so I wanted one too."

"We appreciate it. What year is it, any chance you know kid?"

"Ha ha. That's a good one! They ask everyone that all the time at the soup kitchen. I got to get going. It's getting dark, and my mom hates it when I ride my bike out at night. Good luck!" The kid rides off.

"I don't know Sire, I think we're supposed to be where we're not, or we're not where we think we are." Otto shook his head.

"I think you're right, Squire. Otto, listen, a noise. I know that noise. I heard it a few days ago when I was where I said I was." The king perked his ears, opened them up like a clam, or a flower screaming for bees. "Listen, that sound is from that buggy I was in. It's getting closer." Bugwit slapped Otto on the arm, "listen, listen, it's coming closer."

"I hear it too. What is it? It sounds like crashing metal, or thunder."

Something was coming their way. They could see it now, it was progressively moving faster, as fast as a horse. It too large wheels and a big iron casing. A light was coming from the top of it. Glass was all around the front. They could see a man inside. They froze, fear struck them as they thought it might run them over. It didn't; it came to a complete stop, like the boy on the bicycle.

A large man, wearing a strange hat, a shield cascading the front of it; as well as the same one appearing on the man's coat.

"You gentleman lost? I can get you back to town, if you're lost. What the hell you doing out this way. This is private property." The man takes a breath, looks at the two of them. "You men have I.D.?"

"I.D.?" Otto opens up first. Bugwit repeats him.

"Yeah, identification? Don't bust me now boys. Been drinking?"

"Not sure what you mean" said Bugwit. "Yes, at the festival."

"Well, you both look harmless enough. Let me take you back into town. Looks like you both might need a cleaning up. Drop you off at Church of the Holy Mary."

Bugwit and Otto didn't know what to do. "Get in that thing?" Otto asks, laughs, then a bit apprehensive. "No, I think we'll just keep to walking, since we didn't do anything wrong, Sir." Otto says to the man. His eyes are on the weapon around his waist. He's from the future; they're in the future. First the boy, then this future machine that has wheels.

"No, really. You have a little walk ahead of you. The boy told me he saw you out here. So I ran out here to check you two out. Small town. Kids talk in soda-shops."

"Well thanks kind Sir, it really is ok. We'll just walk. We know where we are anyways. We come out here to clear our minds. We were heading to the kitchen any hows'."

"Well, ok, if you insist. I'll let this all go back to the pond, as they say. You have a good afternoon. And stay out of these parts. It's no man's land. In town, you get yourself some food. There at the church." The cop didn't believe their story, but he insisted leaving them be as they were. Let them walk their way into town. Maybe get a better look at them that way. "Well, just stay on this here old path a mile or so and you'll see us. Do you a favor and take care of yourselves. Have a good day."

Bugwit and Otto looked at each other and then responded to the man. "Have a good day" And then they walked some more.

When they felt they had enough, they came to a road, paved of rock. It again had yellow lines like the one Bugwit saw. It looked empty and deserted, at least for a while in its own time and land. But there was a hut, one made of a kind of glass and metal chairs inside. Benches like in the Meadhall, back at the castle. They decided to take a break and sit down. They faded their eyes into the wishing wild weed stalks flowing brisk in the autumn air. Then they heard the sound again. This time it was much louder, and with much more force. Another buggy, Bugwit thought. But it was larger in size, this one, much larger, it could fit all his guards inside he thought, as it came up and closer to where they were sitting.

"What is it?" Otto, it's bigger then that man's machine.

"I know. I's a floating ship."

It came up to them in hurry, and with such loud piercing sounds, squelching its roar and breath as it came to a complete stop, right next to the both of them. A door opened. A woman behind a large wheel sat in her chair.

"Getting in?" she asked.

"Where are you going?"

"This bus goes up north, first stop Paterson. Take us an hour and half or so, but it's express."

Otto and Bugwit looked at each other. They shook their frazzled heads in agreement. "Yeah, we're getting in."

They got on the bus. They took a seat as two others were in their own.

Like a moving church, Otto thought.

They rode it and onto a bigger road. Their eyes opened wide.

They knew they were somewhere else when they reached town an hour and a half later. They were in something only the great minds of Straphos and Kilton talked about. Mind games from the land of Elsra. It was a devilish sight. Buggies were everywhere, going this way and that way, roaring with ground moving sound. Frightened, but quickly overcome. They saw others, in different kinds of clothing. Something Straphos and Brighten would only dream about. Unless they knew something, thought Bugwit.

They never talked about it at Church, nor in the cellars. The pints of mead would only bring existential thoughts of life and the hereafter. But they didn't dream of places like this. The bus came to a stop. The two in the back got off the bus, so Bugwit and Otto followed. Their legs hurt a little from sitting so long. But the blue sky opened up when they came outside of the machine. And a breath of fresh air followed.

"Where are we?" Otto opened a little.

"A big city." Bugwit walked up to someone on a bench. "Where are we. What is this place called?" Bugwit asks the man, holding a very large, yet very thin book.

"You're in Paterson."

"Where's Paterson? Paterson, Jersey England?"

"No," said the man. Looking tired, holding a bottle of what looked to be some good mead, but different. "No, silly. Jeez. That's funny mister. And so are your clothes. Paterson, New Jersey. This isn't Canada. If you think you walked all that way."

Otto looked at Bugwit. Then at the man, "what country is it here. We're from somewhere else."

"United States silly. My you boys got the worm worse than I do. I hate to see what it does to people. I always said once the worm gets in, there's no way getting that worm out. You know what I mean, mister?" The man took a swig of his bottle.

Bugwit got nervous, felt a need to defend himself, of the sudden fear and paranoia. "Well of course we heard of The United States, and Paterson. We're just testing your wits there mate. No really, we were looking for a place." Bugwit pushes Otto to the side, and whispers in his ear. "Listen, here old man. Is there a Church here. We're supposed to be going to a church. Holy Mary. Do you know where it is?"

The man looked at them both with big beady eyes, and said. "Ha! Of course I know where that is. But you have to give me something, like food or money, and I'll tell you."

They both felt haggled, but just a little.

"I'll tell you," said the man.

Bugwit reached into his pocket, knowing the man looked poor and degenerate. "Heres a five pound gold piece. Now tell me."

"My fools gold, ha. No way." The man jerked his neck at the sky and spit on the ground.

"It's real gold" said Bugwit.

"Real gold? Is it now. Hmm, odd fellow like yourself, well I may just believe you. Let me have it here then." He took the piece and looked at it, close. "Hmm real gold it looks like. You're the fool for giving it to me mister, but I'll take it," said the man. "Eight blocks down and make a left, that's Mulberry Street. Then it's on your right just half a block in."

"That's it?" Otto said.

"That's it. What else you want? said the man.

"Come Otto. Let's have a look." Bugwit pulls his arm and begins moving them both in the direction the man had given. "I think we gave the man too much. We need to be careful about our currency. Come on."

They walked as hundreds, thousands of people posed everywhere, beneath these large monuments of houses on top of houses, and buildings of castles, none had ever scene.

"Where are we Sire?" Otto seemed scared, excited.

"Paterson, New Jersey, my friend."

Chapter Three

Mystery at Hobart Manor

"Come on Otto. Let's find us some good mead around here. The day was dismal and got dark real sudden. By the looks of everyone on the street, they weren't in their home town, nor country. People in bright color uniforms, holding those future weapons appeared to be on every street corner. It was an ominous omen. Mead was their escape back, temporary; but still an escape.

They shifted aimlessly through open markets of thin books on the floor and rock jewelry that didn't look real, and glass windows, with fake people standing in them wearing odd clothing. It was a strange place, thought Bugwit. "There has got to be some good mead, my friend. We just have to hunt it down. We saw that man back there drinking something."

They walked a few blocks, passing all sorts of illusions made real, in a world that looked so busy, busier than London. They stopped at the corner, to take a breath. A light was there; and when it turned green, they saw a little man inside a box, glowing. It were as if he were walking. So they walked in the direction everyone was walking, thinking it was the right thing to do.

"There Sire, look. That market place of bottles, there in the window. All those signs glowing too." The night was coming in. Choking on Otto's words. "Maybe there is some mead in there."

They were both trying to read the signs. They appeared to be in English, most of them, but they were slightly off in their description to what they were both used to reading.

"This one, here. Hooligans. It looks like they'd be having food. Smells good. Don't you think Otto?"

"It does smell good. Charcoaled meat. Look too, and a pint sign of ale. Let's go in."

Otto pulls open the door. Holds it for his King. They both enter to the sound of music and laughter. And lots of people talking.

"This looks like, and smells like they'd serve good mead and food." Otto looks at his King. "What do you think Sire?"

"I think you are mighty correct in your assumption." Bugwit walks to the center of the room, a large square table of sorts with chairs assembled the gathering into what looked to be a fine group of people, sitting there, drinking.

Bugwit approached the bar, he asked the man behind it where he could get some mead, or ale. "Here said to the man. Guinness good for you?"

"Yes, make that two," said Bugwit, and put a gold coin on the table.

"Oh we don't take gold here, my that is some coin. Real gold is it?"

"Yes, I'm from overseas, and it's our currency there."

"Well, I'll tell you what," said the bartender. "You give me this coin here and I'll give you the next couple rounds."

"That's what we were presuming," said Bugwit."

The bartender took the coin, and put it in his pocket. He then proceeded to walk over to the tap, and pour the men some beer. "These old folks don't know what they got anymore." He uttered beneath his breath. "Gotta be worth hundreds." He finished up the tap and walks back over to Bugwit and Otto, sitting at the bar. "You two dressed up for the Halloween Parade?"

"Halloween Parade, oh yeah. I guess we are," says Bugwit.

"Well it passed through here this mornin, you know that right?" the man says. "But got to give it to you, those are some outfits." He takes the pretzel holder from the bar and refills it; puts it back down. "Here you go, incase you're a little hungry. Eat some pretzels."

Otto laughs, "what a strange word, pretzel." He bumps his shoulder into Bugwit. "I like this place." Otto then lifts up his pint to his King. "To you Sire! To us finding the New World!"

"Thank you Otto, but I'm not sure we're out of the woods just yet." He picks up a napkin, wipes his mouth of the foamy beer. "I think by looking around, things may have changed a little too much, and we may be in need of trying to find our way home sooner. We need to find a portal here, something to take us back."

"Mead Keeper!"

The bartender turns, and faces the two.

"Where is there a forum, where the educated go and meet, and talk of things like stars and constellations, books and wisdom, and things that are invented. Is there a place like that here?" Bugwit shrinks, though his seat somewhat won't allow it.

"Oh boy, you two sure ain't from around here are you? The University of course. Let me guess, you both crawled in a cave a hundred years ago and just decided to come out now. Either that or the Dead tour is doing fairly well. Get those rug-rats in here from time to time. William Paterson University, there on the hill. Bill on the Hill we call it. That's the local school here, but there are plenty more. What is it you're looking for?"

"Oh just stuff, curious about these parts. You're right. we're from England, you know. It's different there." Bugwit takes a strong slugging swig of his ale. "Ah! This is very good mead, indeed, Keeper. Round us up two more."

"Well I could have guessed you two were from England just listening to you. That's a no brainer, but you must be tucked in their somewhere deep. Those accents sure weren't tough on the ears." The bartender didn't know what to say, so he went quickly to the tap. Something wasn't right about those two, he thought to himself. The glasses filled with heavy Guinness beer and was about to put the lucky shamrock on top, but thought that was Scottish luck, not English luck, so he left the froth nice and clean.

"Here you go," he said. "On the house!"

"Well, thank you. Said Bugwit, feeling a buzz in his head roll around marbles, waking up his senses. He looked around the room. Everyone inside seemed to be normal except for a few standing out, as if they were going to a masquerade. "What day is it, a special holiday?" Bugwit leans over to Otto. "It must be right? Halloween the man said."

"I don't think people dress up like that every day. Like the festival we were at before. I don't know Otto. Sure doesn't feel right," Bugwit said to Otto.

Otto is staring into his glass. "Halloween. Sounds fun. This mead sure is good, say Sire. Maybe we should head on the gentleman's advice and go to the University."

Bugwit sits there, thinks. The beer is making him think. He's thinking of Jay back at the castle, he's wondering how he's going to return. What a frivolous mess he's gotten himself into again; this time he's also agreeing with his wife thinking he'd been better off sleeping it off today. Instead of going galavanting through the hills and what lies within them.

"Halloween. Must be like our Maypole. All the kids and women all dressed up." Bugwit looks to Otto. "We should find this meeting place. This university." Bugwit gulps his mead. "Thirsty boy! I'm thirsty as a horse after a full day carrying!"

"Sire, if the University is named after the town, wouldn't it be close?"

"I assume it would be Otto. We could probably walk. I don't like those buggies out there, they make noise. And that man on the big bus gave us such a problem when we tried to give him a gold piece."

"True, Sire," Otto agreed. "We should walk. We're better cover that way. No one will spot us."

"Hey Sir, Mead Keep, point us in the direction of the University you spoke of. We'd like to go over to it, possibly see an acquaintance of ours."

"Sure thing. Take the 28. It will take you right there."

"What's the 28?" asks Otto.

"That's the bus you'll want to take," the bartender laughed. "Boy you two are funny."

"Well, we'd like to walk if that's OK with you." Bugwit gives the man another gold piece.

"Well then, no you keep that. I can't take any more from you. It's that way. The man points. "Go out the door and just follow that road to the right. It will go for a mile and then up hill for a quarter mile. Well, you might not understand miles since you're from England, but if you take a right, and walk for a half hour you'll see signs for William Paterson University. It will be on your right." The barkeep couldn't take much more, but glad he could help.

"Thank you kind Sir." Otto says.

Bugwit gulps the rest of his mead. "Come on, put on your coat. Let's go for a walk. This Halloween he speaks of, whether we are in a strange land with strange folks, or this day is some freak holiday we portal'd ourselves into."

"I think you're right Sire. Halloween is a weird and odd name for a holiday. The future or did we come to another planet?"

"No, I think we're in the future my young lad. How to get back is our quest." Bugwit leads Otto and holds the door for him as they enter back outside, into the crisp air. The fall time surrounds them with autumn colors and feelings that excite, rather than depress. Their mead had sunken in, and they both could feel a strong buzz from the fermented yeast, and barley. "Ah! What a lovely day!"

"Absolutely is my King!" Otto smiles. Passersby walk aimlessly around them, tens of them, twenty or more. They were everywhere. And younglings in costume looked odd yet familiar.

They took a right and walked. About a half mile into it, they came to an odd brick building. It had an old name stenciled in paint, peeling off the walls. There was an ally way. They both looked down it, it was dark and long. Rusty lonely pales cascaded the avenue of lifeless space. They both knew they had such things in their land, but none as dark, and fearful. They had their own ghosts, and ghouls, frightening things that dared them not to open their mouths, nor they'd come for you. They knew these places, and this ally spoke of it. They both stopped, for a second, in its calling. They could hear someone back there, at the end of the dark hallway. Bugwit saw her first, as it came forward. It looked like the woman from before, only more of a mist and a voice. "You took my tree." They could both hear her. Whisper, into the darkness and down the ally way to their ears.

"Come on Otto, lets go. Enough of her," said Bugwit. And they passed, down the brick building. The sun beamed for a second on the dry white paint, contrasting the red bricks with scorching innuendo, and foreboding omens. At least for the now they were past it. And down the road. Trees leaned over, a path gave them a place to walk. It was concrete layered by square brick patterns. They came to the place that the man told them they would, as it began to walk itself uphill.

The junction was different. There were lights on both sides of the road, as they towered thirty feet into the sky, giving them a sense of safety, a feeling of relief. Every so minute or so a roaring buggy would pass them with passengers inside. They could see too that some of them would be laughing and tossing about in their costumes. Those buggies too would go up the hill.

"We must be getting close," said Otto. "And it looks like everyone around here is having a good time. Maybe it's still the same day as when we were at the festival, or the same place."

"Maybe."

They walked, up a tired hill, but constantly hearing sounds of festivity and delight. They were in the spirits of hearing something good to them, since craving their home took space on their thinking. They needed to find this University; or better, the people pertaining substance to it.

They came to a large sign, again spraying the letters of the name William Paterson on it. They walked in, as a walkway was granted, they assumed to any one who came there. It led down and into a pit. The buildings were of nothing they had ever seen before. It was just dusk, and people were scattering around, some in costume, some not. Bugwit and Otto didn't care much because by now, they assumed they were fitting in with the holiday. Rather beginners luck, or planned that way; they assumed the first.

They came to a building at the end of the walk, all the other buildings were on each side of them. It said Student Center on it, so the two of them walked in. Students and workers automatically looked at them, the two could feel it. So they walked back out and faced the wind.

"That's not the place. We need a library. Let's look for a Library." They walked around, and after ten minutes actually found luck. They stood in front of a large glass building. People were going inside, holding things on their backs. Large pockets. Bugwit and Otto decided to go in. As they did, they left nothing to chance. There was no plan B. They were just looking for answers.

Bugwit walked up to the man behind a large wooden table, a counter top. It had a modern device on it, a box that flashed green and white letters.

"Can I help you?" the man said.

Bugwit knew he didn't have much time, as if his disguise would seep through his thin facade. "Ah yes. We are here looking for books on the supernatural, and great philosophers dealing with the supernatural." Bugwit stepped back, as if he thought he said too much.

"Ah, sure, that's fine, I can point you to where that would be. Let's see, upstairs there is a section in the back. Let me show you." The man got out from behind the desk, walked them up the stairs. "It's slow today, I can show you." He opened up another door leading to another hall of books. Books were everywhere.

Bugwit had never seen so many books.

"Here," said the man. "Here. Here look, all the supernatural materials are in this isle. Help yourself, enjoy and I'll be back downstairs if you need me."

Bugwit immediately took his eyes off the man and grazed the shelf, peering into each and every title that he could see; but when he turned to thank the man, the man was gone. Otto, standing there just shook his hands as if he didn't see the man leave either. Interesting, Bugwit thought, and went back investigating the books. He pounded through. Stars and Beyond, Metamorphosis, Chariots of the Gods, Ghosts of New England. Witches and Wtichcraft. Nothing he saw caught his attention. He continued. Strange Lands, Dimensions Not Seen, Nothing caught his eye. Then it hit him. Something small, tucked below. As if a beam of light came across the room and pointed at the book itself.

"Here is something. I found something. The Halloween Tree, by Ray Bradbury. Maybe this will say something." Bugwit took the book. Looked at Otto as if he'd found stolen treasure. "This will tell us." He took a seat at the table, and began to read. It looked different than his formal studies at reading the English Language, but he could spot a few words he understood. "There must be something here," he continued. His thumbs and fingers gripped the pages as his eyes heavily laid themselves on the paper. A tree, he thought, that tree.

226

"Otto looked at Bugwit," I hear music, and it's not coming from this building. "I hear it outside."

"Otto, this book is peculiar and filled with such insane and delightful pictures, and the story looks profound. They must have found that tree. Maybe we should go back to the Barrens." Bugwit thought, maybe it was too far away, and they got lucky landing where they did.

"Music, Sire!" Let's go outside and follow the music. It sounds very different. I hear drums and pounding sounds."

Bugwit could hear it too. They followed the sound, Bugwit put the book down by the time they reached the door, on a table there by the door's side wall.

They pushed the front door to the Library open, as they greeted themselves once again to the night. There were lanterns everywhere, kids all gathered with adults around little tables and chairs. The path that led to the Student Center was filled with people walking towards it. Something was going on down there, so they followed their instincts, and matched step with the others.

When they got to the bottom of the hill, people were everywhere, in costume it seemed. "A party, another festival Sire," Otto exclaimed with sheer excitement.

"It does appear that way," Bugwit agreed. "And where there is a festival there is mead. I can smell it on them Otto, I can smell it on them!"

They both laughed. Bugwit went up to a youngster, dressed like someone from his time, his place, but he was alone and holding a red cup, made of a funny looking substance. "Where do I get me a cup to fill my mead, my friend?" Bugwit asked.

"Over there, at that table." The young man points to a table. A few people are standing by it, and behind it in chairs. They all seem so young. But it's not like they ever saw young people before. There were attending adults with them, so they tried to mimic their personas the best they could, to fit in and blend. It seemed to be working.

The two of them, Otto and Bugwit walked up to the table. Two really friendly women were behind it, one was holding cups, and the other was holding a tin silver looking box. Would you like a cup

Professor? They are five dollars each, but the Staff drinks for free. Would you like two?"

Bugwit laughed, they think he is a Professor at the University. He agreed with their assumptions and took the cups from the women, as they generously gave them from across the table. "Thank you, as the both of you look very lovely in your costumes." One was dressed as a Meadmaid with her pony tails hanging down. The other was a ghostly figure, all white in her face, with her teeth hanging out of her mouth. It was odd to see such a costume, thought Bugwit, but he was not stranger to the darker side of the magic world; that he could assure himself.

As he was telling himself to be warned of things he could not see, but suggested in his mind; as things weren't as they seemed. This day was like no other Bugwit thought, but delighted in the merry of what he was witnessing. There was a sense of peace he could not explain. The music was coming from the left side of the field through two boxes propelled on stilts six feet off the ground. A man dressed like a ghoul was also behind another small table. It looked as though he was operating the system which was running the music. His head was bobbing with the beat.

"Are you a friend of Dr. Dave's?" The woman asked Bugwit.

"I am." Bugwit said. He smiled then walked away, towards the boxes producing the music. "Strange world, we live in. Like when I dream, only I am here now." He looked at the mead barrel, and walked over to it. There was a young man there.

"Here, let me fill that for you Professor." Again. "Happy Halloween!" he said and began to fill his cup. "Nice night, isn't it?" The boy looked at Bugwit. "You're a friend of Dr. Dave's; aren't you?" Again, Dr. Dave. Who is this Dr. Dave? Bugwit thought to himself that he must find out.

"Yes, as a matter of fact I am. Have you seen him, I am looking for him." Bugwit sounded as if he knew him, though he knew better than to make his lie less obvious. I was with him, and now he must have drifted away into the crowd, I assume."

The boy laughed and gave Bugwit his cup. Otto wasn't far behind, rushing ahead he handed the boy his cup, and assumed he would fill it as well. The boy did. "Those are some costumes you and the Professor have," he said to Otto.

"Thank you," Otto said; and took the cup of filled mead from the boy. "This is some kind of new music?" Otto asked.

"Well, yeah, I guess. Happy Halloween!" said the boy. "You don't like it?"

"Yeah, it's OK, where...," Otto began to talk about where he was from, but refrained." I mean, in my home, we listen to it all the time." He then took a nervous swig of beer, and with one last utter, "well, I'll best be finding my friend. Thank you for the mead, Sir kind Sir."

"Oh you're welcome. Enjoy it!" the young man said. And then went back to just sitting there on his stool, waiting for the next person to have his cup filled.

Otto walked over and caught up to Bugwit. The music was blaring, but somehow Bugwit was enjoying it. So was Otto. Bugwit kept thinking about how that much amplification was coming out of just two small boxes. He could see there was a string, a thick shiny orange rope on the ground leading to the Student Center. It must have something to do with that rope, Bugwit thought.

"It's getting late," Bugwit said to Otto. "I wonder what Jay must be thinking about all of this. We must find our portal back." He takes a breath, thinks. "That tree, and that book. But something told me that the book might be made up. I don't know, Squire."

Otto shook his head. "I love it here. Maybe it's a trap. Or maybe we should look for the tree again."

"This Dr. Dave," I wonder. Maybe we should talk to him. Maybe he knows how to get out of here."

It was then, Bugwit caught a shadow nearing his personal space. The same feeling he got back in the ally way. He could see someone or something just fifty feet away or so, although his eyes weren't as good as they used to be, he could feel it. It was a man, and he was wearing a hat, a strange topped off hat. The man appeared, but as soon as he was there, in front of Bugwit; he was gone. A small group of younglings gathered in his space. Music that sounded like angels singing to a rhythm snare left Bugwit shaken for a second. But as much as he was shaken, he quickly gathered his composure, taking a long gulp of his beer. "How do we get back. How do we?" He thought on that. Drank some more of his mead, leaving chills down his arms and body.

"Come on, let's go and find Dr. Dave. He must be here somewhere." Bugwit looked and sounded as though there was a good chance they wouldn't run into him. But maybe saying it would increase their odds. That was always the first rule of magic. You have to say the words in order for the trick to reveal itself. "Come on, let's go into the Student Center."

They both walked away from the speakers, and through a plethora of costume'd younglings, laughing in their mead suds. They came to the huge glass doors and opened them. A sense of refreshing relief came upon them, as the spooky atmosphere of the outside seemed to immediately vanish. Instead, the inside was like a palace from Egypt or Rome. Marble floors and high ceilings decorated their minds in hope that maybe they had landed here, at the University for a reason.

There was a desk, and a person dressed up like another ghostly figure behind it. Bugwit walked up to it.

"How can I help you?" The young woman behind the desk asked.

"We're looking for Dr. Dave. Have you seen him?"

"Well, he would be up in the English Department. You might want to check him there. Do you know where it is?" she asked.

Bugwit thought. "No I'm visiting, and I'm not sure. You can you guide me."

"Well," she said. "If you go out of here and up that walk in which you came it's the building adjacent to the Library. It's in the Atrium. He's in 203 I believe. I used to have him for Romantic Literature. It's funny that you ask."

"Great!" Bugwit exclaimed. "The Atrium. I shall find such a place if such a place exists!" he laughs, as if she would get his joke. She got it halfheartedly and smiled back at him.

"Thank you so much," Otto chimed in. They walked back over into the center of the room, where to the left was a food hall, and a staircase leading downstairs. They could hear a piano playing from the staircase.

230

"Listen, again. Music. It sounds like a piano forte, Sire."

"It does," agreed Bugwit. "Let's check it out."

They walked towards the staircase, it was long and quite a ways down. The University was set on a hill, as they found out walking up it on their way. Little hills set themselves inside, on the grounds, and even in the buildings themselves. Bugwit and Otto could not keep themselves from following the music. It was coming from the bottom of the staircase. They were also surprised that not many party goers were inside, as opposed to outside. It would make sense, Bugwit thought to himself. "Come on," he said, and tugged Otto's sleeve.

They walked down what seemed like a set of fifty steps, all the way to the bottom. There were two rooms to choose from at the bottom of the stairs. To the left was what looked like a carnival, shaped boxes of lights and bells. To the right was where the music was coming from. It said Billy Pat's Pub on it. So they walked inside.

It was dark, again. Lights were lit at the walls, where fire would be, only large glass bulbs in their place. A band of musical players were on a stage, including a man playing an odd looking piano forte. Others were playing instruments that were plugged into large black boxes behind them. The music was loud. The people inside were all going crazy in the center of the room, hardly an excuse for dance, thought Bugwit.

Both walked down the side of the room. Otto was thinking that there might be more mead, he could smell it on the floors. But after a once around the place, they felt they might want to go to the Atrium. They were constantly going the opposite way in which their advisors, friendly ones at that, were telling them to go; or at least, this is what Bugwit felt.

"Come on, let's go. Let's find the Atrium." Bugwit then pulled Otto's arm again. He was beginning to miss home. He needed to express that somehow. As much as the night was alluring, it wasn't real. He needed a sense of reality to go on, something to hold onto. He clenched his coat, felt the fleece, and remembered his wife, back home. "Come on Otto. I'm sure Dr. Dave is around here somewhere."

They left the room, immediately the noise caved in on itself, as silence and quiet again filled the empty halls of the Student Center.

They walked through it, and up the long stairs. By the time they got to the top, they needed to stop and take a deep breath. The party was outside, just beyond the colossus glass doors. They opened them and went back outside. Both of them still holding their red cup they got from before. And both of them were somewhat beginning to feel the effects of all the mead they drank during the phase of the day. People were everywhere. They both walked, hither and thither on through. When they got through the people, they proceeded to walk up the path. The people went away, just a few in costume passed them, as they too had red cups; they were laughing and singing. But as they got to the top of the hill, where the Atrium sat, there was silence, and a dead night above. Just the moon dangling there, in the sky with its sinister smile, half the promise of the Sun.

"There. There it is. That seems fitting," said Otto. Atrium was printed in big white letters across the doorway. "It could not have been easier, Sire!"

"I believe you correct." Bugwit laughed in agreement.

Otto leaned in and opened the door for Bugwit, "after you Sire."

They both walked in. The room was large and empty, in a triangular shape with many rooms. A large staircase encouraged the space at the end of the room. It led to a second floor, with more rooms.

It was dark out, and it looked as though everyone must be at the festivities down below, where they just were. The Atrium could barly hold the secrets of a whisper. Bugwit walked over to the wall. There was a map there hanging and notes posted. He read some of them. Book Club Wednesday Night. Read before Writing. Ride Needed Upstate. Free Food. Free food, Bugwit thought. And kept reading down the board. Haunted Hay Ride. Ladies Night Tuesdays at Billy Pats Pub. There seemed to be not as much information as he'd like. Then he saw something there, in the corner of the posting board. Vanishing Tree Site Tour and Guide. Bugwit saw a number on the bottom of the paper posted. It was small, but he could read it. He didn't know what the number was for, but maybe a clue to something; he wasn't sure. So Bugwit took the poster and put it in his pocket. "Upstairs, come on. Let's go upstairs. Here," he looked at Otto. "Read this." Bugwit handed him the poster paper, pointing his fingers on the words; Vanishing Tree.

Bugwit gave Otto the paper, "come on."

They both walked towards the stairs, Bugwit leading the way. The hall was dark, and vacant of anyone. Why he'd be here, they didn't know. But up the stairs they went, again thinking that this University is one of many stairs. When they got to the top of the staircase, they turned left and walked towards what looked like a floating hall of doorways. Each one residing a room, Bugwit thought. "Over here." And to the left they went, again down a long floating hallway. It was one gigantic overhanging balcony of sorts. The rooms weren't part of the walkway. On each door that they came to, as there were many, they had a name printed on the door. They assumed these names belonged to the people who were behind the door. Little homes for them maybe, or just a place for them to teach. Otto was just as unsure as Bugwit. They walked farther down the hall. Otto spotted his name first.

"Here," Otto said. "Dr. Dave B."

"That's it. That's Dr. Dave's home. Knock on the door. See if he's there." Bugwit got a little excited, but realized he was still a stranger in a strange land. "Knock gently."

Otto knocked with little force on the cold wooden door. "There is no answer," said Otto to Bugwit. "He's not there."

"Hmm, let me think," Bugwit said. And to that he did, just that.

It kind of shocked them both when the door opened.

"Hello, can I help you?" a man behind the door spoke.

It must be Dr. Dave, thought Bugwit. "Why yes, are you Dr. Dave?"

"Why who sent you? No kidding, of course I am. But seriously who sent you?" Dr. Dave tucked back, waving them both to come in. "Come in, seriously, I'm kidding. How can I help you both. Great costumes by the way." He tails them to have a seat. They do.

"This flier, about a disappearing tree. Can you tell us about it?" Bugwit asked. "I mean, we really can't say where we're from, but someone told us to see you."

"That's it? All this way to ask me that?" Dr. Dave hangs his head low. "But of course. The Vanishing Tree. Sigma Tao Delta puts it on every year. Legend has it, that the first year of the college opening, at Halloween time, a tree down by Hobart Hall vanished. Right there. Just disappeared."

"Can you take us there?" Otto asked, anxious, nervous as a cat out in the rain.

"Well, I can tell you how to get there. They do ghost tours on campus, and that's a stop. The vanishing tree, who'd of known it would get so much press, but it does. Thought people might be interested in eternal salvation through literature today, but it's the ghost tours they care about." Dr. Dave looks at his desk, a pile of paper lay there, as if Dr. Dave was weigh deep in thought and studies. "It's right outside this door," he points. Down the hill to Hobart Manor. You can't miss it."

"Well that would be easy enough," thought Bugwit. "Come on! Let's give it a try." They both thanked Dr. Dave and left the building. They walked down a long walk that had buildings on each side of the path. Then it got dark, and a lonely path sat in despair. A sign came before them holding an arrow to walk strait ahead. Hobart Manor.

"Must be a famous building to have a sign," said Otto.

"Maybe. But there it is Otto. Right there. When they got there, there were a few people hanging around, again in costume. Bugwit thought that maybe they were there for the Vanishing Tree tour.

Bugwit walked up to one of them, a man dressed in all black and white make-up on his face. "Where is the spot of the Vanishing Tree?" Bugwit asked the man, a slight hesitance in his speech.

The gentleman looked at Bugwit, silence in his reproach, awkward but friendly. He pointed to the middle of a mound just in front of Hobart Manor. "There," he said. "Right there. Vanished a hundred years ago, right before two people who saw it disappear.

Bugwit walked over to the mound, nothing was there. The man either was right, or there never was a tree. But hoping that he knew a thing or two about vanishing trees, he was in the right place. Otto walked over to him. The night was darkening all around them. The people were all beginning to walk back up hill, towards the party and

234

the music. Only the one man with the painted white face stayed behind.

"What should we do?" Otto asked Bugwit.

"Nothing. Listen, just listen. Try and remember the tree." Bugwit picked up a leaf that blew his way. He looked at it. By the time he could see colors, Bugwit and Otto were no longer there, only the man with the white painted face. The tree could hear him, as he wiped away his wind-teared eye. "Happy Halloween," he said. Just in case they couldn't hear, thought the man. In the rare odd happenstance things found themselves gone again, he said it again; "happy Halloween."

Dr. Dave showed up a minute later. He stood next to the white faced man. Somehow his suspicions we're right. "I knew that man," he said.

Both stood there, staring in blank amazement and bone chilling disbelief, there before them, as if on cue appeared the tree, a hundred years since its vanishing. Bugwit and Otto were gone.

Chapter Four

Dr. Dave

Bugwit screamed when he woke up. He was lying face down in the dirt, near home. Otto was also there. The two of them found themselves under a tree, near their home pond. Slumbering as if put to sleep by a magic wand, and then through a wormhole of twisted space and vision, colors of stars passing. The day was deep in wonder already. How they got there, and how they left was a mystery; but it worked. They were no longer at Hobart Manor. And the power of the tree had taken them by surprise; yet, to their destination, which was home.

Otto heard Bugwit's loud yelp and woke immediately after. "Are you OK Sire? My we don't look like we're there any longer, it looks as though we're now here! Wow Sire, what a magnificent site! To see home."

Bugwit clawed the dirt. The travel took a little out of him. He felt for a tree; it was behind his left shoulder. He then picked himself up. "Ah! Yes! It looks as though we made it Mate."

"The pond looks serendipitously beautiful, as if it all came to this, Sire." Otto laughed, pulled himself up. "Come on, Sire, let's have a swim in the pond!"

"Best we be heading back to the Castle, I'm sure Jay is worried sick to where we are!"

They began walking back, half an hour's walk they figured, knowing exactly where they were. In shock of everything that had happened, all started to make sense. Where there is no thought, there is the sound of silence. A silent sound breathing with you rather than against you. With the tide, with the flow. They traveled, kicking rocks.

"Sire, I wonder how long it's been that we've been gone. It looks a little different, don't you think. I see newer buildings and bigger markets ahead."

"No," said Bugwit, "no, they've been there. We just don't get out into town much, and being we passed town going out, it doesn't look the same coming back in."

"That must be it. You are King for a reason I suppose." Otto scratched his head again, and skipped. Merrily. "Can we stop at the market for some fresh fruits?" Otto asked.

"That sounds splendid, Otto. I think we should do just that!" Bugwit laughed. Otto laughed with him.

They stopped at the market, picked up some fresh fruits. The locals were happy to see their King about with his Squire. A few as much, as if it mattered. But they were happy none the less; the townsfolk. They were laughing and singing, dancing like fire lilies and giggling along like schooling children, such their parents drowning themselves in good mead. Again.

"Must have landed back on a holiday, again Sire," Otto guessed.

"It looks that way." The King now was scratching his head. "It sure does look that way."

They fizzled on their time, and both sharing the same thought of a glass of fresh mead. It was on their mind, so just one wouldn't hurt. Otto pulled Bugwit's arm, "just one Sire, maybe we should have a cup, and toast to our arrival back home!"

Bugwit agreed, after hesitating for a second, at first. "Just one, then we must be going!"

They headed over to the hall, hundreds of people were inside, at long boarded wooden tables. There was laughter, and singing. People in the corner whispering secrets, and bumbling over their mead. Waitress women in tails went from table to table, supplying each and every person with the daily needs of mead, and maybe a kiss on the cheek. Otto and Bugwit quickly sat down, and were given both on demand, as the townsfolk knew just well that it was King Bugwit Hampsterfur and his Squire Otto. But they've been gone a while, and now that their back, the townies gleefully sang and shouted outright praise for their returned King.

"Otto this is splendid indeed!" Bugwit exclaimed.

"Yes it is! I've never felt better Sire!" Otto returned.

The atmosphere was enthralling and inviting, it's seductive nature into the arts surrounding the Maypole holiday was like walking into fresh cold water on a blistering day. And the two had seen so much over these past two days, that their brains alone needed a slight vacation. This made the mead go down easier, and the thoughts rather clear for the thinking. Mead had that talent.

Then he saw her. She was sitting there, waiting as if no one could fill a vacant chair. Bugwit had a feeling, that feeling of Deja Vu.

He excused himself. "Otto I must see something, wait here." The King walked over and sat himself down next to the tired looking woman.

"Are you OK?" he asked the woman. Her hands held her face from looking any lower than she already was. "How can I help?"

The woman looked up and immediately felt the intuition to be correct on hearing the familiarity of his voice. "Bugwit! You're back! You're back, I can't believe these tired eyes. It's you, it's really really you!"

"Jay! my what happened, you look tired, my love. I'm sorry I went away to the tree! I should've stayed. I can't believe I didn't listen to you."

"You're back, you've been gone so long."

"Only a day or two," appeased the King.

"A day or two? Are you crazy! Have you also gone mad? I've been waiting a whole year for you! It's been a year since Maypole, and today is the anniversary!" She cried; she took him by his arms and cried. "I can't believe it Bugwit! Where did you go?"

"I went to another time. The future where Buggies had roaring sounds and the towns were cities, and they had places like Universities where people read and studied in grandiose libraries. And they had mead. I had a glass of their mead, and it wasn't that good. But I missed you so much, and wanted to come back." Bugwit took Jay into her arms, and felt the love as if it were only yesterday that he left.

Her love was there as if it were years. They were back, and that was the most superfluous, and frivolous adventure turn itself around. Bugwit knew, maybe a walk around the pond might do the trick, as if it actually might help his confused mind. But that two might take the
238

fearless vision of a King, to do that correctly holding a spoon of oil might be suggested. That now would be his task. "Come on, let's go home," he said to his wife, and they all went walking through the great hall of mead. Out into the air, thoughts meandering as they joyfully walked on through the town.

It was getting later in the day as the castle approached. Home truly is where the heart resides, thought Bugwit.

"Look what showed up on our great lawn the day you left." Jay Pointed. It was a tree. "It magically appeared that day. Isn't that strange."

It was the last thing Bugwit wanted to see. "Yes, strange. Very strange indeed."

They walked down the great road leading to their home, passing the tree there on the right. Bugwit didn't remember a thing about going through his own front gate, into his castle. He was completely passed out in his large comforting bed by the time he could even dream about where he'd been.

He dreamt of no fanfare at the fairgrounds, no horses pulling carts of fresh vegetables and fruits. He dreamt of that place, he had just been, but only this time as an outsider looking in. He could see where he was, and how people had individual lives, hurts, and pain. He dreamt of walking along a path for a while, but after that he couldn't remember just what he had seen. It was more of a feeling that he was there, rather than a visual realization. He was guided by faith over reason. Instinct over thought.

When Bugwit woke up, he found himself home, a sense of sudden comfort arose with a long yawn and stretch. He was happy, a sense of glee floated like clouds around his head. The mead from days before lingered, though not as much as he suddenly thought. He felt glad to be alive, King of his castle, glad his wife was happy to see him back. Though a year hardly seemed believable now. How could it be that he was gone for a whole entire year? It was a day to him. He quickly got up and put on some clothing, a set of his favorite shoes and walked towards the mirror. "I don't look any older," he said to himself, tilting his head back and forth in the mirror.

He didn't see himself walk down the main hall, nor pass the paintings decorating its sides. The wooden floor almost did the walking for him. He was in his living quarters before he could even open his eyes. Otto was still tucked away in his quarters around back, where most of the castle staff slept, or at least Bugwit thought.

"Ahh! Back home! How pleasant it is, and to see such a beautiful site indeed!" Bugwit walked into the kitchen area. His wife Jay was sipping coffee.

"Good morning my love!" she said, with a gigantic smile on her face! "Good morning! Eggs and biscuits, fresh mango and strawberries. And some potatoes for some good energy." It was nice for Jay to see her husband. She walked around the table and gave him a kiss the size of her smile. "I love you Bugwit!"

Bugwit kissed her back. "I love you too! What does the day hold for us today, I wonder, with everything being such a surprise of late." He scratched the dirt from his eyes and laughed. "My how good it is, a year you say, Jay. My that is such a long time for me to be gone. I don't remember. It seems like a dream, but really just a day for me."

"No," Jay said; "it's been a year. I waited so long. Every night by the window, watching a hollow moon sing to me lonely songs of desperation upon your return. Oh Bugwit, don't go wandering off any more."

"Oh no, no more wandering. Plus I want to look after my collections. My wood carvings are coming along wonderful Dear!"

Bugwit laughed, ate his food, gobbled it down he was so hungry. Turkeys looked as happy as Bugwit. The day was glorious, and somehow Bugwit knew this, and he wanted to play on. "I have a new look on life, for some reason. I want to play my piano forte, immediately!"

Bugwit picked himself up after ten whole minutes of devouring his food. He went straight to the piano forte and started playing the song he had heard at the Student Center, yesterday, a year ago; four years ago. He wanted to remember something or someone. He tried, but couldn't quite grasp it. He tried to save his own life for the moment it felt, but he couldn't hit the chord. He played his favorites, those he grew up with, melodies circling like demented children

240

around his head. He laughed! It was hysterical to him that his wife thought he was gone a year. He couldn't bear to conceive such a preoccupation of the mind for so long. Bugwit played more, and it hurt him and helped him. He heard angels accompany him, saw them sitting beside him. If only he knew the secrets, if only he had the courage to seek them out. Bah! Enough of that, he thought. He played all morning. Jay came in and sat down and listened for a while, shaking her head in joyful approval of why Kings are Kings. But none the less, no one has to be a King, in order to play some piano forte well. Bugwit had that talent, like he had in all the arts, growing up under his Queen Mother of the Land of Moore. He didn't question things as much follow them, but had his own voice, and stood stern for the epiphanies that came his way insightfully. He was content for an old man, though not thinking of himself as old. He saw himself in the mirror, like this very morning and thought of himself OK, as a King, a ruler of his people. Ruler or not, he thought. He liked his home, and the people were there, and he let them be. That was his care.

"I have to go to my work shop. I want to work on some of my new figurines. They've been tough to carve."

"I love your figurines!" Queen Jay would say. "I can't wait to see them. I've missed you working on them."

"They are coming along magically, and beautifully. Some are wood, some are rock, and marble. I need to paint them now." Bugwit picked himself off the piano forte stool and grabbed his garbs doing so, almost falling on himself. They laughed and he walked, not before kissing her and wishing her a pleasant hour or so while he worked diligently. Down the hall, and out the side door, into another hall. Doors were on both sides, doors containing much space, but not as many folk. Bugwit laughed at the notions of the day, and the thoughts days brung! "Alas! We can get to work, for once." He mumbled to himself, bumbling a little in his walk.

Outside in the courtyard, there was a shed, or what Bugwit called his workshop. Inside were his trinkets, his sculptures, his paintings. But today he had a calling to work on his figurines. He picked them up, one by one staring at them. There was a princess, and a wizard. There was a horseman, and woodsman. There was his little fairy as well, that he'd put on one of his wooden horses. Ten O Clock turned to Twelve O Clock, and then to Two O Clock, according to the sun dial, a generous gift from the townsfolk, given to him on his fortieth birthday. He went through each and every figurine and painted them with grace and respect, as if for reasons he couldn't understand. They were his friends, for reasons no one else might understand.

The wizard began talking first, saying things like "are you awake King Sire?" Or things like "You have to go back." Back where, he thought. Where he just was. Or go back to the time when childhood had dreams, and visions that meant something. More than dementia setting in for an old king. The queen figurine, he named Jay. He was fond of her, and tried to make her as beautiful as his loving wife. He wanted his kingdom of figurines to be a gift to himself, as well as a gift for Jay.

Something was tugging, as he was listening to the wizard speak. His mind had been lost, he'd felt. Maybe that was why he wandered so much. Maybe that was why he loved his mead. Bugwit sat there. Alone, he felt. He was exhausted from his trip, but in love with his newly carved figures. He looked outside for a second, through the square window at the other end of the room. He could see the courtyard from there. He started walking back to his chair when he could here his wife, Queen Jay calling.

"Bugwit! Come at once! You have a visitor."

"He could hear Jay from the room, he buckled up his tail coat and put his figurines back on the shelf. "I'll be there in one second Love!" Opening the door, and seeing the sun cut the chord from his work, the personalities there he'd create in front of him. Making the non-real, real. That was the magic. The magic was inside the imagination. "I'll be right there!" He hurried on over to the main living courters of the castle. "I wonder who it is," he muttered to himself.

He came to the front of the castle, by-passing his quarters all together, by going around the left side lawn. This way he was able to see right away who was at the door. When he got there, Jay was standing at the stoop, with another man. The gentleman appeared to be dressed in a white long coat.

"Oh Bugwit. This is Doctor Stansford, he wants to ask you a few questions." Jay looked at her husband, still a little out of breath.

Another Doctor in town? he thought. A new hospice going up in town, he wasn't sure. But by the rate of things moving as they were, he would assume new religions sprouting as well. "Doctor, hello. What can I give for you today."

Dr. Stansford stood there, not doing much to get his first words out. "Where were you a couple days ago. And tell me the truth. Have you seen this man?" The Dr. pulled out a white piece of paper. It was a photo of Dr. Dave.

"Well, yes, I saw him but not around here. Far away and supposedly a year ago at that." Bugwit scratched his head, not knowing what to make of the man in the strange long white coat. One he has never seen before.

"Well, that answers some questions," the man said. "Where did you see him?"

"Well, at a University. Is that all? I must get to my figurines. They're waiting for me in the back, and I've been into a project I can't stop. Do you understand? Plus, I'm the King, and I can have moments to myself. People tend not to understand that."

"A King you say. Well, it is a fairly large home you do have, Sir. I must say. It reminds me of an old castle I used to visit over at the park. It's very nice indeed, Sir." The man stood there.

Bugwit nodding his head. Strange this man, talking of things of such. Bugwit began to get nervous, twitching. I am King, he would say to himself. I've been ruler of the Land of Moore for some time now, a long long while. Most beards can't be grown in such length as it is long. "Is that all Doctor?"

"I guess that will be it, for the day. I may come again if I have more questions."

"Sounds fair as the ground." Bugwit waved him good bye and walked back around the castle in which he had come.

He went back to his workshop, confused who the man was, and what he may have wanted with all of that. And it's strange how he could recognize Dr. Dave in the photo.

"Yes it is," said the Wizard carving. "It's strange how you've come such a far way, and to a far away land such as this, and now it may all go away."

"Don't say such things," said Bugwit to the Wizard carving. He thought about the year missing. He thought about the tree in the front yard that wasn't there before all this vanishing and disappearing stuff. "I mind you Wizard, I have it all under control. You need not worry about a thing!" He carried on, walking back and forth in his wood shop, occasionally looking out the window for relief, or solace. "I have it all under control."

There was a bird he'd carved just days prior. It was a parrot, and he'd like to think it had a mind of it's own. There was also a new squirrel he made for Jay, but hadn't given it to her yet. Who was that man, and the strange white coat, something he could swear of never seeing before this day! He muttered along the wall, and almost had it with the change in sudden weather. He went back outside, into the courtyard. His surroundings felt smaller, less grandiose, less majestic. He wanted answers and couldn't seem to grab any. He walked back into his home. The chair in the corner felt as lonely. The dogs were all sleeping. The staff were on vacation. He stood there, looking at his wife, thinking of his age, not liking what was happening to him. He stood there with his hands wide to either side and shook his head.

"What is it Dear?" she asked him, as he came into the kitchen.

"That man on the paper, I know him from somewhere, I think."

"Who was he?" she asked.

"I met him yesterday, at a University. Briefly there. But I'm remembering something else. I remember sitting in a room with lots of people, all sitting there saying things that were clever and smart. And we all felt good about that." Bugwit started pacing the kitchen. "It's all so familiar, yet I'm here and I don't quite understand that."

"Well, you were gone a while," Jay said. "I waited for you. You said there was a tree, and now there are trees everywhere! And no one knows frankly what to make good heed of it!"

"Take me to the tree." Bugwit looked at his wife. "Let's go to that tree again."

"I can't, I won't let you go there again. Play the piano forte, carve some wooden figures! Do anything but go near that tree!" She begged and cried aloud. She was happy he was home, and that was all that mattered. It were the little things, she knew that. Bugwit's imagination always got the best of him. She knew that too.

"Listen to me Bugwit. There are things out there, you don't know. I love you so much, the flowers sing songs when you leave, how much my heart does break every time you go! We have love Bugwit, me and you, we go together. If you go, you really don't go anywhere!"

Bugwit looked at his hands, they've gotten so small, and rustic, then he looked at his wife, and never saw such a beautiful lady. "I love you so much, and I'm sorry for the folly and ridiculousness, the running of the mind and my imagination. I can't help but love you, because I do. But yes, there are things out there. Maybe I need to tend to them, maybe I don't. Maybe I'm like the others, and maybe I'm not. Oh my love of loves." He took her in his arms, and hugged her with all the love he could ever feel. "Thank you. You know I need to say that. You made me a king, that of my heart. That is what a king needs. I know that."

Jay cried, there wiping her lips and nose. His arms felt warm, and comfortable, knowing like home.

"I'm a broken man," said Bugwit; "but I'm a happy man at that. I will always love you."

"As I will always love you Bugwit!" Jay laughed. Bugwit laughed back with her. They were both crying. They didn't know much of what was going on. Pick the potatoes, the flowers, skim the milk, life's chores weren't exactly going to solve her riddles and problems, but she could do the best she could, and that was ok with her. Bugwit always needed help.

"I'm going for a walk, I want to see the tree. I won't go anywhere. But I have a feeling about something, and I just need to see it."

"Please, don't be long Bugwit. And don't go too close to it. I fear it like a rabid rabbit."

"I won't go too near. You have my word."

Bugwit thought to himself. He had everything in the world, in his mind's eye. What was left there for the seeking. Old wisdom from the East calmed his heart at times, books he's read were somewhat there for the taking. But there was nothing as compared to a good woman's love, and he knew that. Still, he could hear the tree. As if there was some unfinished business. As if someone down Bugwit's line got the best of him, put him away, locked him up in his own room.

"Jay, here wait." Bugwit said. He walked back into the work shed, and came out of it not a minute later. "Here, this is for you." Bugwit gave his Queen and wife a carved squirrel.

"He's beautiful! I love him. Thank you my love."

Bugwit again hugged his wife, they laughed again. It was a mutual understanding that these carved figurines meant something to the both of them. They would get them through times, holidays, rainy days. They were like children for those who didn't have children. He walked on the side of the house. With his aim now on a tree in front of the house. He wasn't sure if he'd seen it before. But Jay was insistent on saying that it has been there a year now, the length of time Bugwit had been gone.

When Bugwit got to the tree, he stood there, gazing like a lost sheep. His eyes, bluer than the sky gazed forward. Life was in that tree he thought. Did it see him, or was it just like a wooden door, standing propped up in the middle of the front lawn. He went over to it. Sat down, laying his back on it like he's always done when a good tree came along on his walks. This one was different. It said to himself that he'd been gone a while, without apparently knowing it. If that were true, then how could that be? Where did the time go.

He thought about it. He could see someone else coming up from behind the house. Recognizably fast, he could see that it was Otto. Jay was right behind him. He couldn't exactly understand why they were coming towards him. The wind was quiet, and was creating its own atmosphere. The leaves on the tree were gently falling. As if it were a portal, Bugwit could almost guess, he dreamt of slipping through it, again.

"Come on Bugwit. You've been here long enough." Otto came up to him.

246

"But we were there. Weren't we?" Bugwit nodded his head, bowing the overbearing sun coming down.

"You could say that," Otto concluded.

"Where were we?" Bugwit asked. The wind and the sun making a silent moment worth a word or two.

"I don't know Sire. I don't know"

"I'm not sure either," Bugwit said, and drifted off to sleep. Jay was running towards the tree. Otto was sitting down next to the tree with Bugwit by the time Jay got there.

"He just passed out. Bugwit, Bugwit. Wake up. Wake up!" Jay was tugging at his shoulder. "Get up, it's too early to pass out now." She looked at him.

Bug snapped out of it. He woke up, he felt maybe the tree put him in a daze. He felt himself sinking, gliding, moving towards another time and land. But he could hear Jay, so he tried to stay alert, as much as he could, and remain where he was.

"Oh good, you're awake. My oh my, you must be under some spell Bugwit!" She nervously paced outside on the front lawn.

"You okay Sire?" Otto asked.

Bugwit scratched his head, rubbed his eyes. "Yeah, I'm okay. I just felt something take over me. And I saw someone over on that side of a door. I saw someone as I felt I was falling." He gathered himself up, "here help me." Otto took his hand and he perked himself up next to the tree, using the bark as support. "Here."

"Here you go," said Otto, pulling the King up on his feet; "You okay? Sire?"

"Yeah, whoa. I saw something there. I felt it again."

"I know, you must have, the way you be looking and all, there passed out on the tree. Thought you might leave us again."

"No, well best we all head inside," said Jay.

They walked along the driveway again leading up to the house. That's when they heard the sound behind them. It sounded like one of those roaring buggies Bugwit saw not just the other day. Only this time, it was on this side of the tree. The sound grew louder, and louder, and then they saw it. It was coming up the drive, pounding large pulses into the air, sounding like ten lions, ten horses in pain, driving their coach. They couldn't quite understand, but Bugwit and Otto had seen them in the other place, the Land of the Future Forgotten. The car stopped right at the vanishing line of where they were walking, not ten feet away.

A man got out of the odd looking buggy. It was square and had stripes of red and blue on it. "I don't have much to say, but just the mail. How you folks, doing?"

"The mail?" Bugwit took it from the man's hand. "Why we have an odd carrier pigeon delivering mail for us. How wonderful! My did we go somewhere again, those buggies were from the other Land, I tell you." said Bugwit.

On the envelope it was addressed to Bill Hampstefur, and it had a return address. It was from Dr. Dave at the University. He tucked it into his coat pocket. A sudden fear overwhelmed him. He didn't want to see this yet, he was thinking. He knew about the Land, he always did. But it was coming back to him. He felt it, like he had felt that Deja Vu.

Bugwit opened the letter. He read it. Then he went to bed, hoping it wasn't real. Hoping maybe it would say something different.

Dear Bill,

Hope you are of well mind. Things are pleasant on the outside, overlooking the hills. Not much has changed except for the air and space you once filled. Nothing can replace absence but the source. We wish for you to return, and come back, but ultimately that's up to you. It's been 5 years since anyone has heard from or seen you. Laughter is the best medicine. We did laugh a lot then. Life is life, can't change that, but maybe we can alter it a little for the better. It's all in our head. I wish you the best of health and happiness my old friend, and hope to see you soon, as we all do.

Best,

Dr. Dave

Chapter Five

Bill and The Vanishing Tree

"What is the truth?" Bugwit asked, after raising the hand. I mean you can sit there on the desk and say what the truth is but if I don't see what you're trying to do, then the point is irrelevant."

The teacher, Dr. Dave sat there, mystified by what Bugwit was saying. But none the less he just sat there on the desk, sitting in a Buddha yoga position, legs crossed, not saying a word. Then he jumped off his desk and drank some smart water. Still no words from the teacher, he just sat there. An hour would go by, and still no word from the Dr. Dave. This went on for an extra ten minutes or so. The class was Romantic Literature.

Then he spoke. "OK, we've come this far. I'm glad you are good. Hanging in there. I wanted to show you something. Something I wrestled with for a couple weeks before preparing for this class. How many are familiar with Romantic Literature? Is it different then Eastern Literature? I'm glad you asked that question Bugwit. Let's see how many are left. Eighteen of you. Out of twenty. Two walked out, not bad. Well the lucky ones stayed I would presume."

The class laughed. Bugwit was laughing along too. He couldn't quite understand Dr. Dave's point, but thought he did when a thought came to him. It's been of late not feeling as well, and coming to class feeling tired. He couldn't understand why he'd decided to go back to school at 40. It was kind of demoralizing and out of place. Like a plastic fish in an aquarium, a stuffed Zebra in a zoo.

"Read Frankenstein by Tomorrow, the first three chapters. I will see you then."

Bugwit picked up his notebook and put it in his bag. All the students left the room, happy, frazzled, questions answered.

That night, in his room, Bugwit sat at his desk. "I can't take the insanity," he muttered to himself. "I've been doing this too long.

Always a student. Always a professor who knows more than myself. It's ludicrous. I can't take not having to graduate anything in life." He looked at his book. Frankenstein, by Mary Shelly. What would he be able to learn from a Monster losing his shit on society. He didn't know. He knew it was more than just a Monster. Later on they would discuss it in class and how human and angelic Frankenstein was. But now, Bugwit just looked outside the window of his small one bedroom apartment. They were expecting snow. He could see traces of it fall on his sill. It reminded him of how lonely the human soul actually was. He picked up the book and began to read. The snow began falling like angels, little ones all lit up like winter fire flies.

An hour went by. Things understood sat dormant for years now took another meaning at life. If it weren't too late; though in life he'd been reminded it was never too late, as much as he wished to believe it. Wishful thinking was also one of his shortcomings.

A loud knock threw Bugwit off his chair. Waves of written memories came to a sudden halt. "Who is it?" Without reservation he knew who it was, so without further investigation, Bugwit just gave in and told the visitor to come in.

"Hey Bill. What are you up to?" Otto closed the door behind him. "I got some nice nugs, fresh stuff. Green as the Emerald City. Check this out." Otto pulled out a jar of some nice fresh greenery. Bugwit took it from his hand, noticing a generous giving by his friend.

"Yeah, I want to smoke this stuff. My what a strange night it is, Otto. The snow outside is beginning to come down harder. And that moon.

"How was class today? I was down at the school earlier for Theatre Arts. Ha! Maybe they'll cancel tomorrow due to some serious inclement weather. What do you think Bill?"

"I think you're crazy. They never close that school." Bugwit put his book down.

"Well, we're there to learn aren't we. Why would we want to miss a day in class." They both laughed.

"Otto my friend. I have the strangest professor. He just sat on his desk for an hour and looked at everyone without saying anything. He just sat there and didn't say a word. And after an hour of this he then
250

spoke up. It was so strange. Bill looked at the slow moving ring clock on the wall. Eight O Clock on the knob. Last night Otto came up at Eight O Clock, and the night before that as well. The apartment dorms were a mile off campus. Students who live in the F Dorm have to drive a mile over to the campus. It's mainly for adults who wouldn't fit into the age gap left behind for them; those who go back to school later in life, like Otto and Bill.

Otto tucks in a little green into a small rectangular pipe. He lights it up, takes a few puffs and then hands it to his friend. "Here my good friend. Is Jay coming by tonight? You two have been seeing each other quite a while now."

Bill takes the bowl from his friend's hand, lights it up and takes a few puffs. "Yes we have. Yeah, she'll be over soon. We're going to watch a movie she said she picked up at the library. Santa Clause Conquers the Martians. I used to watch it when I was five or four. We used to see it at our cousins on Christmas Eve." Bill looked out the window. Strange night he thought, illuminating the way it was. Snowflakes so silent he could almost hear them scream. Something lost in it all, he thought. An innocence, something maybe as trivial as that. But he saw it.

How he used to run everyday, at the field, doing laps around the high school. Odd how there was something in the air then that no longer was there now. There was a tugging, and a pulling in his own suspicions on how life should be, and how it used to be. Being older was one thing; being a student at the age of 40 was another.

"It's nice out tonight, don't you think?" Bill looked at his friend. "Kind of spooky out there in the afterglow of it all."

"It's true. It's a silent night, like the song. Do you have a manger for the holidays, you don't even have a tree." Otto laughs at his friend. He knew a few things about friendship as well. We may all go mad in the end, but that word 'friend' lingers and cuts through, even after years of discourse. A friend is someone who says I'm human just like you, and we all fall down like old bad horses. We all fall and the friend says, I'm your friend, and that's that. Otto took the bowl back after it being handed to him. "This is some good shit, don't you think?"

"Yeah, some good shit." Bill looked over at the book on the desk, Frankenstein. What did he know about English Literature, or Romantic Literature; what was it supposed to do. Was literature a spell put on by authors who write them? Were they somehow their justification for living through lives of misunderstandings and misfortune? Does the soul, and the brain get to write that stuff down, so people can see that they too were once like them. Maybe even a friend to talk about it to.

People in Bill's life came passing by like window washers across his mind's eye. The imagination is greater; he thought of Einstein. But it's a dangerous place, he also thought. He took back the bowl and tugged a few hits off of it. More snow fell and blended in with the white smoke filled room. Squid-like fumes gripped the walls, harmless ghosts creeping up the ceiling.

A knocking on the door alarmed them both. They looked at each other and laughed.

Bill walked over to the door and opened it. It was Jay, and Bill was quite happy to see her. It was a daily affirmation, a ritual of a mutual understanding between them. Bill and Jay, or Jaybird, as he would call her sometimes.

"Hey sweetheart," Bill kissed Jay on her red cold lips. She kissed him back, and took off her coat.

"Hey Hun," she said. "Hello Otto."

"Hi Jay, I guess I should be going." Otto looked at his friend. "Here, have a little of this for later." He handed him a small nugget of the greenery.

"Thanks," Bill said. Otto left the room, and walked back to his own flat which was just down the hall.

The two sat on Bill's bed. They smoked a little; and then Bill turned the television on and inserted the movie. "I can't believe you found this!" he said.

"I can't believe it either. Magic, I swear it popped out in front of me, and you mentioning last month I thought it was the most magical thing I've seen. Maybe a few other things, but this just gleamed when I spotted it."

"This movie was the most magical movie growing up too." Bill said. They laughed. They watched the movie and no matter whether it made any sense or not, they were enjoying it. The snow came down in flurries and even harder at times. But the night itself was a lesson in love, and the many definitions that lie there within it.

Between the two, love meant more than 'I love you' and more than a kiss goodnight. It was good to see the fleeting memories spared by meaningful moments. The night flew by, and Santa won the war with the Martians. Bill and Jay kind of thought he would. It was kind of expected. Jay slept next to Bill. They both dreamt of a land they would someday go. Where they were King and Queen of many people. When they woke, the outside was covered in white blanketed snow. Their cars were completely covered. The sun was an hour or two past yawning. It was a miraculous day. Bill had class, and Jay had to get to work.

Frankenstein; it was hardly on Bill's mind leaving the apartments. His car was completely covered, so it took a minute or two to clean it. Jay was by his side cleaning her own car off. The snow was wet and heavy, and created for horrible driving weather. But the day doesn't stop itself. Reasons why people go out in the first place, one might have to wonder. But they do. They do in droves.

"Who has read the novel so far?" Dr. Dave asked the class. "The reason I sat there on the desk. Does anyone have any idea of why I did that?"

"I do," a girl in the front row says. "You wanted to be God."

"That's a good one, but yes and no on that." Dr. Dave smiles and laughs with the rest of the class. Sara who answered the question joined in reluctantly.

"Because you wanted us to appreciate what comes to us in silence." Jeremy says, sitting next to Sara.

"Good answer. I like that one." Dr. Dave pauses, walks around the room. He draws a picture on the board with the chalk. It's a monster, Frankenstein. "Who has read the first three chapters of Frankenstein?"

Everyone raises their hands, but only about fifteen actually did the assignment. The other few kind of half raised their hands.

"Alright. Well, who is Victor Frankenstein?" Dr. Dave looks around the room and points to Bugwit. You, Bill..., Hampsterfur. Where the hell did you get that name too. What a name. Who is Frankenstein?"

"Well, he's the Monster's creator. Victor is the creator, or the man that goes mad looking for Frankenstein after he creates him.

"Good, good. Are we monsters?'"

Everyone laughs. But there is a serious moment. The room quiets down. Bill looks out the window. There is snow falling again. The sky is gray, pale of any color. "Yes, we're monsters that somehow were taught to behave."

"You believe that?" Dr. Dave asks Bill.

"Well, really I believe that we're angels, but kind of deformed angels. Real angels too." Everyone laughs again. "No, really," Bill exclaims. "I think the bible is kind of correct saying the angels were thrown out of Heaven. Why else would we be here? We just don't have wings. We have everything else angels have. Eyes and arms, and feet and bare breasts and bones. We're a lot like angels. Only we fell."

"I think he's right." Eoni in the back of the room yells out. "He's right. We're fucked up angels that have fallen from the grace of Heaven."

Joey Turple, plays for the football team yells out. "Well, how do you explain aliens? Are they angels too?"

"We're all from something big," says Bill. "You just don't realize how a few words in a few books can make us think differently. It only takes a twist of the mind to convince him that's he's something he's not."

"Who was the Wretch? or have we gotten that far? in the book, I'm not sure. Who was the Wretch?"

"He's the Monster, says Mary. "He's the creator's creation."

"And what does he represent?" Dr. Dave looks at his drawing of Frankenstein on the board. He points to it, gives a grinning smile and laughs. "What does this man represent?"

"Broken God. Broken Man."

"Sounds like a good Indian poem. Good I like that one." Dr. Dave sits in his chair. He had brought in a Frankenberry Cereal Box today to show the class. And a miniature model set of the infamous monster. He had made it when he was young, in grammar school. But it made good show and tell. It sat there on the desk. No one can really see beyond the curtain, or the real meanings of why we even talk about books like Frankenstein or The Monk, or Les Miserables, War and Peace. By the time any one really does get to think about such stuff, their mind is gone. If one were to dig there, one might find a gone mind. "Broken God." He pauses. "OK, read the next couple chapters for the next class."

Dr. Dave walks behind his desk. The students with more respect than they realize pass him, waving goodnight to him as they do. Bill did the same. But as Bill was passing him, Dr. Dave opened up and said a few words. Bill couldn't quite understand him. He thought he could, but maybe made out a word or two. "Stay away from that tree," he said. That's what Bugwit heard. "Stay away from that tree."

Bugwit didn't say anything in return. He just pretended to have heard what he did, or pretended not to hear, wherever the sound-waves travel, they followed him down the hall. Bill's friend, tapped him on the shoulder.

Bill turned around, caught by surprise. Almost falling forward towards the stairs. "Oh hey, Murry, you caught me taken back. Jesus, you headed back to the apartments?"

"There's a party going on later if you're interested. At Mary and Laura's place."

Bill was taking in his breath. "I have to go and read this book. I think I may stop at the Library first. What time is the party?"

"Eight O Clock," Murry said.

The two walked for a second in silence both down the long stairwell.

"I'm not sure. I will let you know later." Bill said his goodbye to Murry. A quick hello and goodbye. As he was headed towards the Library, he thought to walk through the Atrium. As He did, he noticed something. A DeJa Vu. But it wasn't as clear as when he left the Atrium, as the Library sits on the other side, he noticed another DeJa Vu. This one was more clear to him, it sank in deeper. He stood outside the building, just thinking. He thought of his age again, and how old he

255

was to go back to school. He looked at the Library doors, and then at the windows. He looked at the grand scale size of the building. "Where have I seen this place before?" he asked himself. "I've been here before." He then walked inside, leaving those thoughts behind.

For the next two hours, Bill read Frankenstein. "Something isn't right," Bill thought to himself. He felt alone, in a big place. Horrifying walls, wall paper and books. long lonely corridors with more silent people. He knew the place. He's been going to this particular school now for twenty odd years. He wasn't a newborn when it came to school; though at times, he felt he was a never ending freshman. Never a senior. Always a groomsman, never a groom. He bowled over thoughts looking at that book written two hundred years ago. Somebody thought to put body parts together and call him God's son. Sick world, Bill thought.

He left the Library, completely not thinking about Mary and Laura's party. He thought of his friend Murry briefly, but thought of nothing as the front doors to the library shut behind him. The air was cold, bitter and ringing frozen thoughts at the ears. Knives cut through this kind of cold. Bill felt alone. He thought of his girl Jay, and love; but he felt alone. He couldn't explain it. He hopped on the shuttle that would take him to the other parking lot where his car was. The bus driver looked at him through her rearview. He was the only one on the shuttle. The ride was around and about, through hoops of visual outdoor landscapes, passing the great and small buildings of William Paterson. Eventually stopping at the last intended location, Lot D- an old Indian Guides hot spot, as it was a camping ground posing also as a park for the locals to come and get away. Since there was very little parking on campus, the University turned the park into Lot D. Bill parked there because he knew he was guaranteed a spot, since parking at the campus was always nearly impossible, none to zilch.

The drive in his 1970 SS Camaro hugged the road, slush moving aside to the grip wall tire, hugging the half-frozen water. The radio played Beatle songs, sometimes they'd throw in a few other groups, but it was usually around this time a Beatle block would take over. The thoughts of sound and lights from the sky came to overwhelming conclusions that he was some kind of viewer of things in some kind of dream. The DeJa Vu back there was more than that, it had ulterior motives showing up like that. Bill was meeting Jay back at the apartment, not less than an hour. He had time to gather things. When he pulled up to the place, he parked the car as usual in a side spot marked 3 in yellow paint. Snow was covering the stopper, yielding a mound of four feet or so. Bill got out, and walked himself inside the two front doors. He walked up two flights of stairs to his floor. When he got to the door, there was a note on it. He didn't think to open it just yet, so he opened the door first and put his things down. He took the note and slit the tape holding the fold.

Don't go near the tree. Come back. Dr Dave

Bill had no idea what the note meant. He thought at first a prank. Then that feeling again he had at the library. A sudden Deja Vu hit him hard, like a punch to the stomach. He looked at the note and quickly put it down on the desk. Who's fucking with him, that was what he was thinking. Otto wouldn't do it, it made no sense. But to see, Bill walked himself down the hall and knocked on Otto's door. No one answered. He wasn't home. Carrying on, Bill walked back to his own place. The strangest things have been happening. Magic was real, his deeper questions on life, and odd occurrences, like coincidences and epiphanies. It was like that; he was feeling these things. And the moments were increasing. And the snow kept falling. Bill looked at the note again as he put it on his desk. The white paper matched the white on the window sill, and the snow outside. He gazed without thought into the vast abyss wilderness there before him. He started to ask himself questions again as they came one by one without permission. A beam of light from the lamp a good twenty five yards from his window shined brightly, casting an emphasis on the silence. The sound it does make, like a high pitch frequency only dogs can hear in the harrowing loneliness of the night, blinding to those who can see, and deafening to those who can't.

Jay knocked and Bill answered.

"Hi Hun!" She kissed him on the lips, gave him a hug. And took off her jacket. Bill took it from her and placed it on the bed. "It's cold out there, really cold."

"I know. What's that in your hand. You got another movie?"

"It's Santa Clause Conquers the Martians. You said you used to watch it as a kid and I saw it in the library so I just had to get it."

Bill froze silent like concrete to feet. He stood there not being able to move. The wind off the sill came in laughing. "What movie?"

"Santa Clause Conquers the Martians."

"We saw that last night, right?" Bill had to ask. He couldn't be thinking thoughts that were completely illogical, not even Philosophy 101 threw him easier tests to handle. "You're kidding right?"

"What do you mean? Last night we saw Eyes Wide Shut. You don't remember us watching. You were reading Frankenstein. Are you OK Bill. Bugwit, are you OK?"

"Bugwit," said Bill. He walked over to the window sill and looked out. "Put in the movie," he said, with a blank dead stare into the falling snow. "Gone a year," he mumbled to himself. He looked out at the lamp, could hear the electricity again. This time the dogs outside began to bark. He could hear that too. "It'll be fun. Put the movie in Hun."

"Are you OK Bill?" Jay came over and put her hand on her boyfriend's shoulder.

"Yeah I'm OK," Bill replied taking her hand from his shoulder, looking at the pale snow fall. Each lonely little flake, one by one falling into the emptiness that seemed to be all around him. Time lasting forever; as if he could name each one by their name.

Afterword

He knew before he even wanted to hear her voice again, he knew. Turning around as if she *were* there, but she wasn't. There was only a book on his desk, Catcher in the Rye, and some papers to thoughts about a novel he was thinking of starting. He walked over, picked up the the orange worn out paperback with the little drawn horse on the cover. Salinger only wrote one or two books; he thought to himself, yet he nailed it on the head.

"Jay?" He called again. She wasn't there, he knew that now. He still wanted to call out for her. As if she were real. There, as if that day were yesterday. Yet somehow in the magic of it all, he could still hear her voice. "A year away," again he mumbled to himself. He looked at the book by Salinger, the title. He put the book back down on the desk and picked up the piece of paper next to it. All typed out, as if he were to put them all in a play. "Call it Pilate's Dilemma with a Witch", or "They Don't Let You Scream Here". He laughed. It had some names penciled in on it, *Laura*, *Oscar*, and *Arthur*. *Mari* and *Kate*, and *Oliver*, *Irie*, *Osbrin*, and Jay.

He had lots of names when he thought about it. He looked down at them. He kind of liked the way they were all crossed out, like missing kids on a campus, or a flier up on a poll. Like the Catcherman finally came by and took them up one by one. As if it were the sweetest part of the cake. Or how the snow tasted when it hit your tongue on a freezing cold day. One by one as they fell from grace, one by one as they fell from heaven.